'Utterly **—it's Lisa M best work to date,** which is really saying something'
KEVIN BARRY

'**Sharp and satisfying** . . . a compelling, sleazy demi-monde of drug dealers, sex workers and property developers'
GUARDIAN

'A **richly savage writer** and an incisive chronicler of her home country'
THE TIMES

'A raw, intense novel, **full of tenderness, humour and above all humanity**'
MARY COSTELLO

'Stylish and **relentlessly original**' NICOLE FLATTERY

'A **belting** read of drink, drugs, music and finally getting to grips with the past'

THE GLOSS

'There's a gang of powerful young women writers in Ireland right now.
But the one they should all be looking up to is Lisa McInerney'

HOT PRESS MAGAZINE

'Few [Irish writers] have their finger on the **pulse of contemporary society** as **strongly as Lisa McInerney**'

SUNDAY BUSINESS POST REVIEW

'Bright and inventive, the dialogue **funny, sharp** and revealing of **character**'

IRISH TIMES CULTURE

THE RULES OF REVELATION

Lisa McInerney

JOHN MURRAY

First published in Great Britain in 2021 by John Murray (Publishers)
An Hachette UK company

This paperback edition published in 2022

1

A CIP catalogue record for this title is available from the British Library

Paperback ISBN 978-1-473-66893-5
eBook ISBN 978-1-473-66892-8

Typeset in Sabon MT by Hewer Text UK Ltd, Edinburgh
Printed and bound in Great Britain by Clays Ltd, Elcograf S.p.A.

John Murray policy is to use papers that are natural, renewable and
recyclable products and made from wood grown in sustainable forests.
The logging and manufacturing processes are expected to conform
to the environmental regulations of the country of origin.

John Murray (Publishers)
Carmelite House
50 Victoria Embankment
London EC4Y 0DZ

www.johnmurraypress.co.uk

For Louise

Cork City made its own music. Amid its hearts beating, its throats noising, its port sounds and traffic and footfall, it might have been difficult to isolate the sounds of one man's ambition, only that his foot fell heavier now, by God he'd filled out a bit. The problem was that he heard the music that his city made and had a bone to pick with it. Maybe it would have been wise to have kept him away. But that was the way of things, and this was only the start of it.

The name of this soloist was Ryan Cusack. He had black hair, brown eyes, tragus piercings, five siblings, three fillings, two passports and a dead mother. He was coming up on twenty-four years of age. He was Karine D'Arcy's ex-boyfriend, best friend, biggest problem, childhood sweetheart. He was the bane or the love of her life and the father of her two-and-a-half-year-old son, Diarmaid. He made the breath catch in her throat. He made her want to kick holes in doors. He was on the screen of her phone, bare-chested, bleary-eyed, maybe a small bit bombed, over nine thousand kilometres away.

'Ah, D'Arcy,' he said. 'Did I wake you?'

'You did,' Karine said. She lay on her bed and held her phone in front of her face. 'But it's not your fault, because it's way too early for me to be panned out on the couch. What time is it there?'

'It's half six and it's Sunday morning.'

'You look stoned, boy.'

'Jesus, I wish. Naw, girl. Soju.'

He passed his phone to his left hand. There was light from a lamp behind him, to his right. He was sitting on his bed. He was alone, or he seemed to be alone. For eighteen months Karine had seen him only on screens and for three years she had not been his girlfriend, and despite their history, their son and the games they played with one another by custom she supposed she had no right to pry.

'Have you been out all night?' she asked.

'What? I'm home early.'

'Dylan's here.'

'Oh, God forbid I'd eat into his evening. Poor Dylan. Poor ould dote. Where is he?'

'He's in the sitting room.'

'And where are you?'

'In my bedroom.'

'Are you dressed?'

'Ah, cheek of you!'

He laughed and leaned back and she glimpsed the ink wash tattoo that had been started in Cork with a dragon across his shoulders and down his spine. In his time away he had added to it. Now the dragon flew in a sky of black cirrus that wound into whorls and delicate lines down his right arm to his wrist, and came down the right side of his torso too, in tendrils that stretched to his hip and on to his belly. There was a cloud-obscured moon on the side of his ribcage. She had seen the expanded tattoo only in photographs and on FaceTime and had expressed mild disapproval, feeling distant from him in an unexpected way. She hadn't told him that. She had said instead, 'Why anyone would put themselves through that I just don't know.'

'*Mi perdoni*,' he said now. 'Old habits.' The phone moved so that she could no longer see the design on his arm. 'Is my baby in bed?' he asked.

'For the last couple of hours.'

Ryan lay down. He held the phone over his face and his other arm over the top of his head. There was a dreamy quality to the line then: 'C'mere, I'm coming home.'

'When? Like, just for a visit, or . . .?'

'We're gonna record an album,' he said. 'This time we do it in the same country.'

'People would say it's about time.'

'Are you saying it's about time?'

Karine looked at the corner of her screen and her own image there, a duplicate of what he could see of her. She brought her left thumb to her lips. 'Diarmaid will be remembering things from now on. Or knowing that it's not right for his dad to be so far away. So it's about time. And in terms of the band.'

'I need to be with Diarmaid,' he said. 'Lord Urchin, take or leave. That'll either be brilliant or a fucking disaster.'

'Maybe Cork misses the racket you make.'

'I sincerely doubt that, girl.'

'How soon?'

'Ah, a month or two yet. We have to raise the sponds. Book work holidays, book the studio . . . write the fucking thing.'

'Joseph never said.'

'We only decided today. Yesterday. Jesus, I don't know when I am, looking at you.'

'That's soju for you,' she said.

According to her friends, Karine D'Arcy should have thought of herself as a soloist as well. They took the actions of her ex-boyfriend as insult on injury. They said that she should feel independent, architect of her own destiny, or doom, if it came to it. But Karine had always considered herself one in a system. One daughter of three, one dancer of a crew, one friend of a squad. Something to someone. There was little she could do about the fact that she was defined by a man's absence. She was the mother of a boy whose father lived varying great distances away. She looked like she'd been abandoned. She was compelled to remind people that she was complicit in that abandonment, that Ryan worked abroad because he'd been given permission to work abroad. There was never a bad word said in front of Diarmaid because she wanted Diarmaid to be sure he had a father who loved him; he wasn't sired by a fella who'd turn up only on birthdays and Christmas Eve, and there were plenty of them around.

After the call with Ryan she sat a few minutes in her bedroom. Her boyfriend, Dylan Moloney, was drinking beer in her parents' living room and watching the end of a horror film, waiting on her to define herself by attachment to him.

Karine thought of the whorls tattooed on Ryan's arm and the skimming clouds on his side. She thought of a lean, dark dragon parting cirrus waves, breaking into the lower atmosphere and laying waste to everything beneath him. She thought of Cork in flames and she could hardly fill her lungs. She felt her dancer's body underneath the one motherhood had given her. And she could have picked out the notes, just then. She could have written it, the piece that was about to play.

It was said that Ireland was reinventing herself, as if this was some rare event and the country wasn't in a constant state of dithering. Postcolonial, post-Catholic, post-Tiger, post-Brexit, junctures tracked by little ould invigilators peering out windows with net curtains bunched in their fists, and every new collapse portending a new wave of Notions. It was said that Ireland always knew what she was, even if she didn't stick with it for long. But how could she? What was she at, legalising same-sex marriage and revolting over women's healthcare and *céad míle fáilte* and fuck off back to where you came from and *divide et impera* and bishops on the school board and wanting everything and claiming to have fuck-all?

It was 2019 and a funny time to be Irish. At no time in Ireland's history was it not a funny time to be Irish.

A little ould invigilator now sat at a wooden counter in a third-floor apartment in Cork city centre. She was not altogether welcome here but she was altogether comfortable; she was comfortable in most settings, because a couple of decades before she had decided she might as well be. She was little by anyone's standards: she was five foot three and comprised mostly of cardigans. She was ould by her own insistence. She was sixty-eight and held no truck with the idea that antiquity was delayed by good diet and modern medicine, because youth meant contributing and conforming, youth was a pain in the arse, and therefore youth would not be conferred on her at her age. Her name was Maureen Phelan, or Mo Looney on occasion. She was in great nick and wasn't keen on people knowing it.

The apartment belonged to her only son, who'd been put in her by Dominic Looney, a man she hadn't seen since the middle of July, 1969. She'd named the child James; he had gone with Jimmy. He had been raised on the northside of Cork by his grandparents while his hussy of a mother did her penance working office jobs in London and speaking disrespectfully to brickies who made overtures in the Irish clubs. He had come down with an awful dose of chivalry nine years previous, and had insisted on her coming home to Cork to rejoice in her dotage under his watchful eye. He had put her up in a series of fancy flats. He had arranged days out with her two grandchildren. He had heartily buffed the gouges she'd cut into his city. He would be fifty in less than a year. For a while it hadn't looked like he would make that milestone.

His eyebrows and eyelashes had come back, thank Jesus, but he'd gone awful skinny and shook.

He put a cup of tea in front of her and turned to finish making his own. He looked as if he'd just gotten out of bed – bags under his eyes, slightly slack-jawed, shuffling – though surely he was up hours.

'Five of them,' she told him. 'Four fellas and a girl. Now, it wouldn't be my kind of music but he has a lovely voice, Jimmy.'

Her son sourly said, 'Plenty times I heard that little fucker singing, plenty different tunes and not one of them stirring.'

'Oh, don't be such an old goat. The lad has a gift, will you let him make use of it?'

'But that's it, girl. I don't remember him asking me.'

'I wonder sometimes if it isn't half-cracked that carry-on makes you. Make a fool of the law often enough and you start thinking you must be the law.'

Jimmy turned and leant back against his kitchen worktop. He folded his arms and held his mug on the opposite forearm and said, 'Ah, will you put a cork in it?'

'I will not,' she said. '*I don't remember him asking me.*
Grandeur, that is. You think you can survive anything now, that's
what's wrong with you.'

'Did you just come over to tell me Ryan Cusack wants to be a
fucking troubadour?'

'I came over to see you,' she said, sincerely. She saw plenty of
people. Living in a city, you couldn't help seeing people. They
teemed and hubbubed and spilled out of buildings. She didn't know
that many of them. She had joined book clubs and taken classes and
got along with the other participants well enough because the Irish
were a garrulous lot and the new Irish either garrulous themselves
or quick to get the hang of it. But she tended to trigger disquiet in
people sooner or later. She'd say the wrong thing or ask the wrong
question and they'd retreat like politicians after a general election,
smiling benignly, walking arseways. She didn't mind too much –
plenty more where they came from – but on occasion she needed to
talk to someone whose life threaded through her own, at least for
the sake of consistency of context. A new pal would need a thorough induction before she could talk to them about Ryan Cusack
and the steps he was taking, bold as brass. Jimmy knew young
Cusack well. He had been his employer. He had brought him to the
coalface; he was probably now the founder of the feast.

Which was, perhaps, a reason she should not have been talking
to Jimmy about Ryan, because what was she doing but precipitat-
ing his demanding his due? But it was easier ask forgiveness than
permission. And she had divilment in her, Maureen, she liked to
tug rugs from under people, she liked a halt applied to a gallop,
she liked reactions, and she was looking for one now.

Jimmy coughed at her.

'I hope it's brandy did that to you,' she said.

'I'm not able for it at all any more.'

'Well, then.'

'Certain levels,' he said, 'of social engagement are expected.'

'You're in remission, Jimmy.'

'Which to most fellas means back in business, therefore back in
business is what I must be.'

'You'd think a man like you wouldn't need to worry about what other people think.'

'Ah, Maureen, you have a bit of a wobble, and all around you langers are getting big fucking ideas. D'you know what, a long way down the list of my headaches is the minstrel boy hightailing it on me.'

She sighed as if to concede a point and said, 'He did all right out of you, I suppose.'

'And what do you mean by that?'

'Well,' she said, and paused to sip, 'the good people of this city would say that you broke far more than you built.'

'The good people lack imagination—'

'And yet you could have built them a folk hero.'

'Oh, you think he'll get that far, do you?'

'Can't you ask him when he's home?'

'I will,' Jimmy said. 'Oh, don't you worry. Mister Cusack will be brought in to me by his ear.'

'So he can ask for your permission, is it?'

'You know I know when you're trying to put a match to me,' he said. 'You're not that opaque, girl.'

'Ah, maybe you're right.' She clapped the mug down on the counter to see if he'd flinch. 'He outfoxed you, and I'm glad he outfoxed you.'

'Chemotherapy outfoxed me,' Jimmy said. 'Or ran the whole fucking hunt over me. Cusack saw his chance and skedaddled, is all.'

'Well.' They sat quietly until she realised each of them thought that in silence they'd outfox the other. She finished her tea. 'I'll hit the road,' she said, presenting the mug. He took it from her. She put her coat on. 'Think of yourself as a patron of the arts, Jimmy,' she said. 'Like one of them old Italian merchant princes.'

Outside the day was bright but wild and had already sprung on her a couple of showers. She followed the Lee and stopped to look at old maps behind glass in a rare-book shop. She thought about patrons. Men and women with plenty money and a dawning horror of their own mortality. Syphilis-mad nobles with a *grá* for

7

gold and cartography. Ecclesiastical plutocrats commissioning paintings of lustrous saints. The merchant princes ordering texts of convenient philosophy, their own Bibles. How could a world recover from that sort of scales-tipping?

She had seen a documentary about merchant princes on one of the channels a few weeks ago and what she took from it was that there was no distinction to be made between your common-or-garden capitalist and the degenerate she'd given birth to. The things he got up to, or at least the things he'd gotten up to when he was a stronger man, knocked great lumps out of the city, and was the city not asking for it? Feck the city, she thought when she was feeling belligerent, which was more and more these days and maybe a result of her insisting on having a hoary head, but when she sighed and simmered down, she thought it was a great pity that most of Cork didn't know what she'd been made go through so she really couldn't hold it against them, and Jimmy's carry-on – wheeling or dealing or banging fellas' heads together or whatever it was – was unforgiveable, but still the result of her country deciding to make shit of her in 1970. Unforgiveable but understandable and hardly unforeseen.

Jimmy had once knocked around with a lad called Tony Cusack, who had brought his own little divil into the world. Maureen had not known Ryan as a child; she had recognised him as a young man only because he was the spit of his father. She'd found him to be wide-eyed, foul-mouthed and uneasy enough in his mannerisms to suggest that he struggled with his morals or suffered from his nerves. Apart from that she supposed he was easy on the eye. She wasn't in the business of falling in love with twenty-year-old boys but it helped that there was nothing gammy about him. He did a bit for Jimmy. A bit of what, she didn't know. Drug dealing, she assumed; he wasn't solid enough for strong-arming. She had befriended him without his scrutinising her motives; he had been in the market for a friend. For a few weeks she had him coming over for the tay and the chats and in the course of that found out there was the cut of a musician to him. He said his mother had taught him to play piano, but after she died, his father had sold the piano. Maureen had realised that his father had sold it to Jimmy's ex-wife, Deirdre, and had eventually arranged to have the piano, otherwise gathering dust, stored in her apartment, but there was no way of producing this gift without revealing to Ryan that she'd known his lineage from the start. He didn't take it well. It was one of the only times in her life she hadn't enjoyed yanking the rug out from under someone.

Owing to some scheme or another Jimmy moved Ryan abroad. Jimmy wouldn't tell her how to get a hold of him, and with her having said plenty wrong things and asked plenty wrong questions Ryan wasn't forthcoming with his contact details. She learned how to get the best results from internet searches. She got her granddaughter, Ellie, to show her how to navigate social media and though Ryan seemed to have no social media presence she found a couple of his siblings and through them discerned that Ryan was now the father of a small boy and was in a sort of exile, as she had once been: Jimmy had moved him from Cork to Naples to Dublin to Liverpool. He kept moving even when Jimmy got sick and was forced into convalescence: Berlin, then Seoul, which she thought was mad carry-on, lepping all over the world like that with a small son at home. What was it keeping him away when his gender precluded him from feeling shame, when the twenty-first century had put paid to most of that, anyway? She couldn't figure it out.

When he recorded a new piano piece – arrangements he sold through a stock music website – she bought it. When she learned he had written the music for a video game she bought the game, though she couldn't make head nor tail of it, and so only heard the first piece in the soundtrack. She tried to make Ellie play the game instead; Ellie said it was weird. Ellie was fourteen and found almost everything weird.

When Ryan started a band with the three other lads and the girl, Maureen assumed at first he had come back to Cork. She checked the siblings' accounts and took a walk by the father's estate and finally went to the band's website, ticked off at her old pet's evasiveness. It turned out he was still in Seoul, that they intended to record over the internet as an experiment. Maureen bought the songs and nodded along. She didn't know at first that the voice on the recordings was Ryan's. He didn't seem the type to sing.

She would be pleased if Jimmy paused to wonder if he wasn't doing the right thing in giving his protégés the means of self-production.

Now she kept going. Along by the Lee, crossing at Parnell Bridge. Without her and her suffering there would never have been a Jimmy, and therefore no resources for Ryan Cusack to expend globetrotting and making music. It was not a stretch to think that without Maureen Phelan there would not have been a Cork five-piece called Lord Urchin. She felt like a dark matriarch, not malevolent, but pragmatic, in tune to all the rhythms of the city. Really, she felt like a patron. Really was she not mother to a great merchant prince?

It was a funny time to be Irish. There weren't even generations between flips. The Irish hated the EU for demanding that austerity be implemented, post-Crash; the Irish loved the EU for being something the Brits hated, post-Brexit. The Irish were losing their best and their brightest to emigration; Dublin was full to bursting and no one could afford to live in it. The priests were dying off; design start-ups were kept afloat with 'Christ on a Bike' T-shirts and tea towels with 'Jesus, Mary and Joseph' embroidered on them. Who'd want a United Ireland, sure wouldn't the six counties bleed the Republic dry? Young wans were wearing ironic slogan necklaces saying 'Brits Out' because there might be a United Ireland soon. To be Irish was to be certain that things were going Ireland's way at last, and certain that there wasn't a hope in hell with Ireland's luck. To be Irish was to be resentful, flippant, European, nationalistic, demented. The island of saints and scholars and not a saint left among them. People writing books and shooting films and doing pop-up gigs in town squares. People recording themselves performing poetry on the Atlantic shore, sneering out at Canada. What could you do except keep trying to tell the story of it? To be young and gifted and damp.

For four years all was as grand as Georgie Fitzsimons could hope for and then the little prick decided to reinvent himself as a rock star.

She googled him intermittently, on each occasion hoping for a report of a harsh prison sentence or his badly losing a fist fight on Patrick Street. For a long time she could type his name into the search bar and find that all he had to that name was muzak, And I bet he's very proud of that, she thought, the absolute state of him. For a long break she was sated by the state of him and didn't google him at all. And then, one morning in late spring, over her bowl of porridge in the kitchen of her flat share in Croydon, an idle search returned an article in the *Echo* about a band called Lord Urchin who had recorded some songs over the internet and, buoyed by the response, were about to record a full-length album in Union Studios, near the School of Music in Cork city centre.

Lord Urchin is the project of Mayfield cousins Joseph O'Donnell and Ryan Cusack. Cusack first found success in dance music production with credits for Some Song She'd Never Heard Of *and has remixed* Some Wagon *and* Some Other Shower of Langers *and is now based in* fucking Seoul?

Fucking Seoul! she fumed, walking down Brigstock Road with an unruly umbrella. How did he get to Seoul? He surely had a criminal record as long as Blarney Street, who'd let that lad into Seoul? Maybe she had the wrong Ryan Cusack. Maybe there were two of them in Mayfield. On the train she looked him up again. There were not two of them in Mayfield. Fucking Seoul! she raged.

When she got to the office she downloaded the Lord Urchin songs. 'Jessica,' she called, and her colleague stuck her head up over her computer monitor. 'C'mere and listen to this for me.'

Jessica's parents were from Clonmel. She had been brought up on GAA and the Pogues and was surprised to hear that sex work was a thing in Ireland, too. She came around the desk. She had been eating fruit salad and sucked her thumb and first finger purposefully. Georgie pulled the headphones out of their socket and turned the PC speakers on. She played half of the first song, then switched to the second.

'You know I prefer Adele,' Jessica said.

'I know the fella that made this,' Georgie said. 'He used to be a drug dealer. And not a hanging-around-doorways-shivering-in-an-anorak drug dealer. A bloody champion.'

Georgie worked in an office with peach-paint walls answering calls to a support line for sex workers wanting to leave the trade. They were funded by a Christian group, but so far no one had asked her to convert any callers, and she thought herself versed enough in these people's Verses to be able to spot any slithery proselytising. Georgie liked this job. It made her feel useful in an unfamiliar way. She was now the kind of woman who wore straight-legged trousers and went for Friday evening drinks, she was the kind of woman who was invited to hen parties.

'The guy singing?' asked Jessica.

'I think so?' Georgie leaned over and opened the browser again. She pulled up the *Echo* article.

'Don't they have a photo?' Jessica said.

'Oh, he couldn't make the photoshoot, he lives in fucking Seoul. They must be giving visas to any old good-for-nothing. Maybe I'll apply, maybe they'll let me out there to . . .' She couldn't think of a mean enough term. 'Make stupid songs,' she said, stupidly.

The question is whether the five-piece can tap that same magic when working for the first time in each other's company, but Corkonian fans are keen to find out. The International Recordings EP can be purchased . . .

'Purchased!' Georgie spat. 'Oh, you can drag the man out of dealing, but you can't drag the dealer out of the man.'

Jessica laughed diplomatically and went off to answer the phone.

There were no photographs on the website either, just monochrome logos for Lord Urchin and its label, Catalyst Music. Georgie thought about emailing Catalyst Music. *Did you know*

one of your musicians was a drug dealer? You should . . . What?
Recall the songs? The songs were out there; there was nothing she
could do about the songs. She read reviews by Hot Press and
Goldenplec and Niallergy. She read a short interview with a bandmate called Izzy King in the *Examiner*, but it was about a previous band she'd been in, so there weren't many pertinent details.

Her phone started ringing too.

Between calls, Georgie opened a new document and wrote
about Cusack's bad habits. She found it difficult to strike a balance
between providing convincing detail and withholding stuff that
would identify her. She asked Jessica for her input. Jessica knew
enough about Georgie to be her friend, which meant that Jessica
knew the bare minimum. She was not the best barometer. She
switched the phones off for their lunch break and asked why
Georgie was bothering.

'I feel like people should know.'

'But devil's advocate . . .' Jessica took another tub of fruit salad
from her bag. 'Couldn't people say, "You can't talk, Georgie, you
were up to no good and all"?'

'Yeah, well I'm not going to mention that, girl.'

Georgie had changed quite a bit in four years. In Cork she had
had long, dark brown hair. Now she had a sunflower-blonde bob.
In Cork she had been scraggy-limbed and drawn. Now she had
plumped up and looked hearty and genial. Disarmed. Declawed.

In Cork City she'd had a boyfriend. Robbie. They were together
six years before he ended up on the wrong side of an argument
with a gangland aristocrat named Jimmy Phelan: 'J.P.' to cops
and robbers both. Because lads ending up on the wrong side of
arguments with gangland aristocrats wasn't the kind of thing
people talked about freely, she had to find this out at great cost to
herself. She went looking for Robbie and in so doing pissed off
J.P., who decided there was one foolproof way to shut her up. As
luck would have it her death was made the responsibility of a
callow feen called Ryan Cusack, from whom she'd bought a fair
amount of cocaine over the years. Ryan Cusack didn't kill her,
but stuck her on a flight to England. He reneged not out of pity,

but out of cowardice, which didn't stop him threatening to kill her if he ever saw her in Cork again.

She took him at his word and cowered in London. A powerful man thought that she was dead, and as Snow White to the Woodsman she had promised his underling that she'd pay for her life with her silence. For two years she didn't contact her parents. Hearing her voice on the phone after all that time seemed to do them more harm than good. Easier forgive a troubled dead girl than a thirty-year-old calamity.

'You put the heart crossways on your father when he picked up,' her mother said.

'Sorry.'

'He's on tablets, Georgina.'

'Because of me?'

'Sure what else would give him angina?'

Now Georgie typed through Jessica eating her lunch, making tea, turning the phones back on, starting on reports that they were supposed to do together. At 4:32 p.m., she emailed the essay to Hot Press and Goldenplec and Nialler9.

'Do you think anyone will care?' Jessica asked.

'Probably not.'

' "Probably not" means his band isn't important enough, which is good.'

'But it really sticks in my craw. That he got away—'

'You got away.'

'Yeah, but I wasn't a drug dealer. And he gets to come and go as he pleases, he gets to sing about it. The audacity of him.'

'That's men for you,' Jessica said. 'You can't do anything about audacity.'

'I can try,' Georgie said.

Young and gifted and damp and looking to glory in it, looking to wallow in isolation, just them and the Atlantic, just them and their Irishness and the stories in their bones. Hence Inishbofin, thirty minutes off the coast of Connemara by ferry. And with them, instruments, laptops, slabs and spirits.

Damp, yes, sure wasn't there something in the water? Sure wasn't everyone saying it, and saying it in plenty differing tones? There's something in the water, and everyone's excelling/There's something in the water and everyone's lost the run of themselves/ There's something in the water, the endless rain keeps everyone indoors, singing songs by the hearth/There's something in the water, if Irish Water wasn't such a joke of a utility company maybe they could engineer it out again, get all of these millennials into honest work/Michael O'Leary should run the country/ Yeah, run it into the ground.

Every morning they woke up and checked the Irish Times app to see if World War Three had started or if Donegal had sunk into the sea. The country joked about its love of the Death Notices and here they were, to a man bound to a global death watch . . .

Mel assumed it was Joseph who'd come up with it, for Joseph seemed to be the boss, despite his anarcho-syndicalism posturing. It appeared on the Lord Urchin homepage the morning she travelled to Galway.

Art and honesty are inseparable.
You must reveal something about yourself with
everything you create.
These are our rules.

What Mel was meant to reveal about herself she didn't know. Maybe it didn't apply to her, being a spare pair of hands.

She sat on the train and looked out at rolling fields, fields, fields and thought of her mother's grey face the morning after Tony Cusack broke their front window. 'I just want you to know,' she remembered her saying, chin in the air. 'I just want you to know that I offered that boy nothing but friendship. I just want you to know that he's lying.'

But this was not her revelation, and so it didn't count.

Maybe the members of Lord Urchin had simply agreed to hereafter insist on disclosure, given how rocky their road had been.

First Orson Rotimi and Izzy King's band – Multiple Bears, a dance-punk outfit that the bloggers were buzzed about – was mangled by allegations that its frontman was a demon for the underage fans. They'd jumped ship and with Joseph O'Donnell, Davy Carroll and Ryan Cusack had started Lord Urchin, notable for its members living on two different continents and creating songs by recording and swapping and building sound files over the internet. This was notable, so *The International Recordings* EP enjoyed modest but promising success. And then Izzy King, insufferably cool alumna of underground bands like Scruffy the Janitor and Maud Gone Mad, past associations with perverts all but forgotten, broke her hand. Just as the bloggers and street photographers and influencers were registering their awe, just as the country retreat was paid for and the studio booked.

Joseph told Mel that he wanted to be honest, that there were other session musicians he'd worked with before that both he and Izzy would have preferred, but it was short notice and no one was free. Mel was pleased with his offer, but didn't fall for his lie; Izzy didn't want creative input from whoever was taking her place during her recovery and no seasoned session musician would put up with that. Mel would, not because she was weak, but because she would hardly find a more solid introduction to the scene at home.

Orson Rotimi was standing outside of Ceannt station's cafe when she arrived. He shook her hand but didn't offer to take her bag or tell her where he'd parked or ask how her journey had been. He led her to the car park around the corner. He had laid the back seat of his Hyundai flat so she would have room for her luggage and guitar. He and Izzy, Davy and Joseph had been on Inishbofin two nights already. He acted as though they were a unit, and putting Mel up was a minor imposition.

'How much of a drive do we have?' she asked as he started the engine, by way of initiating conversation. She already knew it would be about an hour and a half.

'About ninety kilometres,' he said, by way of being a gowl.

'Ah yeah, about an hour and a half so,' Mel said. 'Given the terrain, like. I bet it's gorgeous, is it? I've never been to Connemara.'

'How long have you been playing guitar?' he asked. 'You look about twelve.'

'I'm twenty-three,' Mel said. 'Playing four years, thereabouts.'

She just about heard him scoff. She leaned back and stared out the passenger window. Galway City was alive in the sunshine, like there was geothermal energy jouncing people along its footpaths. She could have said, Just let me out, so. The people here look like they want to jam.

'Izzy can still do a bit,' Orson said. 'She'd have done the lot if the doctor hadn't put the shits up Joseph.'

'How's her hand?'

'Her cast came off the day before yesterday. So I dunno if we'll need you for long.'

Beyond Galway City the way cut between lake-splattered lowlands and a spine of brown mountains. They dodged tour buses and sheep snoozing on the road and drove through Clifden, which to Mel was disappointingly bustling, and on to a more appropriately remote Cleggan, where Orson parked in someone's stony field. He was civil enough to carry her guitar to the ferry, and off it again once docked on the island. He marched ahead and she followed, pulling faces at his back.

The house was a mix of old and new, an elegant addition of glass, wood and stone cladding to a period building. 'This is the business,' Mel said, and Orson obliged with, 'It's grand, isn't it?'

Izzy King was magnanimous, smiling, tactile. Her hair came halfway down her back and was black at the roots, petrol blue at the tips. Her eyeliner was dramatically flicked out. Davy Carroll was strapping and energetic and clearly did not wish to shatter any stereotypes about drummers. Joseph O'Donnell looked the same as ever: dourly handsome, like a funeral director's son.

Izzy showed Mel to her room and told her what time the local shop was open and identified the best spots for mobile coverage, 'Not that Joseph thinks anyone should care.' Downstairs they ate spiced chickpeas with couscous and flatbread and drank lip-staining wine. They talked about whether there was such a thing as a guilty pleasure, they intersected neoliberalism and treason, they argued about the ethics of tagging superior street artists' graffiti; everyone was full of shit and Mel could not have been happier. For dessert there were bottles of local craft beer – 'Bogger Bräu', Davy called it – and they got stuck in while Joseph went through the vision for the album and 'the drab shit', as he put it, incorrectly: the terms of employment. 'Think of Catalyst Music as an artists' collective,' he said, though it wasn't strictly an artists' collective, unless one was willing to think of accountants as artists. 'A marriage, so,' Joseph clarified, 'between art and finance. The finance gets the art out into the world.'

'Natalie and Colm, lords to the urchins,' Davy said.

'Joseph, you forgot something,' Izzy said.

He turned towards her, one elbow on its corresponding knee, and made a face that Mel didn't like because it looked cheerful and yet sarcastic, a sitcom face. 'What's that, Isobel?'

Izzy looked at Mel. 'Art and honesty are inseparable. You must reveal something about yourself with everything you create. What, Melanie, do you plan to reveal to the world?'

'It's just Mel,' Mel said.

'It's just Mel! A great revelation indeed!' Davy said.

The bandmates laughed and Mel, bandmate now too, she supposed, laughed with them. So it was in the manner of an experienced teacher to a room full of rowdy kids that Natalie Grogan walked in, saying 'Mighty craic going on in here,' with a tidy, red smile.

After her came a tall, very blond guy with a Norn Iron accent. That was Colm McArdle. Mel had missed out on the local scenes indebted to his energy, but couldn't have missed the many social media references to those scenes: the Catalyst club night, the indie record label, the rap/spoken word trail he'd overseen with the arts festival, and this whole thing, of course, this collaborative company, this ambitious album. He was over for an introductory hug as soon as he noticed her.

As Colm pulled away, she saw Ryan with Joseph locked in a proper embrace.

'You must be exhausted,' Orson said, as the lads let each other go. 'Only landed and we pull you out here to the wilds.'

'I'm as well off, to be honest,' Ryan said, and this sounded trite, like he said it just for the sake of saying something. He looked at Mel and she smiled and stepped forward.

'Hey Ryan, long time no see.'

He was suddenly very pale and she was not at all surprised. 'Linda,' he said.

'It's Mel now,' Mel said. 'No one calls me Linda these days.'

. . . because everywhere the water was rising. Sex, drugs and rock and roll; that was all that was left. Eat, drink and be merry, for we are completely fucking fucked.

Or make a song and dance about it. Maybe that's what you're here for.

Track 1: *Find My Way Back*

All I had to do was book the flight, pack up some bits, sell off the others, *annyeong* and out the gap. Except what then? I'd get back to Ireland into thunderous complication because I had fucked things up beyond forgiveness, beyond explanation, even. There were boys in Cork I knew would be happy to kill me. I thought the Shades would demand that I help them with their enquiries, given the way things were before I left, or the way I'd left things . . . I didn't know what enquiries they might have had. I didn't feel the reverberations from all that way away. I bounced around the world. There was no form to what I was running from. Dread, I suppose, potential that spidered off into all of the ridiculous places I could imagine.

That was the clamouring stuff, the lurid stuff. There was the practical stuff too. Like whether there would be any opportunities at home. What would I get out of a studio job at home? Twenty euro more than I'd get on the dole? Whose couch would I be crashing on? Even if there were studio jobs in Cork, everyone in Cork knew me, everyone in Cork knew what I used to do when I was a young fella, and I can't take back any of it. Even if I could I wouldn't know where to start: how do you measure what damage you did when you personally saw the last of it wrapped tight in a half-kilo block on a table top just before a courier took it away? All I can be sure of is the damage it did to me, but who'd care? I could show photographs of bruises, medical reports, prescriptions, receipts for days spent on the tear trying to drink away all sorts, and who'd fucking care?

And the private stuff: who was I in Cork? Did I like who I was in Cork? Was it better for my son to see me how I really was or to see me as a distant but respectable fella? If I came back to Cork would I just turn into my own dad?

Would you ever want me back?

'Find My Way Back' started coming together just after we'd made the EP. I didn't think it was a song, at first. It was just me jotting out knots and bumps to see how I felt about them in a different format. Writing things down is a habit you got me into. Do you remember? You brought me a notebook after I had that meltdown on the Jazz Weekend and told me if I wasn't going to talk to you to write stuff down instead. D'you know what I used to do with it? I used to write letters to my mam. I used to write letters to a woman I could hardly remember. I dunno what I was at. I was a bit lost. I was doing a lot of drugs. Making one insane decision after another, 'decision' being too confident a term in this context. I still dunno how I survived it, I think only because I went up a gear after I found out Diarmaid was on the way.

So I would write shit down, first to my mam and then to myself and then thoughts that weren't addressing anyone in particular, just lines that went well together. Do you know you made me a songwriter? Is that a kind of alchemy? Is that always going to be the way with you?

I was writing down all of these thoughts about going home and they started looking like desperate wayfinding and so I saw what the song might look like. They come out like that, sometimes, like a welt rising in a mass of words. Home terrified me but I needed to be home. As much as I wanted to stay away reinventing myself, designing a new, sharper, tidier nature, I had to turn my face back to all I'd done. I had to rescue what was still healthy and I had to tend to all that was sick or brittle, I had to go home, I had to book the flight, pack up some bits, sell off the others, say *annyeong* and be brave for the first time in my life.

A year back, Georgie had written a letter to the other important boyfriend of her time in Cork, David Coughlan.

They had met at a Christian retreat in West Cork and bonded over ridicule of the kind of people who went on Christian retreats in West Cork. In London, Georgie had usually said 'long story' whenever anyone had asked her how she'd managed to get knocked up at a Christian retreat, but it wasn't a long story really. She'd been a mess, so what harm in allowing some watery-eyed zealots to pay for her bed and board in the middle of nowhere? David, a gambling addict, came to the retreat at the command of his born-again father. Thinking Georgie was but a gullible waif with an alcohol problem, he charged into a courtship hinging on trysts in the laundry room. Her pregnancy, he said, signified approval from a god with a great sense of humour. The shock at finding out she was actually a sex worker on a career break drove him to religious homecoming and full custody.

In her letter to David Coughlan, Georgie said something along the lines of: Dear David, I have moved to London to reinvent myself as an upstanding woman. I will learn office etiquette and household budgeting. Perhaps at some point we can work on a reintroduction. Very sincerely, Georgina Fitzsimons.

He wrote back something along the lines of: Dear Georgie, if you are very evidently not a whore by then, perhaps you can take Harmony to Fota for a day just before she begins to menstruate, that would be very helpful as I'm still a massive prude and gobshite. Here is a photo. Disingenuously, David Coughlan.

It had been Georgie's intention to contact David as soon as she arrived back in Cork but when it came to it, it couldn't come to it, it could still be that she was a dead woman. What if she arranged a reunion and then had to renege because some brute had a gun to her head? She refused to die proving David Coughlan right.

She thought such things dryly. She made out that she was so bitter she had become fearless. She did not succeed in fooling herself. Ryan Cusack's was a hell of a transformation: blaggard to bard. There had to have been at least tacit approval from gangland aristocracy; she knew enough of the trade to be sure that bosses didn't allow their subordinates to cavort around the globe. In London, a possibility had come to her and made her giddy. Unless there was no need for anyone's approval. Unless it was that Jimmy Phelan had had his grip loosened for him.

She had searched for mentions of 'Jimmy Phelan' or 'James Phelan' online and turned up nothing significant. Confirmation would require her travelling. She booked work holidays.

Whether grips had been loosened or not, she couldn't stay in Cork City. There were streets Georgie had to avoid and people she was not ready to risk meeting. She had been researching Airbnb rates in commuter towns when Jessica suggested she stay in her uncle's family's mobile home in a park by the beach, twenty kilometres south of the city.

'He won't be needing it?' Georgie asked.

'He won't be going this year,' Jessica said, and added, 'Believe me,' which Georgie thought was an invitation to gossip, but Jessica would say nothing more.

Jessica's uncle had purchased a hotspot for the mobile home. The signal strength was patchy. Videos didn't play smoothly, but Georgie could email fine. She grumbled and wondered whether this was a sign. Whether she should navigate by signs.

On her second morning in the mobile home, she did as she'd seen other women in the park do, she took a cup of tea outside. She leaned against the mobile home, the sea to her right, and looked in the direction of the city. She thought about identifying eyries from which she could observe her weakening saboteur. She imagined him being jeered by the good people, the ones who didn't loiter on low walls, or frequent bookmakers, or hire women by the hour.

When Georgie was a little girl, eight-ish, her mother had announced that an uncle was going to join them for Christmas dinner. Georgie didn't remember hearing of the uncle before then. She was excited. She prepared for the visit by drawing the uncle a special picture, composing a poem, and setting the table like it was set in books, with side plates, napkins, polished glasses, fruit squash in a jug. The uncle too would be like uncles in books, a rogue, or conspirator. When he arrived he was silent and rubicund in the way she now knew denoted alcoholism. He breathed through his mouth. He stared into space. Her mother spoke to him at the top of her voice. Georgie was embarrassed presenting the picture and when her mother asked her to recite her poem she pretended to have forgotten it. She was still embarrassed. She did not know why. That she was still embarrassed was itself embarrassing.

She was reminded of the uncle, sometimes, as she prepared for an arrival: when her boss, Mr Love, was due into the office, when she had Jessica over for coffee. It made her slow down so it was helpful, in an uncomfortable way. She was reminded of it now because it occurred to her that this flap of hers was in preparation for Cusack's arrival back in Cork. She had felt compelled to come back and that was because hurting Cusack from London could only ever give her rudimentary satisfaction. She wanted to see him at the point of understanding why he'd been hurt. She wanted to send him whispers on a cold breeze. *You brought this on yourself. Are you so arrogant to think you'd get away with it?*

'I should have killed her when I was told to!' he would weep, he would quail, he would vomit with the fear of it.

Now a woman approached from the direction of the main road. She wore a knitted hat, a fleece jacket and black gloves that seemed made for a man; she could have been a weathered forty or a lucky sixty-five. She said, 'Are you here with Paschal?' and sounded blandly Irish; she didn't even have a Cork accent.

'Who?'

'Paschal. Ah, come on, the man who owns this mobile home.'

Georgie automatically looked over her shoulder. 'I'm renting it from him, I suppose.'

'You suppose? He's not meant to be renting it out.'

'Well, it's more that I'm borrowing it.'

'What's that mean? Did you break in?'

'I did not.'

'You'd want to tell him to call me, because this isn't on at all.'

'I don't even know the man,' Georgie said. 'It's his niece I know. I'm on a break, she said I could stay here.'

The woman put her hands on her hips and stared into space, shaking her head. 'I don't know about this at all.'

'I'm here two days already,' Georgie said, indignantly.

'Well it's only now I got wind of it. Where's Paschal?'

'I. Don't. Know.'

'That lad burnt his bridges,' the woman said, 'and if he thinks he can be making money letting all and sundry into my park, he has another thing coming. Sell the mobile home, tell him. That's the only thing he can do now.'

'I can't tell him, because I don't know him. I only know his niece.'

'Don't be taking that tone with me.'

Georgie raised her eyes to heaven and in doing so remembered school corridors and cranky pimps in quick succession, as though the relevant phases of her life had occurred simultaneously. Learning on her back, felt up in uniform, Georgie and her attitude problem, needing talking-tos from spinsters and gangsters.

She looked towards the sea. The woman made an impatient noise and said, 'What kind of break is it if you're here on your own?'

Mad creatures, lone women, and maybe owing to the woman's unkind intent or to the overlap of memories, Georgie fixed on a whopper. 'I'm writing a book,' she said.

'About Paschal's carry-on, is it?'

'It's fiction.'

'Well you couldn't make that fecker up.' The woman had softened. 'What's your story about?'

'It's a thriller,' Georgie said. 'About a woman who had her daughter taken off her so she's out for revenge on the gangsters who did it.'

The woman nodded. 'My sister writes. They meet the odd time in the library in Carrigaline. How long are you staying? I'll have to talk to Paschal,' though now she seemed willing to manage under Paschal's apparent idiocy. 'I'm Carmel. I'm in the house just to the left of the entrance. And your own name?' She held out a hand.

Georgie took it. 'Gia,' she said.

'Fancy name,' Carmel wondered.

'Suits the stories,' Georgie said.

She found details for some suitable journalists. She had a type in mind: young, attuned to issues of social justice, easily riled. She sent some messages to see if one would bite and one did, probably more out of politeness than interest but Georgie liked the look of her regardless. The journalist said that she had fifteen minutes in Cork City in the morning, so perhaps a quick coffee. Georgie deduced that the journalist had deduced she'd be a godawful gobdaw and so she dressed as if she was going to the office.

She breathed deep and decided her new curves and sunflower-blonde bob made her sufficiently anonymous. There wasn't much chance that she would run into Cusack; based on the information in those irksome Izzy King video blogs, if he was already in Ireland he'd be in the band's rural hideaway, writing songs that congratulated himself on his post-dealing artistry. Georgie considered that she might be seen by an associate of the old aggressor, J.P. Hardly, she decided. You'd want to be up close, looking in her eyes. What chance that J.P. had ever seen her as a human being? The fact that men at their most repugnant did not see women as equals could at times be a great advantage. But even accounting for the bob and the extra pounds and the indifference of men, Georgie thought she could turn a corner and there he'd be, Jimmy Phelan, narrowing his eyes, curdling the air, scattering henchmen with the flick of a wrist. The thing with misconduct was that it moved around. There was no distinct area in the city where you were guaranteed to avoid the wicked. At Parnell Place, Georgie started to mutter, 'Oh God, oh God,' because she wasn't Gia, or writing a crime novel, only telling lies about a plot that might have been based on her own life. The city pulsated. It had no memory, it was defined by memory. People tied to place, and bound to their fucked-up histories, their imperfect relationships.

Medbh Lucey wore a short dress in a geometric print. Her startlingly red lipstick was applied as if by fountain pen. She was tall and stout and quite conspicuous.

'Young musicians with sketchy pasts is more a matter for publicists than journalists,' she said. 'I appreciate that you're thrown by it, but I'm not sure it means much.'

They sat at the window counter in a tiny coffee shop. The guy serving had asked Georgie what roast she wanted and was disheartened when she shrugged. There were jars of hard biscuits by the cash register and a smartarsed slogan chalked on the board outside.

'Young fellas make mistakes,' said Medbh. 'People love redemption stories, but they're for lifestyle magazines. What you're telling me belongs in a press release. I don't cover historical petty crimes.'

'It wasn't petty. The Ryan Cusack I knew could buy and sell you.' Georgie blew into her unascertained roast and said, 'It's not historical either.'

'In what sense?'

'This album's being produced by his own company, right? Where'd they get the money? Fair enough if he was remixing Rihanna or whoever, but he's not, he's remixing people I've never heard of. And he comes from nothing, he's so rough you'd want a Garda escort visiting his house. I know Cusack because I used move in similar circles, right, which is a big thing for me to say to you.'

'Now I'm inclined to think this is a personal grudge.'

'He was once hired to kill me.'

'Excuse me?'

'Off the record,' Georgie said.

Medbh grabbed her bag. 'All right, this is getting silly, and I have very boring but very real court cases to write up.'

'I wouldn't say this in court, I'm not completely stupid.'

'You wouldn't lie under oath, is it?'

'I'm not lying. Look, do you know Jimmy Phelan?'

'I've heard the name.'

'If you do court reports you know what kind of fella he is. Cusack used work for him. I always knew Cusack was involved with dodgy people, even though he was just a kid. It was only when he came for me with a gun I realised how dodgy. Why would I lie about something so awful?'

Medbh slid the bag over her wrist and folded her arms. 'If you wanted to get in a dig at Mr Phelan you might have done it two years ago. Is it because he's on the mend? Is that what's riled you? Why use Cusack? Was he your only point of contact with Phelan?'

'Wait,' Georgie said. 'Cusack is my problem. What he leads you to is your business.' She picked at a knot on the wood of the counter. 'A lot of us got caught in Cork's undertow. Some of us drowned. Personal grudge . . . Girl, you're right. On behalf of those of us who got caught in the undertow, I'm asking you for help in making sure the ones who thrived on it don't continue to. That's all.'

'Why not go to the Gardaí, then?'

'What would they do? Ask him how much he paid for his clothes?'

'I'll have a think about it,' Medbh said, and made for the door. 'I appreciate you getting in touch, Gia.'

Georgie swivelled. 'What happened to Jimmy Phelan? You said two years ago?'

'He was ill. Private citizen, of course, but the man's name comes up in certain circumstances.'

'Ill? Very ill?'

Medbh nodded. 'Cancer. Don't ask me what sort.'

'Well now that makes a lot of sense,' Georgie said.

Izzy said her jaw was acting up and Mel donated two ibuprofen tablets she'd found at the bottom of her satchel. Izzy swallowed them with red wine, stuck a finger in her mouth and felt warily along the backs of her gums. 'Does anyone else have painkillers?' she asked. 'For later?' She did not look like a woman who was suffering. Mel wasn't sure whether Izzy was being graceful in hiding her pain, which was gendered behaviour and socially enforced, therefore Izzy should not be judged for it. Or whether Izzy was at ease but looking for attention: equally irritating, equally gendered.

Mel's head had been fucked with this shit for a good while now.

Four years in Glasgow made plenty time to relearn what it was to be Mel Duane after almost nineteen on the northside of Cork. Mel's father had said that Glasgow and Cork were actually very alike. Mel had found them nothing alike but knew it was because she walked differently in either city, went to different places and found different denizens. Glasgow, or her experience of Glasgow, needed a different kind of tough. Now back on home soil Mel was set for unlearning, which was a more private undertaking.

They were drinking in the sitting room of the house on Inishbofin: Mel, Izzy, Joseph, Davy and Orson. Natalie and Ryan had gone up to the bedroom assigned to him. Colm was at the kitchen table with his laptop, having tetchily claimed to have work to do.

Joseph, Davy and Orson thought about Izzy's need for painkillers; they looked at her, and then at each other.

'Weed?' Davy said.

'Ryan might have coke,' Izzy said. 'I can rub it on my gums.'

'Ryan has no coke, where would Ryan get coke?' Joseph said. 'Your options are wine and weed, girl. Though you raise an interesting point. It might be nice to have some chemicals. Yokes. Or trips, even.'

They all agreed that this would be good. Izzy left the room in a hurry but returned a couple of minutes later. 'Ryan's not upstairs,' she said, and then, just to Mel, 'Come look for him with me.' An order, not a request. Gendered again. Women clump. They deal with men in groups, so that they can confer or coordinate pincer attacks. Mel wanted no part of this and yet she smiled and nodded and got to her feet. Thank you for the camaraderie. Thank you for thinking of me so soon as armour. Thank you for latching on. Thank you so bloody much.

There was no one in Ryan's room. Izzy called through the bathroom door keyhole and Natalie called back, saying that Ryan must be knocking around somewhere. Izzy led Mel to the yard and they found him facing the strait and the distant mainland. He was juddering, biting the side of his hand. When he spotted Mel he spat the hand out and his eyes darted around her as though she was some fearsome authority.

'I think I'm getting wisdom teeth,' Izzy told him. 'Spare me some sleeping pills or Valium?'

He replied, 'Why would I have sleeping pills or Valium?'

'You're a touchy boy. I meant whatever got you through the long-haul.'

'A skinful and an aisle seat.'

'A skinful it is, then. Pub?'

'There's gatt inside.'

'Yes but!' Izzy said. 'The lads think we should try and find some yokes or trips.'

'Around here?' Mel said at an elevated pitch, so that she'd sound jovial.

'This is Wild Ireland,' Izzy said. 'It's full of hippies and loons and they know how to make their own entertainment.'

Ryan once again closed his teeth over the fleshy space between his thumb and index finger.

'And whether we find yokes and trips,' Izzy said to him, 'don't you need a pint?'

They took it easy. It was a short walk, but steeply downhill, and the light was almost gone. Izzy did all of the asking. How's your kid? Seoul, would you recommend it? Did you have to learn the language? Ryan answered politely enough and did not look at Mel.

There was a picnic bench, unoccupied, outside the quayside pub. Izzy said she'd get the first round. Ryan didn't know what he wanted. A pint of something. What did they have? Izzy said, 'Come in with me, sure,' but he said that he'd stay and mind the bench, that he needed to roll a smoke anyway.

'I'd drink fucking anything at this stage,' he said.

'I wanted him to come in,' Izzy told Mel, inside the pub, 'so we could get talking to the locals and he could ask about the drugs. Fellas are judged less. Besides, he's the expert.'

In developing an obsession with Ryan, Mel had not been unusual because they'd all done it at some point. He was Kelly's older brother so it had to be done. Follow him around, eye him up, talk about all the things you'd do to him. Girls could be as full of hot air as the boys they said were full of hot air. Mel stared with whoever else had eyes on him and giggled when prompted, but the staring was undertaken as research, in the manner of an anthropologist who wishes now to live among wolves. Gain his trust, creep closer till you're walking beside him. Copy his gatch and watch what he watches. Mel didn't want to have Ryan kiss her or hold her hand. She wanted him, meaning the stuff of him, his skin, his bones, his blood, his brain; his experience of the terrace, of his family, of his own mother, brief as that was; his sensations, stirred by a fist fight or by his girlfriend's fingers. She wanted to move his lips and to direct how his hand might close over someone else's. She didn't want him but wanted to be him.

She had learned that a daughter was less a person than she was a doll. Daughters were storybook creatures. You dressed them up and fed them bowls of sugar, you gave them frilly names like

Melinda. That her mother followed that kind of doctrine when she lived on a council estate in Ireland was perhaps a small revolution, *There are princesses in these parts too, take your fishwives and fuck off.* As was the case with revolution it was ugly, dresses and pastels and sparkles but ugly all the same. A femininity insolently superficial. When Mel was a young teenager her mother had decorated her room in black and pink and bought two sets of Playboy-logo bedclothes. She didn't justify this except to say it was a pretty aesthetic. She said maybe one day they'd step out with a pair of brothers. She told people Mel wanted perfumes for Christmas and make-up for birthdays and Mel gave bits and pieces of these hauls to Kelly Cusack but otherwise she was not a particularly rebellious kid. How could you rebel against an ethos as volatile as Tara's?

So if the obsession with Ryan didn't spring from love, then it might have been jealousy, and Mel considered this in the context of her being stuck with femininity: he appeared to have choice that she didn't have and control that she didn't have and respect that she didn't have, her being swaddled in pink and doused in perfume. That was a powerful realisation when she could see the drawbacks to being him. She could hear Tony Cusack losing the run of himself through the dividing wall. She knew respect was won only after perfecting swagger and that looked exhausting.

Mel had always hated the name Linda. Linda was a name for a much older woman, one who was settled and not at all strange. The name Melinda was strange in the wrong way. Gilded. Convoluted. When she was a teenager some of her schoolmates called her Malignant Melanoma. She hated Linda but it was the lesser evil. 'Mel' was her father's name for her and it went with the move to Scotland. She had been training as a hair stylist, and her dad helped her arrange to continue her apprenticeship at a salon five minutes from his house. She didn't stick with it. She hadn't wanted to be a stylist; it was her mother's idea. Really, she wanted to be a rock star or a tattoo artist, so she took up drawing and she took up guitar. She chopped her hair off, pierced the nape of her neck, took a job in Burger King, and donated to the charity shop all of her skirts and dresses. The guilt, then, when she realised what had happened. The rejection of her mother's ideals caused her mother to disappear, as if her existence depended on at least one person taking her seriously.

By the time she found out about it her mother hadn't been seen in Cork for three weeks. Mel's aunt Colette, who lived in Dublin, hours away, raised the alarm. No one in Cork, including Grandad Duane, seemed to have noticed that Tara had vanished.

Tara, was impulsive, flirtatious, hyperactive, spiteful, insincere, a lot of things you didn't want your mother to be, and even with some years' distance now Mel didn't think she ever really liked her mother, or loved her, and love was supposed to be the easier of the two. For the first few months after her mother disappeared, she had read a lot about complex parent-child relationships in an effort to find one like theirs. A lot of these accounts were defined by abuse and still almost all mentioned love. My mother is a vicious alcoholic but I love her and I miss her, or, My father beat me with belts but I love him and want to forgive him. There weren't many that said: my mother was distracted and indifferent, so I feel bad that she's missing but not as bad as I should. There had only been leaden sufferance between Mel and Tara, as if each knew innately that there'd been some biological mistake and neither had fully committed to making the best of it.

Tara was crazy for the fellas. For months after she went missing, everyone assumed she'd gone off with a boyfriend and would get in touch as soon as she discovered he wasn't the centre of the universe. But time went on, and there was no word. A Garda appeal, and there was no word. An investigation, numerous people questioned, international lines of enquiry, no word. The Gardaí informed Mel, Auntie Colette and Grandad Duane that a number of those questioned had said Tara had been talking about getting out of Cork City. It turned out she was in significant debt. Could it be that her disappearance was deliberate? Each remaining Duane said that it was possible.

When it came to boyfriends Tara had indeterminate tastes. She paid little attention to age gaps, so rumours abounded about this boy or that boy, arranged encounters. The estate could be mad and exhausting and a lot of the older teenagers had to take pride in savagery. Tara bought them alcohol and asked for dope in return. The smell of smoke and sweat in the sitting room some Sunday mornings. The way her peers would tell Mel that her mother was a tramp.

One evening, with Mel and Tara both in pyjamas watching *Geordie Shore*, Tony Cusack took a hurley to their sitting room window and kept at it till both panes of the double-glazing were smashed.

'He's fifteen, you sick fucking cunt!' he roared. 'He's fucking fifteen!'

Tara denied everything. A kindly judge ordered Tony into rehab. Ryan took off from home. The aftermath was excruciating. It took Kelly and Mel weeks to get back to normal. Tony was supposed to pay for the window but he never did.

On occasion in Scotland, Mel aggressively remembered the obsession with Ryan. How weird she must have seemed to him, how lovesick, and as it wasn't lovesick she was at all she was able to rise a temper towards him for potentially having characterised her in such an arrogant way, when he was just a study and not a very good one at that because he was a perpetual outsider, too arty to be normal and too delinquent to be properly popular. She tried to make a decision as to what it said about her. Maybe that she had never been Melinda at all, that she'd thought of Ryan as a sentry standing close to a door she hoped he might open for her. She read about the genderqueer community and observed their activists. She wished she was braver and held it against her mother's ideals that she wasn't. She brought up the possibility of *they* as a useful pronoun and her father said it sounded precious, and though her deciding gender didn't matter was the opposite ethos to her mother's, Mel was reminded of Tara, and alarmed by the idea that she might be closer to Tara than she'd lowered herself to think, in terms of preciousness. And so *She* would do, *Her* would do, because Mel was comprised of more than just Mel but *She/Her* would keep people from realising that Tara's defects were bobbing around in there, uninvited.

Now, on the picnic bench on the quay, Mel watched Ryan make short work of his pint and realised it was arrogant to assume he wasn't as much a stranger to her as she was to him. She had known him as a kid; she had not spoken to him since she'd left Ireland. He'd have been nineteen or twenty and it was probably something like, 'Any sca?' and he'd probably responded with, 'Fuck-all' because his scandalous behaviour he always kept to himself. She was ten months younger than him and three months older than Kelly, who had become Mel's best friend by default. He took music for the Junior Cert and she heard him playing piano through the wall or when she was at his house to see Kelly; at school he smoked at the back of the pitch and sold hash to the bigger boys; in the estate at night he played football and drank vodka from a Club Orange bottle. What he was like as a man was something she did not know. Exhausted by sca, she supposed. Embarrassed by her presence, undoubtedly. Reverted to shyness too; this was an educated guess. He had as a child been guarded, unsure of himself. In this they were alike. In this, Tara would have seen something to make use of.

Being musical it made sense that he could hold a note, but until Lord Urchin she'd never heard him sing. While she was in Scotland, growing calluses on her fingers, he'd been DJing around Cork and setting up Catalyst Music with Natalie Grogan and Colm McArdle. He'd sold remixes and actually got royalties, though for unenviable, corporate pursuits: stock music, stuff like that. Then some highly illegal mishap or another had driven him to Italy, his mother's country, and he had only occasionally been home since. The odd time she'd thought to ask Kelly how he was getting on, but Kelly was as guarded as he was, only in an extraverted way that Mel thought duplicitous.

But Ryan would hardly be the first introvert frontman. Most of them were painfully awkward, crippled with anxiety before a performance or overcompensating during, jumping off lighting rigs, howling at the moon. It was what happened when vocation slammed into reality. Making art was a compulsion, making art available for judgement was just deserts for the artist's ego.

They sat outside the pub to drink, nudged and niggled by the sea wind. Ryan rolled a second joint as soon as he'd finished the pint.

'I don't want to be carrying you back up the hill,' Izzy told him. 'Trim and all as you are.'

He sparked up.

'I guess you'd have to hit the gym a fair bit in Seoul,' Izzy went on. 'To keep up with all those . . . Seoulites? Seoulians? What d'you call them?'

'Koreans.'

'Oh aren't you smart? Be careful, I think you almost smiled.'

He made sure to contradict her.

'I'm hoping some islander will smell the joint,' Izzy said, 'and assume us kindred spirits. That Joseph's weed? Or did Natalie bring you something interesting?'

He shook his head. 'It's Joe's.'

'I can't imagine Natalie buying weed, somehow.'

'All sorts buy weed.'

'Natalie, though.'

Mel grinned, not because the idea of Natalie buying weed was absurd, but because of Izzy's evident and wildly optimistic belief that she was earthier than Natalie.

Izzy had half of her pint left to drink. She took a mouthful. 'An interesting job all the same,' she said. 'Have you any songs about that?'

'About dealing?' Ryan eyed Izzy's glass as she put it down. 'Oh yeah, the whole album's gonna be an invitation to kneecap me.'

'You don't have to be blatant,' Izzy said. 'The trick to song-writing is to obfuscate confessions and eviscerations. You know "Sanctum"? That I wrote for Maud Gone Mad? Everyone thinks it's about a relationship. Yeah, a relationship with my vagina. *Sancta sanctorum, no false decorum*.'

'Jesus Christ,' Mel said.

Izzy was delighted with herself. 'What? At the time it was necessary. I had to get my vagina off my chest.' When Ryan didn't react she went on, 'Joseph says we have to reveal something about ourselves. Get it all out.'

'Nothing I want to think about ever again.' He looked at the joint between his fingers and said, almost to himself, 'I was twenty months off this shit.'

His gaze fixed between Mel and Izzy's shoulders. Mel turned to see Natalie and Colm walking towards them.

'What are you doing here?' Natalie said to Ryan. 'I thought you'd be fit only for bed.'

After a drag and a pause he replied, 'This is a reconnaissance mission.'

Natalie folded her arms, caught herself, quivered as if keen to look cold instead of matriarchal. 'Reconnaissance for what?' she said.

'Yokes and trips,' Izzy said.

Natalie shot her a glance. 'Why?' she asked Ryan.

'Artistic thrust,' Ryan said. 'And Izzy has a toothache.'

'My jaw is really acting up,' Izzy said. 'I think it could be wisdom teeth.'

'At your age?' Natalie said.

Izzy swivelled her jaw, peeved.

Colm pointed at Natalie. 'Gin and tonic?'

Ryan climbed out of the picnic bench. 'My round.'

This round and then another. The textures of the sea became less visible, more audible. Mel realised there were no streetlights. She looked towards their walk back to the house and tried to remember the state of the road, how steep the hills were.

'Jesus Christ,' Ryan said, standing up, to which came a deep-voiced reply, 'I thought it was you. On Bofin of all places! Well isn't that a tweak to the nipples?'

The newcomer was rangy and loose. His arms swung, his head nodded. In this incessant jittering he claimed more space than he was entitled to, which had in particular an effect on Natalie, who frowned and sat very straight. He didn't know Ryan that well;

they stood in front of each other but they didn't hug. Ryan made a fist and knocked gently and rapidly on its opposite palm. 'It's mad I even recognised you,' said the new guy.

'Are you living here, boy?'

'Sure I'm from here.'

'This is?' Natalie asked, brightly.

'Traolach,' Ryan said, and to the guy, 'That's right, isn't it?'

'Ryan,' said Traolach. 'It is indeed.'

'We met in Ibiza,' Ryan said.

'He got me yokes,' Traolach said.

'Yokes?' said Izzy. 'Interesting.'

The wind coming in off the darkened sea, they went inside and found a table. Izzy squeezed purposefully between Natalie and Mel. Ryan went with his Ibizan crony to the bar, brought the round back, made a fraction of an excuse and fucked off again. Colm took two great draughts of his pint and looked over his shoulder.

'Go after them,' Natalie said. 'Before you inadvertently become a member of our coven.'

Mel watched Natalie watch him lope through the pub's sizable crowd as Izzy said, 'Your boyfriend has sisters, doesn't he?'

'Oh, Ryan?' said Natalie. 'Two. Why?'

Mel was a conditioned witness, having once had a mother who abhorred being told where to be and when, who brought strangers home and made up things she thought would shock them. It hardly mattered whether Mel was naturally or unnaturally reticent; she played the supporting role, she kept sketch, she absorbed. *Oh, Ryan?* Natalie, while watching Colm, needed her boyfriend's name clarified. Mel looked at Izzy and thought that Izzy had noticed this too because Izzy looked suddenly mischievous.

Colm arrived beside the others. He looked back at Natalie.

'He has two,' Mel confirmed, in case they'd forgotten she was just as in the know. Natalie and Izzy looked at her. 'Kelly,' Mel said, 'who's just turned twenty-three. And Niamh, she's sixteen now.'

Izzy turned back to Natalie. 'Do you think they're beautiful?'

'Why do you ask?'

'I have ideas about the way physical advantage manifests in the sexes. I think for women the body is kind of a really old new frontier.'

Natalie chuckled. Izzy jogged her arm. 'Do you think they're beautiful?'

'They take great photographs,' Natalie said. 'I've never met them.'

'You what?'

Natalie shrugged.

'Aren't you with him years?' Izzy said.

Natalie shrugged again.

'Am I prying?' Izzy said. She shot a glance at Mel. Mel said nothing.

'No,' Natalie said. 'But the moment the men decamp we start talking about them? So tedious.'

It was rather a holy response, and one for which Izzy had no comeback. She sucked her lips in and said 'True,' and there was then a lull as she tried to figure out what she could talk about, if not the decamped men; she would not be derailed for long. 'So what's your story, Mel?' she said, pivoting. 'Have you a girlfriend?'

'No,' Mel said.

'Are you looking?'

'Are you asking?'

'Wouldn't that be something?' Izzy laughed. 'One pair of hands, one heart.' She didn't look to see if Mel found this equally amusing. Mel searched out Ryan and the new guy, navigating by Colm's blond head. They were by the bar, Colm with his back to her, Ryan enthralled in profile, and this other fella – Jarlath? Derek? she'd lost it – coming in and out of her eyeline from behind Colm's head, arms spread, hair chestnut-brown and messy, eyes wide, like a provoked bull.

'Clearly I am super gay these days,' Izzy said, dreamily.

'How d'you make that out?' Natalie asked, and Izzy said, 'It's not visual, it's a vibe.' She picked up Natalie's hand, swayed it, opened their palms. Across the room Colm was leaning over the bar, pointing at bottles. 'They're getting another round,' Natalie said.

'The night is a write-off anyway,' Izzy said. 'But my mouth feels better.'

Ryan came over with fresh drinks. Izzy continued to fondle Natalie's hand. Natalie continued to let her. It was possible that she wanted to see where Izzy would go with it. Possible that she wanted to see how Ryan would react. Possible that despite the bang of Michael Kors off her she was a tactile person. Mel took the pint Ryan had offered without looking at her and thought she could down it and just go back to the house, thought too about why she was always hovering at the edge of unwelcoming crowds.

Ryan said, 'Traolach can get us tips.'

'Tips?' Natalie said.

Ryan held out Natalie's gin and tonic. She didn't take it from him. He left it on the table.

'Trips,' he said. 'Is what I meant.'

'You're ossified,' she said.

'I'm not ossified.'

'He's ossified,' Natalie said, crossly, as Ryan headed back.

'Who cares?' Izzy said. 'We're getting trips!'

Mel got up, leaving the pint behind her.

The bathrooms were cramped but clean. Mel took her time washing her hands, staring left of her reflection. There were posters on the wall for upcoming sessions. She wondered how mad the tourist season got around here. Whether there might be a job going. The island didn't have a Burger King but she could wash dishes or make beds; maybe she wouldn't go back to Cork at all.

On the way back to the table where Izzy and Natalie were sitting, she paused by the lads. Colm shifted closer to the bar to make room. The new fella winked at her and said, 'What do you do, anyway? In this band craic?' Ryan took his bank card out of a leather wallet and handed it to the barman. 'Throw in one more of those,' Colm said, gesturing at three clear shots lined up on the bar. Mel decided against saying she was grand.

'Guitar,' she said. 'I'm the understudy.'

'Understudy?' The new fella had an open face, the kind that in certain light looked unhinged. All eyes, all teeth. Mel felt sure that there was no bad in him. This she attributed to his knowing Ryan; Ryan had for years run with the worst cunts in Cork, and Mel thought he wouldn't down shots with any of them.

'Izzy's the real guitarist.' She gestured back at Izzy and Natalie, who were now staring at the screen of a phone in Natalie's hand. 'She broke her hand a few weeks back.'

'Punched the outside wall of De Barra's in Clonakilty when her girlfriend broke up with her,' Colm said. 'Apparently the problem was the nerve of yer wan because Izzy was all set to finish with her. Izzy's not the most mellow individual.'

'She doesn't look like a lunatic,' the new fella said.

'Aye well, she is a fucking lunatic. She's big on YouTube, guitar and songwriting tutorials and all that shite. And buys into all of this mad artist nonsense, because of the ad revenue. She's a very well-thought-out lunatic. 'Mon, so,' Colm said, and handed Mel one of the shots.

She sniffed. Sambuca. The lads threw their necks back. Mel swallowed and puffed her cheeks. Her throat felt coated with oil. The three lads smelled powerfully of it: aniseed and inebriation.

'If she fucked her hand,' the new lad said, 'why didn't ye give her the marching orders? Sure that could take years to set right. Happened to a sham I used to pull pints with in Galway. He broke his hand in a fight. P45, out the door, good luck and thanks.'

'That's excessively capitalist, we'd never hear the end of it,' Colm said. 'We'd be YouTube famous for the wrong reasons.'

The new fella looked at Mel. 'I think understudies are excessively capitalist. You deserve your time in the sun, don't you?'

'I'm not as good as she is,' Mel said. 'Yet.'

Ryan put his shot glass back on the bar and walked off in the direction of the toilets. Mel watched his gait, not as understudy. He wasn't swaying, so she went after him.

'They grew up next door to each other,' she heard Colm tell the new fella.

41

She hovered in the hall outside the toilets, reading more posters, making herself small when Leinster weekenders and French ramblers and young lesbian couples and bohemians needed to get past, and when he came out he looked only mildly put out to see her.

'Are you odd with me?' she asked.

'Why would I be?' Said too quickly.

'Can we get this out into the open, so?'

'Naw, naw, naw, I'd rather not to be honest with you—'

'I haven't seen you since my mam disappeared, you haven't asked me about her or mentioned her but that's grand, Ryan, let's assume you asked the polite questions and let's assume I said "No word but sure what can you do?" and let's assume you thought, "Good fucking riddance" but didn't let it show on your face and let's just go from there.'

'Jesus Christ, Linda.'

'Mel,' she said.

He joined his hands at the back of his neck and looked at the ceiling. Her throat was still heated by alcohol, her breath sweet. She kept looking at him.

'Joseph obviously thinks it's all in the past,' she said. 'I don't want to bust his balloon, like, I'm happy he asked me here, I want what you want, to play music, that's all.'

He said, 'Can we just—'

'Yeah, we have,' she said. 'That was the point.'

She returned to her pint, and by extension to Izzy and Natalie, feeling more merry through firm disclosure or maybe just the shot of sambuca. Izzy was reproachful under a thin mask of amusement. 'You're not one of those girls, are you?' she said. 'The *all my friends are lads* girls. Coz that's unusual in queer people. It'd be very, very strange.' Mel could feel a dislike for Izzy developing as a mild headache; this was entirely down to Colm's appraisal of Izzy's character, which meant it was fertilised meanness, and that Mel should be ashamed of it.

Izzy became welcoming again. She snuggled against Mel and said, 'Wait till you see this.'

'Izzy,' Natalie warned.

'What? You'll be telling them all tomorrow anyway.' Izzy looked at Mel and went on, 'Just let Natalie tell Ryan, OK?'

'Tell Ryan what?' Mel said.

Izzy gestured and Natalie sighed and held her phone out. Mel took it.

On the screen was a comment on Izzy's YouTube channel, under a vlog Izzy had made about the beginning of the writing process. The writer had called themselves 'Anne Alias'.

I would wish you all the best with this project but as Ryan Cusack is involved I think I'll pass thanks. For those of you who are not already aware he was one of Corks biggest drug dealers a couple of years back and certainly never shy of a few bob so basically if you are all wondering how a bunch of kids can make an album just like that off they're own bat there might be an answer in that for you. they say its well for some. Never mind the damage he did as long as he gets a second or a 3rd or however many chances. He might be trying to forget but why should he be allowed to???

It hadn't gleaned any responses of its own, other than one from Michael Sheehan, a feen Mel knew from school, which read, 'haha youd want to watch what your saying if thats the case. Go way you gowl.'

Izzy took the phone, held it out so that Mel could see it, and followed the link back to Anne's profile page. The account was new. 'Begrudgery,' she said. 'Whoever it is will run out of steam. By the time we get back to Cork it'll be business as usual and the only undesirable comments will be from men telling me I'm a shit guitarist coz my tits keep getting in the way.'

'What a tool,' Mel said.

'Well the tool might have inspired this.' Natalie took the phone, opened her emails, scrolled and presented.

Mel read.

Hi guys, my name is Medbh Lucey and I'm a journalist. Congratulations on *The International Recordings EP*. I enjoyed it immensely and am really looking forward to the album. I'd love to arrange an interview with Lord Urchin for a piece focused particularly on the band's background and on the working-class voice angle. Specifically it would be great if Ryan Cusack was available for a chat. My number is . . .

'Coincidence?' Natalie asked.

Mel shrugged.

'Jesus Christ,' Natalie said. 'He is going to fucking freak.'

'But everyone knows Ryan used to sell a bit,' Mel said. 'Who cares?'

'A bit?' Natalie laughed, cheerlessly. 'You're either extremely innocent, Mel, or completely degenerate.'

'If you say so.' Mel took a draught of her pint.

'Natalie, Mel's a temp,' Izzy said, gently. 'She doesn't need to be invested.'

Traolach –

Mel could now remember his name.

– hugged Ryan goodbye, and offered her a respectful fist-bump, and said that being an understudy was very sporting, lunacy even better thought-out, and told her to keep her eyes on the prize. He pointed at his eyes, then at her. He meant for her to laugh and so she did.

The walk back to the house took a while, so featureless was the road in the dark. Mel made herself fall into step with Izzy and Natalie and listened to them worry. Natalie had not yet told Ryan about the detractor's comment or the journalist's email. Izzy said, 'What makes it worse is that he's already on edge, because he doesn't like you,' and turned to Mel.

'Ha? I've known Ryan since we were children.'

Izzy said she had eyes. That Ryan was awkward when he saw Mel at the house, then fretful, that he didn't smile once in the pub.

Natalie said he was jetlagged and Mel was keen to agree.

But Izzy pressed. What was it? Too many games of doctors and nurses?

Mel was in her own way ossified. She was trusting, then vigilant, then overconfident, which led to apathy, which prompted contradiction, so then she felt unsure of herself and alone. She thought she might laugh and then she worried that she'd be judged for laughing. These feelings came in sequence, and so, not being concurrent, she was at the mercy of this current state, and it happened that it was 'trusting'.

She told them that something happened years ago and she thought it was behind them but clearly it was not.

In the darkness she could only get the gist of their reactions.

'Maybe he's told you this?' to Natalie, who didn't respond.

So Mel prefaced that it was a bit fucked-up.

'Oh, the more fucked-up the better,' said Izzy.

The lads were many metres ahead. Fine long legs on them both. Mel thought that her mother would approve and this made her want to shut up again, but she'd started now, and the silence beside her was hungry.

'I don't know if you know anything about my mam?'

There was a pause, then Natalie said that they knew she was missing, and were very sorry. She hadn't mentioned it because she wasn't sure if Mel would want it to become part of the conversation, but of course she was here if Mel would like to talk. Natalie was good at holy responses.

Mel said, 'Yeah. Thanks. Yeah, she disappeared off the face of the earth a few years back. Honestly, if you knew my mam, you wouldn't be shocked, she's seriously impulsive. Actually, she's pretty loo-lah. And mad for fellas. I don't know if you'd call her a hopeless romantic, she's just a real . . .'

She remembered Izzy's question and turned to her. 'One of *those* girls.'

'Right,' Izzy said.

'Years ago anyway, Ryan had this video on his phone that he'd made with Karine, y'know, his son's mam. It was definitely

nothing crazy, she was just giving him a blowjob or something.'
She thought about adding *Sorry* for Natalie's sake, then thought
that would suggest the story was more dramatic than it was.
'*Years* ago,' she stressed, instead. 'He was fifteen, like. He got
really langers one night at my gaff, with my mam. I wasn't there,
I was in Dublin with my dad . . .' She heard either Natalie or Izzy
take a breath before a pronouncement and hurried to shut it
down. 'Oh here, I know that sounds dodgy but my mam thought
she was a teenager, like. I'd to stop her making the place a full-
time party gaff. Kelly told me after that Ryan had a fight that
night with Tony – their dad – so it's not a surprise, really, that my
mam brought him in, Tony can be a nightmare. Anyway, I don't
know if he showed the video to my mam or something, but she
knew it was on his phone and she took it upon herself to tell his
dad about it, trolling maybe, my mam and Tony did not get along,
and she was no prude, like, the fucking opposite actually. And
because my mam was so into the fellas, Tony jumped to conclu-
sions and accused my mam of carrying on with Ryan. He went
ballistic, even though my mam swore there was nothing. It was a
mess coz we were next-door neighbours. I guess it's still a mess in
Ryan's head. I don't give a fuck, in terms of my mam I have bigger
things to worry about, you know?'

Izzy said, 'Ryan told me this before.'

At the Electric Picnic festival. Years back. Izzy remembered him
telling her about the neighbour. When Natalie sharply asked why
he'd tell such a thing to Izzy and not to her, Izzy was blasé. Oh,
you know Ryan, he was off his nut on some substance or another.
She was playing with Scruffy the Janitor at the time, not at the
Picnic, obviously, they were never mainstream. Just they went for
the session. Joseph brought Ryan and Ryan brought Karine and
the two of them were in this mutual strop. So Izzy took Ryan
aside and said to him, Joseph told me that your girlfriend was
with some other guy and since then you can't stop cheating on
her, but look, it's wrecking all of our buzzes, surely you should
just break up?

To which he had responded,

Don't tell anyone but I cheated on her first.

He said something about the woman next door and Izzy told him, look, own it. Is it that big a deal that a MILF had her wicked way with you? No, it's not.

Mel asked for clarification but had already begun to feel the dull downward motion of self-reproach; she had recognised delusion and was now mourning it.

'Oh God. Yeah, shit. Sorry. His dad was right, Mel.'

Natalie was laughing furiously. '*Ryan*? My Ryan?'

'Look, no offence,' Izzy said. 'But isn't that why his ex is his ex? Because at the time, at least, he was a bit, y'know, cheaty?'

'Cheaty? At fifteen? With someone's *mother*?'

Izzy sniffed, 'That's what he told me.' Her head turned towards Natalie meant their voices were further muffled, and Mel had to strain to hear.

Natalie said that she knew everything about Ryan, almost as if it's what she did for a living.

Izzy just said that shame worked on men too, surely Natalie never thought otherwise?

Mel put a hand on her stomach and thought about falling over. Remind them of their focus, beyond the paltry *Oh God yeah shit sorry his dad was right*.

'You're telling me he had sex with Mel's mother when he was a kid, an actual child? Because holy shit, Izzy, I wouldn't have brought that up, that's such a headache, no wonder he's ossified!'

'That's what he told me. And he felt so shitty about it he started whoring around just so he could cheat on his girlfriend and not feel shitty about it.'

'That makes no sense.'

'A balance of power thing. It was quite mad, I wrote it down in one of my journals, I made it into a kind of meditation on fear of a powerful female, I could look for it if you like?'

The shape of Natalie's head leaned out from behind Izzy's. A second *Oh God yeah shit sorry*.

Mel could think of no answer but, 'Yeah, thanks,' a condolences answer she had to deploy still, on occasions when others remembered that Tara was gone. They were approaching the house. In darkness smudged by indoor lights she saw Ryan and Colm nearing the front door, pausing before entering, and again feelings came to her in sequence, she was now at the mercy of disappointment, and she was afraid of what that might turn into.

Track 2: Deoksugung Doldam-gil

There's an urban legend about the stone wall road of Deoksugung Palace that says any couple that walks it will break up. I'm not 100 per cent sure but it has something to do with the divorce courts once being down that way, so the superstition has roots. They all do, really: you blame your luck on something you did or didn't do and before you know it, it's in the marrow all the way down your family tree. The myth of Deoksugung Doldam-gil isn't much of a deterrent. Plenty of couples walk it. It's unbeliev-able in the autumn when it's splashed with yellow and orange leaves. But you know the way superstition works on me. The easi-est way to deal with bad luck sometimes is to pretend it wasn't luck, that you had some say over it, even if you didn't know it at the time. It comes from the same place as religion; inventing rules for a senseless condition.

I said yes to Seoul because I thought it'd feel like penance (and still if you asked me I'd say I'm only culturally Catholic). I threw myself into work, I thought work would distract me and Jesus, they like to work in Seoul, but it turned out I liked the work and I liked the city and there's fierce overlap between Ireland and Korea when you know where to look for it. I was bouncing off the walls most of the time – I didn't sleep well and I was drinking too much – but quiet times I felt like I was starting to know who I was and even threatening to like who I was. But you weren't there, so it never felt as good as it should have.

The last time I'd seen you had been in Berlin. Seoul should've been the nail in the coffin. I thought about whether I owed it to you to make sure it was. I was thinking, OK, according to the rhythm I've got going, I'm supposed to be here, and Karine is supposed to be there, and so long as Diarmaid's OK I have nothing to complain about. But then you'd sign off a message with 'Miss you xxx' or at the end of a call you'd say, 'Love you, be good' and I told myself not to read into it but of course I read into it. I welcomed the dogsbody work in the studio if it gave me time to obsess over something you'd said that week. It was like being a kid all over again. I liked Seoul but in terms of its primary function it was failing me. I was like, Jesus, Cusack, do you have to move to Mars? Is she here with you? No, she's not here with you. Because she doesn't want to be. Repeat after me in English, Italian and Korean, you daft prick.

One day I had nothing to do, which was a novelty. I had the day off, which was one thing, and then Ji-hun fucked off home to see his mammy. He doesn't have any patience for touristy carry-on so I thought I'd take advantage of his absence and do Deoksugung Palace because Maddalena in my Korean class had raved about the changing of the guard. I went in along with the idea of being an eejity foreigner, taking a bunch of selfies and laughing at myself but my head wasn't in it at all. *Miss you, love you, be good.* What the fuck did it mean? Were you being affectionate in a platonic sense, were you talking to me how you'd talk to Louise or your sisters? Did you mean for me to say it back? If I said it back in the right way would you come to me? And I stood then on Deoksugung Doldam-gil and questioned if the urban legend worked for head-wrecked individuals. If I took off down the road would I do great but necessary damage?

So I did.

I wrote the lyrics on Bofin. We'd had the guts of the song already, based first on a bit I'd come up with out in Seoul. It had been born in Korea and we called it Korean Air for the craic. I didn't have it about anything in particular. It was just this sweet structure we'd built around a lament.

I was after having this weird, quasi-spat with Joseph. He was asking me if I was OK, only he wasn't, he was actually saying I was clearly odd with Mel so would I ever get over myself? So that

I wouldn't lose it with him I went into the living room and I listened to some of the scratch tracks and tried to get to the current in the melody. I thought about you, thought about the enquiries Traolach was making on my behalf and then, fucking hell, I had it, I had 'Deoksugung Doldam-gil'.

In Seoul I had been all about trying to kill the hope that kept jumping around in my chest, keeping me ravenous and wide awake, only to realise it hadn't been tied to place, that I felt it just as hard on Bofin. No distance would make this go away, and no ritual would lift it.

She had a new vocation sprung on her. She was north of the Lee one morning, minding her own business, when one of three wans wearing anoraks and sensible trousers asked, 'Is this the point for the tour?'

'Is this the what for the what?' Maureen said.

'The meeting point for the walking tour,' the one on the right said in an accent Maureen thought was probably German, and then, 'Oh! Sorry. I thought you were the guide.'

'I'm not,' Maureen said, 'though I suppose I have the shoes for it.' The footpath by the entrance to the development in which Jimmy had bought her apartment was cracked and uneven; she had taken to exercising caution and wearing clodhoppers.

'I think we are in the wrong place,' said one of the wans.

It was twenty past the hour. 'It'd be the wrong time for a tour, surely,' Maureen said. 'Though if you walked a few steps that way you'd get a different time again. The four liars, you see.'

One of the wans dutifully asked, 'Four liars?'

'That's what they call the Shandon clock. Four faces, four different times. They did repairs on it a few years ago but could do nothing about the lying. It's all in the mechanism, apparently, that the four clocks will have four different ideas of the time. It's in the inner workings of the Irish to be liberal with the truth. Not that you'd like that, aren't you fierce punctual? Germans!'

The three wans laughed. 'I didn't think my accent was so strong,' said the middle one, and the one on the left said, 'We're from Rottweil, in the south.'

'Is that a city?'

'A town. A very old town.'

Maureen was disappointed. She wanted to talk about southern cities and geographical camaraderie. She'd developed a speech on the subject after a conversation at a bus stop, six months ago, with a stocky pup from Kraków. 'How long are you waiting on your guide?' she asked.

'I think almost thirty minutes. We rang the bells in the tower while we were waiting. Maybe he came and left again.'

'Not a bit of it,' Maureen said. 'Thirty minutes is a bit much even for the fellas around here. You must have the wrong place, because Corkonians would leave you waiting but they wouldn't leave you down. And in the spirit of that statement, I'll escort you to where you were supposed to end up. I'm Cork born and bred, I know where I'm going.'

'Oh, that isn't necessary, we wouldn't like to trouble you.'

'No trouble,' Maureen said, wild-eyed.

She led the wans to the Butter Museum and the Firkin Crane, and recounted what she remembered about Cork's dairy industry, which wasn't much, so she told them instead about a recent case involving an Irish butter-smuggling ring in Wisconsin. The name of the butter involved was Kerrygold, but she didn't want to confuse the Germans by invoking the neighbours; Cork butter, she told them, was the best in the world. 'The social welfare', she said, 'used to give out butter vouchers, that's how important butter was. The elderly, the infirm, the layabouts all got subsidised butter. God be with the days.'

They stopped at Griffith Bridge and Maureen looked back towards Shandon, hands on her hips. 'I'd say there's not much else on the Northside for you.' She thought hard. 'The old gaol is out Sunday's Well.'

'Yes,' said the wan on the right. 'We visited on Wednesday.'

'My mother was from Sunday's Well. They have waxworks in that gaol and I swear to God, two or three of them are the head off her.'

'She looked like them?' clarified the wan in the middle.

'She was an ould bitch,' Maureen said, 'with a face like a half-chewed toffee.'

53

'Like a half-chewed toffee?'

'And the toffee you get in Ireland would glue your jaw shut,' Maureen said, staring. She recovered and waved an arm. 'That's the Northside, now. Less about places of interest, more about people of interest. Ten minutes up there and you'd come to the North Mon, where all the great lads went to school. Terence MacSwiney and Frank O'Connor and Niall Tóibín and our own Taoiseach Jack Lynch and Rory Gallagher, God rest their souls.'

'I've read Frank O'Connor's stories,' said the wan on the right.

'I haven't,' Maureen said. 'Cork is a very male place. But then I suppose isn't that the way of history? It's all fecking men. Here now they're proud of Roy Keane – oh, a fine Northside boy – and Cillian Murphy and Jonathan Rhys-Whatshisname and Denis Irwin and the little fecker on Game of Thrones. Jesus, is the only woman we had Danny La fecking Rue?'

'These are celebrities,' the wan in the middle said.

'Well. In so far as they can be, around here. Come down now this way, I want to show you something.'

They walked westwards along a disquietingly high Lee. Maureen stopped at the footbridge at the end of the quay. 'This is Saint Vincent's bridge.'

Two of the wans took photographs through the latticed steel.

'And there,' Maureen pointed, 'is where I used to live. A ground floor flat in a done-up townhouse, though you wouldn't know that now because it went up in flames a few years back. I was only in it when I found out it used to be a brothel.'

'How long ago?' one of the wans asked; Maureen was looking too intently at her old home to identify the speaker.

'Was it a brothel? Just before I moved in.'

'It's illegal in Ireland?'

'Brothel-keeping is,' said Maureen, who had done her research, and considered herself better informed than the average nana. 'But didn't I tell you? This is a fierce male city.'

'Fierce meaning violent?'

'Fierce meaning very.'

Few people moved on the opposite quay. This Maureen had noticed about her time living here. The quays on both sides of the Lee here were quieter than they should have been, not in a peaceful way but in a way that suggested suspicion. Maureen had lived alone with two empty floors above her. The walls were imbued with bad feeling, down to her actions as much as the men who'd occupied their leisure there. It could have been that she was giving it unnatural shadows, that she was shook now with sentiment, assigning meaning to meagre things.

'Fierce. Very. Violently,' she added. 'One time I stopped a lad jumping into the Lee from this footbridge. Just before Christmas, three and a half years ago now. That's the violence of the male too, isn't it? When they finish wrecking all around them, they turn on themselves.'

None of the wans spoke. Maureen exhaled and turned to them.

'Though things grow in the cracks of all sorts of wrecks,' she said. 'And it's far from parched, this city. *Corcach Mór Mumhan*, the great marsh of Munster. The Lee keeps bursting its banks. I think sometimes it's putting manners on the place. I'm sure you don't want to hear about brothels and suicide attempts, but there's light and dark and every city has plenty of both. What you see now' – she flicked a wrist at the river's course – 'is the fruits of my labours, or the labours of my generation.'

One of the wans saw the opening and asked, 'Are there many Europeans here?'

'We're all Europeans,' Maureen said, sternly. '*Continentals* is what I'd call you. Yes, yes, the place is hopping with you. But I wasn't saying the only people here are the children of the natives. I mean . . .'

'Ireland is changing a lot.'

'It isn't changing enough,' Maureen said, and because the wans looked restless she said, 'Germans are pure mad for sausages.'

The wan who looked least perplexed said, 'You mean, mad about?'

'What we'll do,' Maureen said, 'is go along the south bank here to the Opera House and the Crawford gallery, up to the Huguenot

55

Cemetery, on to Pana, down Mutton Lane so you can see the mural and in then through the English Market, where you'll find the best sausages in Ireland. And before I leave you I'll point out the Port of Cork, which is on the second largest harbour in the world. We're a pirate's city, damn good at coming second. But have you ever heard the saying . . .?' She paused. She had a show-manship, Maureen Phelan, and on this occasion she thought it wasn't going to get her into trouble. 'Ireland', she said, 'would sink without its Cork.'

The world was dangerous now. The streets were full of people with unknowable motives. The chances of dying in an accident at home were significant. At any moment your body could turn against you and your cells could multiply until they cracked whatever it was that was holding you together. Worse things, too. Inexplicable ailments that baffled doctors. Sudden onset allsorts.

Since Diarmaid was born Karine found the world impossibly fragile. When he was a tiny baby she would crook her finger under his nose and wait for his breath to graze her skin. Now the thou-sand deaths she foresaw came about as a result of his innocence and her negligence. She scrolled through Instagram and he drowned in the bath. She looked into her bag to find her purse and a lunatic snatched him. Mostly she stumbled and knocked him off the footpath and into traffic. More than once she had sobbed, imagining in detail these scenarios.

Caution or gloom had never been her natural state and this was why she was this morning standing on a sprung dance floor, wear-ing cropped tracksuit bottoms and a white vest, red-faced, sweat-ing and stroppy. *Dance like no one is watching*, except her oldest friend was watching and judging good-oh.

'You're not hitting it hard enough,' Louise said. 'Hit. Hold. Keep it clean. Jesus, you're dancing like you're four vodkas into a hen party.'

Karine said, 'Yeah, thanks a million,' and went back to the middle of the floor.

'What d'you want me to say, girl?' asked Louise. 'Oh, Karine, that's it, babes, sitting on your arse for years but right back to where you were in the space of a fortnight. You're unreal.' She punched a button on the sound system and the intro came in. Karine cocked her hip and put her weight on her left leg.

'Better,' Louise said afterwards, as Karine dragged her forearm across her mouth. 'You can't forget your face, though. You're supposed to be like this bad bitch but you're still doing the big eyes and the lip-biting.'

'Must be coz I dance like I'm at a hen party.'

'You said you wanted to be pushed,' Louise said. 'There are beginners classes on Thursdays at seven, like.'

'I'm not a fucking beginner.'

'Prove it, so, girl.'

Karine swabbed her forehead and neck. The first four classes she had spent on the verge of tears, and rather than experiencing an endorphin rush afterwards she had been disappointed and queasy. Her throat had been sore. Her thighs and bum ached. She'd considered quitting and it wasn't pride that kept her chin up but its opposite. She had cornered Louise and bawled for her help catching up.

'Ready to go again?' Louise asked. Her arse was poured into grey marl leggings.

Karine fixed her puckered waistband. To her thumbs her belly felt cold. 'With bad bitch facial expressions,' she said.

Louise folded her arms. 'I'm trying to get you to think about the vibe you're selling. You're tough, right? A grown woman. Confident, strong. We don't do this for the boys.'

'Ah, I'm aware of that?'

'Why are you at this, then?' Louise demonstrated, running her hands over her breasts and hips and dropping low.

'Not once did I do that!'

Louise's top lip pulled back to her gum. 'Why are you here?'

Karine was here because she needed something that wasn't Diarmaid, some grown-up diversion, or some means of reconnecting with herself, and with that some respite from the paranoia of motherhood, some way of remembering how fearlessly she used to tackle things, how well she used to sleep.

'I know what you've told me,' Louise said, 'but I see the timing. Everyone knows this is because of Ryan.'

'It isn't, and who's everyone?'

'Don't mind *Who's everyone?* Second he says he's coming home you're dolled up in Nike and asking about squats. Lie to yourself all you want, Karine, but don't lie to me. I've rubbed your back and let you snot up my shoulders too many times.' As Karine performed incredulity, Louise went on, 'It's been almost two years. Well. Supposed to have been.'

'I'm here because I want what was a huge part of my life back—'

'Yeah, Ryan.'

'Dance, Louise, and you know it.'

'You're trying to tell me Ryan has nothing to do with this?'

'Maybe he does,' Karine said. 'Maybe coz I spend all day watching Paw Patrol and he's out there doing remixes and soundtracks and the most creative thing I've finished lately is a colouring book and I have an honours degree, girl, I have an honours degree and a flabby belly and stretch marks and he doesn't even have a fucking Leaving Cert.'

Louise sucked her teeth and said, 'You're giddy as balls.'

'Maybe dancing has me giddy as balls?'

'I'd like to think that. Because d'you know what really annoys me? Dance is the one thing that was all you, not him. That's why you couldn't keep it up, and you're only able to come back to it now that it's about him.'

'This is motivating me, is it?'

'This is me asking you to leave him out of this.' Louise brought her finger to hover again over the switch. 'Do you want to go again or what?'

Karine inhaled sharply and went back to the middle of the floor.

Karine's father had given up his morning to look after his grandson and Karine was grateful without cause. Gary D'Arcy appreciated time to mould his only male descendant. If left to lean to the other way God knows how the child would turn out.

Karine was like her father: fair, hazel-eyed, short and hot-headed. When she was little she didn't like to be told that she was like her father, because, having a moustache, he was clearly a boy. When she was a teenager being told she was like her father was worse again, because he was a man who'd rant at the sea for being wet. Her mam used to say to him, 'You'll give yourself a stroke one of these days, Gary,' but then she also used to say to him 'Gar?' at regular intervals from all corners of the house – *Gar? Gar? Gaaar?* – which drove Karine and her sisters barmy, so it was no wonder their father was always on the brink of some personal Krakatau.

She sat at the kitchen table and he made her a coffee.

'How was it, girl?' he asked.

'Terrible. All the length of one wall is a mirror and I swear to God, Dad, I looked like a potato being fucked down Patrick's Hill.'

'G'wan outta that. You'll get the hang of it again.'

She went, *Mmm.*

'And sure it's very healthy.'

'Healthy? Oh my God, Dad.'

'What? Is it not healthy?'

'That's like something you read now in a magazine. Were you at the dentist's?'

He was genuinely offended. 'You're a saucy bitch,' he said.

'Aw Dad,' she said. 'I'm only at you. It's comical, like.'

It wasn't comical; she was simply relieved, though why should she have been relieved? Why should her father not have been encouraging? She had imagined him disapproving, detracting. Saying things like, *Dancing, and you don't even have a job. Less dancing and you wouldn't have turned out how you turned out.* An invented version of her father, poisoned by the prejudices of an age she'd only read about.

A cheerful song came from the television in the sitting room. Karine tried to ration Diarmaid's television time but *Ah will you let him watch the telly?* Gary would say. *Ah he's only a child.* Or, *It didn't do you any harm, girl.* Or, *That's not something that other langer is dictating to you, is it?*

Now it occurred to Gary that he hadn't yet brought up that other langer.

'When's that other langer back, anyway?'

'A couple of weeks.'

'Wouldn't you think he'd come to Cork first to see his son?'

'He had to go to Inishbofin first. I told you.'

'Inishbofin's the new Spike Island, is it?'

'Stop, Dad, you're a howl.'

The afternoon was ahead of her and after the spat with Louise she didn't feel like hanging around just to stew. She'd been saving for a summer outfit, so she and Diarmaid ambled to the bus stop. The breeze tousled their hair and rippled their sleeves. Car bonnets glinted. An old man in a burgundy jumper was mangling a 99 outside the shop. Karine's thighs felt weak and her skin sensitive, even under her clothes. Every time Diarmaid tried to pull his hand from hers she carried him until he forgot whatever it was he'd wanted to poke at. This was something she wasn't supposed to do. *You'll spoil him*, her mother would warn. It was amazing the amount of ways you could accidentally damage your child.

In town they shopped first for Diarmaid, and found pyjamas, bright chino shorts to go with a white shirt, and a set of socks with animal faces. Karine hoped he would be captivated with his new threads long enough to allow her a browse in Opera Lane. He set to cribbing ten minutes in. There were too many people around, teenagers cawing and focused girls laden with bags, all able for heels and with a hand free for carrying iced coffees. Karine grabbed a flowing vest, a bralet and matching knickers. There were denim shorts she wanted that looked too small. She threw a glance at the changing rooms. Diarmaid lay on the floor and mewled.

'OK,' she said. 'We'll pay the girl for these and we'll go home.'

Tony Cusack spotted them before she saw him. He was leaning on the railing beside the bus stop. Diarmaid pointed, 'Nonno!' and pulled her hand. She held on.

Tony was Nonno, despite being Ryan's Irish parent. It was for the sake of convenience and too of difference, so that Gary D'Arcy wouldn't have conniptions.

'Well Derry, where are you going?' Tony held out both arms to Diarmaid and picked him up before Karine could wrinkle her nose and test the air.

'Going to see Daddy.'

'Daddy?'

'Not yet,' Karine said. 'Soon. We're going home now,' she reminded Diarmaid.

'We got jammies in the shop,' Diarmaid said. 'My jammies has triangles.'

'I'd swear he's avoiding me.' The sun was in Tony's eyes. 'He won't pick up his phone.'

'The coverage is really bad out there,' Karine said.

'I need to talk to him before he comes back here but sure he's still making points. And he was no angel, my lad. Not like this little man here.' He tsked. 'Is that how I'm supposed to get a hold of him now? Through his ould doll?' But he didn't look indignant. His voice was heavy and slow.

Karine held her arms out. Diarmaid pulled at his grandfather's hoodie strings and ignored her. She retrieved him anyway, telling Tony, 'He'll phone you back once the missed call notification comes through, honestly, it's very patchy out there.' She balanced Diarmaid on her hip. 'Everything all right, like?' Everything might well have been. It was not so unusual to see Tony half-cut at half three.

He said, 'I don't think he should come back here.'

'What d'you mean?' she said. 'Why?'

He looked the other way, out of the sun, and she thought she had to decide now how drunk he was, whether it was kindest to humour him or safest to walk away. They saw Tony regularly but it was difficult to arrange visits around his hurdling on and off the wagon. Ryan was inconsistent on the matter: he wanted his father to have a relationship with Diarmaid, and he wanted his father to fall into a sinkhole. He wanted Tony to whistle softly and say,

Jesus, didn't you make an unbelievable child? and yet, if you were to put this to Ryan, he'd jump up as if scalded and say he didn't need Tony's approval, where would he be going trying to impress that clown?

Now Tony made a frustrated noise and she worried that he was not simply being dramatic, that there was a grievance to unpick.

'You could do with a coffee,' she told him.

He looked at her. He had passed deep brown eyes to his son, and so on to his grandson. His too was the dark wavy hair, the naturally morose expression. There was a meekness in Tony that made it seem as if he was always looking up at you, but there was nothing meek in his having given Ryan bruises and dire neuroses over the years, and nothing meek about his reputation for being whiskey-sick and evil-mouthed. The man was an unaffected puzzle: he was quick to anger and he was easily hurt.

A sixteen-year-old Karine had once allowed her boyfriend to film her giving him a blowjob, an indulgence after Tony had sold his mother's piano. Tony had found the video on Ryan's phone and every so often the shame of it came back up on her in a bitter, hot bloom. It did so again now as Tony said grand, fair enough, a coffee. A lump rose in her throat. She pressed her face to Diarmaid's so she wouldn't have to look at his grandfather. She was angry then that this task had fallen to her. Let someone else sober him up, she thought. Doesn't he have six kids of his own to disappoint?

The last time Karine had seen Ryan.

Berlin, almost two years ago. Her second time over.

The first time she'd visited he had only been in Germany a month. He was living in a one-bedroom apartment in Moabit with white walls, red kitchen cabinets and a corner sofa. She went for two nights with Louise; if it went smoothly she had promised to bring Diarmaid later. Louise stood in the middle of the apartment with her arms folded and asked, 'Ah, how are you affording this?'

'Not drugs,' Ryan told her, after a vexed pause.

He brought them out shopping and drinking and shrugged when Louise said there was no way she was attempting Berghain, thank you very much, and was attentive and affable and, with Karine, especially tactile. She kissed him in a narrow bar with a mirrored ceiling when Louise was in the toilets.

'D'you think she'll sleep on the couch tonight?' he said in her ear.

'Oh she will, yeah,' she said, rolling her eyes and catching their reflection in the ceiling: his arm around her waist, his hand drifting, her arm held up against his chest, her fingertips against his throat. She looked smaller, and proud.

Back at the apartment they had tea and toast and then she and Louise retired; he had given them his bed. Karine waited fifteen minutes, slipped out and padded to the door.

'Where d'you think you're going?' Louise asked, drowsily.

'I can't sleep.'

'Yeah, I bet he can't either.'

Ryan, on the L-shaped couch, held up his blanket and she snuggled in beside him. In the dark he kissed her lips and the tip of her nose, then went up on one elbow and kissed her neck, slid a hand under her cami and on to her breast.

'Have you had sex on this couch?' she asked.

He laughed softly. 'No.'

'Have you had sex in the bed?'

He laughed again but this time too late.

'Yeah,' he said.

'With who?'

'. . . My girlfriend.'

There was a reason he answered in this manner: he assumed she was checking that he had not fucked half of Berlin. She got up and went to the kitchen cabinets and began to cry, and he followed and pulled her against his chest. 'I don't want to be on the couch,' she wept, and in the morning she told him it was the drink that made her so daft and that of course he had a right to be with Natalie, given how clear Karine had been on the subject of their

63

own relationship, in what shared state they best got along and all that.

'Why does this keep happening, then?' he asked. This was fair. It had been happening since Diarmaid was four months old. She would be intrepid and Ryan would be easily led.

The second time she visited Berlin was from a Tuesday to a Friday with Diarmaid, who had just turned one. She carried him on her knee and thought the whole way about not only plane crashes but sudden bumps on the runway, unprecedented turbulence, fellow passengers drunk on mini booze bottles falling on top of them on their way down the aisle. Ryan was waiting at Arrivals. She told him she wasn't getting back on the plane, that she'd learn German and raise Diarmaid in Berlin. Ryan held Diarmaid as she gathered herself. 'No need,' he said. 'We'll drive to Napoli and raise him a good Italian boy, like his *papà*.'

'As opposed to being a bold Irish boy, is it?'

'I can be both,' he said, and it was true that duality came naturally to him, as likely in a composite sense as conflicting sense. They stayed in each of those three nights. They conferred, argued, drank and joked. They had sex in his bed.

That was their last physical meeting. She had seen him since on screens. He wasn't keen on social media so she became an emissary; she guarded his vulnerabilities and brandished his stories. He would usually call in the early afternoon in Ireland. Sometimes he'd be in his flat, sometimes in a corridor at the studio, sometimes in a restaurant. Diarmaid would sit on the couch with the iPad and they'd *raiméis* for a bit. Or sometimes he'd call her after a night out. His mouth a little looser. His requests a little cheekier. And sometimes she gave in, and it felt harmless.

The day came when she had to say to him, 'I've met someone'.

He didn't knock his laptop off the table. 'Is he sound?' he asked, head tilted, right hand over his mouth.

'Yeah, he's all right, like.'

'Who is he?'

'Dylan Moloney. You don't know him, he's from Douglas.'

'Of course he is.'

'Maybe he knows Natalie,' she smiled, sourly.

'Maybe.'

She had recovered by the time she brought the coffees to their table. She sat with Diarmaid contained on her right, facing Tony, who offered Diarmaid a teaspoon of foam from his cappuccino. 'Don't give him that,' she said.

'No coffee in it.' He tilted the spoon. 'See? There's not much you can tell me about smallies, come back to me when you have a couple more.'

Diarmaid took the foam from the spoon and looked up at Karine, delighted with himself. Other times his grandfather would be just as delighted with himself for reminding her how much more experienced he was, only now he was bothered; he sank in on himself, chin to his chest.

He said to her, 'You know as well as I do.'

'Know what?'

'What he used to get up to. Ryan.'

She didn't respond, which was to admit it.

'You should be telling him the same thing,' Tony said. 'Maybe he'll listen to you.'

'What do you want me to say?' It didn't seem necessary to mask her aggravation, Tony being in the condition he was in; she was aggravated as much by that condition as his vague warnings and yet here she was. *And yet here I am* could make a motto, she thought.

'There'd be fellas looking for him,' Tony said.

'Why would there be fellas looking for him? He's out of all that now, Tony, he's been away two years. He owes no one anything.'

'That's not how any of them lads operate.'

'If they weren't looking for him during the past couple of years, they'd hardly need him now. If Ryan's not worried about it, neither should you be.'

Bringing Tony for a coffee was a gesture, but she wasn't sure of what, or what she thought she might prove. That she felt associated, maybe. In Louise's voice she told herself, *Well look at you, always saving a Cusack from himself.* Under the table she flexed her toes. Her calves and thighs were as lead. Diarmaid began to remove sugar sachets from the bowl at the edge of their table. He counted loudly and Karine praised him.

'They've already been looking for him,' Tony said.

She darted him a look. 'Who's "they"?'

'J.P. was up at the house. I told him what you're saying now. He says he only wants to see how Ryan is getting on, he wants to hear it from the horse's mouth.'

Karine hunched her shoulders.

'I don't want Ryan to come back to that,' said Tony. 'Will you tell him?'

Karine deceitfully said, 'If your calls don't get through then mine won't either.'

'He'll talk to you before me. I know that much.'

Her options now were between leaving and listening to more of this dark stuff. This would leave her vulnerable to reawakened paranoia. She totted up the cost. But she did not want to leave.

She ordered Tony a second coffee.

'I don't know if I'll manage that, girl.'

'You will,' she said.

For their first six years, Ryan had lived in a city bigger than Karine could navigate. He kept odd hours. He spent social gatherings outside on his phone, smoking. There were friends he didn't want her to know or whom he couldn't bear to see be nice to her. He knew where things were; this was not a bad thing per se but something nonetheless disconcerting, something she took as proof of his maturity; in mapping out the city he was going in directions that had never occurred to her. He grew cagey and suffered bouts of insomnia. He became more pragmatic, which in him was nothing more than a coping mechanism; as many excuses as he could find for himself, he could find a dozen more for his father or mother or for Dan, his boss, the other recipient of his devotion. Karine, resident of a more manageable city, regretted the benefits of his career but made use of them anyway; often she couldn't see a way around it. She could afford to be generous. She could make use of his constant state of apology to get favours and tokens. She didn't get shit from anyone, not that she'd have taken shit from anyone. She was always something to someone and so she was, for a time, a little gangster's moll.

But what else was she going to be? She'd been with him since they were fifteen; it was unthinkable that she just leave him to it. There were witching hours suffered together; he whispered things like, *I can't tell you but trust me* ... She was with him when guards bothered him on the street and it never felt rebellious, only uncomfortable. She didn't like the way the guards looked at her. Whatever lines she drew he crossed them; he fucked other girls, he fell into coke binges, he shouted, he pushed her up against walls as she kicked his shins and called him things she knew would hurt him. But these offenses were performed without arrogance or elation or any sense of giddy liberty; his behaviour wasn't a privilege of his position, but the price he paid for it. He was sorry, he said. He was so sorry, he didn't know what was happening to him. He had strayed too far and couldn't manage the terrain.

At that point, Karine was adamant that he quit. She was an advocate for the tidier city. She told him that the prosperous cunts of the swollen city would never own him. That Dan or J.P. would never own him. She had taken it for granted that if he was no longer part of the swollen city, then he would be contained safely in hers. Only he couldn't find his way home. He had twisted the Northside for himself; he had made it so there might have been dangers around every corner, he had made the ground uneven, he had made his neighbours hate him. And so even now, years later, he was not at home but offshore, ignoring his father's calls.

Of course, the thing was that her city was only made seem small by the widening boundaries of his. Louise was right: it was all about him.

Tony Cusack said, 'I want him home too but I can't see him hurt again, not when he has the small fella to worry about. Talk sense into him, girl.'

Karine put both arms around Diarmaid and kissed the top of his head.

'Karine,' said Tony.

Karine said, 'I dance. Did you know that? That I'm a dancer?'

He frowned at her and then at the tabletop. 'I did.'

She narrowed her eyes. 'Did Ryan tell you?'

'I suppose he must have.'

'He usually just says I'm a nurse. He's obsessed with that coz he thinks it's the opposite of him, like. I'm not a nurse, I just have the degree. But I dance. That's important in its own way. He plays piano and I dance.'

'There's two of you in it, no one would say otherwise.'

'Only you're putting this on my shoulders like you don't even know there's more to me than him.'

'I know full well,' he told the table.

'Do you,' she said, dully.

Diarmaid dragged on her neck. He wanted to go on the bus, to get sweets, to see Grandad. Karine told Tony they'd better ship out and he agreed and rubbed his temples. Karine got him a glass of tap water and looked away while he downed it.

'I will tell him,' she said. 'I don't want to see him go backwards either. To be fair, I think he has more cop on these days.'

'But I told you, girl,' Tony said. 'That's not how any of them fellas operate.'

It must have been that Maureen's countenance was not so interesting as to linger in the memory for the best part of a decade. She stared, but Tony Cusack's mind was elsewhere. He didn't look at her once. She considered a coughing fit.

The three Germans had insisted on tipping her twenty euro. She decided to spend some of it on a sticky bun and a pot of tea while she self-evaluated. The Germans were happy with her histories and homilies. It was as she thought: people could be very receptive to the truth if it was sufficiently ugly. It was humdrum truths they despised.

She thought that she would like to show more people around. Not just tourists, but the new Irish. But the old Irish who had lost their knowledge of their city. But miscreants! But those who needed to see the damage they'd done! TDs, robbers, the Chamber of Commerce! She would like a mandate to have a word.

Tony Cusack came in when she had almost finished her bun. A prime candidate. A man who needed to be dragged up and down the quays and asked what he was at, knocking around with Jimmy when he had six children at home to feed and clothe and put through school, giving the same dangerous idea to his son? If he had been on his own, she would have plonked herself beside him and taken his confession, but he was with a blonde girl and a dark-haired toddler boy whose lineage was obvious and whose presence gladdened her greatly.

The blonde girl's eyes were large and her demeanour calm, some feline quality, though Maureen was not so deluded as to overlook her own narrative sensibilities in coming to this conclusion. She was remembering Ryan – his restlessness, his short fuse, his contrary hunger for praise – and based on Ryan had come up with a woman who'd give birth to his son. Feline, meaning graceful, clever, cool until provoked. She would like to introduce herself, shake this girl's hand, look directly at her face. She wanted the measure of her, for of course this girl was her own person, not made to smooth out his faults. But she saw her in conjunction, she saw her as the keeper of intimacies, the person most familiar with her old pet's soul. Maureen had seen herself in a similar role, one time, with a bearded boy called Dominic Looney.

She watched the blonde girl carry the little fella to the counter. She watched Tony's grandson point at the cakes, cuddle his mother, parrot thank-yous at the cashier. She wondered what had possessed them, Ryan and this girl, to spark into being another little life. Whether it was their intention in their greed for one another.

Tony and his grandson's mother had only low words to say to one another. She bought him two coffees. He rubbed his chin or forehead frequently. On occasion his chest bulged.

She followed them out of the cafe and kept her distance as they made their way to the bus stop. There they parted ways. Carrying the little boy, the blonde girl walked towards and past Maureen, away from the river. Maureen watched Tony lean against the side of the bus shelter with his arms folded. Now she could make him recognise her. Instead she turned and followed the girl and the little boy.

They went into the Centra on the Grand Parade. The girl set the child down and they wandered between the displays, holding hands. Maureen picked up a box of Mr Kipling Viennese Whirls. The girl and her little boy took a bottle of water from the drinks fridge, then he held his arms out and she picked him up. Maureen went up beside them. 'Well hello,' she smiled at the little lad. 'Hello there, dotey thing. What's your name?'

He stuck his finger in his mouth and pushed his face into his mother's shoulder.

'Ah, dotey,' Maureen said. 'He's shy. Will you not tell me your name, craitur?'

The girl smiled. 'This is Diarmaid.'

'Diarmaid!' Maureen said. 'How old is he?'

'He'll be three in August.'

'He will,' Maureen affirmed. 'He will, that's right. He's very like his father.'

'Excuse me?' the girl said. Maureen headed for the till, tugging at Diarmaid's right foot as she passed.

'Ryan,' she said, putting her biscuits on the counter. 'God, he's very like Ryan.'

The girl followed. 'How d'you know Ryan?' Her tone was suspicious.

Maureen gave the cashier a fiver and turned back. 'Don't I know his grandmother?' she said. This was not a lie. She remembered Noreen Cusack from years ago.

'How d'you know me, then?' the girl asked.

'Should I not? You were with him long enough.'

This was the point the girl should have relaxed and smiled and granted that this was true. Instead she held the child closer and stepped past Maureen to the counter. 'Well he's fierce like him,' Maureen went on, softly. 'And like his grandad too.'

The girl finished paying. 'He is,' she said. 'Doesn't bode well.'

Maureen tittered but the girl only sighed.

'Why would you say that?' Maureen asked.

The girl finished paying and stood back, a cardboard display between her and Maureen. The little fella reached for something Maureen couldn't see; his mother let him. 'People always say he looks like Ryan,' she said. 'No one ever says he looks like me. I mean, he doesn't, but no one even lies out of kindness. I'm the one who had him, like, I was sixteen hours in labour, he was nearly nine pounds.'

'Well, he has your nose,' Maureen said.

'He does not,' the girl said, vehemently.

Maureen let on as if the idea had only just come to her. 'I suppose it's a strange compliment. Like that the child looking like its father proves its mother's virtue.'

'Excuse me?' the girl said, again.

'Or that it's a compliment to the child, or to the fella. Cork is like that with fellas, don't you think?'

'Well I don't know but I'll tell you what, all day people have been talking about Ryan to me and it's wrecking my head a bit.'

'I'm sorry,' Maureen said. 'But sure I don't know you, so I can't be asking after you.'

The girl crossly conceded.

'Fair play to you for spotting the pattern, though,' Maureen said. 'I was only thinking about it earlier and here I am, I suppose, on the surface just as bad as the rest of them. He's a credit to you, little Diarmaid, he's a dotey boy.'

'Sure you only think he's dotey because he looks like his father,' said the girl.

'Not at all, haven't you a lovely rig-out on him.'

'That's true, I do change his clothes the odd time.'

Maureen, who appreciated sarcastic women, smiled broadly. The girl raised her eyes to heaven.

'When's he home, anyway?' Maureen asked.

'Who, Ryan? How'd you know he's coming home?'

'Isn't it on the little website they have?'

There was an odd beat and the girl said, 'Is that really how Nana Cusack's friends track Ryan? Online?'

'We all have access to the internet,' Maureen said.

'Funny things you'd be looking up,' said the girl. Her goodbye was a light, slow headshake. She left the shop, the child pointing merrily at this and that over her shoulder, and Maureen felt tetchy enough to think it was no wonder Cork chose to exalt its men if the young wans were so odd. She changed her mind a moment later. It just wasn't a nice feeling to be triggering disquiet so soon.

Track 3: Up and Lose

It's not the piano that endeared me to Dan, because he was cold, by necessity and by conditioning; I was prodigious when it came to selling drugs, and that was the main thing. But the piano gave me an extra layer. If he'd been looking for a sign I wasn't a gobshite who got lucky with a customer base of bigger gobshites, that was it.

He asked how I knew how to play and I told him my mam taught me.

He was like, Your mammy, is it? On your mammy's lap?

He was tickled when I didn't apologise for it, when I just went, Yeah, my mam.

You remember my dad sold my mam's piano and what a mess I was over it. You remember years after that I bought the digital piano but I don't know if you noticed me going demented trying to figure out how to fit it into the life Dan had me living. I was gonna use it electronically, just one line in a dance track. I was gonna use it as something to do with my hands when I was scheming as per the stupid stipulations of my job. I wasn't gonna use it at all because I didn't deserve it. Or I was too hard a feen for piano. Piano? Would you be well? And it wasn't like Dan was saying any of this shit to me, because that I wasn't an ordinary soldier was the reason he kept me close. He talked to me about all sorts – Buddhism, Marxism, consequentialism, solipsism, all the fucking isms – because he thought I was on his wavelength. Dan came from fuck-all, too, but even he believed piano wasn't for the likes of us.

But singing's a thing you do in the car or under your breath as you're making toast or when you're langers and thinking about a thirty-two-county republic. I came to singing easier than I came back to piano because singing doesn't make me special, loads of people can carry a tune. There's something vulgar about it, like.

When we were kids you were always telling me to go for *X Factor*. I wouldn't have, in a million years, but maybe there were ideas sown. You made me a songwriter, maybe you made me a singer, too. Weekends in the flat Dan had put me in on Blarney Street, when me and you would be listening to tunes and talking shit and smoking, you'd be like, Sing this one with me, or you'd show me some dance routine you'd come up with. It felt like it was the only thing happening to anyone, anywhere. You and me, a few steps, a few notes, a tiny world. Take each other's clothes off like we'd discovered that as well. I didn't want to know any better.

No one would believe me and I don't blame them, but I swear to you, I never thought Dan would die. Even though J.P. mandated it, even though I knew Shakespeare was a mé-féiner, I had all of Dan's philosophy in my head and up to the last fucking minute I was full sure I could save him. I could say now it was a lesson learned, only how crass is that? Dan's gone, coz I was never capable of changing J.P.'s mind, I only ever had the capacity to make things worse. And it feels like the complexities of it, the give and take, happened only down at my level. The likes of J.P. don't have to compromise. They decree what they decree, and the rest of us try to live under it.

'Up and Lose' is probably the vaguest of my songs. Songwriters should keep their lyrics on some border between personal and universal so that a song means something, but can be taken as their own by anyone who needs it. 'Up and Lose' is superficially about creativity, putting a shape to a strong feeling. Kicking a few doors in. *Have you up and lost your mind, sonny? Naw, boy, just being creative, as is my right.* But also it's about feeling powerful even though you know, you fucking *know* how powerless you actually are. The noble idiocy in thinking you have everything when the world is keeping so much from you. Whether that's the world's intention.

Putting it together I was thinking about reality-TV singing competitions, the people who won them and ended up back gutting fish for a living, how I'm still at Grade 4 in piano because the formal learning ended when my mam died, how all of Dan's isms didn't help him, in the end. How anyone with talent can sing or rap but not excel on an instrument because it costs too much to access that knowledge. Thinking about how naive I was on Blarney Street to think I had the world when no one even wanted me to cross the river, but how, in a way, I did have the world and I should have been happy with it. Whether ravenous ambition is its own sort of oppression, and whether the rich need to lose, rather than the poor need to win. How I come from fuck-all but I shouldn't be trying to better myself because what does that say about me, if I swallowed that line, if I believed I wasn't good enough for being from where I was from, for being my mother's son?

I have the brains and the scars she gave me. I have piano and I have poverty and I ran myself ragged years ago trying to figure it out. I'm woke and I don't want to get up. I raised myself and I did a terrible job. I'm the terrace, I'm Dan, I'm you. I am my mother's son and this is what happens when I open my mouth.

In a hotel bar in Carrigaline, Medbh asked Georgie if she'd ever thought of writing her own story. Teenage runaway to sex worker on the fringes of gangland Ireland, reinvented as a social-justice warrior. More than an article or an essay: a memoir, a whole book. It could be explosive.

'Never thought about it, to be honest.'

'No?' Medbh held her coffee in both hands and blew, and with the warm light from the glass behind her, and her bright lipstick, she looked to Georgie like a magazine image of femininity. If, for whatever churlish reason, she knocked the cup out of Medbh's hands, she imagined Medbh would mop the spill competently and fetchingly. 'I could help you,' Medbh went on. 'Why don't you think about it, put some ideas in an email to me?'

'I don't know if I'd be able,' Georgie said.

'I told you, I'll help.'

'I mean able as in, able in my head.'

'I'm going to send you a link to an essay I read recently about how owning your own narrative is crucial to self-acceptance. I know, I know,' she said, to Georgie's pulled face. 'A bit American. But I think someone like you, who has a history so . . . imbued, would get a lot out of it.'

'Imbued with what?' Georgie said.

Medbh thought about it and said, 'Imbued with meaning,' and before Georgie could ask her to expand again, said, 'It could be really, really important,' with a certainty that discouraged Georgie from asking why her real life should be anyone's cautionary tale or parable and so, on the way back to the mobile home, she leaned

76

her head on the bus window and let the notion of recounting her own history rattle about.

The problem would not be in recalling the necessary; the problem was that she couldn't see how important the effort could be. People would get the guts through the merest gist: some girls are easily manipulated, some men think it's their right, no eye-opener in that. The worst people found the climb the easiest, and once on top spread out effortlessly. The likes of Jimmy Phelan, say. How much had he ever known of the scale of industry dependent on him? It was said he had his profitable enterprise, and his lesser businesses were just money-laundering operations. So did he think, ever, of the girls in the brothels, or the street dealers, or the people whose debts the moneylenders bought and sold? Or did he just say, *You're a headache, so you can die.* Think of the power involved in that, being able to decree death without having to, well, get the hands dirty, as the saying went. To find some young fella trying to make a name for himself. To be so sure he'd do as he was told.

Passengers got on and off the bus. Another young woman sat beside her and opened a news app. Georgie peered. UNIVERSITIES ARE BASTIONS OF PRIVILEGE, the headline read. Georgie and her neighbour made eye contact. The neighbour slowly tilted her phone the wrong way.

The people surprised to hear their city was rotten could not be trusted to save Georgie from the people who made it so. But she was back here, and what did that say about her stubbornness, or psychosis? She had lurched back here as if tugged.

A tug, now, at the back of her head. The person behind had pulled her hair. She gave it the benefit of the doubt. People were clumsy and she had plenty on her mind. Her hair was tugged again.

Georgie turned around. Behind her sat two teenage girls, one dark, one blonde. Both wore messy high buns and school uniforms. 'What?' Georgie said.

'What?' echoed the blonde one.

'You pulled my hair, do you want something?'

'Ah, no one pulled your hair?'

'Mature,' Georgie said. She turned around and stared at the back of the bus driver's head. Her hair was tugged again. She ignored it. A fourth time, and she ignored it again. She remembered being so bored as a teenager she'd run away from home and become entwined with a 22-year-old layabout who she'd since been encouraged to think of as her first pimp. She had never been so bored as to be aggressive. Though perhaps she should have been. Perhaps that was why Cusack's misspent adolescence had brought him to bigger things. Perhaps she should have kicked Robbie in the balls when first he put to her that it wouldn't kill her to keep the landlord sweet, *Would it, Georgie? I don't know what the fuck we'll do this month otherwise* . . .

Her hair was tugged again.

Georgie snapped around. One knee bumped the thigh of the woman beside her. She curled one arm against the back of her seat and hung the other over the top. 'Are you finished?' she asked the teenagers.

The blonde one made the saucy face again. 'Excuse me?'

'You're pulling my hair.'

'Why would I pull your hair?'

Georgie smiled widely. She made a fist with the hand against the back of her seat. She couldn't think of anything to say. 'What?' sneered the blonde girl, as the dark one tittered, looking towards the front of the bus. Georgie pushed her tongue against the back of her teeth. She kept smiling.

'You're fucking weird,' said the blonde one.

Georgie reverted to a smirk. She turned around. The woman beside her scrolled up her screen with her index finger. Georgie took a stab at sisterly telepathy and begged her to get up and move seats, allow Georgie an escape route, but the woman had fixed on obliviousness or the mocking little weapons behind them were cluttering up the frequency, being sisters too. At times like this Georgie wondered if they weren't worse than men. The ignorance required to see the odds stacked and the state of the ground they'd need to tread and still to decide to make it worse again, as if by pulling apart the women around them they'd score points, or just camouflage themselves beneath the debris.

The teenagers began to pull Georgie's neighbour's hair instead and Georgie's neighbour didn't react. She must have thought she was being adult and dignified but it was obvious to Georgie that she was intimidated, having seen the measly impact of Georgie's confronting the agitators. Maybe she thought Georgie would stick up for her too. *What is it?* Georgie telepathically crowed. *What is it, girl? Your own fault. Your silence didn't save you. I could have told you your silence wouldn't*, and this thought made her blanch.

She thought that her silence would save her, in that making noise would lead J.P. to her. And then she thought that her silence was saving him too, and all of the men of the city who'd jumped at the chance to exploit her. And now she thought that she might throw up.

The woman beside her kept scrolling on her phone, stony-faced, as the girls behind her yanked and giggled, yanked and giggled.

They got up for their stop at Crosshaven and gave Georgie's hair one last ferocious wrench. She brought her hand to the back of her head. The girls descended from the bus and through the window she saw that they were not cackling or high-fiving but seemed to have already forgotten their mischief. Georgie shot up and shoved past her neighbour, who tutted after her. The bus driver tutted too. He had to open his door again for her.

The girls were looking in the blonde one's schoolbag, their heads touching. There being no one else around, Georgie changed her mind on confronting them. There were two of them. They were evidently belligerent. They would take strength from each other and she was alone. Just her luck that there happened to be a chunk of walling stone to hand. It was light enough for her to throw it easily, and it hit the blonde girl on the right shoulder and caused her to totter forwards, drop her school bag and cry out.

Georgie took off at full tilt.

Into a housing estate, out into a field on the other side, across the pasture and behind a small shed, gulping on the ground there for twenty minutes, circumnavigating the village and waiting, weeping at a bus stop on the far end, travelling into Cork City to throw them all off the scent, into a pharmacy on Patrick's Street and eventually back to the beach wearing a beanie and a pair of glasses with clear lenses.

She stood in the bathroom of the mobile home after wrecking one towel and leaving a vibrant splodge beside the sink. Her head was itching. She was crying. She was sure she would be identified, arrested and charged for taking a chunk out of a child's shoulder, a promising student, perhaps, a good girl from a good home who'd just been having a bad day and was now permanently altered, unable to play camogie or the concertina, stricken with nerve damage and her exams coming up and everything. Georgie had bought two boxes of home hair dye. She was trying light brown first, and then had a dark brown to apply over it. Articles online said that her hair could react badly to the cheap dye, it might go green or grey. She was supposed to do a patch test and wait forty-eight hours before dyeing her hair and she did not have that luxury. Her scalp tingled and so she imagined her head blistering and her hair falling out in chunks.

Medbh's sitting room was tiny and tidy but well put-together. She had graphic prints on the walls, colourful upholstery and a turntable. The room didn't get a lot of natural light, so Medbh had both floor and table lamps. 'Let's start,' she said. She placed two mugs on the coffee table, put her laptop on a cushion on her lap, and sat back.

Georgie perched on the other end of the couch and said, 'It's hard to imagine any of this matters.' It was three days since she'd hit the teenager with the walling stone and she had not been able to convince herself that she would get away with it. She'd been reading local news obsessively. Her hair had a weird hue in the daylight and Medbh had briefly gritted her teeth when she'd opened her apartment door.

'We'll outline,' Medbh said, 'and then we'll know. Anyway, everyone likes talking about themselves.'

'I don't.'

'You haven't given it a shot. What makes you special is that you actually have something to say.' Medbh gave Georgie a look that wasn't wholly patient, then began typing. 'Tell me where you grew up,' she said. 'What was your family like?'

Georgie was an only child. Her father was forty-two when she was born, her mother almost forty, and Georgie suspected her parents had found in each other a last resort. Her father was an oldest son bequeathed a small farm. The land swallowed him; he worked all hours on sickly, finicky soil; he conversed falteringly; he had faith in God because God felt as vital and unremarkable a presence as the town's doctor or publican. Georgie's mother did not seem to have strong feelings about anything, therefore it was impossible to buy her thoughtful gifts or to engage her in lively conversation. 'Well, I don't know,' was something she said an awful lot.

There were girls at school who would never have accepted Georgie even if she'd grown up brilliant or beautiful. Her house was not right for sleepovers or, later on, drinking vodka and Coke before nights out. Her school books were subsidised, her runners own-brand. When she was in sixth class she tried to make out that her name was Georgia instead of Georgina; no one believed her, and she never really recovered from it. In secondary school she became one of the rowdier girls because there didn't seem to be any point in waiting to blossom. Nor was there any point in knuckling down towards an impressive Leaving Cert. Her parents couldn't stretch to the grinds and summer Gaeltacht courses. Ambition was a strange language. Rarely did they ask how she was managing with homework.

Georgie and the other contrary girls smoked on the way to and from school, drank cans of cider on Saturdays and befriended older boys who smelled of cannabis. When Georgie was fifteen and a half she told her mother she was staying the night at Alison O'Keeffe's but instead got the bus to Cork City to stay with one of the cannabis boys. Alison O'Keeffe was a popular girl and would no more have Georgie stay over than a delegation of nuns. That Georgie's mother didn't know Alison was of finer stock than her cemented in Georgie's mind that she was misunderstood. She phoned her mother from the older boy's mobile and in an even voice told her she wasn't coming home, that her parents shouldn't bother looking for her because even if they found her, she wasn't going to budge. She intended to stay only the weekend in Cork, to punish her parents for not knowing her better. But then she waited another day, and another, and so on, and then she met Robbie, who gave her his bed in return for her virginity.

Her parents called the guards and came to the city. They did the whole of Cork looking for her five, six times in the span of a fortnight. The guards put out a missing-person appeal and there was a thrill in Georgie's seeing her face on a couple of shop windows and on a couple of news websites. She called her parents to tell them she was fine so could they please stop looking? This was relayed to the guards, and Georgie wasn't sure but she assumed the guards lost interest because there was no immediate danger of her being cut into pieces by deranged men. After a while of this – the harried Gardaí's indifference and Georgie's own arrogant bullshitting – her parents gave in. Maybe they had Mass said for her. Maybe the neighbours came to the Mass but otherwise avoided them.

'Maybe I'll come home for Christmas Day,' she told her mother on the phone that first year, though when Christmas came, she decided it wasn't a good idea. All her mother did was let out a short sigh and ask, under her breath, where all this was coming from.

'Maybe if you're good to him, he'll be good to us,' Robbie said, churning his hands. 'What would it take, ten minutes? Ten minutes for the rest of the month's rent? I won't like it either, girl.'

Practicalities were not what Medbh or anyone else wanted to hear. Georgie liked to read crime fiction, specifically books in which broken but brilliant detectives caught broken but brilliant serial killers. She would not be interested in a book in which a detective solved a case by thorough process of elimination and the killer wasn't excited by his crimes because it felt bad to be acting the bollocks. Georgie understood the drug of an innocent's suffering. Medbh would not want to hear about the boring home life that drove Georgie to distraction, or about her slide into commonsensical prostitution. It would be better if she'd had a demonic father and a mother who indulged his urges, if she'd made a desperate bid for freedom and ended up in thrall to a slippery pimp who'd sold her to dozens a day, every day.

Her story did not feel monstrous enough and as she recounted it to Medbh in Medbh's tidy flat Georgie waited for Medbh to stop her, to press her, or to laugh at her indulgent victimhood. Medbh did not, but she did say *Hmm* a lot, and pressed her lips together either in thought, or as a way of refreshing their brilliant ruby colour.

'And so why was there a hit out on you?' she asked in the end, in a calm tone that made the dramatic turn of phrase sound twice as absurd.

'Because I knew too much,' Georgie replied, which was just as dramatic even though it was true. 'Please let's say no more about it.'

'Whatever you knew too much of,' said Medbh, 'we can assume part of his story, not yours.'

And the lines on this were also so brilliant, so clean, that Georgie nodded sadly and said, 'OK.'

Mel was stuck with disappointment, a cowardly emotion because it was meant to be buried, it was defeat that went nowhere and could be channelled into nothing, it was not meant to be anyone's imposition. Mel felt forced into it because she was not meant to confront Ryan with what Izzy had disclosed on his behalf. It would have been cruel, definitely unsightly and irreparably damaging to the vibe. She could not decide whether she wanted Natalie to have given Ryan a heads-up, which would mean they'd be working towards the same goal – suppression of a private fact – which would muddy the waters in terms of whether her passive behaviour could be classified as feminine, because she would like to think she was just being Mel and not your common-or-garden girl. *Angry? I'm just disappointed.* Or whether she wanted Natalie to have said nothing at all, only maybe to have asked him probing questions or given him sympathetic, unreadable looks. That way, it would disappear quickly.

Izzy was in on top of her all day, every day, Izzy had Found a Friend, and that would be a noble gesture if Izzy had not also Given this Friend a Land, which soured any overtures she was trying to make; no one could switch off to the extent that they forgot the person they were talking to was born of a degenerate mother with a taste for teenage boys. And who wanted a new friend who knew that kind of thing? Friendship rarely had to blossom out of brutal honesty, and Mel had come home to Ireland to be reborn, not to keep kicking up the same old dirt, making the same old excuses and apologies. She didn't blame Ryan, really. The reason the whole thing was so awful was that at his age he'd been blameless, legally speaking anyway. She was just pissed off that she had to carry this around with her when she'd packed so lightly for the journey home.

They were writing chords and lyrics and she was aping Izzy well – taking Izzy's ideas to make them sound as Izzy would if her hand wasn't banjaxed – but she could feel the weight of it the whole time, as could Ryan, whose head bowed further and further, who must have a terrible crick in his neck.

Izzy had ideas about theme and form and they were, each one, shot through with gender politics. For example, Izzy said that women could carry heavier loads because women's bodies were meant to be vessels. Within the woman was always some space to be filled whether or not she ever wished to fill it; in a sense a woman was hollow and a man was solid, and Mel felt this as a threat but Izzy did not. She went on and on about it in the writing sessions. She said that such ideas ran through her like chemical imbalances, stimulating and euphoric, which made Izzy as intimidating to Mel as the sort of body they both inhabited.

The lads were not disturbed by these ideas; they seemed instead not to understand them. Izzy supposed loudly that there was nothing surprising about that, because men weren't interested in any experience which didn't mirror their own. This made Mel feel even more distinct from the lads, even more sequestered by Izzy, who was tactile or grabby depending on how confident Mel felt on any given day, and the days were flying by and Izzy's ideas seemed more and more insistent, and so sometimes Mel thought she was being churlish in not wanting to be on Izzy's side –

Mel, tell 'em!

Mel, you know what I mean, right?

See how Mel coaxed out that guitar line, Mel gets it, Mel gets me

– and sometimes she felt as though her own ideas, her own body, her own fucking self was weak and woeful next to this force of nature, Izzy King, who held her own and fought her corner and said she would never stop advocating for women's voices and looked pointedly and reassuringly at Mel as she did so.

Remembering this kept Mel awake when she needed to sleep, and she thought of 'women's voices' and how they birthed into sound ideas about femininity or the rejection of femininity, and she wondered how they did it and why they were not at war with themselves, as she was –

Janelle Monáe Patti Smith Alanis Morissette Nina Simone Róisín Murphy Tori Amos Denise Chaila Sarah Slean Kathleen Hanna Christine McVie Sister Rosetta Karin Dreijer

– just like them her job was to find the extraordinary in the ordinary and word it in such a manner that it brought everyone who heard her closer to insight, but unlike them she couldn't, being at war with herself, being out of sync in sickening perpetuity, she felt like words came to her in specific lyrics in the correct order but she could only ever find the first couple, and the rest of the line stayed just out of her grasp, as if she had caught the first few words of a scintillating secret but lost the rest and had to make it up based on her own narrow understanding of the scandal. And now with Lord Urchin, Izzy kept putting her arm around Mel's waist and saying things like 'We are Tracey Emin's Bed, the lads are the Great Exhibition at the Crystal Palace!' – when for Mel Crystal Palace was a football team.

Not that it mattered to Izzy who Mel was, so long as she remained a receptacle for Izzy's ideas, a vessel, as it were. And not that it mattered to Ryan, only what Mel was evocative of. How, then, could she not be disappointed?

Regarding the comment underneath Izzy's vlog and the request from the journalist, Ryan did exactly as Natalie had predicted. Mel didn't witness this but read it on his face afterwards. He was pale to the point of being a little green. He didn't recover from the jetlag; he spent much time sitting on the wall outside the house, smoking joints and staring at his phone, which was odd as his phone could hardly pick up the Wi-Fi from there; Mel even went out to check.

The bandmates argued about it the evening Natalie and Colm left. Izzy was the most vocal. She said that it wasn't right for one of five to be interviewed, that Lord Urchin was a unit, not Ryan's backing band. 'How would you all like it,' she asked, 'if I was interviewed because I'm a female guitarist in a male-dominated industry? The spotlight would just be on me, which would set a terrible precedent.' She did not look as if she thought this would set a terrible precedent.

'This journalist says she's interested in the working-class voice angle,' Joseph replied. 'And Natalie thinks that's code for "bould-little-drug-dealing-bastard voice". So we have to be so careful. Ignore it and we might have lost our best chance of setting our own agenda. Like if we do this right, we'll grab attention, we won't have just another debut album, we'll be the band that recorded on two separate continents with a big political declaration of arrival—'

'Joe,' Ryan said. 'Joe, stall the fuck on. There'll be no declaration.'

'What kind of world are you living in, boy? You can't just go, "Oh, the juicy thing? I'm not telling you about the juicy thing".'

'Yeah, I can, that's kind of a stipulation of the fucking world I'm living in.'

'Ryan boy, I'd love to launch an album at people who only care about the music but I don't think there are enough of those to cover the costs of recording the fucking thing. Likes of us don't give two shits about ex-drug dealers but other fuckers give multiple shits. They need their questions answered. Do not think you can hide from this.'

'Joe, I'm not worried about music journalists and fucking gig-goers!'

Izzy stood up. 'Ryan absolutely needs to come clean. What I'm saying is that he can come clean as part of an ensemble. We all have our stories.'

Ryan did not stand to face her, but lifted his chin and raised his voice further, 'I have fuck-all to come clean about.'

Joseph gently put it to Ryan that if he had nothing to come clean about then he would hardly be so worried about the consequences of coming clean; he was being contradictory even here, among friends, and this is why he had to get his story straight.

Come clean was the term Ryan couldn't get past. Izzy said it was just a turn of phrase. Ryan said nothing was just a turn of phrase. Izzy condescendingly supposed it was just like a baby lyricist to get tangled in semantics. 'If it really bothers you that much,' she teased, 'you must have an awful lot of secrets.'

Mel tried to shoot her a warning look, but Izzy would not meet her eyes.

The juicy thing? Izzy could hardly keep a lid on the juicy thing.

'God forbid I'm saying this to you for your own good, Ryan,' she said. 'Honestly, I think you need to own your past.'

'Own my past? What fucking self-help books have you been reading, girl?'

'It's not the first time I've told you that,' Izzy said, as if just remembering it, and he looked at her as if uninterested in remembering it himself, but it came up on him. He dropped his head as Joseph started speaking again. He stared at his lap.

Inishbofin was a changeable place. So vividly green under a threatening sky, or after rain. Then so boggy and bleak. There were no trees. In the sunshine the beaches were better than any. The roads were pitted, hardly roads at all. No streetlights but what bodily harm would come to a visitor on Bofin? You might crack a kneecap. You might graze your palms. But if it wasn't a lonely place, if its winds wouldn't leave you winded, if it wouldn't rip away whatever bit of you was curling at the corners. You were further out than the map indicated. You needed a sense of self.

This was the kind of thing Traolach liked to tell them when he came by. Not that Natalie had raised any objection to him in the few nights she'd spent on Bofin, but he seemed to do particularly well in Natalie's absence; he latched on to Ryan so fiercely that Mel felt he'd guessed some awful secret had been unearthed and some awful shit was about to go down. He put himself between Ryan and Mel as though by magnetic navigation and worked on her as if trying to distract her. One night he yanked up his T-shirt to show her a surgery scar and stared over the bunched cloth as if expecting her amazement that he was still kicking. Another night he went on about how one might determine, in terms of increasing the volume of a substance by miniscule increments, for example grains of chilli powder, which was the particular straw that broke the camel's back. He talked about Tibet and Salvia divinorum and was an agreeable enough waste of time.

'I'm not saying that Bofin isn't sinking under the weight of arty fuckers,' he said. 'It's just you'd wonder what urban arty fuckers would get out of it.'

Mel thought that Traolach had hit on something. She wondered why Joseph had picked such an isolated place. Was it supposed to make the mind more fertile, as a fire in a room depleted of oxygen will burn furiously once a window's cracked?

The writing sessions took shape. Davy and Orson got a rhythm going. Between them, the eking out of a vibe. Davy, the bones of it, Orson, the blood. Joseph and Izzy sat picking and listening, drawing sundry routes now open to them. After a while one tried a melody and the other took strands to rework, and the instigator took those reworked notes and expanded on them. Mel took Izzy's lead, aping her basic sequence and then, watching her eyes, bringing it into focus. Joseph nodded steadily as she hit the groove intended. 'See, that', Orson said pointing at Izzy, 'is melancholy, so I think more like this . . .' And he put forward a gorgeous, slumping line, and turned the air electric with words of a new language.

Ryan recorded and wrote notes at intervals, hunched over.

Mel was combustible, and knew that Ryan could sense it. When she caught his eye, he looked away. When she spoke to him, he answered as though she was someone he'd met in a waiting room. Izzy kept gently goading him. She made suggestive comments. She had found a dud note and was determined to hear him sing it. She said that revelation was only the first step, confrontation had to follow. Thinking this was something to do with art and albums, Joseph and Davy and Orson agreed. Mel asked Izzy to stop, told her she was making her itchy; Izzy apologised, toned it down but did not stop. It would have been better for Ryan to be as reactive as Mel felt. He went the other way. He went still.

'I can see why you'd think Bofin would be a good place to string together a few tunes,' Traolach said, one night, maybe to all of them or maybe just to Ryan. 'But I can see why it wouldn't work on you as well. Keep the blood pumping,' he said. 'Keep her lit.'

And so the following afternoon they tried an amalgamation of hurling and rounders in the garden. It was true that in fixing beats and melodies they had kept long hours on various intoxicants and were not eating regularly. In Glasgow, Mel lifted weights and did careful meal prep; her father assumed it was a fitness thing. But that she was biologically predisposed towards softness alarmed her. She was only on Inishbofin a week and she felt like shit. Headachey, heavy, her body ready to escape however she'd hemmed it. She clattered the sliotar like Setanta taking on a pack of hounds, making Izzy flinch.

Izzy was restless. The fresh air had gone to her head and she had decided it was past time the promised acid went to her head. Exercise was one thing; imagine the benefits of widening the sky. 'We should really have sorted those trips by now,' she said to Ryan as the game was wrapped up.

He went, *Oh*. He looked at Mel and just as quickly looked away. Mel saw him make a decision, and in that decision, a bad mistake.

'Dunno about that,' he said, to Izzy. 'I've too much going on in my head to be dropping acid.'

'You don't have to,' Izzy said. 'Just get trips for the rest of us.'

He did not raise his voice. 'That's what I'm good for, is it?'

'You're the one with that kind of relationship with Traolach.'

'Traolach's not a dealer. He was just trying to help us out.'

'Let him help us out, then.'

He tsked.

Izzy leaned in. 'You don't want trips, so no one gets trips? How puritanical. Here's the unexpected price you pay for having an ex-dealer frontman.'

Izzy's tone was as it often was. Open to interpretation. Finely balanced between joke and barb. Therefore she was able to deny responsibility for whatever reaction came. Mel didn't think she would ever be able to train herself to be so cunning. She thought that Ryan would have to puzzle the meaning out of what Izzy had said but instead he responded plainly, 'Get your own fucking trips,' and Mel thought, well, she might have liked to train herself to wield this sort of fearless certainty instead, but for its consequences. Izzy was taken aback only briefly, then indignation came off her in waves.

Track 4: Animal

I don't know if you'll remember this the way I remember it, but the first time we had sex make me go loop-the-loop. You said we'd moved too fast and that we had to pretend we hadn't done it at all coz otherwise it'd go to my head, but it had already gone to my head. We didn't do it again for weeks but I was replaying it all the time. I couldn't hear a word any teacher said to me. I always had to sit with my elbow in my crotch and God help me, if I caught the line of your bra under your shirt, I'd to put my head between my knees. At home my dad would be phoning me to see where I was and stunned when I'd tell him I'd been in bed since half nine. He'd come up the stairs and gawp in at me. What're you at? he'd say. Are you fucking sick or what?

You laugh, I was demented. My brain was going ninety. You'd have killed me if you knew what I was doing to you in my mind. PornHub could've come to me for ideas.

Fellas aren't supposed to overthink it. *You fuck now. That's all it is.* What it means to want to fuck is meant to be beyond you; what's driving you to it, other than feeling good. Before what happened on Bofin happened, you'd have thought I was mad if I said sometimes it's clear that my dick does what it's meant to, regardless of where the rest of me is. Sometimes it's frightening to know that I'm stuck in this body and this body is treacherous and easily broken. And sometimes it's not frightening, just . . . right.

There's a list of people who've gone for the most fucking responsive part of me. Dan booted me in the balls when he found out I'd been fucking Natalie, which in hindsight is fair enough. A sham in Liverpool brought a knee to them; that was just business.

And it's instinctive for J.P. to go for where it'll hurt the most. He took a handful once, like you'd see in a gangster film, wrenched and squeezed till the tears rolled down my cheeks and the bile came up my throat. He knows how to use your own biology, or what's sacred about your own biology, against you. So he threatens you with all the ways you can be violated, because that's the curse of not being allowed to overthink it, it becomes so important that it's instinctive, it gets knotted through you: your place as a fella, the role of the body you're in.

How quick it was to put Dan down.

How easy it was for Tara Duane to get what she wanted out of me.

How right it was to make you pregnant.

So 'Animal' is a song about sex and that's fairly obvious. It's not an entirely positive treatment of the subject but I didn't want it to be.

It could have been. Me and you fit together. I don't know if that's a case of luck in finding the right person or the result of us growing up together and figuring it out together, but I like what you like and you like what I like, and whether we're naturally compatible or we made ourselves compatible is an unnecessary distinction. So we go slow and look into each other's eyes, or I make you come with my mouth and my fingers first, or I watch your arse jiggle as I go in and out of you from behind, or we make a hames of it and fall over laughing because even when it's bad, it's unreal. After a stupid argument? Unreal. After my dad was shitty to me? Unreal. After I'd pick you up from a night out with your buddies? Oh God, unfuckingreal.

It's almost as good afterwards, when you're in bed beside me, reading something on your phone or giving out about someone or trying to decide what we'll do for breakfast, and I'm on my own phone, or agreeing with you that such-and-such is a fucking clown, or saying maybe you should go get the coffee for once in your life, and we're both naked and I know you're still wet from me and that even going off for a shower doesn't mean we won't do it again in a few minutes. It's not just me being a fella that has me so always up for it. Things were never like that with other girls, not even Natalie, and she worked hard at it. Nah, it's you. It's the taste of you, it's your perfect little tits, it's the look you give me when you want it hard but it'd ruin what we're doing to tell me to go hard. I know you, and I fucking love that I know you, and sometimes I think that if it wasn't for you having a bit more cop on than me we'd stay in bed till we starved.

I was so excited about you coming to Bofin. I was so sure of what was going to happen, like, the same thing that always happened when we hadn't seen one another in a while. Dylan wouldn't be a problem because I was there now and what would you want with Dylan when you could get the better of me? I sang placeholders as we made 'Animal' what it is now, this dark beast of a song, but I was already there or thereabouts on the real lyrics.

So yeah, no one's going to give me a prize for subtlety with the lyrics of 'Animal'. Only thing I can say is that I'm not sure if sex is the animal, or I'm the animal, or you're the animal. Yeah, you. You're not performing when you arch your back or take hold of my dick or kiss me so hard you could break my jaw when you're going to come. On Bofin I thought, you're this creature that's stronger than me, wilder than me, tougher than me, and you're what's going to tear me limb from limb. I couldn't wait to taste the copper in my mouth.

I've been dancing, Karine told herself. I am lithe and blissful. I am provocative and strong. She swayed down the aisle of the train carriage with Diarmaid on her hip. She got a few looks and gave a few back. Her new shorts dug into her belly.

Not to go was the imperative thing. Not to be dictated to, not to have her arm twisted or her heartstrings plucked. But he'd made so much sense: a friend of a friend had a holiday rental on Inishbofin that was free all week, Ryan would rent it for the final three nights of the band's stay on the island, Karine and Diarmaid could come for a little break. He could wait longer to see Diarmaid, of course he could, but it was hard to wait when there were other options. He'd borrow a car and come to Galway to collect them from the train. He'd pay for the train tickets, too. All she had to do was throw a few bits in a bag, he'd do the rest, he'd make it easy.

'Didn't I warn you?' Louise said. 'Are you such a dope as to not know what he's after?'

Karine's mother chose the other extreme and claimed not to understand it at all. Karine showed her the internet listing for the cottage. She said that the weather was supposed to stay nice and that she could bring Diarmaid to the beach. Her mother frowned. Wouldn't this reintroduction work better in Diarmaid's own home, where he was comfortable, where he was secure? Amazing the ways you could damage your child.

'For God's sake,' Karine laughed, 'he'll be fine'.

To which her mother just said, 'Karine, love, I hope you know what you're doing.'

95

A secure person would go because there were sensible reasons to go. The holiday cottage, the weather, the beach. Karine was a secure person and so what harm? Such things good parents do.

But oh God, her heart when she saw him at the station. She didn't know if she had expected him to have changed; he looked the same but he wasn't the same, he had twenty months of separate experiences, new languages, songs written; just then the span between meetings seemed beautiful. She held their son's hand and rubbed the other off the side of her bag.

Ryan went down on his haunches.

'Ciao, Derry.'

Diarmaid went in behind Karine's leg and looked out at Ryan with his thumb in his mouth. 'Ciao, Daddy,' he said. He put his forehead to the back of Karine's thigh. 'Hi, Dad,' he said again, and giggled, and after a bit allowed himself to be picked up.

Ryan put his free arm around Karine's shoulder. She pressed her nose to his chest and closed her eyes.

'Jesus, it's good to see you,' he said.

What both confused and delighted Karine was knowing that this was not how a straight woman interacted with her ex. Her straight friends had exes: boys they had outgrown, men who had outgrown them, or guys revealed to be bastards or cowards. And sometimes her friends saw them on social media or on the street or in a pub and said, Oh great, there's Whatshisface, that's my day ruined, who's he with? what's he up to? state of him. If it came to it the friend might greet the ex, enquire as to his health or after his parents. In general, though, the ex was a relic about which the friend had no contemporary information. Even the fathers of her friends' babies, the decent ones who had outgrown or been outgrown, became unknowable again. They did their duty and maintained polite relations with the mothers. All of Karine's friends had at least two exes. Karine had a sort-of-ex, a maybe-ex, someone whose importance couldn't fit in a syllable, and in this sense she felt like her friends didn't understand, which sometimes made her feel special and sometimes lonely.

When she messaged Louise to let her know she was going to Inishbofin, Louise had not responded for hours and when she did it was to say *I suppose you are such a dope then* and after that, *My advice: don't shave your legs* and after that, *Not that you ever listen to me anyway, girl*.

They went first for lunch in the city centre. Diarmaid sat on the table and Ryan held his waist and told him they'd make sandcastles and go swimming and see the moo-cows *le mucche* and the birdies *gli uccelli* and go on the boat *la barca* over the sea *il mare* . . . Karine thought about how to begin relaying his father's message. There was time yet. It was safe here; he was safe here, ordinary except in his history with her. On the ferry she sat indoors, minding the bags. Ryan took Diarmaid out to see the waves. He hooked his arm around a pole and stood well back and still she watched as if he'd lurch forward and fling Diarmaid overboard. Diarmaid put both hands around Ryan's neck and looked at the water, mesmerised.

They came in after ten minutes and sat beside her. She took Diarmaid and tucked his hair behind his ears. 'I badly want a fag,' Ryan said, stretching.

'Well then why'd you start again, eejit?'

'Coz I'm an eejit.'

Diarmaid took Karine's phone and sat on her lap to play with it. She opened an app for him.

'D'you think I deserve to be a musician?' Ryan said.

'You are a musician.'

He arched his back, hands behind his head. 'But do I deserve it?'

'You're good enough. I've always told you that.'

'No, I mean given the shit I used to get up to.'

'Oh,' Karine said. Only for the warmth of his thigh pressed to hers she might have said, *Right, yes, the shit you used to get up to, turns out that hasn't gone away*. Instead she said, 'I don't think it works like that.'

He scrolled on his phone and passed it to her. Diarmaid reached for it. Karine held it in front of her face. 'What's on your phone, Dad?' Diarmaid asked.

A video of Joseph and Izzy King titled 'Makin' Jam'. A reply reading:

How many likes would this video get if people knew this band was funded by drug profits. Ryan Cusacks own record label run on ryan Cusacks dirty –

The reply cut into a hyperlink.
'Should I click this?' Karine said.
'I've read it twenty times, it should load.'

– money. For what will become obvious reasons this blog will be anonymous. I am a person who knows Ryan Cusack outside of music. Ryan Cusack comes from a deprived background and Im sure he makes no secret of that. However it begs the question, where did he get the money to set up a record label (Catalyst Music) to promote his band Lord Urchin. The fact of the matter is that before this he was a drug dealer and there are plenty of people in Cork who would confirm this. I do not mean that Ryan Cusack was standing around on the street selling small quantities, in fact he was responsible for selling large quantities and as he is still in his early twenties I think this will pose a further question –

'What is this shit?' Karine said.
'It's not shit, though, is it?'
Diarmaid tugged at her. 'Bold word,' he said.
The writer went on to say that Ryan had been successful suspiciously early on, and therefore had to be a psychopath, because normal drug dealers couldn't make half as much in twice the time. Further along there was a rant about the damage drugs did to a city. A lament for hypothetical dead kids. A plea for people to 'ask questions about this band and the man who financed it' and 'to come to the right conclusion'.

'*Deprived*. Like, whoever wrote this is not just a gowl, they're a sanctimonious gowl.' Karine sat up straight. 'Why don't you just delete the stupid comment?'

'This is one of many,' Ryan said. 'Every time Natalie deletes one, another pops up. People have started to reply to them, tagging Natalie or defending me which is worse again.'

Karine closed her hand around the screen. 'Who could have written this?'

'It could be one of fifty different people. It could be a fucking syndicate. People I fucked over years ago. The ould dolls of people I fucked over years ago. Anyone who drinks with my dad. Neighbours. My sister.'

'Kelly? Ryan.'

'She always said I was a jammy prick. I dunno. Could be your ould fella, for fuck's sake.'

Diarmaid clambered over and stood on Ryan's lap. He placed his hands on his father's cheeks and said very seriously to him, 'Dad. Dad.'

'What?'

'No bold words.'

'Who said no bold words?'

'Grandad.'

'Oh,' Ryan said. 'Daddy'll be good, so.'

Adding to the muddle in her head were thoughts inspired by muscle under skin, by power differential. Ryan had always been lean and he had always been stronger than her. That was the reality for most girls. You let him in, you hope you can handle him.

The cosmic joke was that even if things went perfectly, even if he was the gentlest, most chivalrous soul, if you had a child with him it would physically change you, it would push you out of shape and make you scared of everything. In the marks on her body she saw the damage he'd done. She had never marked him. When Natalie looked at his body she didn't see signs of his history with Karine, she couldn't tell whether he'd ever been touched.

It made no sense to resent this. It was just the way it was.

She watched him fiddle with a thermostat panel in the cottage he had rented for them. She and Diarmaid wandered about looking in cupboards and tracing out corners and she did not have to resort to stealing glances; her sort-of-ex, her maybe-ex was engrossed in profile. In profile being the angle most graphic, she'd thought from the beginning, when she'd been boy-mad, or him-mad, when she had to steal glances. When they'd shared a classroom. She and her friends would joke about perving on boys but when she genuinely liked the boy it felt wrong to think of it in those terms. She would feel ashamed for looking at him and not because she thought it was a breach of his sovereignty or masculinity or whatever it was but because lascivious looking seemed a bit desperate or even aggressive, not feminine. She would take in the little bump in his throat, the flatness of his stomach, the small of his back. She saw how he might look in vulnerable states. Sleeping. Showering. Getting dressed. The boys in her class would joke about masturbation and she would be furious that they'd made her think of him in that state too and she did think about it, and wondered how often and what kind of girls he liked and what kinds of things he'd done with girls he liked and what kinds of things had been done to him.

When they started going out, it thrilled her to have him stand over her and push against her, tug at her clothes, tilt his head and whisper in her ear. She held him off because it was proper to hold him off; she wasn't sure what she wanted but it was more than she was supposed to give. She wondered why this was coming into her head nine years later, with all that they'd made together, and realised she was meant to hold him off again. That was what was doing the damage.

He asked that first night if he could stay. There were so many things they should have discussed first but she just said, 'I want you to.' She had thought about it on the way to Galway and had resolved that she'd quiz him on his recent history and insist on his using condoms, but she hadn't taken any with her, and she didn't quiz him and didn't want to insist. She brought him inside her the way she always had and when she imagined the pill failing, there was a crazy joy in it. Craziest was the contradiction: feeling so at home in her body while aching to lose control of it. She let him in, she wanted him unmanageable.

And then still entangled, shining after one another, Ryan said, 'I love you.'

'I love you too,' she said. It was the easiest thing in the world.

'No, listen.' He went up on one elbow and leaned over her. 'Not, *I love you, mate*. I love you, I want to be with you.'

'You're with me now.'

'All the time, I mean.'

'That's a big thing you're saying.'

'It's not really. Why else would I be in bed with you?'

It was easy to consider what he was suggesting because she'd gone there so often she'd made shortcuts. She was herself around him; they made each other laugh; they wanted similar things; she couldn't imagine she'd ever be sick of looking at him. It was comfortable, for a fantasy, but a fantasy was what it was. Reality was the mess he'd made, and the son she was meant to shield from it.

'You're homesick,' she told him. 'That's all.'

'Maybe. But I'm home now.'

He got up in the morning with Diarmaid, and an hour later they brought her tea and toast. She sat up in bed, wearing Ryan's T-shirt, and Diarmaid read his father's tattoo for them like it was a story. She showered and changed the sheets, and when she came back to them they were playing on the floor in front of the fireplace and the stacked firewood so clean it looked fake. She wanted to tell Ryan nothing of nosy drug barons, or even of his father. She reached for his hand and he got up. She put her hands around his neck and kissed him; she wanted his heartbeat to quicken. Maybe it wasn't selfish if in the end it would be for his own good. To keep him here, blissfully ignorant, dazed.

But she stepped back.

'I met your dad the other day. He said he was trying to ring you.'

Ryan put a hand on his forehead. 'Yeah, coverage is shit here though.'

'When I couldn't get through you rang me back.'

'I wasn't able for him, to be honest with you.'

'Only he was trying to tell you that J.P. was looking for you.'

Ryan moved his hand through his hair, over his crown, back to his forehead. He glazed over, briefly, before looking at her again.

'I'm sorry,' she said. 'I should have told you this yesterday, only I figured there was no rush, Diarmaid seeing you again was what was important.'

Her seeing him again. Her having him to herself, knowing full well how he'd be.

'Yeah,' he said. 'Of course. What did J.P. say to him, do you know?'

'That he wanted to talk to you, see how you were doing. He wanted it from the horse's mouth, apparently.'

'It might be nothing, so,' Ryan said. He had glazed over again.

'It's been years, boy.'

'Time moves slowly in that business. Makes you good at waiting. I have nothing to offer him, D'Arcy.'

'In terms of?'

'I'm useless to him. I have no input on anything he does, I have no control over anything I set up for him. He'd have come looking for me earlier if he wanted something specific. Unless my dad says he's been looking for me all along?'

She shook her head.

'He's just trying to put the shits up me, then,' Ryan said.

'Why would he bother?'

'Because throwing his weight around reminds him that he's got weight on him yet. I'd say it's about him and not me. Unless . . .'

She waited.

'Unless he's seen those comments,' Ryan said. 'And he thinks that anyone digging dirt on me will eventually get to him.'

'What are the odds?' she said. 'He didn't show any interest when the EP came out. Why would he be scouring the internet for you now?' She remembered the grey-haired woman in the shop on the Grand Parade then. Maybe it wasn't just Karine who thought about Ryan every day.

'I don't know,' Ryan said. 'The game makes you wary as well as patient. I might be being paranoid, am I?' He didn't look to her for the answer.

'Your dad thinks you shouldn't come back to Cork,' Karine admitted, and later, after Joseph had come looking for him, after they'd gone to the house where the band was writing and she'd said hello to everyone, after they'd spent the afternoon apart – her with Diarmaid, him with his music – after they'd reunited, kissed and held each other like it was all settled, he came around to his father's idea.

'Maybe he's got a point.'

'He doesn't have a point,' Karine said. Conscience made her correct herself. 'I don't want him to have a point.'

They were on the beach, just the three of them. Ryan had bought a yellow-and-black football in the island shop; he nudged it a few metres and Diarmaid waddled after it. When Diarmaid was born Karine told Ryan that she wouldn't assume him to be active over nurturing, that she wouldn't dress him exclusively in blue and give him only plastic toolboxes and train sets for his birthdays. And so maybe this was regressive as well as selfish, her sitting and smiling in the background while her son played football with his dad. She knew she was overthinking it and that there was a current of pleasure in her overthinking it, some strange, sad pull to the old-fashioned.

Ryan stood beside her as Diarmaid went after the ball. 'I don't get on well in Cork, like. Maybe if I go home now, I'll undo all the work I did on myself.' She looked at him and he went on. 'Small shit. Just I learned to breathe and stuff, I was making an effort and it wasn't too difficult because I wasn't acting the bollocks for a living any more. Jesus, I'm still four and a half hours from home and already I'm back on the draw, I'm not even getting stoned, I'm just managing symptoms.'

Diarmaid picked up the ball and dropped it again. Karine looked east, to the mainland. The Twelve Bens cut waves into the sky. She imagined a warning in their shadow. Maybe she would never live in the same Ireland as Ryan. How might the landscape look had she been a hawkish girl from a feckless family, a better gangster's moll? She felt her normality as a slur on him.

'Diarmaid needs you,' she said.

'I know. I don't want to let him down. Would the dad he'd get in Cork let him down?'

'The alternative is a dad he sees on screens.'

'I dunno,' Ryan said. 'You could come with me.'

'What? Where would I be going?'

Diarmaid flopped on to the sand to dig out a shell. Ryan put his hands in his pockets. 'Seoul's unreal, like,' he said, looking straight at her.

'Ryan, are you fucking mad?'

He kept looking at her.

'I've nothing to offer Korea, Ryan, I don't think they just let people's exes wander in along.'

'You were never my ex,' he said.

She shook her head but didn't correct him.

'What would happen back in Cork?' he asked. 'Between you and me?'

She couldn't make herself lie. 'Probably end up tearing each other's heads off.'

Diarmaid picked up the ball and threw it off to the left. Ryan retrieved it and nudged it towards him again. Karine joined her hands on her lap and ran a thumb over her knuckles.

'This isn't real,' she said. 'This is like Oisín in Tír na nÓg. Once we go back to the mainland we'll crumble to dust.'

'It doesn't have to be Cork,' Ryan said. 'I could buy a gaff in Campania tomorrow, like, I could fucking *buy* one. I'm Italian, Diarmaid's Italian, you're an EU citizen, it's the easiest language in the world to learn.'

'Ryan.'

'You're a nurse, like, everywhere wants nurses.' He recovered the ball again, and nudged it a little further away. Diarmaid squealed and took off after it.

'My whole life is in Cork, boy. My family. Your family. All my friends. I've never lived anywhere but Cork. Italian? I don't even speak Irish, for fuck's sake.'

'You don't feel that you need to be with me, then?'

'I need to put Diarmaid first. You think we wouldn't end up tearing each other's heads off in Italy? You know what we're like, Ryan.'

'I'm not the fella I was. You've to take a chance, sometimes. Don't you?'

She said, 'What was your original plan? Before I told you what your dad said. Where were you going to live when you got home?'

'Dunno.'

'Dunno like you hadn't thought about it or Dunno like with Natalie? Or is that actually the same answer?'

'Dunno, like I have options. I needed to see how things were going before I got a gaff.'

'How things were going with what?'

'Work,' he said. 'You.'

'You're still with Natalie, aren't you?'

'Not really.'

'What's "not really"?'

'I've been nearly two years in Korea.'

'Yeah, but "not really" means you haven't actually broken up, have you?'

'What'd you tell Dylan before you came here?'

Diarmaid carried the ball back over and threw it at Ryan's feet. Ryan rolled it away again.

'D'you see how we're revving up?' Karine said. 'See how we're quizzing each other?'

'I don't mind you quizzing me.'

'But you interrupt it to ask about Dylan.'

'Can't I be curious?'

'Can't you accept Dylan is my business?'

'Right, well Natalie's mine.' He turned to her. He did not look defiant or exasperated. 'I came home for you,' he said.

'You came home for Joseph,' she said, reproachfully.

'I came home for you. And fuck Cork and fuck Jimmy Phelan and fuck Natalie and fuck tearing each other's heads off and fuck common sense. Gimme whatever stipulations. I'll show you how much I mean it.'

It was supposed appropriate that there would be a hooley on the band's last night on the island. After dinner, back at the cottage, Ryan put an arm around her waist and pulled her on to his lap. 'Come by for one?' he said. 'It'll give me an excuse to fuck away off early.' She asked him if it wasn't irresponsible to bring Diarmaid to a party. 'It'd be a stretch to call it a party,' he said.

'You don't much like being in a band, do you, boy?'

'It's not that,' he said. 'The rest of them don't want to be in a band with someone the internet says is a delinquent.'

'Did they tell you that, or are you just assuming?'

'I'm assuming and I'm right to assume,' he said, glumly.

She wasn't sure about that. She thought that being musicians they were probably morally flexible, even militantly liberal. It was a given that Joseph would be on Ryan's side. Linda Duane she remembered as Kelly's buddy, and if she was Kelly's buddy she'd be mouthy about ethics but lost as to their practical application. The rest of the bandmates she didn't know, but she'd gleaned that Izzy King was from the tamer end of Cork, and wasn't it an unwritten rule that she'd think of this as an opportunity to borrow some street cred? That was the kind of lip-licking idiocy you'd get from those who didn't often knock around with real people. Izzy was a tiresome yoke, gauche and pretty in a calculated way that set Karine's teeth on edge.

They gathered in the front room at the band's retreat, aired out and tidied in preparation for their leaving. Orson put on a play-list. Izzy did some impressions of Karen O and Kae Tempest. Davy skipped tracks on Azealia Banks, which led to a discussion on separating art from artist, and how, in Davy's opinion, that could never be fully achieved. To this Ryan put his elbows on his knees and joined his hands behind his neck.

They began to talk about the booked studio time. Joseph said he was sure they would have the album recorded quickly, based on how they had worked during their time on Bofin, their collective certainty about how the finished thing should sound.

'It's all so male, though,' Izzy said.

'Oh Christ,' Orson groaned, and because of this Izzy said, 'Come on, don't you think it's very male, Mel?'

Linda Duane said, 'I'm staying out of this,' and chuckled unconvincingly.

'What's this Mel thing?' Karine asked.

'All Ryan's songs are very male,' Izzy answered. 'They're all about how desperately hard it is to be a boy.'

'But he is a boy,' Karine said.

'Don't mind her,' Ryan said. He held his arms out to Diarmaid. He didn't look at Izzy. 'She's cranky with me because I wouldn't get her drugs.'

Izzy gaped. 'Where did that come from?'

'From you telling me you were cranky with me because I wouldn't get you drugs.'

'You can be a hostile little prick, Ryan, can't you?'

'This is what happens,' Joseph said, 'when you've been holed up together, making shit up for art. It's time, all right, to withdraw.' His composure was false and impressive.

'What I was actually asking,' Karine said, 'was why you're Mel.' She pointed at Linda Duane. 'Not why it's all so male.'

Linda Duane shrugged. 'I hate the name Linda.'

'You look different,' Karine said. 'So I was thinking it was an identity thing, like.'

'I suppose, yeah. I mean, Linda is such a feminine name and it doesn't suit me really.'

Izzy softly snorted, and Linda-now-Mel swivelled with an elbow on her knee and said, 'Why're you snorting at me, girl?'

'I'm laughing because,' Izzy said, sternly, 'I thought Caroline was asking about male lyrics and it turned out she was asking about *Mel*.'

'It's Karine,' Karine said. 'Did you not get your MMR, girl?'

'Sorry, what?'

'Yeah, deaf as a post, mumps I'd say, very sad,' Karine said. She was rewarded with very similar smirks from Ryan and Mel and she twinkled back at them. 'I'm going to go after this anyway,' she said.

'And Ryan will go with you,' Izzy said. 'Rather than staying here and talking this through.'

'Talking what through?' he said. Diarmaid, in his arms, leaned back against his chest and looked at Izzy, then up at the underside of Ryan's chin. 'Dad,' he said, 'let's watch Chase,' to which Ryan responded with a kiss on the top of Diarmaid's head and a murmured *'Presto'*.

'Oh, what's the point?' Izzy said. 'You're playing a different role now. Daddy, not drugs, I get it.'

'Sorry?' said Karine.

'No apology necessary,' said Izzy.

'There's no point in this,' Joseph said. He went to the fridge and pulled out beers for the beer drinkers and waved the bottle of white at Karine. 'For the road, girl?' And in the jiffy it took for Karine to decline the offer Izzy had started again.

'Why don't you write lyrics about this kind of thing?' she asked Ryan, gesturing at Diarmaid. 'Is it because it's new to you, or doesn't feel real? What?'

'What are you getting at now? Why don't I write songs about being a dad? A minute ago I was too male and now I'm not male enough.'

'I'm just looking for meaning in your life. Stuff you can draw from that will lead you away from lyrics about being a lovelorn hetero.' Izzy crossed her wrists at her knees and purported to stifle a yawn. 'I mean, you're about to make this big statement in an interview about how you're a reformed drug dealer, don't you think your songs should feel more anarchic?'

'What big statement?' Karine asked.

'Fuck,' Ryan said to Izzy. 'I really wish I'd gotten you those trips.' He shook his head at Karine. 'I'll tell you later,' he said.

'Given the circumstances,' Izzy said, 'you should play the part of the class warrior. For example, the stuff you've done. Dealing drugs and whatever goes with drug dealing. What I'm saying is that if you had any sense you'd be writing political lyrics.'

'The personal is political,' Davy droned, holding his palms up, swaying his head, and Karine wanted him to infer from her smile that she was grateful he was trying.

Izzy said, 'It's not like you don't have that kind of darkness in you, Ryan.' She swigged and sat forward. 'A journalist wants to rip us apart before we've even begun because you were a drug dealer. The male-est of the male professions. You were a fucking gangster, write a song about that!'

'All right.' Karine stood up. 'Great wrap party. I'm going to put my son to bed.'

'He shouldn't be here anyway,' Izzy said.

'Yeah, clearly.' Karine took Diarmaid from Ryan's lap and looked around for his jacket.

'I'm heading off too,' Ryan said. 'I'll see you all for the ferry. Drink some water before bed,' he said, to Izzy, 'and whatever problem you have with me, fucking work on it.'

'Oh, no one is on your side more than me, Ryan. Don't snort at me,' she said. 'I'm serious. You want to explore darker themes, I am here for you. Let's go fucking alpha. The working-class hero–villain divide. Let's record songs called, "How I Razed the City that Raised Me". Or about how all the slutty sluts offered it up to you for free drugs. Let's record songs about how you're terrified of women because you had sex with Mel's mother when you were fifteen, Ryan.'

Conjunct inhalation, something that might have seemed melodramatic had it been prompted by a stranger's assassination, and Karine bundled their son into her arms and Mel let out a brutish cough and Joseph said, 'Izzy, what the actual fuck is wrong with you?'

'Nothing's wrong with me.' Izzy clipped the lip of her beer bottle with her teeth.

I don't know what he thinks about, Karine had once conceded, but that's about it, and that's as natural as it gets. Certainly her own mind could be a sinkhole of morbidity and pettiness and she would not want anyone getting in there because her thoughts were not reflective of her person, as contradictory and all as that seemed. If she stewed, sometimes, on lesser slights, that didn't make her a bad friend. Or if she wondered what might happen if she sat on the wrong lap or set the trap of a mad hint, that didn't make her a bad woman. She knew everything else about Ryan, so what did it matter if she couldn't tell what he was thinking? If his feelings were strong enough she was sure she'd pick up on them; likewise, if her feelings were strong enough – if she began to obsess over a lesser slight or the wrong lap – she was sure he'd figure it out. A thought was just that: fleeting and faint and not indicative.

She knew that Ryan's first kiss had been with Lauren Sheehan, that his middle name was Gennaro but that for some reason he didn't mind, that he was two inches shorter than his brother Cian and that for some reason he minded that immensely, and that his most embarrassing memory was of his mother slapping him soundly on the arse after his sister pulled six boxes of Special K off the shelves in Dunnes, because he wasn't able for the injustice of it and had cried all the way home.

She knew the rumours. She'd heard some. Others he'd relayed. Rumours from when they were eighteen and nineteen she'd learned to listen to. That phase he'd gone through, fucking whichever girl would have him; he'd taught her to pay heed. Before was different. He brought up what people had said and showed her how he'd been hurt by it.

'My ould fella', he told her, 'isn't as bad as people say he is. He's only drunk, is all. What I'm trying to say . . .'

What was he trying to say?

The usual prefixes. *I dunno. Nawthin.* She had to wait for the rest of it. Fellas picked fights with him at school over his father. What does he do to you, Ryan? Just a black eye or a sore hole too? Eventually he'd come out with, 'Nothing like that ever happened. You don't need to worry. I'm completely fucking normal.' There'd been words said about the mad neighbour. Tony had broken her window and Ryan had said he didn't know why. His dad lost the plot without rhyme or reason. That was true. There was a rumour about the mad neighbour having fucked Ryan but Karine hadn't even bothered bringing it up with him; she'd only have wounded him.

That he was a separate person with his own brain had never offended her the way her friends said it should. *You can't trust him, girl, what does sorry mean coming from him?* What choice was there except trust? Sufferance? Without trust there was only screeching malice and the worst possible version of herself. She knew his history, his politics, his humour, how he moved, what he wanted. He was honest, most of the time. He was honest when he wanted to be anything but.

And now it turned out she knew fuck-all and she was excavating new histories and trying to fit new patterns and she was cold with the effort of it. 'Are you going to tell me what that was about?' she asked him, coming down the road from the band's house to the cottage. The light was waning. He was carrying Diarmaid. Diarmaid had his hands around Ryan's neck, his chin on Ryan's shoulder. He was watching the road stretch behind them. He was too young to be so vigilant and so she thought it was simply that he was tired. Yet it felt like he'd quickly learned when it was best to be silent.

Nor did Ryan say anything. He bit his bottom lip and let his breath out through his teeth.

'It requires an explanation, doesn't it? Because it's very specifically . . . What the fuck, Ryan?'

'I don't know what to say to you.'

'I wouldn't turn it over too much, boy.'

He didn't continue. She felt it wasn't belligerence but a lump in his throat or a genuine loss for words, none of his spoken languages having the right constitution, and when she started quietly losing it and asking him whether he was a sociopath or a coward he took to opening and closing his mouth as if cycling through those languages trying to find a phrase. And she, not knowing him after all, couldn't guess what he had to tell her, though knowing how the world felt when she'd just been let down, she was sure that there was truth in it. She didn't know the form it would take but she knew it was going to wound her.

They reached the cottage and he handed Diarmaid to her, put his hands in his pockets and kept going along the road.

'Ryan,' she said. 'For the love of God. What, are you going to swim away?'

She had the armour of motherhood. When she and Diarmaid went indoors she lifted her voice. She told a story and ran a bath. She told him Daddy had a pain in his tummy. She had to wrap him in a towel and carry him to answer Joseph's knocking. 'He's not here,' she said, letting him in. Diarmaid squirmed and threw his head back and whinged.

'What the hell was that?' Joseph said.

'Oh, you tell me. You surely asked her where she got her notions.'

'I don't know what's going on,' he said.

She had always said that Joseph was a better liar than Ryan and yet look.

Diarmaid straightened and threw his head back again. She stood him on the floor. 'Stop it now,' she said, 'or I'll be cross,' and it felt humiliating to have her anger diluted. Motherhood an armour; armour to bind.

Joseph put one hand on his forehead and said, 'Mel's just gone through her, if that makes you feel any better.'

'Why would that make me feel better?'

He shook his head. 'Look, if it's true it's like, what? Nine years ago? It's irrelevant.'

'Me and Ryan were together from the night of his fifteenth birthday. And Linda – Mel – was Tara's daughter the whole of her life. It's relevant.'

'Don't get emotional,' he said.

'Don't tell me to not get emotional.'

'Sorry.' He looked away. 'Where did he go?'

'Down the road, with his shoulders up at his ears and his mouth shut.'

'I'll find him.'

'No, Joseph, you'll sit with Diarmaid. His pyjamas are on the bed upstairs, his toothbrush is by the sink, we're on *The Gruffalo*.'

'No, coz how it is—'

'I'm telling, not asking,' she said. 'No way am I letting Ryan bounce a story off you before he gets back to me.'

She found him standing at the door of the quayside pub with a brown-haired and blank-smiled fella she didn't recognise. She stopped on the road and Ryan looked at her, and down, and pulled on a cigarette. She thought she might comment on this, except it was a bit late now and he looked so pathetic, like the paltry weight in the cigarette was the only thing keeping him from reeling off to one side and falling down.

'I don't want to make a show of you,' she told him.

He took another drag. She looked pointedly at his companion, who nodded slowly in return. She cocked her head. He kept nodding.

'Like, if you don't mind,' she said.

'This a domestic?' he said.

'Yeah, boy. So why don't you leave us to it?' In what was left of the light she discerned a nod from Ryan. The other stubbed out his own cigarette and went into the pub.

The lapping of water against quay stone was gentle and degenerative and dogged. Ryan followed her up the road to a grassy patch where there was a low wall and a couple of weathered benches. He stubbed out the cigarette on the wall and with nowhere to leave the butt, ground it against the stone again, sat down, put effort into it.

'Tara Duane,' Karine said. On the cottage behind them, an outdoor light went on but hardly reached. She moved closer to him. 'When you were fifteen. But the first time you kissed me was on your fifteenth birthday, so either you were with a literal hag between kissing me and asking me if I'd be your girlfriend, which was, what, a whole fucking day, which means you were lying when you told me I was your first. Or you were with a literal hag after you asked me to be your girlfriend, which means that the start of me and you, which was the only segment of our history that wasn't a fucking disaster, was in actual fact a fucking disaster.' She had not expected to choke up. What was the point in boohooing over some decade-old arseholery, except that the story was important, the component parts important, as elements that could not be broken down or altered, the primary constituents of value and significance and the bloody fucking sense of the pair of them?

'It wasn't like that,' he said, and stood up again.

'It wasn't like that but it was like something, yeah? Go on, tell me what it *was*.'

'I don't know how to tell you.'

'Well, imagine you're telling Izzy.'

'I don't know what I told her. Years ago. I'd had a skinful, I told her . . . I don't remember, I was feeling really fucking bad about it.' He brought the insides of his wrists to his eye sockets. He squeezed his temples.

'When you were fifteen,' Karine said, 'you decided you were going to have sex with the creepy bitch next door.'

'I didn't decide to.'

'Oh, sorry. You instinctively had sex with the creepy bitch next door. So typical for a fella, throw all the shapes about how this wan's a whore or that wan's a whore and then take a stab anyway because, like, the whore's right there, it'd be a shame to waste her.'

He shook his head.

'What, you figured you needed to learn a few things? Or, oh Jesus, or was this because I said we rushed into sex and you thought, oh whoops though, my dick's awake now and if I don't keep it in constant use they'll come and take it off me?'

'Jesus, no.'

'Well, boy, I've run out of theories so you better enlighten me.'

'I can't enlighten you, I don't know what to say to you.'

'How about the fucking truth?'

'I can't tell you the truth, I don't fucking remember, I was langers, I was beyond langers, I was fucking demented.'

'Yeah, I'd have said you'd have to be.'

'You don't understand, girl. This isn't me trying to get away with it. It wasn't like a party scenario.'

'I see what you're doing. Coz I did that, didn't I? I let another fella take me to my Debs because my stupid boyfriend was banged up and it was weird and awful and I drank too much and I let Niall Vaughan have sex with me, and oh, correct me if I'm misremembering, but didn't you give me lorry-loads of shit for that, even though you were in prison and therefore I could reasonably assume that I was single? You acted like you were single, didn't you? You didn't ask if I minded the risk of my boyfriend going to prison because he cared more about his boss than he did about me.' She wiped her nose with the back of her hand. 'And didn't you heap shit on me for Niall? Didn't you bawl like a baby and then hold me down on the bed and then not speak to me for, what was it, a week or something?'

'That's why, though,' he said. 'That's why I lost the plot. Because whatever wrong things I did, you weren't supposed to—'

'*I* wasn't supposed to? The fucking hypocrisy, Ryan!'

'You don't understand—'

'Oh no, I fucking do—'

'I didn't want to have anything to do with her, you wanted it with Vaughan, you were drunk but you wanted it.'

'What the fuck do you mean by that?'

'I mean he didn't hurt you, did he hurt you?'

She clutched her arms. 'Are you saying she hurt you?'

'I don't know. Yeah. I don't know.'

'Ryan.'

He ground his wrists back into his sockets. He turned his back. Karine sat on a bench, clutching her arms. She leaned over her belly. 'Ryan,' she said. 'Turn around.'

He stood for a minute with his hands knotted behind his neck. He turned in stages. In profile he said, 'I swear to God there's fuck-all I remember about this.' To the grass at his feet he said, 'Like, if he'd hurt you, I'd have killed him.' And to her knees and her folded arms he said, 'I don't know why I said anything to Izzy. I thought she wouldn't remember after, I thought it'd make me feel better, like Confession, I was outta my head.' He stood with his hands by his side. 'I never even said it to Joseph. I thought only my dad knew this.'

'Your dad?'

'It was after we made that video. She was the one who told him it was on my phone.'

'How did she know it was on your phone?'

'I don't know,' he said. 'She must have found it because I swear to God, girl, I'd never have showed that to anyone, the idea of it being just between us was the best bit. It drives me mad. I can't think about it.'

'You're going to have to, boy, because you're telling me this mad bitch found a video of us, of *me*, and you don't know how? Like what, was it online?'

'Course it fucking wasn't.' He quaked as if the image of friends leering over a flickering screen had come to him too.

'Did you share that video, Ryan?'

'Karine, listen to me. Never, never. It never left my phone, no one ever saw it except my dad and her—'

'So she stole your phone?'

'I don't know! I swear to God, Karine. I swear to God.'

He sat back down on the wall and put his face in his hands. She crossed her legs and drew in her shoulders. He let his hands fall. He held them, palms up, on his lap.

'My dad sold my mam's piano,' he said. 'You let me make the video to cheer me up coz it was a bad time, the piano was just one part of it, I wasn't getting on with my dad at all. That week he clatters me over something, probably even then I couldn't have told you what, and he leaves me with a black eye and the black eye annoys him even more. One night he comes home mouldy and I know I'll get another one if it enters his head. I says I'll make myself scarce coz he'll be asleep soon enough so I go into the garden to wait it out and out she comes then and says to me, Ryan, come in here to me boy, wait it out in here with me, you poor fucking idiot.'

Karine watched his fingers coil into claws.

'I knew what she was like,' he said. 'I thought if she got weird with me I'd just hop the wall again, it wasn't her first time getting weird with me.'

'So you saw it coming.'

'Not this,' he said. 'A few times she tried to get cuddly or she'd flash a bit of tit, like, I'd laugh about it, what's this fucking loon think she's at? But this time she's like, "Have a whiskey to warm you up" and "Fuck it, have another one" and she gives me a few cans and I was already smoking, I was out of it so fast. Next thing she's on top of me.'

'Like what?' Karine said. 'Doing what?'

'I don't even remember lying down, the only thing I remember is her on top of me. Like, she has my fucking . . .'

He screwed up his nose. The next sound he made was, she thought, a scrapped word rather than a sigh; he brought his wrists to his eyes again.

'See how I didn't need you to know this?' he said, to his forearms.

'I still don't understand,' Karine said.

'She has my jocks down and she's on top of me,' he said. 'I remember pushing her off me and that's the bit I don't want to remember, because I don't remember asking her to fuck me and if I pushed her off me then that's a strong hint that I didn't ask because I didn't want.'

The light in the cottage behind them went off as if timed to spare him. Karine dragged her sleeves tight over her arms. 'Jesus Christ,' she said.

She couldn't tell if he'd teared up, if he was just drawn from the effort.

'Why didn't you tell me?' she said. 'You told me about your dad, like . . . and still you told your dad about this and not me—'

'I didn't tell my dad about it, not till he bate it out of me.'

'Because of the video?'

'Y'know, how'd she find it? Was I going around showing her stuff like this? Was I letting her get a kick out of me? He fucking hated that wan. He assumed the worst and he was right. How could I tell you, girl? You'd have finished with me, I'd have fucking hung myself.'

'I wouldn't have blamed you.'

'Why wouldn't you have blamed me?'

'Ryan. You know what that was.'

'I do,' he said. 'It was me being a fucking idiot.'

'You were fifteen,' she said. 'Jesus, this could happen to you now and it still wouldn't be your fault.'

'I don't know that it wasn't my fault,' he said. 'I don't remember.'

'Because a grown woman basically drugged you.'

He stood up. He put his hands in his pockets and looked over his shoulder to the sea. 'You were sixteen,' he said. 'You think you'd have made more sense of it? You hadn't done a Leaving or gotten a degree or fucked Niall fucking Vaughan. You think you wouldn't have broken up with me? It's neither here nor there anyway. I knew this would make shit of everything and look.'

'How has this made shit of everything?'

'Tell me it hasn't,' he said, dully. 'Tell me you still fucking love me.'

Of course she did, she told him; that he assumed she might not testified to his keeping the story to himself for too long. Little things flared in her mind now, petty arguments, overreactions, the time he'd written to her from prison and included an ostensible non-sequitur about how conniving Tara Duane was, the fact that he was averse to letting her on top when they had sex . . . that most of all, actually. Bedroom dominance that on occasion she'd suspected as a product of anxiety, and God, he could be uptight. She no longer felt faint and hollow; she grew more solid as he went to pieces, as wicked as that was. And he followed her back to the cottage with his head down and his hands in fists.

He told Joseph that he didn't want to talk about it, though Joseph kept insisting.

'Does it matter?' Ryan said. 'At the end of the day?'

Joseph looked at Karine and said, 'Well, I dunno, I don't want you shook, like,' and after getting no reaction, said, 'I don't want our hard work undone over Izzy's blather. For fuck's sake, boy, you know what she's like.'

'Bit of a shit-stirrer,' Karine said. 'Is that it?'

Joseph put one hand on the kitchen counter. He spread his fingers and leaned down. 'She's all about being provocative,' he said. 'She goes too far.'

'It doesn't matter a fuck,' Ryan said, as if answering his own question. 'Was she lying, was she? Was she fucking wrong?'

He was swaying to calm himself and the movement was quietly improper. This vulnerability was new. Was suggestive. Karine wanted Joseph to leave.

Joseph said, 'C'mere, we were all cracked then. You can't blame kids for being kids.'

'I'm done with it,' Ryan said. 'Go back to the house, boy, shrug it off on my behalf, will you? I don't want to see Linda, I don't want to see Izzy, I don't want some great big fucking debate, I don't want any more reminding of the things that are wrong with me.'

After a pause, Joseph gave Ryan a hesitant hug and tapped his cheek. 'It'll make more sense tomorrow.'

After he left Ryan and Karine stayed standing, him looking at the floor, swaying his head or his hips, rolling his shoulders, rubbing his neck. He said, 'D'you want me to go?'

'No.'

'I don't want to talk about it any more.'

'We won't talk about it, then.'

She took his hands in hers, then slid up to his elbows, then to his shoulders. He stopped moving. He closed his eyes. 'This couldn't have happened at a worse time,' he said. 'I had a case to state, y'know?'

'D'you want to go to bed?'

He blinked. 'Seriously?'

'You don't want to?'

'No, I do,' he said. 'I just didn't expect . . .'

She kissed him. 'Let me check on our son.'

Diarmaid was sleeping soundly. She padded around his room,

double-checking what she'd packed and the outfit she'd laid out for their return trip. She stopped in the doorway and put one hand to her neck. She thought Ryan too might feel transformed.

He was standing, diffident, newly defined, at the window in the bedroom. She put her hands on his waist and pushed his T-shirt over his shoulders. She put her cheek to his chest and listened. They lay back on the bed. She traced the lines on his skin. She thought maybe she was imagining nervousness on his part and still she took pleasure in her mercy, for mercy felt powerful. He knelt to undress them both. She pressed her hands to his shoulders and he seemed not to understand. She pushed him again and he fell back.

She looked at her hands on his chest, rising and falling. 'Don't you trust me?'

He went up on his elbows. She straddled him, felt him hard against her, kept one hand on his sternum and moved the other down to part herself.

He said, 'What are you doing?'

He sat up straight and unseated her.

'Are you fucking serious?' he said.

She curled one leg underneath her. She wanted to be bold and tell him, *Yes*, then exactly how to feel as she rewrote his history. Instead she cleared her throat and clasped her hands as he said, 'Does it turn you on or something?'

'Does what turn me on?'

'What I fucking told you.'

She shook her head. He mimicked her.

'Jesus Christ,' he said.

'All I want to do is show you—'

'No, no. I show you. I relive it, you lift it from me, is that it?'

'No,' she said, though *Yes*, that was it, and in spitting it out he'd broken it.

'D'you see why you don't tell these stories?' he said. 'D'you see now what these fucking stories do?' He got up and in the dark looked around desperately for his clothes.

'Ryan,' she said. 'You're overreacting a small bit.'

'Am I fuck.'

She held his wrist and he yanked out of her grasp. 'Jesus,' she said, and then, 'Ryan,' and then, 'Ryan, I'm sorry, sit down.' He got most of the way dressed; he couldn't find a second sock and swore softly, hand to forehead.

'I can't cope with it, Karine, you can't be thinking that way about me.'

'What way?'

'See what it's done already?' He dropped to all fours and rose again with the sock in his hand. And this she thought so declarative, and young, almost, or helpless; she wanted him to lie down so she could hold his head in her lap and stroke his cheek. She wasn't so simple as to always need him rough. She could have him bite her or grab her or talk filth to her and still want to mind him from the world, from himself.

He said, 'I hope she's fucking dead.'

She got to her knees on the bed and shuffled towards him. He stepped back. She sank again.

'Ryan.'

How many times in the past had his own name soothed him? He couldn't let it now.

'Since she went missing I've hoped she's fucking dead. And all that kept it manageable was knowing you had no idea.' He knocked a fist to the side of his head and she jumped. 'It's grand in here,' he said, through his teeth. 'And now it's not in here and I don't know what the fuck it's going to do.'

Tara Angela Duane was born on the second of November, 1972. Her parents' names were Maurice and Ann. After she left school, she got a job answering phones in an estate agent's in the city centre. After that she worked as a hotel receptionist. After that she had Mel. She never lost her phone voice; she was very, very good on the phone.

For a while she liked yoga. She bought all the gear and joined classes at the complex. For a while she liked chat rooms. She planned her days around when various people would be online and talked about visiting new friends in the Netherlands, Turkey and Brazil. For a while she liked cake decorating, which she called sugarcraft. She subscribed to magazines and said she might open her own cupcake business.

For a while she liked activism. She went to meetings in hotels in town and joined a feminist collective. She nominated herself for a place on the board of the feminist collective. She fell out with the feminist collective and spent the subsequent months calling them privileged puritans on Facebook. She lost interest in the feminist collective and for a while then she liked learning Russian.

She earned money as a virtual assistant. She earned money as a customer-service chat operative. She earned money as an ad-clicker. She earned money in data entry. She earned money selling natural cosmetics. She earned money as an agony aunt. She showed Mel the archive. It was a sex therapist's column for an online publication in the United States.

'You're not a therapist, Mam,' Mel said.

Tara waved a hand at the screen. 'The evidence says otherwise.'

'Her name isn't Kayla Lam, either,' Kelly Cusack said, as they pored over the archive on Mel's laptop in the bedroom Kelly shared with her little sister, Niamh, who was way too small to hang out with them and way too big to be cute in her efforts to do so.

'Obviously she can't use her real name,' Mel said, doubtfully.

'She's great at the American words, like.'

'Yeah, but how hard is it to throw in the odd "awesome"?'

'Kayla Lam says women shouldn't be obliged to host baby showers for moms from out-of-town. Kayla Lam says "grad school" and "roommate" and "sweater". Kayla Lam says if your therapist isn't supportive you should find a new therapist.'

'Oh my God, like, I hate it when my therapist isn't supportive.'

'We should really find more supportive therapists.'

They curled up in hysterics, and thereafter were huge Kayla Lam fans, and read her advice to one another in their best impressions of Tara's everyday voice and Tara's phone voice. One day Kayla Lam's column was reformatted to include in its header a photograph of a smiling woman who looked nothing like Tara and, egged on by Kelly, Mel had offered her mother condolences at having been replaced. Tara gave Mel a look.

'Just that Kayla Lam has a new photo?' Mel said.

'Calum who?'

Tara rarely went to parent-teacher meetings because she didn't like the other parents. Certainly, the other parents didn't like her, even the ones who had never put her window in. 'I'm so much younger than the other mothers,' Tara said, 'and they're threatened by me, because they have internalised misogyny,' and for a time Mel thought that internalised misogyny was a kind of communal madness, like Bieber Fever or sightings of evil clowns.

Kelly said the other parents didn't like Tara for all sorts of reasons. One: Tara smiled too much and too broadly, which was untrustworthy. Another: Tara over-shared, which was annoying. A further: she was drunk or otherwise half-cracked a fair bit of the time, which she didn't acknowledge, which was insincere.

And yeah of course the other women didn't like her; she'd get up on a gust of wind.

Mel suspected Kelly was being particularly mean because she didn't have a mother any more and was, therefore, stubborn in her views on maternal standards.

After Mel moved to Scotland, for a while Tara liked messaging her at all hours. She sent her selfies, memes and inspirational quotes. Mel didn't know whether she grew tired of that, or whether Mel's indifference discouraged her, but for a while she kept it sporadic, then she was very quiet indeed, and if there was a new man on the scene she was not keen on taking selfies with him. For a while after that she talked about maybe getting out of the city, because maybe she'd like to keep chickens, maybe she'd like to harvest seaweed for homemade beauty creams.

It was not a stretch to surmise that for a while she had liked a fifteen-year-old Ryan Cusack; Ryan, but narrower, shorter, softer-faced, to complement her, light-footed, flat-chested, and so defiantly impulsive.

This was what Mel was thinking about on the ferry from Bofin to Cleggan. Things Tara had liked. Manifestations of who Tara really was, things she had found, for a time, integral to her personality. Her personality being the great mystery. Her sins barely shedding light on it. How was it that you could be created by a stranger? That you could live for eighteen years with one? Was it a defect in Tara that made her so nebulous? Was it a defect in Mel?

Things Tara had liked. That was all Mel had. A ghost in the mirror. A handful of air.

A truncated name. The guilt of an unloved child.

She and Kelly met on Paul Street when Mel got back to the city. They hugged by the counter of a soulless pub and sat at opposite ends of a tall table, Mel holding the neck of her guitar case between her knees. Kelly was in an uncharacteristically pretty dress, a leather jacket and ankle boots. Her hair was shiny and thick and swept over one shoulder. 'God, girl, you're looking well,' Mel said.

'Bread soda for shampoo and vinegar for conditioner,' Kelly said.

'No way! It's—'

'Would you be well? Extensions, girl. Aoife did them. Some stylist you'd have made.'

'I don't need to hear that, I might have to go back to it yet. Did you see the comments online?'

'Cian saw them,' Kelly said. 'Why, have you some there?' She gestured at Mel's phone. Mel checked the band's social media channels and Kelly stood and looked over her shoulder. Natalie had already done the day's housekeeping, but Mel googled and found a discussion on the Ireland subreddit. Someone had posted screenshots of three of the comments and typed:

- ■ Cork band Lord Urchin. Singer used to deal. Potentially used the profits to fund upcoming album.
    - → Hello lads, we're the guards.
        - ↘ Hello guards, we're the lads.
    - → When I said we should get the dealer scum off our streets that isn't what I meant.
    - → I couldn't give a fiddler's fuck. Lad has a rare pair of lungs.
        - ↘ Having met a trader or two in my day I have to say they're usually psychotic so I'd like to think there are lads and lungs more deserving of your support there pal.
    - → Did he used to DJ at Catalyst in Cork? Dont know if hes connected, doesnt look the part in fairness.
        - ↘ He OWNS Catalyst and he's only out of his teens. He's a bowsie. You don't have to be Sherlock Holmes to work it out.

Kelly tsked and went back to her seat. 'Joseph should have seen this coming.'

Mel put the phone on the table. 'Who'd you think's leaving the comments?'

'How would I know?'

Mel flipped her beer mat and said, 'D'you think it could have been my mam?'

'Why, have you heard from your mam?'

'No.'

'Why d'you think it's your mam, so?'

'I don't know. I've been thinking about the thing that happened with our window.'

'Fuck's sake, the problem there wasn't your mam hating Ryan. What put that mess into your head?'

'It came up on Bofin.'

Kelly thumped her glass down. 'What?'

'Yeah. Apparently they . . . did. Ryan and my mam.'

'Jesus. What kind of songs are you sickos writing?'

'It wasn't like that. He was odd with me when he got there, Izzy noticed, asked me about it and like a gowl I told her about your dad and our window. And then she said that Ryan had told her about it years back. That he'd been with his neighbour. So.' Mel rested her chin on her hand and closed her eyes. 'I said nothing, like. Didn't want to be bringing that up, I'd be sick. But then Izzy fell out with him, he was meant to get her trips and he didn't, so last night she dropped him in it in front of everyone. Karine and all, like. "Ryan fucked his next-door neighbour when he was fifteen!" And me sitting there *mortified*.'

'Izzy? The tit from YouTube? Please tell me he's not flahing her as well.'

'As well as who?'

'Ah, what d'you think Karine was doing there?'

'That could have been a friends thing.'

'It was not a friends thing. Hopping on and off each other is how those two say hello. She used to fly to Berlin to see him and she wouldn't cross the road for anyone else. God, Linda, you're so innocent.'

'Mel.'

'Sorry. Mel.' Kelly finished her drink and, without asking Mel if she'd like another, headed to the bar. She returned carrying two bottles. 'He's such a whore,' she said, pouring. 'I'm not surprised about your mam. I always thought they did.'

'Ah, no you didn't.'

'Privately I did. Just I had to stick up for my brother.' She sipped. 'I'd say she'd fuck orphans off a lifeboat, that Izzy wan. Isn't she some bitch? In front of Karine, like. About your mam! Why didn't you thump her?'

'Oh yeah, then what would you have? A Norrie weapon assaulting a lovely girl from West Cork. I'd have ended up in court.'

'Fuck that, I'd have mangled her. Hurt my brother? You'd want to be ready for me.'

'You just called him a whore.'

'So? He is a whore. But that's irrelevant, because he can be a whore till the cows come home but selling cannabis to kiddies is awful carry-on. So how far can this band go, really? Ryan isn't Jay-Z, he's not going to get away with it.' They sat for a few minutes, then, as if there'd been no pause, Kelly said, 'Take it as an omen, girl. Be a musician in Scotland. You shouldn't have come back at all.'

'Brexit has everything up in a heap.'

'Everything's permanently up in a heap here, I've fucking altitude sickness, like.' She nodded at Mel's bottle. 'Down that and we'll move on, this gaff is a morgue.'

Mel poured. 'I shouldn't have gone away in the first place.'

Kelly watched the filling glass. 'Listen,' she said. 'Ease up on the what-ifs, take it from someone who knows. What if I'd gotten up out of bed the night my mam died? What if I'd taken the keys off her? What if I'd taken the bottle off her? Don't go there, you'll only break your own melt. Besides, it was probably Tara's plan all along to get rid of you. How would she have gone to India if you were still hanging around?'

'You still think she's in India, do you?'

'She was meeting that Hindu fella, didn't Michelle Busteed say?'

'They have WhatsApp in India too.'

'Look, it's shitty, but your mam wanted to disappear. She owed money all around her, everyone said she was demanding the corporation move her every other week. Did she try to stop you moving to Glasgow?'

Mel rubbed her forehead. 'No.'

'Was it her idea?'

Mel could hardly remember. 'Probably.'

'There's no way to say this gently, girl. She was a shitty mother, you're better off.'

'No, I bet there was a way of saying that gently.'

'Fuck it. I stand by it.'

'I should have come straight back. When it was obvious the guards had no interest. I could have done a bit of hunting.'

'Yeah, and you'd have ended up hounded by whoever lent her the sponds in the first place. What are you on about? You were eighteen, what could you have done?'

'I've felt bad about it for years. And Izzy brought up the Ryan thing again, and I feel worse. I didn't know my mam at all.'

Kelly sat back. She tapped her nails off the tabletop and peered around the pub, intermittently shaking her head, aggravated but trying her best to be charitable.

We could all do with a few days' breathing space, Joseph had said, in a group text. *So let's just hit Union Studios on Monday morning, hungry as fuck.*

Mel assumed that he had forgotten to remove her from the group and was waiting on a cold addendum. There was no way she could return to reproducing Izzy's lines after a mere weekend's lung exercises; this had to be an ending. Her own mother did her frontman when he was underage. The necessity of her expeditiously fucking off would be put to her with a concerned frown, a soft hand on her arm. On the ferry back to Cleggan she'd found herself hoping he hadn't been a virgin and that experience had taken the edge off it. Now she said to Kelly, 'What d'you mean, he's a whore?' and Kelly replied, 'Isn't that why Karine gave him the shove?'

'But when he was fifteen, like?'

'D'you not remember him? Pure septic, like. And the wans then following him around.'

Mel thought about what kind of girl Karine had been. 'But d'you think he was . . .'

'Was what?'

Mel shook her head.

The few drinks before heading to Grandad Duane's house were a mistake. Bringing Kelly was a mistake; she loitered outside the house next door, trying to be unobtrusive, but this made Grandad Duane nervous. He was generally opposed to people born after 1975, and here now in his sitting room was a granddaughter who'd gone to Scotland in dresses with hair to her elbows and had landed back on top of him with literal baggage, an undercut and weird piercings. Was it any wonder he wouldn't let her stay?

'Why didn't you ring me first?' he said. 'You don't ring me from one end of the year to the other.'

Mel put one fist over the other and said, 'I don't like the phone.'

'You arrive up here from the pub,' he said. 'Without a by-your-leave. Telling me you don't like the phone! Jesus Christ, I'm at the age now I'm entitled to my space. I have no bed for you.'

They argued for fifteen minutes, till he gave her twenty euro, pointed at Kelly outside inspecting her nails, and told her it was clear she had plenty of places to go.

'But if you had any sense,' he said, 'you'd go to the airport, and back to your father.'

She returned to Kelly and they struggled with the bags and guitar to the bus stop, Kelly agreeing with every word Mel said about her awful grandfather, cold yoke that he was and always had been. Imagine being in the same city as Tara and not noticing her going missing. Imagine thinking of your own progeny as an imposition, imagine the concept of entitlement to seclusion *at whatever age* making a defensible excuse. They got the bus back up the hill. Mel felt sick. This was because she had been drinking on an empty stomach so she talked herself out of making it portentous. She looked at Kelly, and Kelly's eyes seemed tired and the skin below them speckled with dried mascara, as though she'd been walking through thick smoke.

'He was always a bollocks,' Kelly said. 'He never even used to get you Christmas presents. Fuck him, like.'

Kelly had the knack of making the world seem more cruel than had ever crossed your mind. Her unwavering support was meant to compensate for her snapping all the lights out.

She had moved into the city centre a year or so back, but she said she'd planned to head up home this evening anyway. The city centre wasn't far enough away to break her pull to home, something that was probably necessary if Kelly was ever to see the world in full colour. Kelly could do with a sea between her and the terrace. Mel, having a sea, felt now like a museum visitor. The terrace was comprised of six near-identical houses facing a bulging, dipping green that was scratched with trodden pathways. It was a faithful but not wholly successful recreation of the site of her formative years. *It is very good*, she thought. *Very believable. Only small things jar. The air smells different to how it used to smell, I think. I do not remember as much space. Good job otherwise, and thank you.*

They walked past the house in which Mel had grown up and stopped at the Cusacks' gate. Mel looked at her old home. There were potted plants by the front door and two wheelie bins at the bottom of the little drive. There was a topless, blonde fashion doll face down in the overgrown grass, one arm stretched over her head.

'What are the new neighbours like?' Mel asked.

Kelly said there was a mother and three children. When the mother had first applied for a house she had only one child but the list was long and her fertility unrelenting. They weren't the worst. They'd erected stained wooden boards on top of the concrete wall between their back gardens for privacy. 'Or she didn't want to be looking at us,' Kelly said.

They came into the Cusacks' narrow hall. Both interior doors were open. The newel post was buried underneath a mound of jackets. The walls were painted a light blue, and there were crayon marks still, though Ronan, the youngest, was fourteen. Crayon marks, scuff marks, marks where the front door had slapped off the wall behind it.

'Can I use the toilet?' Mel asked, and Kelly stared at her as if she had sprouted a second head and said, '*An bhfuil cead agam dul amach, más é do thoil é?*'

Mel made a face.

'*Tá cead agat*, girl,' Kelly said, beatifically.

Kelly's bathroom was exactly as tiny as Mel's old bathroom and laid out the same. There were towels on the floor, too many shampoo and body-wash bottles around the bath, toilet roll tubes on the sill. Mel reached over the bath and opened her palm on the tiled wall between Kelly's house and the house she'd once lived in. She bowed her head, as if in prayer, then straightened to scoff at herself, and headed back to the downstairs hall.

Kelly was directly in front of her in the kitchen, head in the fridge. To Mel's left, in the armchair by the living room's far wall, sat Tony Cusack. 'Hey, Tony,' she said, and he looked over. His hair had grown out into thick curls flecked with grey. There were red blotches under his eyes. He looked confused. She remembered when he'd seen her last she had the long hair and feminine wardrobe. 'It's Linda,' she said. 'From next door.'

'Jesus,' he said. 'Linda, girl.' His eyes were bloodshot. His complexion was sandy around the blotches. Maybe he was just stoned. 'Where are you these days?'

'I was in Glasgow with my dad but I'm home now for a bit.'

'What's here for you?' The Irish question: What's here for you? What was here for *you*? she might have asked. What's ever at home? Tony realised he had asked a question suited only to those whose mothers had not run off on them. 'Ryan's home tonight himself,' he said.

'No coincidence. We were actually working together.'

'Linda,' Kelly shouted, from the kitchen. 'D'you want a can?'

Mel smiled at Tony and went to the kitchen. 'Mel,' she said. 'And yeah, else I'm going to get early-onset hangover.'

Kelly snapped open three cans of lager, brought one in to her father, returned and sat at the kitchen table. Mel sat opposite her. 'What am I gonna do?' she said.

'Jesus, we're hardly gonna kick you out. Stay here till you get sorted. My dad won't give a shit. OK, when you sign on, you'll have to go, because that'll complicate claims, but while you're looking for a room, you can have my old bed. Niamh won't mind. She's going mad in all the testosterone.'

'What d'you think Ryan's gonna say to that?'

'What, like he's the man of the house? If he cribs you just tell him to fuck off.' To Mel's pained look she said, 'It's either that or Cork Airport and haggis for dinner again!'

'I can't ask your dad, Kelly, I'd be mortified.'

'Fuck asking,' Kelly said. 'I'll tell him for you.'

'You haven't changed a bit, anyway.'

'What fucking changes around here?' Kelly said, though on the bus she had detailed pregnancies, affairs, emigrants to Australia and Canada, diplomas and degrees, sentences for assault, possession for sale or supply, theft. *What fucking changes around here?* Everything, Mel thought. Fucking everything but the superficies.

Can in hand, Kelly went to the living room door, told her father that Mel would be staying for a few nights, and came back again.

They went upstairs to Kelly's old bedroom. She and Niamh had shared the big one at the front, with Ronan too when he was little. He'd long since moved into the back bedroom: the boys' room. How well he knew when to segregate. It was an act that made the awkwardness of puberty many times more awkward. Which wasn't the point, Mel supposed; the idea was to be around others of the same sex specifically to avoid awkwardness, but didn't it just underline that you were now so very separate from, theoretically an object of desire for the opposite sex? Either you seized the mantle or experienced some personal cataclysm, as had been the case with her. Maybe segregation was a relief to ordinary people who didn't ask such questions. She thought of her grandfather, finally able to enjoy the misanthropy he'd spent decades designing.

Niamh was lying on her back on her bed with her phone held a few inches from her face. She had round cheeks that made her eyes look small and wary, and lips that turned up at the corners.

She tended to look subtly mocking. It was probably the best way to go about things if you were a younger Cusack.

She was only mildly put out that Mel was going to share her room. She took an armful of clothes off Kelly's bed and plumped the pillow doubtfully. 'The lads are noisy,' she said. 'So there's no point whinging about it.'

'I don't whinge,' Mel said.

'The neighbours whinge,' Niamh said, nodding at the left and right walls. 'The lads are always hopping things off each other's heads.'

'Linda'll sort them out,' Kelly said.

'It's Mel,' Mel said.

'Mel?' said Niamh.

'I prefer Mel to Linda. So it's Mel.'

After a pause Niamh said, 'My friends call me Neecee. Niamh C, like?'

'MC Neesee, Saint Anxious of Assisi,' Kelly said, to which Niamh said, 'We're nowhere near Assisi, though,' to which Kelly said, 'Like you'd know,' and Niamh, disguising retreat in abrupt boredom said, 'D'you think Ryan will bring chips?'

'How would I know? Fucking ask him.'

Niamh rapidly tapped her screen.

'Oh my God,' Kelly said, to the ceiling. 'She hasn't seen him in two years but whether or not he brings chips home is the important thing.'

The other three boys – Cian, Cathal, Ronan – came home, one after the other, and one after the other said, 'Oh right, grand,' when Kelly said that Mel was going to stay. This had never been a house in which routine was important. As teenage girls Mel and Kelly had slept as easily in each other's bedrooms as in their own; they shared history in the sense of recorded defeats and cruelties; they had too many things in common. *What fucking changes around here?* Everything, and still you carry it together.

When Ryan arrived, Kelly and Mel were in the kitchen, out of lager and drinking tea. Kelly had just said, 'It's disgusting how disgusting I feel right now,' when the front door opened and if

Mel had thought there was any point in running out the back door she'd have been gone.

Six siblings and their father gathered cacophonously in the living room. Mel waited in the kitchen. She rolled her mug around the surface of the table. Her stomach lurched. Niamh came to the kitchen door triumphantly holding a chip, grinned, and whirled round again.

Kelly came back and began to look through the cabinets. 'I don't think I can clear space for you,' she told Mel. 'You'll just have to pack in whatever bits you buy.'

'That's fine.'

He would lose the plot. He'd rip the cabinets off the walls.

'Dad hardly cooks anyway,' said Kelly. 'They throw on goujons and stuff. They're lazy fuckers.'

Out on her ear. He'd throw her to the footpath. She'd bust both knees and people would come to their doors and stare.

'Don't take any shit from them, is my advice,' said Kelly. She went still until Mel raised her head and met her eyes. 'Don't take shit from him.'

Mel twisted her mouth.

'Don't,' Kelly pressed.

'After what happened, though.'

'All right, what're you gonna do, sleep in the garden?'

It wasn't raining and Mel thought she was tired enough.

'I should try my grandad again,' she said.

He had heard her voice from the hall, and so he came into the kitchen startled. He said, 'What are you doing here?'

Mel put her elbows on the table and inhaled.

Kelly answered for her. 'She's to stay a few days till she finds a gaff.'

'She can't stay here, where'll Dad put her?'

'My old bed? It's all sorted, so wind your neck in.'

'Kelly, there's five already here, you need to be leaving my dad space, not stuffing more bodies into it.'

'Aw come on, boy,' Kelly whined. 'Be neighbourly. I thought you were an excellent neighbour. I heard no one does the neighbours quite like you.'

Ryan lifted his chin and said to Mel in a small voice, 'Thanks, girl. Thanks a lot.'

'It's her mam,' Kelly said, hands on her hips. 'She's allowed talk about it.'

'A story to tell, is that all it is?' Ryan said to Mel, still in the feeble voice; for a moment she thought he might have engineered it for her ears, so well-pitched he had it; for a moment she saw how he could have been that time with her mother, artfully guileless and at first blush so brittle. She snuffed the thought out because the thought was desperate, and ugly for it. It was how she'd learned to make sense of things and she had been trying for years now to override her impulse to assume malice in every element. She grabbed her knuckles with her thumbs.

'Look,' Kelly said. 'Linda didn't do anything on you, did she? Whatever went on isn't Linda's fault. So this is the least we can do, like.'

'That's not the point I'm making, the point I'm making is that there's five here already, there's no room.'

'There was eight of us at one stage.'

'Eight when we were fucking twinchy.'

'We weren't that twinchy that we can't fit six now. The bed's empty, like. Anyway, we know what's actually bothering you. I won't ever mention the other thing again. All right? Swear to you.'

'I said that's not the point,' and here he erupted into Italian. Kelly folded her arms as he bent his at the elbows and jabbed at the air both sides of his head.

'Ah, pure rude,' she replied, in English.

Something else in Italian. Rolled rs. His lips jutted. His shoulders went back. He glanced at Mel as though afraid she'd been hiding her translation skills all this time.

'Oh my God,' Kelly said. 'Five months in Naples and you're fucking insufferable.'

. . .

'It was a fucking joke, Ryan, Jesus Christ.'

. . .

'This has nothing to do with you, or what happened on that island where you went to, I dunno, lose your fucking mind by the sounds of it. Were you flahing her, too? That Izzy wan? Is that her problem with you?'

'I was not fucking flahing her,' he spat, and switched language again.

Mel stood up. 'Listen,' she said.

Neither looked at her. Kelly stood firm in a cascade of words Mel could only guess the gist of, till Ryan lowered his voice and rubbed his eyes. The flamboyance of the language might have tired him in the same way the flamboyance of playing piano tired him; they were overcome easily, the boys Mel had grown up with, so dedicated to ready belligerence and paring their words that little feats of expression wore on them.

She moved around Ryan and Kelly and went into the hall. Pain rushed in behind her right eye. She realised she needed water and wondered if she could return to the kitchen for it. She thought of walking the few minutes to the shop but wondered what came after that. Would they even let her back in?

The living room door was open. The younger siblings had dispersed; she heard footsteps on the floor above. Tony was there, though, back in his chair, facing the television, on which was displayed a grey splatter of faces and corridors.

'I'm sorry,' she said. She was drunk enough to be able to say this but no longer drunk enough for the words to come out coolly.

He cleared his throat as if he intended to respond. She waited; he was not forthcoming; she asked, 'Do you know what he's saying?'

'Bits,' Tony said. 'I was never any good at it. She understands every word, and she could say it back to him, too. Only she knows answering in English will rile him. And he knows that asking in Italian will rile her.'

'They're arguing about me,' she said.

'They are and they're not.'

'Should I leave?'

'Do you have somewhere to go?'

She shook her head. The truth, to him, must have looked like impudence. She thought that abandonment should not be so drawn-out. It should be a slammed door, a hateful word, the smell of burning rubber. Now she felt the finality of that abandonment, like she just hadn't appreciated it without the imagery, though it was a deal done years at this point.

'I suppose that's your answer, so,' he said.

She hesitated before sitting, slowly. They watched the television, and in the kitchen the bilingual quarrel continued.

There were dozens of them, all in their later years, some frail but most in fine fettle. You wouldn't know what connected them just to look at them; that was the thing and that used to be the grace in it. That wasn't how it was any more and no harm at all in the upheaval. Now they were talking, confidently, frankly. They were done with hiding their histories. They were flanked by helpers, some of whom shied, smiling, from the cameras, daughters or granddaughters, by the looks of them.

One of the women was only gorgeous. She had long grey hair, half-up, half-down, and she was wearing a scarlet one-shoulder jumpsuit and dangly earrings. This was what got to Maureen, because talk about telling the moral authorities to take a running jump, talk about claiming your place at the table, talk loud, by Jesus, as long as you're talking. Power was just rising off her, the woman in the jumpsuit, and Maureen threw her head back and blinked at the ceiling.

'Well they weren't keeping her down,' she said, when she was able.

On the television, the Magdalene survivors were arriving at the Mansion House in Dublin. Hundreds of well-wishers had turned out to greet them. They waved homemade banners that said 'Welcome Home, Sisters' and 'You Are Heroines' and they were cheering and crying and hugging and though this kind of thing usually gave Maureen indigestion she was terribly moved. She was not at all used to being impaired by compassion. And the grey-haired girl in the jumpsuit, sure that put the cawhake on the composure altogether, her striding past this gathering of allies, looking like a movie star, as if to say, Fallen? Fallen, how? How elevated must I have been, if you could only knock me to here?

'Well, aren't they brilliant?' Maureen said.

On the couch to her left, her granddaughter Ellie graciously went, 'Yeah.'

They were in Ellie's house – Ellie's mother's house, for Deirdre had given Jimmy the boot years ago – watching this documentary and waiting on Deirdre's return from a friend's birthday in Limerick. Ellie was fourteen, her brother Conor fifteen, not quite old enough to stay on their own. Maureen couldn't have said she was babysitting; she didn't cook for them or tell them to do their homework or make sure their clothes were ironed. She was functioning as a party deterrent, she supposed.

'They were locked up by nuns,' Ellie said, stretching and slumping. 'It's very sad.'

'It's a disgrace,' Maureen said. 'It's our great shame.'

'It's so sad,' Ellie stressed, as if sadness were the pure and definitive sense to it, but sadness seemed too resigned to Maureen, too uninvolved, sadness was the hangover of it, *It's sad now and that's the truth, we'll say no more about it.*

'I could have been one of them,' she told Ellie.

She was sure enough that Ellie knew her own composition, that her father was born to a nineteen-year-old banished by her parents for bringing ignominy in on top of them. That her father was then adopted by those same miserable doctrinaires. That they made a bags of raising him. That Ellie would know the extent of her father's own ignominy was perhaps not so certain, but she must at least know that she was not as Ireland would have preferred her. Her father was born in sin and she, then, was a child of divorce. In her blood, therefore, in her guts, she must empathise with the women on the telly. She should still taste that history as salt in sea air. She was too close to it to stop at *sad*.

'You can't say that, Maureen.'

Maureen said, 'Ha?'

'You can't say that,' Ellie repeated, and even looked over to underline the point. 'You can't say it could have been you when it wasn't you, it's like you're trying to get in on it and that's just wrong.'

'Trying to get in on it? I ask you!'

Ellie sat up. There was a bit of her mother to her, but a lot of her father, God love her. Maureen had once read that it was more likely a child would take after its father, because back when they were all living in holes and plucking fleas off one another's shoulders resemblance was all that stopped the males killing the babies; the right cut of the chin or drop of the earlobe and a wee alarm would go off in the backs of their heads. 'Twas instinct to want a lineage, 'twas your only hope of immortality. And so when Maureen felt affection towards her grandchildren she knew she couldn't blame herself, that she was right in thinking that they were bould little feckers and that she genuinely couldn't help forgiving them for it.

'Those ladies had a terrible time,' Ellie said. 'And now everyone is feeling sorry for them and that's why you're saying "It could have been me".'

'Is it that you think I begrudge them the sympathy? That's an awful thing to say.'

'No, it's that I think you're piggybacking on it because girls do that.'

'I haven't been a girl since nineteen-seventy-fecking . . . two.' 1972 being an arbitrary date. She was no maiden, then; she was a mother. She supposed the fellas in London didn't spot the distinction. You'd have to be carrying a placard stating your deviations and peccadilloes before lustful men would cop on to them, and then only if you held it in front of your chest.

'Women then,' Ellie said. 'Coz it's cool to have problems. So now you can't say you have a cold because some girl will be like, *Me too, I had to have therapy for my colds, I sneeze, like, so hard.* So that's what you're doing, you see the ladies on the telly and you're like, *That could have been me, I had it so bad* but you didn't have it bad, Maureen, so it's disrespectful.'

'Disrespectful, would you listen to this? I did have it bad, Ms Ellen, you don't know how bad it was.'

'I know my dad's mam and dad were awful to you, like, I'm not saying they weren't.'

'They were, and my country was, and sent into exile, I was, for the most natural thing—'

'Yeah I know but at least you got to go to England and live your life, like. Those ladies on the telly were locked up and some of them didn't even *have* babies. So like even though it was wrong to be punished for that they didn't even do it in the first place, and then they had to, like, work as slaves for nuns and some of them were institutionalised . . .' One of the women had just used this word in her comments to a reporter. '. . . and Maureen, to all intensive purposes you got off lightly compared to them.'

'Well the thread is there,' Maureen said. 'To be punished without even having committed a sin.'

'Yeah I know, but still if you say "That could have been me" you're making a point only about yourself and not about, like, the thread or the sin or whatever.'

'If I'd have been born ten years earlier it would have been me!'

'Yeah but like if I'd have been born ten years earlier I wouldn't be me, would I? If I'd have been born a hundred years ago I wouldn't have been able to read or something, if I'd have been born ten years later I'd be four now, what's your point?'

'My point is,' Maureen began, but here they heard Deirdre's SUV pull into the driveway. Maureen rose decisively, for it was time now for adult conversation. 'My point is,' she said, 'that it should bring home to you what was done to the Magdalenes, so you should know we're all in this together. And know that there but for the grace of . . .' She stopped herself just in time and wagged a finger by way of a synonym. 'Those who don't learn from history are doomed to repeat it.'

'I've read loads about it,' Ellie said, 'which is why I don't think you can say it was nearly you.'

'Well it fecking was,' Maureen said, off out through the door. She turned on her heel to stick her head back around and say, 'And it's "to all intents and purposes".'

She entrusted her claim to the last word to her grandchild's laziness and returned to the hall. 'You little bitch,' she grumbled. She no longer felt stirred and sisterly but chastised, not by Ellie but by the Magdalene Survivors, as if it were they that had put the words in the girl's mouth. This reaction was silly and she felt chastised by that too. She wasn't suggesting that there weren't levels of suffering inflicted by the old Ireland, just that the suffering sprung from the same sentiment and the variables were sometimes not just down to social class or the strength of the affected family unit, but down to chance; was that not a frightening thing? Would that not put a fire under anyone?

She got to the kettle as Deirdre's key turned in the door.

'Everyone alive?' Deidre called.

'Ah, why wouldn't we be?' Maureen said, and banged two mugs on the counter.

She felt the fact remained that Cork was a male kind of place but she'd be damned if she didn't pull against it a small bit. She had started gathering lists of names and dates, photographs, printouts of old newspaper articles, books. It was terribly hard to find a woman who'd made a dent in the place without a borrowed crosier and this made her feel angry on behalf of Cork and her country, but a little bit relieved in herself, because she was right in thinking her revolutionary capacities would always have been limited to giving birth to a revolutionary; she wasn't, in fact, a slovenly bitch. Lately she was thinking very dark things and that Jimmy could be rebranded as a revolutionary was one of them. That one man's revolution was another man's terrorism. *Man*. Jesus, there she went again. *Jesus*. A man made into a god.

Her sex had seemed a cruel joke when she was a girl. Her body was one that was made to suffer and she didn't feel she had been born only to suffer, though if she had would that not have been very Christ-like? The blasphemy in that. Imagine this *thing*, this dirty, bleeding, debased casing that men lost their minds over daily, imagine saying that thing was godly. *Divine, Heavenly*:

these words were allowed if men blessed you with them but it was a sin to take to heart what they said. Christ was born to suffer and so were women but men were closer to Christ. What did men ever suffer? A bruised ego and the odd swollen ball? Oh, the self-harm, she supposed. As if that were an unconscious way for them to redress the balance based on this lie they told themselves and the world: *like Christ in Gethsemane, we tear our hair out and look to the sky. Father, father, why have you forsaken me?* Because that's what fathers fucking do, Maureen thought, writing it in black marker on a bench in Fitzgerald Park. And if Cork turned its back on her then Cork was very obviously male.

There was a lot of her sort of craziness going around these days. Maybe it was the settled and cosy women of Ireland waking up, at last, or coming out from behind the backs of the men who'd hemmed them in, at last, or growing a conscience, at last; the ordinary women of Ireland had been very good at turning their backs on their sisters when there was some prize of safety in it. Now they were after turning the country on its head and fucking the Church out of it and Maureen was glad of it, but put out because she hadn't seen it coming. First the gay marriage and then the abortion. Outside of Ireland they were talking about harassment and abuse of power and every day there seemed to be some superstar fella in the doldrums over his shitty carry-on coming to light. That gobshite in the White House had probably helped it along, even though he didn't look able to find his arse with both hands. Here Maureen would normally have suffixed with, 'God love him,' but God was no longer in Ireland.

So maybe there were local heroines on the way, young wans of Ellie's age who'd change the face of the city and maybe Cork could be steadied yet, maybe when Maureen got her walking tours going she'd be adding new names every few weeks. *This is where she went to school*, or, *Up there in that women's place is where such-and-such a campaign grew legs.*

Ellie making televised political statements on the quays.

Ellie storming City Hall.

Ellie on hunger strike.

Ellie writing in black marker on park benches, *Don't mind Ould Wans who think they were Magdalenes when they had it easy.*

Maureen thought sometimes that she'd like to have been a proper drinker. Drinking was discouraged in young ladies when she was a young lady, so she'd stuck to acceptable measures with the odd gin and tonic when the occasion called. She thought now that she'd have made a great barstool philosopher. There but for the grace of . . .

She'd have made a great religious leader. There but for the grace of . . .

Maureen had always thought that when Ireland changed she'd be a lighter soul and it was true that the delicious upheavals of the last few years had delighted her, but at the end of it there was a sort of hollow in her identity; now that the idea of a woman had changed she felt that she was somewhere between two states. Neither soft nor stuffy enough to belong to the older species and neither correct enough nor revolutionary enough for the younger.

She put the kettle on when she got in and sat on the couch to look through the collected histories on her coffee table, though she did so with no pleasure, no energy.

It was lavender tea she had reluctantly purchased from a health food shop. She wasn't sleeping this weather. She couldn't make her mind up on what to blame. She was used to blaming the country but she could hardly do that any more, now that Ireland was a paragon or paradise. She supposed she was pleased for Ellie's generation and the great sacrifice in being pleased had knocked her sideways.

She was reading about Terence MacSwiney's widow – Muriel MacSwiney, a great nationalist and a bad mother, so Maureen quickly decided that she was a fan – when the rapping sounded on the door. And sure there was another of Cork's many wayward sons, a sort of son to her himself, she'd once so fervently believed.

'Would you look?' she said when she opened the door, and held her arms out as if presenting him to a legion of peering biddies behind her in the hall, all of them bad at being old and worse at guiding the young.

Nothing gammy at all, sure a young stag with his chin in the air and his nostrils flared. 'Have you been saying shit about me, Maureen?'

'Have I been what?' she said.

'Saying shit about me,' he said.

'To who?' she said.

'To the whole of fucking Ireland,' he said.

'The whole of Ireland? About you? Jesus, what age do you think I am? I wouldn't have anything to say about you if I met your father on the road, Ryan.'

'You did enough damage three years ago,' he told her, first finger out.

'What damage,' she said, 'and you gallivanting around the Far East?'

'Is that the problem, is it? You heard I was doing all right, is that what has you raging?'

'You're some langer,' she said. 'Come in.'

'I will in me shit,' he said, and pushed his chin closer to the outstretched finger. 'If you're behind this, I swear to God, Maureen. I swear to fucking Jesus.'

'I'll ask Jimmy what's eating you.'

'Ask him, do. G'wan, amn't I waiting long enough on him to take another chunk out of me?'

She watched the chin come closer again to the finger. 'Would you not ask yourself what you're at, Ryan, coming to my home at this hour and raving about gossip on my doorstep?'

'Someone is trying to wreck things for me by spreading stories, which is sly and fucking petty carry-on and like something someone's mammy would do.'

'Am I the only mammy you know? What about your son's mammy, didn't you go making a mammy yourself?'

He leaned in again. 'What'd you say?'

'He's a dote.' She smiled. 'Diarmaid. Lovely name. He's the bulb off you.'

'G'wan,' he said. 'G'wan you fucking—'

He was close enough now for her to reach out and take the lobe of his left ear so that's what she did.

'You're a pup,' she said. 'What are you?'

She had him bent almost double and the blood came fast to his cheeks. He yipped in what she'd take as assent; she pulled him forward. 'Get in here,' she said, and he did, because she was merciless and he was mortified; had she an audience she was sure he'd cry with rage. She took him by the ear into the sitting room and wished then she could have dragged him up Patrick's Hill, so enjoyable she found the action. She'd have made a great bully, she'd have made a great and evil nun, there but for the grace of . . .

When she released him she saw that she'd made him speechless; he stood, gaping, rubbing the black stud in his lobe.

'God, you must have been a terrible gangster,' she said.

He hadn't been reared well, she knew, having met the father and seen how easily led and often macerated he was. She'd never met the mother but it wasn't a responsible woman who'd leave her parents in Italy to have six children on a Corkonian council estate. And what kind of well-reared boy became a gangster? She had experience in this sort of thing, her own son having been dragged up by Holy Joes till he was a plague all by himself.

And still Ryan Cusack couldn't figure out what to do about being caught by the ear. Still he was allowing himself to be chastised. If she were him, she'd knock her assailant down before kicking a hole in the door, but she wasn't him, not of the same generation at all. How they could be so soft and yet so self-righteous was a mystery; it was all in the head now, she thought, they were all about connections and rights and responsibilities and confounded by physical jolting.

'Tea?' she said.

'Don't grab me like that,' he said.

'All right so.'

'You could've pulled my fucking ear off.'

'Pity about you. Leaning in over a grandmother like that. And she living alone.'

'You shouldn't have mentioned my young fella to me.'

'Why, aren't you proud of him?'

'Don't be smart.'

'Jesus, Ryan, one of us has to be.'

She remembered how he took his tea; she'd made him enough of the stuff. She started into the task without asking again. When she turned back around he was sitting on the stool in front of his mother's piano, still a bit purple. He didn't refuse the tea but he didn't take the mug from her either. She left it on top of the piano.

'In case I don't ask Jimmy,' she said. 'What's eating you?'

'See, I think you know.'

'I don't know.'

'So it's not you leaving comments on every video we make about how I'm a disgrace to my city? And telling journalists that I used to deal so I don't deserve a go at this music thing? Coz it's like something you'd do for the craic.'

'Who's we?' she said.

He rubbed his nose. 'Me and . . . This thing I've got going.'

'What thing?'

'The music thing.'

'We, the music thing?'

'We, like, the—' it took him some seconds to shape the word – 'band.'

'Your theory is that I'm leaving mean messages on the internet about your band?'

'It's not a theory.'

'I'm sixty-eight, Ryan.'

'That doesn't mean that you wouldn't.'

'Why would I want to drop you in it if doing so could hurt my own boy? If I went around saying you were a little bollocks wouldn't they all want to know who was the big bollocks employing you? And he the apple of my eye, Ryan.'

'Yeah, see, the sarcasm is what makes me think you're trying to get to him and all but he'll blame me for this, when he catches on he'll take the legs off me.'

'Catches on? To the music, is it? Can you do that anonymously? Like the fella above in Limerick with the plastic bag on his face?'

'I don't know,' he said. 'I don't know what the fuck I was thinking.'

She took a mouthful of her own tea, which had gone cold. She grunted and went to refresh it. On her return he carried on, 'I'm fucking trying, like,' and stuck a finger and thumb in his mouth.

'You're looking well,' she said. 'It's obvious you're trying.'

'How'd you know my son's name?'

'Sure I met him with your father.'

'How'd you know I was in Seoul?'

'Because unlike Seoul,' she said, 'this is a small city.'

'Exactly my fucking problem,' he said, into his fist.

'Bastards,' she said.

'What?'

'They're only bastards, Ryan. Whoever's claiming you. I wouldn't mind them.'

'I have to mind them.'

She shrugged. 'You've one thing going for you, though.'

He didn't ask her to elaborate, only looked at her with his forehead corrugated.

She explained, 'The thing between your legs.'

'Ah, Jesus, Maureen.'

'I'm telling you. All of this city's notables have been men. You'll get away with it. Cork loves a pup and a chancer and Cork exalts its men. This is a very male city.'

'A male city? Fuck's sake.'

'Tell me a famous daughter, so.'

'I dunno, Mother Jones?'

'What?' Maureen said, and for the second time today she felt a weight lifting and its absence buckle her. 'Who?'

'That trade union wan. The most dangerous woman in America.' By way of answering her raised eyebrows he scowled and said, 'My cousin has the horn for shit like that.'

'I know the name Mother Jones,' Maureen said, scowling back.

'Worker's rights,' he said. 'All I want now is to work but this work's too good for the likes of me even if I'm good at it . . . My head is wrecked.'

'And mine with you.' Maureen said. 'Mother bloody Jones. For the love of God, do you not see what a curse it is that a man had to tell me that?'

Track 5: Submarines

There was nothing serious between me and Seon-mi. We were buddies more than anything else, just, y'know . . . You'd like her. She's pure sound. She has a batty sense of humour. She has tattoos on her ribcage, where her parents can't see. It was gas how disappointed she was when she realised I wasn't American. She'd spent a couple of years in Los Angeles and couldn't wait to talk about it so when we met for coffee, God, she was at sea altogether.

She got hold of me at a bad time. Not knowing me, she didn't know that. She thought I was always a bampot and she was OK with it. The pace is breakneck in Seoul; no one assumes you've lost your mind if you're on the tear every night, sleeping for five hours and up again for the gym in the morning. I couldn't get my hands on any dope and drink just makes me lairy, so there was nothing to take the edge off. I was bombing it. Say what you like about the Irish, but we'd have you sectioned for that kind of craic.

Seon-mi knew about you and Diarmaid, which would have been a dealbreaker except she'd never planned on bringing me home to Eomma and Appa. I showed her photos. She said Diarmaid was adorable, but I was mad for having him. She said you were very pretty, but that you, too, were mad for having a baby. She says, Ireland must be a very traditional country. I says I'm not sure what you'd call it, but we're divided north and south, in an abusive relationship with the old empire neighbours, good at emigration, fond of the gatt, drenched by the rain, like a bit of Mass on occasion but believe fiercely in ghosts. You tell me. And she'd pinch my arm.

This is after you told me about Dylan. I'd been OK, up to then. Not great, but OK.

I get nightmares since Dan. Sometimes I'm with him and Shakespeare, sitting around in some gaff talking about how we're gonna make shit of some fella, and I have this awful sense of dread all the way through, like they're about to turn on me. Sometimes it's more like sleep paralysis, where J.P. walks into the bedroom and says something unintelligible to me, and I can't move my mouth to ask him to repeat himself, and he waits, and the air gets heavier and heavier. In Seoul I didn't dream about anything but men who wanted to hurt me.

A couple of times around the city I thought I heard gunshots – which'd have been very fucking unlikely – and I was just this instant mess. Shaking, like. Tears in my eyes. A frightened child.

After you told me you were seeing Dylan, I wasn't able to manage nightmares and jelly-legs, I was sure that what I deserved was coming to me. I pushed harder. Slept less and drank like a fish. I was convinced every morning that I'd said something incriminating in broken Korean or, worse, perfect English the night before. Had I told someone that I have two black market trade routes to my name? *Oh yeah, boy, you'd think it'd be psychotic bigwigs behind that shit but it was me, Salerno to Cork and Dublin to Liverpool, just coz I'm a gifted go-between, I'm the Mouth of fucking Sauron.* Immigration would be battering the door down. I'd get twenty years. When I was with Seon-mi I tried to keep a lid on it. She'd be getting ready for work and I'd be in bits all over the apartment, pretending it was just the sloppiness of my dual nationality. This is what I'm like off the draw.

One morning I woke up in Seon-mi's apartment and I could remember drinking with her the night before but not going back to her place. Blacking out like that gives me woeful heebie-jeebies. Guess now we both know why.

She told me I'd gotten some picture messages from you after I passed out. She'd seen on my home screen that they were of Diarmaid, so she'd used my thumb print to unlock the phone. She sat beside me on the bed and went through the photos with my phone on her knees, as if it was her phone and her young fella she was showing me. Like, Look how sweet he is in the little dressing gown. Look, it's got bear ears.

Then she says to me, You don't still want to jump into the Han, do you? Only you'll have to wade in. They'll never let you off the bridges.

What are you talking about? I says, and there's a lick of terror up my spine because what the fuck was I after saying now?

What are *you* talking about? she says, and sticks my phone under my nose and tells me to look at him, look at my son.

I wrote the first few lines of 'Submarines' in the humming dark of the cabin on the twelve-hour flight from Seoul to Heathrow. *I woke alive in her bed. I woke and I was alive.* The rest I only wrote down once I knew you were bringing Diarmaid to me, in the bedroom in the house on Bofin, a baggie of grass beside me on the bed, just in case.

You know the lyrics, girl, you must know what they mean. I knew if I let him be taken from me – I don't mean by you, I mean by the world going against me as the world has every right to do – if I let that happen I might as well wade into the Han, or the Spree or the Mersey or the Lee or the fucking Sarno.

I thought maybe I could write him into the nightmares, taking the place of J.P. Wouldn't it be much better if it's him coming in while I'm lying there, frozen, to tell me to wake up coz the world isn't going to wait for me to get my act together? He's not going to stay small, is he? He's going to get bigger, and watch closer, and judge me if I fail him. I'd know, wouldn't I? It's exactly what I do to my own dad, isn't it?

It's called 'Submarines' because I wanted reminding that you can go underwater and still be safe, if you do it right.

There was conversation on the way home to Cork but it was the dutiful kind. At first Karine put up with it because this Traolach creature was driving them as far as Galway City, so what kind of disclosure could she expect? But on the train her son's father was dedicated to being only that, and as soon as she said, 'Listen . . .' or 'Look . . .', he was up out of his seat, toddler in his arms, babbling about stretching legs or getting Taytos from the trolley. Or pretending not to have heard her at all; in the end he stopped responding to even innocuous openers. In any case she wasn't sure she would have been able to continue from a 'Listen' or a 'Look'. How could she hope to concentrate when she'd found a disorder in her ex-boyfriend's past, which was by definition her past too, and not just in the sense of their having a shared history but also because what was damaging for him should have been formative for her, should have proved her mettle, but instead she hadn't noticed it at all.

He paid for the taxi from the train station to her parents' house. He got out of the car with them and made the right arrangements for the coming week and gave the right response when Diarmaid insisted he come in to see his toys. He didn't leave too soon. Right things and all of it wrong. He didn't have tea or make eye contact. When he was leaving, he said, 'I'll be on to you,' and extended the first finger of his right hand, casually, as he would leaving an acquaintance behind him in a queue.

In the days following recollection kept her occupied, as if poring over exam notes, hoping to understand a lesson she'd disregarded, that it'd precede everything else clicking into place.

Tara Duane she remembered as skinny and peaky and quick to confide but there was never anything enticing about her, except she supposed in her promiscuity, which was obvious enough. She didn't remember how Ryan had acted around her, so he must have acted as all of them did.

What she did remember of Ryan at fifteen was his calamitous honesty, an intelligence that turned easily into rage, the grief she could barely help him with. He told her difficult secrets. He said he was actually luckier than other fellas with alcoholic fathers. His dad smacked him around but he deserved to be smacked around. He sold drugs and terrorised his teachers, he smoked cannabis and took ecstasy and was having sex with his girlfriend. It would all change if he stopped being an impossible son. Tony didn't even want to hit him. Tony was always miserable afterwards.

Now she wondered if she had responded to this calamitous honesty with the sympathy he needed or if she'd in fact been trying to will it all away because he'd always been too much for her to handle. If his next-door neighbour had managed to rape him and he had managed to recover all while Karine was blithely holding his hand or gossiping in his ear or unbuttoning his fly or pushing her lips on to his, what was he to her? A body on to which she was projecting her own likes and dislikes? No wonder she'd tried to lay him flat and make him compliant.

Lightheaded, she performed normality. When Ryan came by to see Diarmaid she didn't push him to talk about what had happened on Bofin. She didn't make a big deal of it when her father said, 'Well here he is, back from the missions at last'; she let Ryan brush it off, standing in front of Gary and smiling faintly at the sitting room carpet. She didn't try to hurry her mother along when Jackie asked him about his plans. She let him talk about sound engineering and being a good dad. She stole glances again. She made guesses about what he was feeling. She admonished herself. She went dancing with Louise.

'Did you shave your legs?' Louise asked, as they were getting changed.

'Yeah.'

'For fuck's sake, Karine.'

'For fuck's sake, Louise. What's it to you, like? You weren't there.'

'And did you break up with Dylan?'

'This has nothing to do with Dylan.'

'Did I get it wrong, girl? Did you fuck your ex last week?'

'It's complicated,' Karine said. 'It's really complicated. I don't want to talk about it, he doesn't want to talk to me, I made a balls of everything, can we just not, for now?' Which shook Louise into a frustrated sort of pity, which made the problem seem less urgent, more amplified, and so after that Karine's recollection meandered. Now it was like casting an eye over exam notes when she'd already assumed failure. Disputing her own definitions, googling, following unrelated links, getting distracted by a better routine on a better dancer's channel.

When Karine thought about postpartum sex, which would be uncomfortable and awkward, she knew it would be easiest with Ryan. And that he'd be open to it. More than. He was so awed by her now; he couldn't do enough for her. It was sixteen weeks since Diarmaid was born. She'd stopped breastfeeding the week before, a couple of months before her mam said she should have even thought about it, but she wanted to have a Christmas drink, wanted to go out-out with her friends, to dress up and dance. Which might at some point mean meeting a fella, getting the shift and maybe more and that required research and preparatory thought and if she needed to practise, per se, then of course it should be with Ryan.

A few days after Christmas, he was minding Diarmaid in her house so that she could go out for a meal with her family. At the restaurant she had a glass of Prosecco, then wine, then one more Prosecco, then said it had gone to her head, and it had. She needed to go home. She'd call a cab. No need for them to cut their night short. She was tired anyway.

Ryan didn't need convincing. She asked if he would stay with her and of course he would, absolutely he would, she thought

155

she'd see his heart pounding under his skin when she took his T-shirt off. The next day she said, 'I don't wanna hurt you, like,' and in a small voice he agreed. No, of course she didn't. Only that she could hardly blame him for thinking it was a reconciliation. The sex had been slow and gentle. Not fucking, like; the other way. As if they were in love. There were intimacies afterwards, like them waking with a start when her mam stuck her head around Karine's bedroom door at 2 a.m., or how Karine told him in the morning not to mind her dad, to go down to Diarmaid and to have a slice of toast or something while she was in the shower. That had to mean something.

It was early afternoon and they were in the sitting room. Diarmaid was lying on Karine's lap, smiling up at her. She felt protective and pragmatic. 'It was lovely, Ryan. And I don't see the harm when it's something just between me and you. But you know what we're like together and it's not fair to subject Diarmaid to it.'

Ryan put his hands in his pockets. He didn't look at her. He said, 'Were we that bad?'

Dylan called over on Tuesday evening. Her parents were in the sitting room and her little sister Yvette was blasting some make-up tutorial upstairs, so Karine brought him into the kitchen and told him she was having an early night. He thought she meant with him. He started bopping about, his hands on her waist, breathing in her ear.

'Jesus!' she said.

She sat with him and held his hands, but it was not easy to break up with someone in soft focus when there was a toddler getting into crannies and faces and essentially acting the way his father did after a Napoli win and a couple of bumps.

'I just don't think this is the right time,' she told Dylan, and in the course of badly explaining herself, she thought that it wouldn't be the worst thing to put what had happened on Inishbofin to the back of her head and try a bit harder with him. Why was it necessary that she come clean when so many people never came clean and so many relationships were still ticking because of it? Would it have been better if she'd come clean to Ryan about the two other boys she'd been with in her first year of college, when he was in gaol? Of course it wouldn't; it'd have killed him. And so maybe she should shut up before she dug herself too deep a hole.

She thought about being with Dylan this time next year. Things would probably be fine and it would do her good to look forward to *fine* and Dylan was grand, decent, she could see why people might call him a catch. He was fit, active, sensible. He didn't smoke or eat cinema popcorn or white bread. He was on the lower end of average height so the extra muscle made him impressively solid. For an athletic fella he had shocking rhythm but that didn't stop him giving it socks on the dance floor; she went with him to his sister's twenty-first and had to hide in the toilet during 'Despacito'. He was afraid of rats. He had a degree in Computer Science. He went like a jackhammer in bed and had made an effort to understand her when she said that wasn't always a good thing. He had no difficulty in understanding what she was saying to him now. He removed his hands from hers. He asked if it had anything to do with her ex.

'It's confusing,' she said. 'Him being back.' She pressed her fist to her cheek. What if all she knew of her normal self was performed normality? What if the true Karine was so awful that artificial words and grinning through bad dancing was the only way anyone would really love her? 'I think he's confused too,' she said. 'Ryan and me were together for such a long time.'

'You're still into him, so?' Dylan asked. Emphasising *him*. Except Dylan didn't know anything about Ryan; she had more sense than to talk about Ryan in front of Dylan. She looked at the ceiling and pursed her lips. 'Ah, you are,' Dylan said, disgusted. 'Right so, yeah, thanks a million.'

'You say *into him* like it's some sort of crush. It's more complicated. There's nothing I can do about him meaning a lot to me,' she wept, and wept harder for not knowing whether this was true. Diarmaid pulled one hand from her face and tried to kiss her better. 'I'm OK,' Karine told him, sobbing and smiling. She was anything but; she was utterly out of order.

Dylan sat back and said, 'For Christ's sake.'

'He's Diarmaid's dad,' Karine said.

'Yeah, I remember, that's how you put it to me, all right. I said it to the lads, she's heading up the country to bring the young fella to see his dad, and they said I was some fool for letting you, and I said, no, you've got her all wrong, she's not one of them. Only you are.'

'You didn't "let" me do anything,' Karine said. 'I didn't ask your permission.'

'The issue isn't the words I'm using, the issue is that you went however many miles out of your way just to ride your ex. Well, I hope he's good to you now. I hope you get more out of him this time than the few cents he pays you in maintenance.' He stood up. Even now he was careful not to drag the chair on the tiles. 'I treated you well, Karine. Y'know? I brought you out. I drove all the way up here to you how many nights, coz you couldn't go out because you had a kid, I met your kid, I bought him presents and all, I didn't even let it bother me that you'd had some other fella's kid.'

Had Diarmaid been able to understand this Karine would have said much more than, 'Yeah, Dylan, oh my God, so unbelievably good of you.'

'Other fellas wouldn't have touched you.'

'You think you were doing me a favour?'

'No, Karine. I'd have thought the way I treated you proved that. But y'know, I won't be so quick next time to give a girl the benefit of the doubt.'

'What doubt?'

'You know what doubt. You know well. Jesus, treat a girl right, like, respect her and what does she do? Runs back to the lad too stupid to wear a condom. Thanks, Karine. So glad I wasted all that time on you.'

Perhaps he thought she would cry harder and apologise, tell him he was right, that she was weak and Ryan an irresponsible lowlife. She wiped her eyes with the flat of her thumb. She would give him neither concession nor the unashamed Northside bitch he wanted her to be, one of *them*. Though either would be a kindness, she said, 'I'm sorry, Dylan, but you have to leave.'

'Don't worry,' he said. 'I'm off. Bye, Diarmaid.' He tousled her son's head, took a step, turned back, told her to delete his number, and then he was gone.

In the winter, just over three years ago, she went to the house he shared with Joseph and when Ryan answered the door to her, she saw relief and gratitude flit over his face. He was always going to be the first person she told, who else do you tell first but the father? Only for his stupid faith in her mercy, he would have been. It was not just how committed he was to this idea of him being the sinner and her being the saint, nor that she had, at that moment, remembered in great definition the topless selfie of Natalie Grogan's that she'd found on his phone a few weeks previous, the one that had shattered their post-fight routine of apology-to-promises-to-sex; it was worse than that, it was the suggestion of this sinner's inherent goodness, his optimism, the glimpse of the gentler self he was always rolling in cocaine and throwing into conflict, and she didn't quite hate him for it but didn't want to accept it either. Not then, seven weeks pregnant and knowing she was going to keep it. Instead she told him she wanted him to delete all of the nudes he'd ever taken or she'd ever sent him, and stood over him till he'd done it and every photograph seemed like a piece of an intricate puzzle, one she'd spent so long composing and didn't at all want to put away.

Midday on Thursday, Karine's mother came in, all business.

'The girl down in Dr Roche's office is going on maternity in a couple of months,' she said. 'Twenty hours a week and only down the road. You need to put something on a CV for yourself.'

'They're hardly interviewing yet,' Karine said.

'If you tell them you're available there might be no interviewing at all.'

'Mam, I can't just land in on top of them going, "I hear yer wan's boxed, sure I'll pick up the phones for yeh."'

'Isn't that the problem with your generation, girl? How'd you think things ever get done? Go and ask, for God's sake.'

Karine caught Dr Roche going out the door to his lunch and he suggested she go with him to the hotel in Montenotte. She could have a coffee as he ate, win him over. He drove as she explained herself. They arrived and parked and sat and ordered and she was still explaining herself. 'And you've never had a job?' he asked. He wiped his mouth violently, bunched up the napkin and tossed it off to the side.

'Not since I was a teenager,' Karine said.

The hotel bar was decorated in green and taupe and mustard. Karine thought that she would like a sitting room in those colours, then thought that she might only have her own sitting room by the time a fully-grown Diarmaid was filling out his CAO form. She had not put her name down with the council. She didn't want to. She didn't fucking want to.

Certain places did this to her. Something evocative in the decor or the crowd or the orientation, how she was ushered in or left to linger, she didn't know. She would think about the future and not know how to get there and the fear would gather in her chest, rise up her throat, and come out as some different poison.

'My mam and dad made sure we got jobs,' she went on, 'so I stacked shelves in Super Valu. But you know, I took maternity leave in my last year of my degree and when my son was born I went back and made up my hours. I was very focused.'

'Super Valu,' said Dr Roche.

'Oh yeah, the little polo shirt and everything.'

She had stopped going in to the Super Valu job after a couple of months, when Ryan's boss got him the little flat on Blarney Street. She managed to pretend she was going to work for a fortnight more before her mother found out. Karine had thought all hell would break loose but her mother only did the 'I'm so disappointed in you' thing. At that point she had obviously given up on disentangling them and Karine wondered now if her mother ever regretted giving in. If she looked at Diarmaid and thought, *Oh God, you're far too early*.

She started talking about her degree again. She told Dr Roche how lucky she'd been to get the internship in Cork, that for a long time it had looked like she'd be going to Waterford. *Ryan saying fine, they'd get a gaff in Youghal, he'd drive between Cork and Waterford, he'd spend every cent he made on petrol.* She told Dr Roche how her mother's sense of purpose had made such an impression on her, that all she wanted to do was help sick people. *Ryan, bruised, bloodied, delirious, wincing. And desecrated, all that time. In turmoil. Self-medicating. Scared shitless.*

'So why have a baby?' Dr Roche asked, picking up the napkin and blowing his nose.

'You can't ask that in an interview.'

'It's not an interview. I haven't advertised the job yet.'

'I wanted to have a baby,' Karine said, and off his pulled face asked, 'What answer were you expecting? Would you ask me this if I was five years older?'

'Well now, it was bad timing, when you were still in college.'

'The absolute gall of yeh,' Karine said.

Dr Roche gaped. She made a shocked face back at him.

'I was only wondering,' Dr Roche said, 'how you coped with it all. With your studies and internship and all of your plans.'

'You were, yeah. The way you worded that question?'

'There's not a thing wrong with asking how you meet challenges, that'd be integral to the role, wouldn't it?'

Karine stared.

'You haven't mentioned a partner,' Dr Roche went on.

'Neither have you,' Karine said. 'Probably coz it's irrelevant.'

'Is it? In a situation like this, I'd wonder whether the girl I hired had support with things like childcare or if she'd be rushing back home every time there was a hiccup. Is it such a bad thing to ask these days where the father is?'

'It is, actually.'

'And why is that?'

'Because, Dr Roche, if I couldn't pick him out of a line-up it wouldn't be any of your business.'

'It would be if it meant you couldn't do your job.'

'What, coz I'd be slutting around with the patients?'

'Listen here, it's about the level of support—'

'It's about you trying to figure out whether I'm rough or respectable.'

'You won't get far, madam, if you jump down people's throats like that.'

'Thanks, so, I'll just sort out my mouth and I'll be flying it.' She finished her coffee, which was cold and made her want to gag; she made a face and hoped he thought he'd provoked it. 'Did you ever in your life meet a nurse who'd put up with that shit?' she asked, getting up. 'D'you know now what you can do? Take your job and stick it up your arse.'

'Well,' he said, 'good luck with your career.'

'Thanks, hun. Good luck finding a wimpy bitch to answer your phones for you.'

It took her almost half an hour to thunder home, where she told her mother that Dr Roche was a dinosaur to whom she wouldn't give her time because he'd implied she was a stupid tramp and she wouldn't be judged, not by him, not by Dylan, not by Jackie either, because her mother looked neither sympathetic nor angry on her daughter's behalf.

'For God's sake, Karine, you'd want to grow up a bit.'

'You can't ask that in an interview, Mam. It's sexist.'

'I don't know what world you're living in, at all. All well and good blithering on about sexism, but you did get pregnant in college, didn't you? You don't have a job. You've no experience. You're living at home and your child's father could be at the other end of the world again in the morning. Come down off that high horse fierce fast and don't be believing everything you read on the internet.'

Karine pushed her bottom lip out so that her chin might stop wobbling. 'I suppose you think Dylan was right too. Thanks a million, like.'

'Karine, I just want you to have a small bit of cop on. You're nearly twenty-five years of age. Getting offended will get you nowhere, I put up with a lot worse from doctors in my day. Is it just lazy you are?'

Karine took Diarmaid's jacket from the back of the kitchen chair and went to find him to put him into it. Her mother followed. 'Where are you going now?'

'Going to see *the father*,' Karine said. 'The only person I know who doesn't think I'm a lazy bitch.'

Her mother just said, 'Is that jacket warm enough?'

Four, five years ago, they were in bed in his gaff, at the height of it or at the depths of it, at the point at which the only thing that mattered was him in her and what that did to the thoughts in her head. His eyes closed as he said it: 'Jesus, you're such a little slut'. At that moment it was the hottest thing anyone had ever said in the history of human discourse.

In the morning she wasn't so sure. It had been difficult enough to allow herself to want him after he'd been with the girl from Italy, and perhaps this was how he had talked to the girl from Italy. Besides all that Karine was embarrassed. It was like he had grabbed for a toy that wasn't his and assumed to show her how to play with it. Always the way with him, and sometimes this suited her and sometimes it caught her off guard. Honestly, she said to herself, you don't know what you fucking want. She was applying foundation, he was getting dressed. Her cheeks flushed when she said, 'You called me a slut last night.'

He reddened as well, gave a little smile. 'Yeah. I kinda got carried away.'

'What made you think that was OK, like?'

'You're not into it,' he said.

She was into his shoulder blades at that moment. The strip of hair that led down from his bellybutton. His hands.

'It's a bit porny, like,' she said.

He winced. Tsked. Said, 'You cloud my head sometimes.'

163

Still he knew her well enough to say it again at exactly the right time. It wasn't that he knew better than she did what she wanted, only that he knew when she felt obliged to tell him lies.

As soon as Karine was out of view of her house she picked Diarmaid up and carried him. She smiled at anyone who greeted them because she was a sincere and sweet person, she must be a sincere and sweet person because the smiling was instinctive, and she had lost her temper only because Dr Roche deserved it. She had Diarmaid because she wanted to. It was not Diarmaid that made things difficult; it was Ireland, it was the housing crisis, it was the cost of living. It was no high-horse position; it was, rather, a reasonable response to the world she was living in, and she did not overreact out of fear of leaving Diarmaid, nor because of the green and taupe and mustard, the space she'd found herself in, the space she was meant to visualise as motivation. It wasn't wrong to have reservations about moving into the kind of life other people had designed for her based on what was deemed respectable. It wasn't wrong to want only to be with Diarmaid, it was a fairly average goal for a mother. Right now she was not displaying ambition, but she was capable of ambition, capable of clear thinking and problem-solving and she was certainly a sweet and sincere person and so why, why the fuck couldn't she see, years ago, what Tara Duane had done to Ryan?

Almost six years ago she sat with Ryan in a waiting room with sash windows that let in too much light. They had been there fifteen minutes in silence when the nurse called his number; when Karine asked 'Should I come with you?' it was the first thing she'd said to him in this building.

'I don't think you're supposed to'.

She already knew this because she'd been here by herself the previous autumn. Blood test, urine test, questions that had made her weepy. The nurse had been surprised and asked Karine if there was anything else. The service was confidential. She could refer or recommend a counsellor. 'No, no,' Karine had said. 'It's

not like that.' Just that she had a stupid boyfriend and felt guilty.
He had never been with anyone else and now she had.

Imperative to let him think he had balanced it with the girl from
Italy. Revenge for Niall Vaughan at her Debs. She waited in pitiless
light. She imagined what questions the nurse was asking him.
What kind of sex was it? Vaginal? Oral? Anal? Did you use a
condom?

Was it unreal? Did you both come?

Karine had been waiting for Ryan to get sick. It was already
evident how much he needed her so it wasn't that she wanted to
draw attention to his weakness, or show him her worth or the
stuff she was learning. Just there was no artifice in sickness. The
more rattled he felt, the closer he was to the boy she'd fallen in
love with. Having to piss into a tube to be told whether he'd
contracted something pernicious wasn't what she had in mind
and all the same it was like she'd willed it this way. Karine was
eighteen and this apparent adulthood came with new cruelties to
suffer and to deploy. Making him attend the STI clinic was an
entirely reasonable and responsible reaction to his confession,
and yet they both knew that wasn't why she'd done it.

She had always felt like there had to be some sexual reluctance on
her part for the sake of the game or of propriety and he'd tried to
dispossess her of that idea, over and over again. She remembered
how, in the little flat on Blarney Street, he was so concerned with
making her come. But this had been after the terrible thing, and
she didn't know what it meant. How could her satisfaction have
been important if he was in recovery? She thought of him at
sixteen, the deep brown of his eyes unreadable.

Diarmaid wanted to walk. At the entrance to Ryan's estate, he
went rigid in her arms. She put him down and clasped his hand.
He slowed her down. He ambled along the pocked pavement,
blind to the guarded faces of matriarchs standing arms crossed
at dividing walls, at whom his mother sweetly and sincerely
smiled.

*   *   *

Eight years ago, she was in bed with him in the Blarney Street flat. Kissing. Removing clothes. And he said to her, 'Will you show me what to do?'

She laughed. 'Ah, you already know what to do?'

'I mean for you.'

This had been on his mind since he'd run off from his dad's house and they no longer had to fuck in a desperate rush. That she felt good, or that she liked having sex with him, wasn't enough. He wanted her clawing his back, shrieking at the ceiling. They had the time to match their inclinations and this had never been the case before. 'What d'you do when you're on your own, like?' he asked.

'Oh my God,' she said.

'Oh my God what?'

She turned out a pout, an eye roll, but he was earnest. She went red as he said, 'I mean, you know already, you could just . . . I really wanna make you happy, like.' He knotted his fingers in hers, just over the pillow and under his breath, went, 'Show me show me show me.'

She and Diarmaid turned on to Tony Cusack's terrace. She hadn't seen it coming that Ryan would want to stay with his father. Nor had Ryan, she suspected, though whether he'd had a terrible row with Natalie — Natalie could not have been pleased with how things had finished on Inishbofin — or he'd fallen to some tender filial instinct, she didn't know.

They let themselves in. Karine belatedly thought Ryan might not be there, given that it was only after lunch, but he came around the kitchen door with his brows knotted and a helpless smile for his son. 'What are you doing here?' he asked Diarmaid, who laughed and ran into the sitting room to his grandfather.

Karine said, 'We thought we'd swing by.'

They followed Diarmaid and watched him chat with Tony. The television was too loud but Ryan didn't move to turn it down. Tony asked Karine, 'How are you getting on, girl?' but looked mildly reproachful. She was not meant to bring Ryan back to Cork with her. She told Tony, 'Grand, now,' and felt rebuked.

'Will we go for a walk?' Ryan said.

'Tea first?'

He flattened his mouth. They went into the kitchen and he put the kettle on. While he was getting mugs she closed out the kitchen door.

'Quiet here today,' she said.

'I'm the only langer who's hanging around at this hour. What are you at, anyway?'

'I'm the langer who never has anything better to do, Ryan,' she said, and he blinked. The kitchen was cleaner than usual. Things usually left out had been put away. The surfaces had been wiped down. 'Did Mel come to her senses and leave?'

'She's down at the studio with the rest of them.'

'Why aren't you there?'

'Getting my head together. Prescribed. I have that interview in a couple of hours.'

'I forgot,' she said. 'The one where Izzy thought you were going to discuss the ins and outs of drug dealing. But you're hardly going to?'

'Be a death sentence if I did.'

'I hope you're being a small bit dramatic there, boy.'

'I don't know what I'm being.' He bowed his head and pinched his eyebrows and looked at her from under his hand. 'He hasn't shown up yet. Maybe I should root him out myself, or fling myself at his feet, I don't know. Maybe I shouldn't draw attention to myself, maybe I'm nothing to him, maybe it's a good sign.'

'You could go stay with Joseph.'

'No. I have to be here. I want to keep an eye on things. My dad is fucked.'

The kettle clicked off but he didn't move to fill the mugs. He said, 'My dad is fucked,' again.

She agreed that he didn't look great.

'It's not just that,' he said, but didn't elaborate, or remember the tea. He stood with his back to the worktop, pinching the bridge of his nose.

She said, 'Ryan, I am really, really sorry for what happened.'

'No, I'm sorry,' he said. 'I reacted all wrong. Pure scalded-cat job. I'm mortified.'

'I didn't want to hurt you.'

'You didn't hurt me,' he said. 'Let's go for a walk or something, seriously, this isn't the place.'

'It is the place because we have someone watching Diarmaid,' she said, 'and I have so much to talk to you about, I can't figure out where to start.'

'You have nothing to talk to me about, girl, I don't want to talk about it.'

'But you have to talk about it—'

'No, I don't,' he said. 'I was doing all right with it, I didn't make the decision to share it with you. It belongs to me, can we just leave it at that?'

'I wasn't able to see it,' she said. 'I'm so angry with myself.'

'Why would you be able to see it? I didn't tell you.'

'But you tell me everything—'

'I don't tell you everything.'

He opened the kitchen door and went out. He returned with Diarmaid in his arms. He left the door open behind him.

'I broke up with Dylan,' she said.

'Did he do something on you?' he asked. Diarmaid wriggled out of his arms and went after something that caught his eye under the stairs. Ryan took a step after him, just the one.

'I did something on him,' Karine said.

'I wouldn't have told him.'

'Everything's changed, so?'

'You let a story like that out and everything changes.'

'Does it really matter?' she said. 'If I know that about you?'

'Yeah, it fucking matters.'

She raised her voice in return. 'Why does it matter?'

'I don't know,' he said. 'It just does.'

'Dylan wasn't happy with me,' she said. 'He didn't see it coming. I did. I knew it going to Inishbofin, I knew why I was going.' She looked straight at him and he wiped his nose with his cuff and looked off to the left. 'God, it didn't last long, did it?'

'I wasn't planning on Izzy opening her stupid mouth.'

'So your plan was to always have this secret, was it?'

'It doesn't belong to you, for fuck's sake.'

'Maybe you should just go back to Korea,' she said. 'You can be whoever then, around no one who knows you or wants to fully know you.'

'I have three months left on my visa.'

She sucked in her bottom lip. 'What are you getting at?'

She counted and at six seconds he said, 'I dunno. Maybe you're right. Maybe you're all fucking right.'

Nine years ago, and Joseph's dad and step-mam had gone to some wedding so he'd thrown a party. She and Ryan were both fifteen, him only just. They were shifting on the couch, her on his lap, their eyes closed, and his mouth had slowed to the extent that she thought she might actually burst. He whispered, 'Will you go upstairs with me?'

Her blood rushed under her skin; she was hot, almost headachy; she enjoyed a series of revelations; so this was what it meant to badly want someone. They took a suit bag and two shoe boxes off the bed in the box room and lay down in the dark. He was contradictory. His tongue was unhurried but the rest of him was almost shaking, like if she pressed down hard she'd set his muscles fitting.

Things progressed to the point where the hem of her dress was pushed up past her bum; his hand was in her knickers; his jeans were undone; it could definitely happen now; it probably would happen now, only for the wetness at the tip of his penis and the thoughts that pushed into her head. Pre-cum. Sperm. Pregnancy. She said, 'Not here,' and pushed on his shoulders.

And the thing was that saying 'Not here' implied Yes, but somewhere else. Some other time, soon. That the only issue was the location. He protested softly. He stayed over loads at Joseph's so this was practically his bedroom. No one would come in.

Only it was too late. Not here. Not in the dark with their clothes half hanging off and a party throbbing downstairs. The stipulations were in place, and it was irrefutably in motion.

Two days later they went on the hop from school and had sex in his bed and when she looked back on it, it was sweet and kind of perfect and she wished she'd known immediately – as they lay under the thin duvet hardly able to make eye contact, so amazed they were at one another – that he wasn't just using her, that he was hopelessly in love.

Track 6: How It Feels to Be Tamed

Natalie drew up the strategy when we were still in Naples. We'd make waves, her as the manager, me as the artist. A lost tough made to realise his worth by a benevolent toff. Did I know I could speak however many languages? Did I know my mother taught me to read music? Did I know my larynx settled into just the right shape for anthems? It stops being luck when you recognise it and make it work for you.

Natalie says nothing superficial is actually superficial, that meaning comes across in visuals before language. She says no one really moves past first impressions, so once something looks right people will have a hard time believing it's not right. She says there's something about what the two of us together imply that people will get off on. She put time and energy into me. She was the one who told me that because I was underage when it happened, my criminal convictions were spent after three years because I hadn't been convicted of anything since. She was the one who told me to run when we heard J.P. was sick. She said she'd be able to deal with him if he came looking for me, that he wouldn't be stupid enough to fuck with a respectable girl like her. I don't know if it was to do with her being minted or being a sociopath but I believed her. She had me constantly on the wrong foot, almost always confused, but that was because I was watching myself play better and talk better and *present* better and I knew it was betrayal. I brought this up with her when it first started coming up on me, in Berlin. 'Ryan,' she said, sternly. 'You're actually of really good stock on one side.'

When I arrived back in Cork from Bofin, after I'd dropped you and Derry up home, I went to her gaff. She let me in, poured me coffee, sat at the kitchen table, opened her laptop, cleared her throat and said, 'You know, when I hired Mel, you might have said—'

Can I stop you there? I says. Mel was Linda when I knew her. I didn't cop on to it till I arrived on the island and sure I could hardly say something then. Natalie said that I could have, if just to her. I said why would I tell her? I didn't know Izzy would remember some bollocks I was spouting at the Picnic four years ago. Anyway, we had other shit to worry about, if Jimmy Phelan was cornering my dad for word on my location.

Natalie goes, 'But it's so subversive that a middle-aged woman would want to fuck a boy. What height were you even, at fifteen? Were you shaving?'

I don't want to talk about it, I says.

'And you!' Natalie says. 'The balls, if you don't mind the pun. I didn't think you had it in you, y'know, to put it in her. The effect your upbringing had on you. It's amazing.'

Can you stop? I says, but no, she kept going. As far as Natalie's concerned, everyone's just an insect in a jar.

'Do you fantasise about older women?' she goes. 'I don't think I count, I'm only twenty-seven.'

'Can we talk about Jimmy Phelan?'

'Do you expect me to save you from him,' she says, 'when you've been out on Inishbofin, wrenching apart my ambitious album project with your sexual history by day, and having tragic vanilla sex with the mother of your son by night?'

And, y'know, she had me there. I didn't deny it. She told me I needed therapy.

'How It Feels to Be Tamed' isn't about Natalie, but it came from the feeling that she gives me. Like I'm standing lost at a crossroads without my phone, waiting for someone whose name I don't know, in a place where I don't speak the language. And then someone like her comes along and points and says, 'That way, I'll show you.' There are rules I've always been bound to but only became aware of when she told me what they were. 'How It Feels to Be Tamed' is about the ways you're supposed to go, and the ways you're not allowed to go, and the people who made those ways. It's about whoever designed my terrace. Whoever had it that young fellas should provide highs and lows for their betters and then be snubbed or threatened or killed for doing it. Whoever let it come about that *il nord* went one way and *il sud* the other. About Ireland, or Italy, or the EU, or whatever entity has responsibility for me, whatever entity I'm responsible to. Waking up to all of it. Seeing it in the girl who's paving a way for me, and only me, because she likes my eyes or my shoulders or my cock. I was picked for rehoming. Go with Natalie, she'll show you where you sleep now.

Fuck that, though. Fuck the burden of it. Fuck the crawl on the skin with it. Fuck staying away because I was told to stay away. Fuck whatever's for my own good.

Is that too heavy? Y'know, you give it drums, a little electronic swagger, get the feet tapping, and maybe no one will hold it against you.

I wasn't surprised when Medbh Lucey got on to Natalie. I'd been expecting a Medbh Lucey for a long time. Natalie prepared me for it. We did practice interviews. She wrote me statements and made me say them back to her. This was my therapy, I think, this was her protecting the album and re-educating an ungrateful protégé. I wondered if she'd ask how I could trust her to keep quiet about all the things I'd done wrong in Cork and Naples and Dublin and Liverpool and Berlin. I wondered if she trusted me to not do anything stupid like get arrested and say the wrong things to the cops. Or tell you everything. All I'd done. All she'd shown me.

'I'm not covering for you any more,' Jessica said. 'Mr Love's catching on and my dad'll kill me if I lose this job.' Georgie said things like, 'I appreciate it,' and, 'I'm sorry, girl,' soothing, deceitful things she'd never had a knack for, so Jessica huffed on the other side of the phone and said, 'Sorry, Georgie, next time he asks me what you're doing, I'm just gonna say I don't know.'

'Fine,' Georgie said. 'Then I suppose I'm staying in Ireland.'

'So if I don't keep lying for you, you're not coming back? That's bloody ridiculous.'

The last packing up of an entire life had felt as it should have felt: significant, substantial. This was down to Ryan Cusack. Before he'd come along with his handgun and his conscience, Georgie had been fading, till she was sure that through her others could see stone walls, traffic on roads, the glittering Lee. Her activities she undertook mechanically, as though if she were more contraption than woman, she'd have been less see-through. She had unwittingly invited the jolt of him. Who'd have thought her drifting around the city, asking if anyone had seen her boyfriend, would piss off so many people? She was like a child with a Ouija board. He'd come in snarling.

This latest packing up of an entire life was far too easy, though she thought she was just dazed, and, with the ease of being dazed, mechanical again. She fucked up her call with Mr Love. She'd planned to insinuate a sob story. He would draw her out and feel terrible for her. He would be too mindful of his gender and their imbalance of power to ask for verifiable details. Being a Christian, he would allow her the leave she needed. She'd appeal to his indoctrinated nature. But she hadn't been able to steer the conversation gracefully. She had sounded shrill and then petulant.

'If I don't see you at work on Monday morning,' he said, 'I'll have to assume you've left the position.'

'I honest to God can't make it Monday morning, Mr Love.'

'That's a shame. You're an asset, you know.'

It was a good thing to be called an asset but it wasn't an emotive word. Something mechanical in it. An asset, a useful object, a thing that performed usefully. Georgie didn't like the word 'perform', or any word that might pertain equally to sex and contraptions. For much of her time with Robbie, performance reviews were delivered online by strange men who claimed to have had sex with her. *Very poor GFE*, they said. *Very defensive. A bad actress.* Hardly an asset. Better if she were more mechanical, but she always had unsightly humanity poking through. *Put me off my anal, let me tell you.*

She phoned her flatmate and said she was going to stay in Ireland. Her flatmate said she better call the letting agency, because she wasn't going to make up the balance of the rent. What was she going to do about her stuff? Georgie had originally hoped Jessica could be wheedled into collecting it, but Jessica was no longer an ally, so Georgie was forced into a stock take. What she'd accumulated was worth far more than the cost of the return flight. She was annoyed with herself for being surprised. Of course it was worth more than the return flight; hadn't Georgie been accruing straight-legged trousers and court shoes and bangles and bed linen for years?

'I'll come over for it,' Georgie said.

Outside of this kind of thing – this mechanical undertaking – the sloughing off of this life without the promise of a better one was undemanding, as if she did not even have to be fully awake for it to happen. The path ahead arranged itself in flat slabs before each dreamy footfall. Going back to London was unthinkable. It wasn't just about revenge, or what she'd set in motion. It would have made sense for her to retreat now to a safe distance, the boiling water flung at the wasps' nest. It was to do with things making sense here, Ireland providing a sort of blatancy she hadn't felt in her years away. There was friction to the mechanics in London, which was perhaps not the worst thing but it was not the right thing either. She hadn't chosen to leave and so therefore she would never be fully comfortable away.

Dramatically, she thought of the famine emigrants, the indentured servants, the boys sent to Van Diemen's Land.

She inspected her bank balance and flew to London with a couple of empty suitcases from Penneys, which she filled tidily and mechanically. She dropped her key to the letting agents and went straight back to the airport. She was terrified that Jessica had somehow found out about her visit and would intercept her to demand the return of the mobile-home key.

She worked on her memoir with Medbh. They settled on an outline and Georgie stuck rigidly to it, wanting to examine nothing except that which she had that day prepared for. It wasn't easy, she told Medbh. Dredging was bad for the soul. Medbh firmly disagreed.

'It might feel like that now,' she said, 'but it is so much healthier to talk about these things. What did shame ever do for Ireland?'

'It's not just shame,' Georgie said.

Old news was stagnant. Even remembering an earlier version of Georgie felt regressive. She was betraying the woman in the straight-legged trousers. And the enterprise made her nostalgic, which she didn't appreciate. When she remembered girls she'd worked with, she found herself missing a few of them. She wondered how they were and whether they'd done runners, too. If she might find them on social media. If that would be appreciated. *Remember Shitarse from up the country? Luna was the only one who'd take him. Remember, Luna? God, you had no standards at all! Was it smack you were on or what?* No. Hardly appreciated.

'Luna?' Medbh asked.

'Not her real name. Duh.'

'It's sad that you didn't know each other's names when really there are few workplaces so intimate—'

'I knew their names,' Georgie said. 'Just professionally they didn't use them, so why should I use them here? It's respect, like.' The truth was she couldn't remember all of the girls' names. Mariella was Masha. Luna was Ruth. There was a Mary, whose working name she couldn't remember. She remembered managers' names. There were fewer managers than girls. If a punter told her his name, she would have made a point of immediately forgetting it. She didn't have fond memories of any punter because when they weren't spiteful pricks they were deluded gobshites. She could have bitten the knobs off the ones who brought her presents.

Medbh had an eye for detail. With her suggested tweaks Georgie's stories became more evocative and less true. The truth didn't matter so much as the effect, Medbh said. There is first the story and then the point of the story. An object only loosely held becomes a tool with intent. It was best that there was a point to Georgie's doing this. *A point to Georgie*, she might have added.

When Georgie asked what preparation Medbh was doing for her interview with Ryan Cusack, Medbh laughed.

'Oh my God, Gia,' she said. 'Will you relax?'

Georgie felt there was a lot at stake but she couldn't get this through to Medbh, not having the right words without Medbh's prodding, or being capable only of the most mechanical relayed stories. He looked unassuming to Medbh's eyes. Like he *smelled* nice. He had always smelled nice and yet look how he'd made shit of Georgie's life. Not looking like a thug while thugging around the city was a strategy; only legitimate people like Medbh could afford to be conspicuous.

The interview was scheduled for a Thursday evening in the Riverbank Inn. Georgie came into town and hung around the university – the last place anyone would find her, and the last place she'd find any of them – and waited for Medbh to phone her. Medbh called earlier than Georgie had anticipated, and they arranged to meet back at her flat. Medbh was home before her, and had the kettle on. She said she hadn't got all she wanted out of him. Certainly no confessions. To which Georgie smiled bitterly.

'Can I listen to the recording?' she asked.

'Oh, I don't know if it's worth your time,' Medbh said.

'Of course it's worth my time.'

Medbh dithered, irritably, but in the end put her phone on the table and opened the app. The file was called '230395 cusack urchin' and its duration wasn't at all long enough.

'So there's me, him and Natalie Grogan,' Medbh told Georgie. 'I guess enjoy?'

MEDBH: So thanks for doing this. It's a very exciting time, *The International Recordings* is great. How are you feeling about the whole thing?

RYAN: Grand, yeah.

Through time or subterfuge, his voice sounded softer than Georgie remembered. She put her elbows on the table.

MEDBH: Right now you're in the studio. How's that going?

RYAN: Grand. We're just putting it together now. We did a couple of weeks on Inishbofin up in Galway, writing and stuff. Digging it out. I think it sounds good.

NATALIE: The album is something we're all really excited about. What you have is five musicians, each with their own ideas, it's been a democratic process and like *The International Recordings*, it's really worked out. We can't wait to share it. This album is about home, identity, very much a post-Crash album, very much of the themes that come to the fore when there's any discussion about how our generation experiences this new Ireland. It's going to mean a lot to a lot of people.

'She sounds posh,' Georgie said.

'I don't know if that's fair,' Medbh said.

MEDBH: Thanks. You agree with that projection, Ryan?

RYAN: I dunno. It's more personal than Natalie's making it sound. You saw the manifesto yoke. Art and honesty, the rules of revelation or whatever.

MEDBH: So you're digging deep?

RYAN: You can't mean anything to anyone if it means nothing to you, y'know? People pick up on that.

MEDBH: Has it got a name?

RYAN: That's a last-minute thing, I'd say.

He gave a short laugh, as if he were embarrassed.

MEDBH: Let's go back to the beginning. Was music always important to you?

RYAN: Oh yeah. My mam had it, like. She studied it for a couple of years in university, then later she used to sing at weddings, stuff like that. There are six of us so she didn't have much time for it, but she taught me how to play and read music, so . . . Yeah, I grew up with it. My dad doesn't play but he's always got some album on. When I was a small fella I was listening to a lot of Stone Roses, Frank and Walters, Underworld. And then Radio Friendly and stuff.

MEDBH: So you aren't exactly rebelling with what you do now.

RYAN: No, no. I'm actually pure boring when you realise I didn't have a hand in any of it.

MEDBH: So did you think of following in your mother's footsteps, doing music at university?

RYAN: No, that door wasn't open to me. My own fault, like. I left school at f—, sixteen. But y'know, I did it in my own way, so I suppose it worked out.

Medbh paused the playback and said, 'He was going to say fifteen there, right?'

'I think so,' Georgie said. She put her chin in her hands and looked at the phone. 'I didn't know that his mother was a musician. Makes sense. Where else would he learn to play piano?'

'It doesn't really matter, does it? It's just colour.'

'Fifteen or sixteen, that's just colour too, so.'

'No, it's not, that's important when it comes to profiling.' Off Georgie's frown she added, 'Varying ages of criminal responsibility, I mean.'

'I met him when he was that age,' Georgie said. 'Fifteen or sixteen.'

'Really? Christ. You didn't . . . uh . . .'

'Fuck him?'

Medbh returned Georgie's glare. 'I'm still learning about the world you lived in, Gia. You can't decide now what is and isn't a stupid question. This grudge you have is personal, isn't it?'

'He never fucked me,' Georgie growled, though she was remembering how easy he found it to lure her off the street the night he failed to kill her. She had underestimated him when he pulled up alongside her and told her to get in his car. She had thought that men were only ever just men and his not being a boy any more meant he wanted what she'd had to give every man before him.

'How did you meet him, then?'

'How do you think? I bought drugs from him.'

'When he was fifteen or sixteen?'

'Don't be shocked, girl. They have their own versions of pimps, the baby dealers. It's not like the big guys wait for them to finish school before they turn them out.'

Medbh nodded for a few seconds before tapping the screen.

MEDBH: You used to run club nights, right?

RYAN: Here, actually, in this place. Me and Colm, another one of the brains behind the Catalyst thing. This is where all that craic started. And then, y'know. Expanded. We did the gigs in Dublin and then that crossover in Berlin.

MEDBH: And you were in Berlin for a while?

RYAN: Only a few months.

MEDBH: Must have been exciting.

RYAN: I was kept busy, like. I did this sound-engineering course, just a short one, to get some formality on to what I already knew. I met my buddy Ji-hun there, turns out he knows the instructor on an unreal course in Korea and like where else would you be going, if you're into sound? So I dunno. We made it work. I went out there two months before it started, straight into Korean classes. Korean is tough. I never had a problem with languages but it shook me.

MEDBH: You have other languages?

RYAN: Yeah, sure my mam was Italian. So that, and the Neapolitan language as well.

MEDBH: And German?

RYAN: Fuck, no. Just enough to get me into Berghain. Good luck finding someone to speak German to you in Berlin.

MEDBH: You say your mother *was* Italian?

RYAN: She died when I was eleven.

MEDBH: I'm sorry.

RYAN: It's grand. Using past tense is probably wrong, I dunno.

MEDBH: So distance was no impediment, then. When you and the others decided to make *The International Recordings*.

RYAN: Doesn't have to be. Producers have been doing it for years. You get a file and add to it. I've remixed people I've never met. Aimee Keohane, never met her and I was in the same city as her.

MEDBH: I didn't know there were remixes of Aimee Keohane's music.

RYAN: Her first single was me. The original was a guitar song. I put the piano and the beats in.

NATALIE: Sorry, Medbh? That's off the record. Ryan isn't credited on that track so we have no claim to it, officially.

RYAN: Yeah. I signed it away. I got 200 euro for that and she made a bomb off it, it's gas. It was a sign, though. Keep doing what you're doing, boy, you can be all right at this.

MEDBH: What were you doing before that?

RYAN: Same thing as I'm doing now, just under the radar. I didn't just fluke something with Aimee Keohane on my first go.

MEDBH: You made enough money though production to send yourself to Berlin and Seoul, so there was a real measure of success, at least financial success.

RYAN: You can make money at it, no one needs to have heard of you to make money at it.

His tone was defensive. Georgie wagged her finger in the air and Medbh gave her a wry look.

NATALIE: Medbh, it was actually Catalyst Music that sent Ryan to Berlin. Of course by then we'd seen the club nights grow, and the remixes et cetera were all put through the company, as a management agency, see?

MEDBH: Actually, Ryan, I wanted to ask you about that. It must have been great to be able to travel. I was wondering if that wasn't daunting, even taking into account that you were sponsored by Catalyst Music.

RYAN: Dunno what you're getting at.

MEDBH: Well, as I said to Natalie in my emails, I'm particularly interested in you as a working-class voice, whether you feel some obligation to your community, in that regard?

RYAN: Yeah, but that's a funny angle to come at it from. That I'd be freaked out by travel.

There was a four-second silence.

RYAN: I spent every summer till I was fifteen in Italy, like. I just told you I speak four languages.

MEDBH: Not at all daunting, then. Do you feel an obligation to your community?

RYAN: What's that mean?

MEDBH: Maybe my language is too formal. Do you consider. yourself a working-class artist? If you look at the titles of the tracks on *The International Recordings*, you could say there's a common theme. 'Beg, Borrow and Steal'; 'No Soul to Sell'; 'Collector'; 'If I Gave it All Up?'

RYAN: I'd say you're reading into things. Have you listened to those songs?

MEDBH: I have. I couldn't help but wonder whether there was a narrative emerging. Where did the titles come from?

RYAN: 'Beg, Borrow and Steal', that's a working-class thing, is it? That's what I look like? A beggar or a debtor or a thief?

Another four-second silence, enough to make Georgie uncomfortable, which she supposed was the point. She looked at Medbh and Medbh nodded.

RYAN: Fucking song's about a fucked-up relationship. Nothing to do with money. Y'know my grandad's a pharmacist. In Naples. My mam went to university in London. I'm not fucking scum, like.
NATALIE: Medbh, you mean more along the lines of getting by, right?
MEDBH: Yeah, exactly. Thanks. So you don't consider yourself working class? That's interesting. To reject that label feels political?
RYAN: I don't reject it. Don't know what it means to you, is all.
MEDBH: I don't equate it with scum, certainly. You're quite sensitive about this. Have you had that accusation levelled at you before?
RYAN: I might have.
MEDBH: As I was preparing for this interview I came across a number of allegations online. I'm sure you know about this, Natalie, because they were largely in the form of comments on the band's social media channels. You know what I'm talking about, Ryan?

Georgie flapped her hands. Medbh frowned and held a finger to her lips.

RYAN: See, I knew this is what you were angling for. Just come out and ask it, like. You don't have to be snakey.
MEDBH: OK, well, talk to me about those allegations.
RYAN: They're comments.
MEDBH: They're persistent.
RYAN: Some fuckers have too much time on their hands.

MEDBH: So there's no truth in them?

RYAN: Tell me what you read.

MEDBH: That you were a drug dealer.

There was another silence. 'Why would you ask him that?' Georgie cried, and Medbh frowned and pointed at the phone.

MEDBH: Would you like to respond, or—

RYAN: Fucking tabloidy bang off that.

MEDBH: I suppose—

RYAN: I'm a hard worker, like. Took me ages to realise that because as a kid you put 'hard work' and 'school' together and I was a little bollocks at school, my mam died and I was fucking miserable, I was constantly fucking angry. I didn't work hard at school, therefore I must be a lazy prick. I figured it out after I left, wait, I'm not a lazy prick, I'll do sixteen-hour days for you, if it's worthwhile and if I'm good at it. D'you know?

MEDBH: Yeah.

RYAN: And when I was growing up, like fourteen, there or thereabouts, I didn't have fucking anything. My dad couldn't keep a hold of money. He'd just piss it away. My grandparents in Napoli would send him money but when it was time to buy schoolbooks or uniforms or just fucking everyday clothes or fucking cereal or bread or fucking whatever, he didn't have a bob. Y'know what that's like? It is fucking mortifying, Medbh. You've to go to school, you don't have the fucking books, your trousers are too short, you worry you're stinking coz there was no shower gel, no soap, no toothpaste, and you fucking starving coz there was fuck-all for breakfast. So when I had the bobs I'd buy as much grass as I could and sell it to people who actually were lazy pricks. Middleman at fourteen. Gonna blame me for that?

Three seconds. Georgie sucked her lips in.

RYAN: Means to an end.

MEDBH: How long did that go on for?

RYAN: Long as it had to.

MEDBH: Which was?

RYAN: D'you know what, you're like a fucking guard.

NATALIE: I mean, it just goes to show, these are sensitive topics. We need to bring these issues to the fore.

RYAN: We do, yeah.

He tsked.

RYAN: This is my fucking problem, it's not everyone else's problem, it's not the Northside's problem. Majority of my neighbours are grand, like. They had cop on and their young fellas and young wans turned out OK. This is my thing.

MEDBH: So how long did it go on for?

RYAN: No length.

MEDBH: Did you ever get caught? Get in trouble?

RYAN: No.

MEDBH: No?

RYAN: Oh yeah, your source has it that I was some sort of boss. That I was selling so much I managed to buy my way into real life, some shit like that?

MEDBH: What's alleged isn't that you were just a teenage entrepreneur.

RYAN: I was, though. I turned twenty-four in March, all of this happened when I was a kid. If I was a boss, I think I'd have had a harder time coming out of it than I did.

MEDBH: What do you mean?

RYAN: I mean fellas who earned fortunes would hardly have fucked off into the music business at twenty.

MEDBH: I don't think that's a stretch.

RYAN: It is a stretch.

MEDBH: You'd know?

RYAN: I don't know anything about it. I was a fucking amateur.

MEDBH: Only I guess the natural question is if you were able to funnel some of the profits from that enterprise into, as you say, legitimate business?

NATALIE: Can I reject that in the strongest possible terms,

185

Medbh? Catalyst Music has never benefitted from any illegal activity and we would take a very dim view of anyone suggesting anything of the sort.

MEDBH: Of course, of course.

In the five-second silence that followed, Georgie said, 'He's lying. Twenty, twenty-one, he was still at it. That's when he—'

RYAN: D'you know who's been talking about me, Medbh?

Georgie lost the end of her sentence.

MEDBH: No, but I think it's an interesting thing to come up now. I can understand why it might be frustrating for you.

RYAN: Someone doesn't want me to do well. Someone or some one of many, fuck it.

MEDBH: You think it's begrudgery?

RYAN: No. It's genuine. Genuinely whoever this is coming from has a problem with me and the shit I did to try and make things easier for myself. It's not fucking jealousy, like. No one likes drug dealers, do they?

MEDBH: If you were fourteen at the time, people would allow for complexities.

RYAN: You think people are nice to fourteen-year-old boys?

MEDBH: A fourteen-year-old is a child.

RYAN: Literally no one gives a shit, Medbh. Once your voice breaks you're not a child, you're a fucking problem.

MEDBH: Must get more and more difficult to prove them wrong, then. Or even more difficult to want to bother to prove them wrong.

RYAN: That's what I'm trying to do now.

MEDBH: What would you tell your younger self, if you could speak to him? How would you steer him right?

RYAN: I wouldn't try to steer him. I'd tell him I never met a moral person who wasn't on some level a thundering hypocrite. D'you want to ask me about the people I sold to?

MEDBH: Sure.

Ryan tsked again.

RYAN: You didn't ask though, did you? It's all about me and where I went wrong. Who the fuck buys drugs from a teenager, Medbh?
MEDBH: Who?
RYAN: Other teenagers, is it? Fair play, girl, yeah. If I say it was a cottage industry, does it leave me off the hook? And everyone else along with me?
MEDBH: Well, this is a great opportunity to explain the context. As you say, you're trying to prove people wrong, so treat this as a second chance—
RYAN: You fucking know.
MEDBH: Sorry?
RYAN: Who's claiming me. You fucking know.
MEDBH: Honestly, Ryan, I don't know what you mean.
RYAN: Why am I so fucking interesting? Who's so bothered about what I get up to? And where do you come in?
MEDBH: I'm just looking to do a profile piece for the Culture section. That's all. I am genuinely interested in a tie-in with social issues, I think these are the questions we're asking now, they're necessary.
RYAN: Yeah, very worthy. Listen, I've to make tracks. Oh. Ha. Literally. Whoever it is that wants to gossip in your ear about me, tell them there's bigger shit going on in Ireland than a langer like me trying to write a few fucking songs, will you?
MEDBH: OK, well, another thing I'm really interested in, as a journalist, is following the money. It's my job to examine corruption, see what's really going on and where.
NATALIE: Sorry, Medbh, I have to hurry you.
MEDBH: I'm not alleging anything about Catalyst Music. Ryan's right, this is more about ... I hate using the term 'Gangland Ireland', but we're talking organised crime here.
RYAN: Fourteen-year-olds selling draw isn't what anyone'd call organised.

MEDBH: Sure, but it's one aspect of the market, isn't it? And you have a platform now, Ryan. So you are a voice. And if you were really so inconsequential, you have very little to worry about, talking to me.

RYAN: I don't know nothing about gangland anything.

MEDBH: No, I think you do. I think you have things to say and I think I could help you say them.

NATALIE: Thanks so much, Medbh. Listen, let me give you a call tomorrow and we'll see if we can't put some sort of shape to this?

MEDBH: Ryan.

NATALIE: Yeah, I'll give you a bell. Thanks again.

MEDBH: Ryan, do you have my number?

RYAN: In a fucking manner of speaking, I do, girl.

MEDBH: The story gets told. Whether in your own words or someone else's.

RYAN: You threatening me?

MEDBH: Just telling you where I stand. As a journalist.

RYAN: As a journalist, OK. Well. I'll look forward to someone else's words on where I went wrong, and someone else's tales on the fucking cunts who own me.

MEDBH: All right, well, you know where I am . . . Bye, guys . . . Jesus Chr—

The recording ended. Georgie leaned forward. 'You think he has things to say and you think you could help him say them?'

Medbh was quickly peeved. 'Elevating this from petty revenge into something beneficial to everyone.'

'That lad pointed a gun at me. It's beneficial to everyone if they know about that. Then they can choose whether or not to listen to him. How is that petty? Did you really just ask him to talk to you the way I'm talking to you? After all I told you about him?'

'Kind of obvious you were both victims,' Medbh said.

'What?'

'You said as much yourself. What did you call them, baby

dealers? There's a lot in this. The gender divide. Drugs for boys, sex work for girls. What does that say about the various gangs in Ireland? What does it say about Ireland? Imagine having both sides of that story, Gia!'

Georgie could only say, 'I don't believe this.'

'Look, Gia. I want you to see the bigger picture, to realise the importance of your testimony. Ryan Cusack? He's *ashamed* of himself. You know how powerful that can be? He will talk about this, he's got snitch written all over him. And also? So not dangerous. He was more interested in protecting himself than trying to intimidate me, which is what you had me expecting. That said, I promise you'll never have to meet him, OK? I understand he's a symbol of a side of Ireland you'd rather not have to deal with any more. And I promise I'll never expose you in any way.'

'What about all you said about women's stories and the patriarchy?'

'It's patriarchal systems that force boys like him into these roles, Gia. You heard him. Never had a pot to piss in, so he took drastic measures to get what he feels the world owed him. This is bigger than a few tawdry stories about sad bastards purchasing sex.'

'That's all my story is to you?'

'Of course not, that's why I've been so hard at it, contextualising it for you.'

Georgie grabbed her bag and got up.

Medbh smiled tenderly. 'OK,' she said. 'You go if you need to. But I know you're smart enough to understand, once you calm down.'

'You're so fucking naive,' Georgie said. 'No wonder he was able to wrap you round his little finger.'

'How is that wrapping me round his little finger? He panicked and stormed off the same way you're storming off. And he'll come back the same way you'll come back. Do me a favour,' she said, as Georgie went for the door. 'Stop with the online campaign. We have him where we want him, nothing more to be gained from pushing that agenda.'

*   *   *

Georgie had seen this coming. She had become attuned to disappointment. It was her theory that this was a female thing, not the instinct, but the disappointment: how the world as it was contrasted with the world as it should be. She didn't ask for much. That there might be an equal chance of things going to shit for fellas, that was all.

Now she wondered what the fuck she was doing here, under the disappointment. She considered phoning Mr Love and pleading for clemency. She would say that Brexit had made her feel unsafe. Mr Love was not a Leaver. She was an asset and would come to her senses. She thought, *Yes, I'll do that.* Mechanically. Though of course she would let on that she was driven by emotion, being female. She pre-empted being disappointed with Mr Love for believing her to be an emotional mess. But was she not being an emotional mess? She had given up her flat and her job to enact paltry revenge, which, after all that, was going to work out in favour of her target. She thought, *Yes, I'm an emotional mess.* Mechanically. She tapped her feet off the floor and scratched her jaw. Her options were too many. Free will was a curse. Someone should have put a hand on her shoulder and told her to sit down. Someone. She went through candidates. Mechanically. Medbh, that first day in the coffee shop. Hand on shoulder, Georgie's arse firmly back in the seat. Will you get over yourself, you crazy bitch? Ryan Cusack made several appearances on this list. Instead of threatening to kill her if she came home, he could have calmly explained why Stansted was her only option. Those times she'd met him to buy coke from him, he could have told her graphic tales about customers without septums, girls who went blue at house parties. Day One he might have said to her, *I'm only fifteen, and one day a woman in a honeybee-print dress will make you feel terrible about this.*

You just didn't know what was going on inside anyone else's head, therefore all movement was deceptive and mechanical. One might think, watching Georgie board the bus to Millstreet, that she was newly homesick, keen to feel the country earth beneath her feet after being tossed about half her life by cities. One might think she was feeling bad for her parents, or perhaps that she wished to take up with her parents the issue of why neither had ever put a hand on her shoulder and told her to sit down.

None of the above. She moved, one foot in front of the other, in this direction. The programmed woman. Wind her up and point her thataway. This is what daughters did. They popped home for visits.

It was a fifteen-minute walk from the town centre to her parents' house. It used to be a walk by hedgerows, crossing at points where she'd be more visible to traffic. Now there was a path most of the way, a housing estate that was no longer new. There was the sound of insects and family cars. One neighbour's bungalow had gone to ruin, its once manicured garden maddened by freedom.

Home was a grey two-storey with a small lawn and two ash trees in front, blocking the light to the sitting room. She knocked and when her mother opened the door Georgie smiled a routine smile. She sat at the kitchen table with routine ease and, as daughters do, accepted the cup of tea. When her father said she was looking well, Georgie said, 'Ah, sure,' with routine modesty.

'You got the kitchen done,' she said to her mother.

'Georgina, it's been fifteen years.'

Time flies and had crashed into the faces of her parents. Her father was seventy-three. In the city a seventy-three-year-old wasn't so old, and so in the city he'd look eighty. He had his cap off on the table in front of him. His fingers were gnarled and yet fat. The skin under her mother's eyes was an almost translucent blue and it brought out indigo in her irises; Georgie hadn't noticed before.

They listened to her talk about London, Friday evening drinks, Mr Love and Jessica, Brigstock Road. About Cork, the redrawing of its boundaries, and regeneration plans. About how her father was right to sell the land. About how people came home in their thirties, about raising families in the country, about seeing places in new light. She had a second cup of tea. Her parents looked at her and not at each other. She talked dismissively of politicians and certain social trends. She suggested the names of old schoolmates they might have updates on. She asked of the comings and goings of the parish. If it were her daughter coming home after half a lifetime, without notice or ceremony, she'd ask her what it all meant, or even what the fuck she thought she was doing. But her parents didn't know how, and this wasn't routine for anybody.

'It's good,' she said, as she came to the end of the things she might possibly say, and felt the machinery seizing up. 'It's good you got the kitchen done. It's good that life went on.'

'We didn't know what to do,' her father said. 'We thought it would be straightforward. The guards would bring you home and . . . I don't remember what we thought we'd do.'

'Give you a talking-to,' her mother said. 'Ground you. We were worried about it. We didn't know how you'd take that sort of thing. You were so saucy, Georgina. The weeks went on. The guards had no interest when you were on the other end of the phone, bold as brass.'

'We've been over this,' Georgie said. She made her face bright.

'I don't blame the guards,' her mother said. 'They don't know how to handle situations like that, sure.'

'We didn't know how to handle it,' her father said to her mother.

'We did not. None of it came naturally. And look what happened.'

'It's just unconventional,' Georgie said. 'It is what it is.'

'You're a grown woman,' said her mother. 'I didn't get you there, I don't even know you.'

'No one ever gets to know their parents till they're adults themselves,' Georgie said. 'We're not as behind as you think we are.'

'One day you might have children,' said Georgie's mother. 'Talk to me then about making up time. We did the kitchen because that was something that was falling down around us we could fix.'

She got up and brought her cup and Georgie's father's cup to the sink and started scrubbing. More mechanics.

Georgie put her hands on her lap. 'I have one,' she said.

'One what?' asked her father, when her mother didn't turn around.

'One child,' Georgie said, and mechanically, so that she might save herself from their expressions, she told her hands that she had a daughter, Harmony Faye Coughlan, who had just turned six, and who lived in East Cork with her father, a pious man, a pillar, a lad who could be trusted around neither bibles nor poker sites, a man led by his emotions who nonetheless always did what was predicted of him. She told them that she did not know what she was meant to do any more than they had known what to do, and that she couldn't tell right from wrong or victim from villain. They watched her, her father sitting and her mother standing, and she did not have to lift her head to know that neither knew the right face to make.

Track 7: Believe in No One

What happened to me didn't belong to you and I felt no need to dig it up for sharing after nine years. I stand by that. So when I say my head was fucked from not being able to talk to you, I mean that being awkward with you actually damaged my sense of myself. I wasn't even that troubled by what had happened the last night in bed in Bofin, definitely not enough to pull away from you the way I had. If I'd been able to talk to you at the time, I'd have told you, Look, girl, just don't hop on top of me because I don't want to be inviting monsters in when I'm fucking you, there are forty other ways I'll fuck you, can we err on the side of caution and just pretend there's no such thing as riding a fella when he's lying flat? But I wasn't able to talk to you, which was a kind of self-harm. My stupid fucked head.

I didn't know what to do with myself. The songs were coming together, and elsewhere my faults were being made sense of. I thought about going back to Seoul but that would have been running away from my own inability to be normal, unfortunately disguised as running away from you. I couldn't leave Diarmaid. Couldn't leave my dad. Every day I made a dozen indelible mistakes. I thought about Lord Urchin falling apart because in not telling tales to Medbh Lucey, I'd inspire her to write a hatchet job. I thought about making up mild stories so that she'd write me off as a waste of time, but even anaemic lies could be enough to get my kneecaps blown off. Meanwhile strangers online analysed or diagnosed me. I read one reply to Anne Alias's daily rants, written by a fella who said he'd boxed the head off me at a house party five years back; he didn't like 'pushers'. I don't remember getting a dawk at a house party except one time from you, but there's nothing you can do about what you get up to in other people's heads. I thought about Medbh. Whether she'd use words like 'pusher' if I didn't do as I was told.

At home in my dad's, I was deep into one of my Luchè/Ntò/Clementino/Rocco chapters, so I was listening to nothing but the confrontational and political and unapologetic and it was making me feel like I had nothing to say and the rest of my life to say it. Why don't the lads get their fucking kneecaps blown off, like? Napoli is a much hairier situation than Cork. In Napoli – in cities all over – you have the dark subculture and music as an observatory on its fringes and here any underworld overlap is overridden by middle-class gobshites wearing gold chains, rapping *ironically*, laughing at junkies. Not that I'm saying ex-dealers need accurate cultural representation, but . . . I mean, it'd be handy.

It was in this state I went to see Gina. She has a first-floor office on Washington Street. I thought first it was going to be like Dan's old office – not exactly a hotspot of lawful enterprise – but no, she's legit. I shouldn't have assumed that I was the only one of the old gang who'd tried to sort themselves out. Gina was as crooked as any of us but only because she was Dan's ould doll. Her natural form was always an innocent craitur.

There was no one else in the office. Gina was typing when I came in. I don't know if you see her ever around town, but God, she looks ordinary. Soft.

She said I had some nerve.

I didn't know how to ask if it was her who was badmouthing me online. I said something like, I'm home and I didn't want you blindsided.

You've a guilty conscience, you mean.

I stood shaking my head even though that's all I am, really, a guilty conscience.

She goes, Ryan, if you have an ounce of decency in you . . .

You'll guess what she asked me. What happened to Dan. *You know*, she goes. *You know.*

I might have gone to see her to prove to myself there was no point in finishing the songs. I was trying to navigate by jumbled frequencies, convinced there was no underworld overlap and looking for it all the same. I told her what I told the guards when they hauled me in the week Diarmaid was born: I don't know what happened to Dan. Expanded with what I could never have told the guards: I know he pissed off the wrong people. My heart broke when he went on the missing list but I wasn't surprised.

Gina knew the context, she didn't want any more context.

I don't know where he is, I told her, and I don't.

Then who does, Ryan?

Dealing creates these weird physical obstructions. It's not just that there are things you can't say, it's that there are things you're no longer able to say. Certain facial expressions blocked off. It's like you're hunched over, cagey, for so long your bones knit to keep you that way. I couldn't answer her because I'm well trained. Conditioned. J.P. knows. Shakespeare. I know part of it. I know Dan's dead coz I saw him die. What they did with him, I don't know. Gina wants confirmation because she already fucking knows but without someone else saying it, she has no one to blame, she can't hide from her own guilt. We all fucking know and no one can say.

Can you find any of that in 'Believe in No One'?

It came from two places. The first was all of the confrontational and political and unapologetic stuff I was listening to, which, after it made me feel useless, started making me feel obligated. If no one else was saying it, then shouldn't I? The second came out of that: the fundamentals of revelation, the workings of the voice. How it depends on will. How easy it is to silence a fella. And in a sphere like the one in which I'd spent the best part of a decade, how you can have networks of silence, all those twists and turns of fear. People who let on they know stuff know nothing. People who do know can't say.

Silence as self-harm.

I think 'Believe in No One' is the first angry song I wrote. It's not coincidental that it's the most electronic of the tracks on the album. I warped the full sounds of the guitar or piano in post and hid them behind shifting inorganics. It sounds class but at the end of the day the swagger comes from artificial enhancements. And it works, y'know. I feel bigger when I sing it.

Anyway, Gina wasn't the orchestrator of the campaign, was she? She's just another fucking idiot trying to keep the head down.

Izzy was sacked. 'Well, sorry to burst your prudish bubbles,' she said – she actually fucking said! – 'you can't sack me, because I quit.' Mel was asked to step in, and Izzy withdrew into an official dispute with Natalie about ownership of riffs and motifs. Before long she was back on YouTube, alluding to artistic assassination.

The studio was as it should be: instruments with the patina of hard-earned articulation, carpet in the live room, a desk bigger than Kelly's bed, soft indoor gloom and everything sounding true as a bell struck once. Senan, the engineer, and Triona, the manager, were calm and decent. There was biscuits and beer in the green room. Mel, Orson and Davy played with the scratch tracks and nailed more sounds than they had any right to.

The cousins lagged behind. Joseph brooded over Izzy. When he played his own lines he made mistakes, and when he didn't make mistakes he said he'd made mistakes. He told Mel and Orson and Davy to go home, he wasn't keeping them, when they argued that his last take had been grand.

'Fucking grand,' he said. 'Fuck off.'

Similar caginess from Ryan. He hadn't finished the lyrics. He said he'd get there, that the thing was to get the rest of it right and then he could finish the vocals. There was a short rebellion from Davy and Orson. If they didn't know the meaning of what they were meant to be playing, then they were just playing *to*, really. They said he was making them feel like session musicians. He said he didn't fucking mean to, for fuck's sake. They held their hands up. He put his energy into playing the piano lines and Mel watched and was inspired and imagined herself in his place. Through the piano lines he was reinstated as a template. When they were all together in the green room, and when Triona made a beeline for her for sororal conversation and support, she was down on herself for not having grown out of this compare and contrast.

On Thursday she found Joseph on one of the green room couches, watching Izzy's latest vlog. He didn't turn it off when she came in. She sat opposite him and took a biscuit.

'This is by no means confined to the boys of Lord Urchin,' a tinny Izzy said. 'Ask any woman in the industry and she'll have a similar tale.'

Joseph rubbed his forehead.

'If Ryan decides that that's the story he wants to tell, then of course I'll be surplus to requirements. I can't project his kind of energy. He will say that it's not a sexist move, because he's replaced one woman with another. But the woman I've been replaced with is far better for him. Quieter. Less experienced. Never said a word during the writing sessions.'

Though Mel didn't open her mouth, Joseph raised a finger and shushed her.

'You'll probably know by now the drama around Ryan, the shit he's alleged to have made money from. On the record, I have no idea what the truth is. I do know that it looks like there's more value in going along with it and making that part of the band's identity than in denying it, so, I don't know, keep an eye out for his video essay on how underprivileged and desperate he was, I'd say.'

Joseph closed the video and held his phone between his knees. Mel took out her own phone and scrolled Instagram. 'Why would she say this shit?' Joseph asked.

'Guess she doesn't want to be associated with skangers,' Mel said. She didn't look up.

'While telling the world that the skangers kicked her out for not being a skanger. And we can hardly explain why she really got the shove, can we?'

'I'd rather we didn't, yeah.'

'What a mess,' he said, and, remembering himself, added, 'You're a lifesaver, Mel. Money doesn't grow on trees for studio bookings, us being skangers, and all.'

'I just think it's good experience,' Mel said.

'That all?'

'No one's asked me,' she said, 'but spending all day with a fella who fucked my mam when he was fifteen is very unpleasant. I'm getting a kick out of the tunes, not out of the situation.'

'Don't feel obliged,' he said.

'I don't,' she said.

Though she did, in some manner too unusual for her to get her head around. Obliged to see it through, or to the music she was trying to perfect. Or to understand Tara through Ryan. No, that was stupid. She understood Tara well enough, even if she'd never really known her. Blood made a person intuitive. She felt obliged to see it through for the love of a good story. *Wait till I tell you about this particular fella*, she would say at a gathering of admirers some years in the future. *Wait till I tell you how I figured out all I needed to know about myself: that I was a bit of a voyeur and a bad mimic.*

She left Joseph and went into the live room, meeting Orson and Davy on the way out. They asked if she wanted to come for some fresh air, but between them she could see Ryan at the piano, so she declined, went into the live room and waited for him to pay her attention.

He, too, was sitting with his phone in his lap, though he wasn't playing a video, he wasn't even scrolling.

'Did you find a gaff yet?' he asked, after a couple of minutes.

'How would I have?' she said.

'This is why nothing's getting fucking finished,' he said.

'It's only Thursday.'

'You're fucking torturing me.'

'I'm getting you out of a fix, I thought.'

'Staying in my fucking dad's house. For fucking free. Like he doesn't have enough to deal with.'

'Fair exchange is no robbery.'

She was determined not to leave before him today, as she'd done all week at his stubborn, silent insistence. He made that task easy. He took off in the early afternoon – a suggestion of Joseph's – so that he could prepare for that evening's interview with the journalist. This was probably not a thing that would have required solemn preparation for anyone else. Perhaps this was why he was so short-tempered, because when she thought about it, it was hardly the worst thing if people knew you'd been seduced by someone older when you were a teenager. It was much worse for her; he could be assumed to have fallen prey to his hormones, whereas she could be tainted by association, raised by a creep, and so raised without morals. She felt affronted by his embarrassment.

She got the bus back to the terrace in the early evening. The Cusack house was peaceful, only Cian in the sitting room, watching a sitcom with an obnoxiously abrupt laugh track, and Niamh in the kitchen, practising dance moves to something equally obnoxious. Mel made herself a toastie and chose the laugh track. Cian didn't have much to say but his was a pleasant sort of indifference. He was twenty-one, tall and strong, quick to smile, dogged about taking nothing seriously. He didn't mind Mel being there, nor would he care if she ran out the door bawling. He didn't ask how her day had been, but made comments about the characters on the television, most of whom he said were some class of langer or another. Mel ate her toastie. The evening sun seeped through the curtains. There was what sounded like a children's riot underway on the green outside.

Ryan came in just after ten and stood in the sitting room doorway.

'Where's my dad?' he asked Cian, who shrugged. 'What?' Ryan said. 'You don't know?'

'I can't be watching him 24/7,' Cian said.

Ryan stared at Cian, then turned to Mel. 'Do you know where he is?'

'No,' she said. 'He wasn't here when I got back.'

'When was that?'

'Around half seven, eight.'

'Hours so,' Ryan said. 'He's gone fucking hours.' He took his mobile out of his pocket and tapped into a call.

'He won't answer you,' Cian said.

Ryan tried three times. In the end he let his arms hang loose and stared into space.

Cian watched, grimacing. 'He's in the Relic,' he said. 'Nowhere else will serve him.'

'If you fucking know, you think you'd go and pull him out of it,' Ryan said.

Cian looked pained, and that was enough for his brother. Ryan went back out the front door. Mel followed and asked herself if she was being nosy, Tara-like, should she want to put a name to it. If he asked – any second now he was going to turn and notice and ask – she could say that his conversation with Cian made her concerned for Tony, who was doing her such a kindness.

'Fuck are you going?' he said, over his shoulder.

'Everything all right, like?' she replied.

That was if 'nosy' could make a synonym for 'ghoulish', because to be Tara-like was to tint benevolent actions with malevolence. Maybe Mel couldn't help herself because she didn't lick it off the stones. It wasn't that she was fond of Tony, because there was nothing left of him to be fond of. So in this particular context she was merely bad-minded, and she could hurry back to the Cusack house and pretend she wasn't bad-minded or she could keep up with Ryan and see what was going on. On the face of it there was nothing wrong with wanting to know, re: her living arrangements, re: her study, re: her impatience with Ryan's embarrassment and the thought that maybe in this he'd have something worse to be embarrassed about.

'I'm just going to get my dad,' Ryan said. 'Is that all right with you, like?'

'How'd your interview go?' she asked.

'Grand.'

'Yeah? She ask you about the dealing thing?'

'You're all business, aren't you?'

'Every day that passes I think maybe this does concern me, like.'

He stopped, briefly, to tell her, 'It doesn't concern you.'

'So I am just a session musician?' she said.

'Yup.' But he didn't tell her to turn back, so she kept on, a few steps back from him.

Tony Cusack was sitting alone at one corner of the counter in the pub Cian said he'd be in. He was leaning over a pint, the head of which had turned the colour of straw. He looked like someone's woe betide.

The place was half-full. They were playing Two Door Cinema Club. It was the season for Thursday night drinks. Mel recognised a handful of people who didn't recognise her, but they recognised Ryan, and nodded to or questioned him, smiling.

Story, boy! Someone told me you were in fucking China!

Hey Ryan, how's tricks?

C'mere timme, those Urchin tunes are fucking daycent and so on; for a lad whose past was catching up with him he sparked a lot of good humour. Mel wanted to be greeted like that, like a person with the capacity to warp the truth behind him. Like a person right in his own skin if not in his own head, so right in it he could do what Ryan had done with her mother at fifteen, to not even have to make such a decision, just be driven to it by fitted skin and opportunity. She couldn't see if he smiled back at any of the people in the pub but she imagined they got from him that sad little closed-mouth grin that had really begun to get on her nerves.

Tony gave no indication that he'd seen Ryan come in but he didn't seem surprised to be interrupted. He took his time looking up to his son's 'What the fuck are you at, like?'

Tony said, 'Ryan,' and half-shut his eyes. 'Ryan,' he tried again, and huffed the air out of his lungs. Ryan did the same, through clenched teeth.

Mel leaned against the bar on Ryan's other side and the barman, filling a pint, nodded at her.

'What are you at?' Ryan asked her.

'Getting a drink,' she said, and to the barman, 'I don't know what I want, vodka and fizzy orange, maybe.'

'C'mere,' Ryan said to the barman, 'what the fuck is wrong with you to be serving him, and the fucking state of him.'

The barman threw Ryan an awkward grimace, put some ice in a glass and brought it to the optic. 'I'm fucking serious,' Ryan told him. 'I'm fucking asking you.'

Mel paid, poured half of the little bottle of fizzy orange into the vodka, and took the bottle and her glass to a nearby table. She sat, closed one hand around the glass and rested her chin in the other. Already she regretted the expensive pettiness of it. Ryan put both hands in his hoodie pockets and cocked his head while his father blew out his cheeks, over and over, as if stifling hiccups. The barman was joined by another for moral support. They said they weren't able to assess drunkenness in someone who wouldn't talk to them and had come in sober.

'Is it not apparent to you?' Ryan said. 'He shouldn't be drinking at all.'

'We can't make that choice for him, boy,' said the first barman. He looked mournful and resigned, as Cian had looked.

'Come on, to fuck,' Ryan said to his father.

Mel swallowed a third of her drink. Tony rose to his feet. Ryan cast an eye over him, turned, and made his way back through the bar. Mel watched Tony as he followed. He swayed but didn't fall in on top of anyone and she imagined that if she had been Ryan, she'd have been praying for Tony to make it out of that pub on his own two feet, trying to keep the colour coming to her cheeks, telling herself *It'll be grand, it's not so much to ask*.

He'd have. *His* cheeks. Telling *himself*.

She finished her vodka and sat willing someone to recognise her and come over, which of course they didn't, her being away since leaving school and no longer being a storybook creature or a sexy little girlfriend-in-waiting.

It was a pretty aesthetic. The *Playboy* thing. It was meant to be pretty and playful. There was no point in gouging out PTSD now. She hadn't thought much about it for years. But she thought now that she knew how it felt to have a parent mortify you, and though her mother's buying tawdry bedclothes for her teenage daughter and his father's public drunkenness were many subjects removed from one another, they were both quite showy, as aberrations went.

Mel had a second vodka to go with the rest of the fizzy orange, then headed back to the terrace. She didn't hurry. Ryan and Tony had arrived at the house before her, but the door was still open, and as she turned into the driveway she saw that it was because Tony had fallen. He was on his side, and his legs were between the door and its frame.

Ryan was standing in the hall, looking at his father.

'He's fucking heavy,' he said, when Mel stopped at the door.

'Cian not here any more?'

'He fucked off out.'

'Where's Niamh?'

'Hiding. Both of them have more sense.'

'D'you want me to help you?'

'If he'd fucking help himself,' he said, and bent to take Tony's underarms. Tony refused to turn; Ryan heaved him on to his back. 'Move your legs,' he said. 'Move them, you cunt.'

Mel caught Tony's shins. She pushed his legs upwards, hoping he'd curl them. Tony grunted and remained a dead weight. Ryan squatted and caught Tony's underarms again and ferociously dragged him far enough so that Mel could step in and close the door behind her. She looked out to the street with her own ferocity as she did so, to discourage rubberneckers. The few kids left on the green might have noticed, but they'd lost interest. She was sure it was Elaine O'Mahony and Donna O'Leary she could see across the green, two great gawpers who, like all the great gawpers, hadn't seen or heard anything when her mother disappeared. She thought of conspiracies, a woman so unpopular that a whole estate let her vanish.

Ryan arched his back and rolled one shoulder. Tony lay on his back, head to one side. His jeans had come a little way down his arse. The exposed skin was ashen.

'This house is pure empty when shit needs doing, isn't it?' Mel said.

'Why would you be at home when this is the shit that needs doing?' Ryan said. 'I could fucking kick him but if I kicked once I wouldn't stop.'

'Don't do that, so.'

'You remember what he was like?' Ryan looked at her from the corner of his eye.

'Loud,' Mel said. 'Crabby enough.'

Ryan looked back down at Tony. 'Kicked me once or twice,' he said.

Mel pursed dry lips. Ryan didn't look ready to kick anyone. Assuming things had not changed that drastically now that he was a father and an artist and an emigrant and respectable, she knew how temper manifested in him. She refused to doubt herself, so she asked, 'Is that why you went to my mam?'

Ryan didn't react except to answer, slowly, 'I didn't want to go home.'

'You must have told your dad,' she said. 'Your dad broke our window.'

'It was only a fucking window,' he said, dully.

'You must have been delighted when she went missing. Both of you.'

'Not really.' Still slow. Still dull. 'When she fucked off, I was still trying to own it. That's what Izzy told me. I couldn't remember so she said if I went to your mam and asked that'd be half of it, at least. Without your mam I had none of it, and all I have now is context.'

'What's that mean?' she said. 'Context?'

'I know now I'm not supposed to blame myself. That was something she did to me.'

'That's the opposite of owning it, Ryan. She was fucking daft, like. You probably had more cop on than her. Can't you just stop looking so offended and saying things like that I'm torturing you? It's me they're judging. Maybe you're annoyed about the drug dealer thing, I don't know. Don't take that out on me.'

'Leave, then. Kick your grandad's door in. Tell him what you told this lump.' He jerked an elbow at his father. 'That no one else will take you.'

'You'd kick me out before you'd wake up to yourself?'

'You don't get it,' he said. 'And I don't see why I have to rip myself open till you get it, but fucking hell, Linda, are you that fucking thick?'

He dropped to his haunches again and tried to put his father sitting, back to the wall. Tony moaned 'Fuck off, Ryan', and slumped. Mel waited as Ryan grunted and pushed and tried to hold Tony up and despaired and sat beside his lopsided father, elbows on knees, head in hands. 'Piss off, Linda,' he said, into his wrists.

'Why am I thick?'

'You think I fancied your mam?' he said, muffled. 'You think I instigated any of that?'

'G'way, instigate. You didn't have to instigate, only respond. She thought she was a teenager, you could've told her you didn't want anything to do with her, the way you'd tell any young wan. Are you trying to say you'd have done it with anyone who came on to you? I dunno, maybe you would've.'

Ryan took his phone from his pocket as Tony, muttering, slumped back to the floor. With the right soundtrack it could have been funny. Crop Ryan out of the picture, with his burning cheeks and the miserable set to his mouth, and maybe. Mel sank too, and shook Tony's shoulder. 'Tony,' she said. 'Come on, now. Get your act together.'

Ryan put his phone to his ear. 'Where'd you go?' he said.

Mel could make out Cian's voice. 'For a takeaway. D'you want a three-in-one?'

'This langer's on the hall floor,' Ryan said. 'I can't lift him.'

A pause. 'Leave him at it.'

'He'll choke or something. He'll vomit and he'll fucking choke.'

'What can you do about it, boy? Four of us together couldn't get him up the stairs.'

'Four of us together,' Ryan said, 'fucking could.'

Another pause. 'I'll be back in a minute, so.'

'What's instigating got to do with it?' Mel said, as Ryan took the phone from his ear.

'I am telling you now,' he said. 'Get out of my house. You can't be that friendless.'

'What if I am that friendless?'

'I'll chance it.'

Mel got up and walked out the front door.

The two weapons were still standing across the way, arms folded, though now she couldn't see if they were Elaine O'Mahony and Donna O'Leary. What was the difference? A weapon's a weapon. A tramp's a tramp. The apple doesn't fall far from the tree.

She walked the few metres to the footpath, intending first to approach them, and then not quite chickening out but losing steam. Apathy wasn't an unusual affliction for this place. There was treachery in thinking that, but apathy stopped her correcting herself; she stood at the Cusacks' front wall and folded her own arms. City night was down, the weak yellow of streetlamps, headlamps, front windows, screen after screen after screen.

She turned to look at her old house. The new resident had installed blinds. They were pulled almost to the bottom. There was a thin rectangle of low, dancing light.

Mel went to her old front door and knocked gently. When there was no movement she tapped on the window and smiled when a woman with thick eyebrows looked out.

The woman came to the front door and said, 'You're next door, are you?'

'Yeah,' Mel said. 'Staying a few weeks. I used to live here though.'

The woman said nothing.

'Here,' Mel said. 'In this house, your house. I lived here something like twelve years.'

The woman wrinkled her nose. 'Are you drunk or what?'

'Me?'

'Keep your voice down. Jesus, I can smell it off you.'

'I had a couple of drinks earlier,' Mel said, 'and you're hardly smelling that. Maybe you're having a stroke.'

'Sorry?'

'I'm only joking with you, calm down. I was standing out and saw the light on, so on a whim—'

'You're all cracked in that house.' The woman tilted her head to gesture, which made Mel think of a confused dog. 'You've me driven demented.'

'How so, girl?'

'Roaring and shouting. You're as noisy!'

Mel had had nothing much to say in either of the two houses, certainly nothing to her mother's insistence on parties, or the bedclothes, or the frills or the niceness. She had nothing much to say to the grown men who came to her bedroom door in the middle of the night, fellas-plural, who leered or whispered till she told them to fuck off. Tara, who loved company, parties, niceness, must have been aware that it was taking them a long time to piss and must have considered that they were drawn to the pink and black bedroom, dying wasps sickened by the meagre time left to them to do damage. Nothing much to say when people told her that Tara was odd because it hurt to hear that Tara was abnormal from people who could confidently define normality. And so she and Kelly sat together, her with nothing much to say and Kelly with everything to say, but neither able to understand whatever had gone so wrong either side of the dividing wall.

'Falling over drunk.' The neighbour's chin crinkled. 'Drugging and all.'

'That's why you've the slats up so in the garden,' Mel said. 'Big snotty head on you. Nawthin wrong at all with them, d'you know they all speak Italian? And play piano and run companies, don't know where you got your notions.'

'I'm going to bed,' the neighbour said, and shut the door.

Mel turned and sighed out at the broader green, and the two still standing on the other side, who she now felt closer to, the weapons, the tramps. She raised a hand and the shapes moved. She took it that they'd raised their hands too, a gesture of solidarity, or raised higher, truth to power. She steamed around the pillar at the end of the wall and back into the Cusack hall, where Ryan was bent over his father, one hand on the man's shoulder, listening to him keen.

'D'you know what?' she said. 'You'd want to realise who your allies are. Being pissy with me? After growing up on opposite sides of the same wall? You were never like this. Yeah, you could play the piano and talk in Italian and God knows what else but you were never up your own hole with it, and I don't know if it's Natalie that has you that way but it's not your dad, and not this terrace, or this estate, or this side of the Old Youghal Road, and it's not my fault Karine can't get her head around the way we carried on when we were kids, running wild, and my mam all about it.'

'My dad's sick.'

'Yeah, and my mam with him. Sorry you're not special.'

'I mean he's fucking sick now.'

'He's demented drunk.'

'He's telling me his chest is hurting.'

Niamh appeared at the top of the stairs. Mel shook her head at her and asked Ryan, 'What do we do?'

'SouthDoc,' Niamh said, from above them. 'We'd to call them before.'

Ryan went to the banisters and looked up at her.

'He got pains before,' Niamh went on. 'He had to go to A&E.'

Ryan took his phone out again.

Mel sat on the stairs, her back to the wall, her foot on the posts, as Ryan and Niamh went through drawers looking for Tony's medical card. A nurse phoned Ryan back and he explained his father's symptoms, pausing before adding the drunken crumpling in the hall. He told the caller he had no transport. He listened and nodded. 'Yeah,' he said. 'Yeah, sound.' The hall door swung in and Ryan looked at whoever was standing there and nodded again. Mel took her feet from the posts and leaned forward. There was a slim man with a shaved head. She thought she recognised him, and smiled.

The visitor didn't look at her, but at Tony, mouth closed.

Ryan hung up and crouched, hand to his father's shoulder.

'D'you need a hand, boy?' said the visitor.

'Not sure it'd do him any good,' Ryan said. The man took a step forward and Ryan put his hand out. 'Leave it,' he said.

'Are you going to come with me?' the visitor said.

'There's an ambulance coming,' Ryan said, 'for my fucking father.'

'He's all right,' the visitor said. 'Come on with me a minute. I've to have a word with you.'

'I'll have a word with you tomorrow,' Ryan snapped.

'You'll have a word with me now,' the visitor said. 'Or the kids'll be calling another ambulance.' He didn't raise his voice.

'You're some cunt,' Ryan told him.

'I'm driven to it,' said the visitor. He stepped back out the door and out of view.

Ryan looked at Mel. 'Cian'll be back any minute,' he said. 'Tell him what's going on.'

'I don't know what's going on,' Mel said, as Niamh bleated 'Ryan?' from the kitchen door.

Ryan nodded at Tony. 'You know what's going on with him. I'll follow him to A&E. I won't be long.' He shook his father's shoulder. 'I won't be long, Dad.'

'Don't be going with that fella,' Tony slurred. 'Have some fucking sense.'

'You're one to talk.' Ryan got up and stretched and went out the door.

Mel followed. Ryan got into the back of an SUV. 'What the fuck is that about?' Mel said, softly.

The SUV turned and drove out of the estate. No one stood outdoors to witness it. No silhouettes in windowpanes. Like when her mother took off, Mel thought. Not a sinner.

Maureen stood on John Redmond Street looking up at the stone plaque on the wall commemorating Mother Jones, born on the northside of Cork City and baptised in the North Cathedral only around the corner.

MARY HARRIS. 1837–1930.
'PRAY FOR THE DEAD AND FIGHT
LIKE HELL FOR THE LIVING.'

'The dead are dead,' Maureen grouched, 'and a prayer is just a bad poem learned by rote.'

It would be no waste of her Friday afternoon to coin some better slogans than this wan had in her day. Pure simple, but wasn't that the point of it? Mottos a child could memorise. Poems recited in a damp schoolroom. Maureen had done a little recent reading on Mary Harris Jones and knew that minding and rousing children was a significant portion of her approach to social justice, and so therefore her legend. She'd lost four children of her own. As it had not broken her, it must have incensed her.

Maureen should have felt admiration towards Mrs Harris Jones but instead she was feeling resentful, interrogated by this plaque. She wanted to say things to it, like, 'Isn't it well for some? Not many of us got the chance to be swept up in that kind of virtuous fervour.' She knew why, and today's self-awareness was making her miserable, and wasn't the kind of carry-on she liked to entertain any day of the week but especially not of a Friday.

There'd been nothing stopping her. Maureen. In London. It wasn't like the Irish in 1970s London had no need of a champion. Or in Ireland; it wasn't like the Irish women behind the high walls had no need of a champion. Or the Irish girls giving up their jobs because they were getting married, or the Irish girls who hadn't a say in how many children they were going to have, or the Irish girls born at the side of the roads, or any of them without borrowed crosiers. And to have this wagon up on the wall, having left Ireland after the famine only to lose four children and a husband and a business in America and go on to incite a nation, made Maureen feel ten inches tall. Mother of a merchant prince indeed. Mother of a dragon sitting on his pile of gold! She had nothing else to preside over, and Jimmy hardly needed and barely wanted her.

She looked around for something to mark the plaque with, a bit of dirt or a flint, even, to scratch it, but there was nothing, and she knew she didn't really want to do such a thing anyway; she was fed up with herself and not with Mrs Harris Jones on the wall; she was sixty-eight and she had no idea what encouragement or compensation she could offer to the country.

It embarrassed her to think that she could have started her walking tours and brought Germans in anoraks all over the streets of her city talking about how its men had shaped it and its women had sat nice and still and watched them, without knowing about Mother Jones and her achievements, without knowing that this plaque was here; Christ almighty, she must have been up and down John Redmond Street a hundred times. She imagined herself beset by Germans who were huge fans of Mother Jones and had come to Cork for the Mother Jones experience, pink in the jowls because she didn't know what they were talking about when they asked in which cathedral the good firebrand was christened, scrambling for excuses as German trade-union enthusiasts shook their heads and fecked their complimentary Corkonian sausages into the gutters.

She plodded east towards the flea market she'd learned was named after the esteemed, the exalted Mrs Harris Jones, and was inside giving dirty looks to old records within a quarter of an hour.

Maureen liked flea markets and car-boot sales. She liked curios and tat and had been to this place more than once. She couldn't remember forming an impression of its name at all, but if she had it would have been that she'd thought Mother Jones to be a common nickname, like Lady Muck or Missus Mop.

'What do you know,' she asked a man presiding over an abundance of denim jackets, 'about the woman this place is named for?'

'Mother Jones?' He had the teeth of a fella fed up of listening to anti-smoking campaigns, and a crown of dusty curls, though both he might have owed to the light. It was the same light you got in pubs with a strong day trade. Light for the impulsive guilty.

'That's the wan.' Maureen pulled at the sleeve of the nearest jacket, which felt too supple to be clean.

'She was a Cork woman,' said the seller. 'Emigrated to America, and fought for worker's rights. There's a plaque up on the wall on John Redmond Street.'

'And c'mere,' Maureen said, 'does everyone in Cork know all about her?'

'Enough do. They have a festival for her, I think. Human rights stuff, talks and poetry.'

'I never knew about her.'

'She wasn't a friend of yours, then?'

Maureen threw out an injurious glare. The seller looked not even a decade younger than her. 'Saucy so-and-so,' she said.

'Sure I'm only codding you.'

'Your jackets smell of diesel,' she told him. 'I'm not codding you.'

She lingered at his stall, rubbing denim between her thumb and first finger and tutting. He had left a black marker on top of a hardback notebook; when he turned his back, she slipped the marker up her jacket sleeve. She moved on slowly and cast an eye over lampshades, second-hand books, bottles of coloured glass, porcelain dolls, military coats. She had a coffee at the little cafe and played conspicuously with the black marker, but its owner did not come looking for it. She took her time because she was otherwise at a loss for occupation. Oh, this was not like her. She pinched the handle of her mug. This was not like her one bit. In London she'd had every right to be down on herself, and she wasn't. She held a grudge but wasn't sunken with it. She should have been down on herself because for all her grudges she trundled on unnoticed. What would the people in London remember of her? That she was the joyless wan who used answer the phones. That she was the wan you couldn't bring to the pubs because she'd turn away the fellas with her acid tongue. And in the end that she was the cracked Irish biddy who lived in the middle bedsit on the middle floor, who thought herself guardian of the building and all its lost souls but who did nothing for anyone but gripe and belittle and rub the wrong way. She rammed the marker into her pocket.

She was continuing on up the road, she decided. Up the hill. She was going to wear the legs off herself.

'Merchant fecking prince,' she said, loudly, halfway up Summerhill North and coincidentally outside the old Chamber of Commerce; a fella with thick stubble, walking past her from the opposite direction, nodded in camaraderie. Even if he hadn't been flaking down the hill she wouldn't have corrected him. Merchant fecking princes, and Mrs Harris Jones the opposite of a patron saint. She wouldn't think much of Maureen, and she living off sour spoils. Not that they'd let Jimmy in the gate of the Chamber of Commerce, and how many of them could he buy or sell? She could only make educated guesses. He was able to keep that big car on the road. He was able to pay for two petulant lumps of children. He was still making money and his sort of merchant prince wasn't guaranteed longevity. His continuance was its own proof.

The sky was grey but light and high. There was a lackadaisical breeze. She was getting clammy in her jacket, so she took it off and carried it over one arm. There were intermittent breaks in the terraces of townhouses where she could see Cork stretch to the south. It was a pleasantly green city looked at from that angle. She came to the cross at St Luke's and turned right. The footpaths here were narrow, the views more frequent and more impressive. She climbed past old money's back gates and Lycra-clad girls carrying patterned water bottles. On either side, weeds poked from the top two feet of old stone. She went left and the street rose ahead of her again. The walls got lower and uglier. She turned her back on the view. She crested the hill, reached the Old Youghal Road, turned right, and sat on the first wall low enough.

'Merchant fecking prince!' She rubbed her thighs. 'And content to keep this place in this condition, because it suits him down to the ground.'

She looked around. There were teenagers in school uniforms. Exam season; they looked peaky and strained and even worse than teenagers usually did. There were old fellas in thick jumpers, walking with their eyes on the footpath. There were mothers with small kids in buggies. 'Encourage your neighbours to better themselves,' she said, 'or say nothing at all, because you want them sick and buying medicine. Agitate, or . . .' She couldn't think of the word. The harder she thought, the more possibilities swam through her head. Depress. Medicate. Put to sleep. Put down. '*Baile na mBocht*!' she screeched, and a woman with an enormous arse swerved around her. 'Ah, what am I going to do to you?' Maureen called after her. The arse bounced on up the road.

Maureen's home-house was here on the Old Youghal Road. She came upon it after ten more minutes on her complaining feet. The house had felt a very long way from anywhere when she was small. It wasn't the way it was now, surrounded by housing estates. Two-storey, detached, grey, with its front door in the middle and small windows either side, it looked outdated. Her parents had raised eight in that house, Maureen and her six siblings, and then Jimmy. They'd agreed to sell it when the mother died, ten years ago. Now there was a car with a dinged bumper parked in front. Maureen thought about someone erecting a plaque to one side of the front door on her behalf.

LADY MUCK A.K.A. MISSUS MOP
MAUREEN PHELAN
1951–SHE'S STILL IN IT
BENEVOLENT AND BELOVED MOTHER
OF AN ECONOMIC REVOLUTIONARY,
BLACK MARKET EXPANSIONIST, PIRATE
OR MERCHANT PRINCE, DEPENDING ON WHO'S ASKING
BORN AND BRED ON THE NORTHSIDE OF CORK
AND SHIPPED OFF TO LONDON,
BECAUSE SHE GOT TOO FRESH WITH US ALL.

Maureen took the black marker out of her jacket pocket and pulled off its cap. Not wanting the bother of having to approach the front door, she bent and poised the nib over the top block on the whitewashed border wall. She couldn't decide whether to lead with Lady Muck or Missus Mop, so instead she wrote:

Don't mind Ould Wans who think they were Magdalenes when they had it easy.

No one stopped her. Maureen reread her admonishment and kept walking.

She went downhill again, through one of the newer estates, on to the concrete footpath and into the dip. The state's intent was to provide green space for children, but the state didn't want the bother of maintaining that space. But then maybe Maureen was wrong in the way she was thinking today, about how greater powers – princes and such – should feel responsible for the lesser, and if lesser was the wrong word, then for those who weren't born to feel the world was already theirs, or mad or belligerent enough to grab what wasn't nailed down.

This was the house. The one with the overgrown lawn and the faded front door. How such a place could produce such a boy she didn't know, but then if people saw her home-house, they wouldn't know how it produced a base prince like Jimmy. Inside the Phelan home-house there had been too many pictures of the Sacred

Heart, which in hindsight would move anyone to evil. In this house, therefore, there might be similar messages, nudges towards art and light. Piles of manuscript paper. In a frame painted gold on the wall over the fireplace, a portrait of Beethoven instead of Holy God.

She leaned back on the front wall, taking the weight off her feet, and looked out over the broad green. There were a lot of small children. She was surprised at this. It was usually the case that the terraces matured over time. Maybe the young mammies were living at home with their parents. That was a nice way to be. Parents supporting their daughters, instead of sending them off to London in such a state that they could only fail.

Mother Jones had to run from the Great Famine and she woke up a nation.

Mother Jones must have been made of mad and belligerent stuff, so.

Then why had Maureen nothing to show for her own madness and belligerence except a criminal son and a few one-time suitors who only thought of her when rooks screamed from the trees outside?

She leaned with her back to the Cusack house for five or more minutes, watching the goings-on, before she heard a door open and close behind her. She looked briefly over her shoulder. Ryan Cusack came up and stood to her left.

'This estate was built long before your time,' she told him. 'Might have been even before your father was born. My mother wasn't one bit happy when the houses were going up. I wouldn't read into that, though, she wasn't one bit happy about anything.'

He didn't respond. He had a fine purple mark on the right side of his jaw.

She clucked her tongue. 'What happened you?'

He held her gaze for a long few seconds, then hardly moved his mouth to say, 'Nawthin.'

'Are you getting into scraps already?' she said. 'And you only just home.'

He did not lean on the wall beside her. He stood looking at his feet, as though she was a rebuking teacher. She hung her jacket over the wall and went through its pockets for her cigarettes. She put her hand into the wrong pocket first, felt the marker, pulled her hand out again as if she'd been bitten.

When she lit up he said, 'Gimme one.'

'I will not,' she said. 'Young boys should have more sense.'

His head stayed bowed, though she could see his eyes dart from green to footpath to his feet.

'This Mother Jones person,' she said at last. 'How'd you know about her?'

'She's from Cork.'

'She was from Cork,' Maureen corrected. 'She's fecking dead, Ryan.'

'I told you, my cousin is into all of that craic.'

'The plight of the working man. Are you not into that craic?' She took a great drag off her cigarette and spat the smoke at the green. 'Are you not?' she snapped.

He rubbed his uninjured cheek. 'Will you just tell me what you want?'

'I don't want anything. You're the one who came out to me.' She took another drag. 'This is as much my place as it is yours, my lad. More. Both my parents were from Cork City.' She pointed her cigarette at him. 'Not to mention your great-grandfather I think was from up the country. Wasn't he?'

'I don't know,' he told his feet.

He had white runners on him, dark jeans, a blue top with a flag on the left breast. She thought it was an Irish flag; a second look told her it was actually the Italian green, white and red. She thought this pretentious.

She gestured at the house. 'How's your dad?'

'He could have asked me himself,' he murmured.

'Who? Your dad?'

'Jimmy. Instead of sending you up.'

'Jimmy didn't tell me to ask after your father.'

'He has my number,' Ryan said. 'Doesn't he? My address. Everything.'

'I told you, Jimmy didn't ask me to ask after your father. Didn't you come to see me the other night? Is it cracked to think I might return the house call?'

'You don't know where I live though.'

'Do I not? You're not very good at hiding it.'

'I'm going to see him now,' Ryan said.

'Who, Jimmy?'

'My dad.' All of this was in a soft monotone, and she wasn't used to that from the customarily sparky little divil.

'Is he not inside?' she asked.

'No, they kept him in. A few days, they said.'

'Are you talking about hospital?'

He looked up at her.

'I didn't know he was sick,' she said. 'What's wrong with him?'

'Why are you doing this?' he said.

'Doing what?'

'Pretending to be here for unrelated reasons.'

'I am here for unrelated reasons,' she said. 'I'm here because this Mother Jones wan has me distracted. It's like you were all keeping her from me.'

He shut his eyes, swayed his head and put his hand over the back of his neck.

'Will you let me in?' she asked.

'No,' he said. 'Why?'

She dropped her cigarette butt and ground it out with a clod-hopper. 'I had a coffee,' she said, 'in the flea market. And now I need a wee.'

'Are you serious?'

'Does that not happen you when you drink coffee?' she wondered. 'God, don't the young men have fine, strong bladders.'

'It's not a good time,' he said.

'Sure it never is, when it comes to piddling. I'm sixty-eight,' she reminded him.

'Grand,' he says. 'But you've to go then.'

She followed him into the hall. The place was the kind of messy you got from having more children than shelves. The air had that sour tinge of cannabis just smoked. She sniffed. Under that, she thought, was oven chips and washing powder.

To her left, the door to the sitting room was open. Inside were balmed out three other Ryans, and she couldn't help but smile in at them.

'Story?' said one of the Other Ryans.

'I'm a friend of your brother's,' she told them.

'She's a friend of Dad's,' Ryan said, beside her. He pointed at the stairs. 'Just at the top.'

'I know my way around,' she told him. 'All of these houses are the same.'

She did not find a Beethoven portrait or manuscript paper, but then she was confined to the hall, the landing and the little bathroom, which was not clean but had all the accoutrements of cleaning: shampoos, body washes, soap, razors. She wasn't going to judge, being an intentionally disorderly person. The toilet seat was up. There was no key in the lock. The best she could do was throw her jacket on the floor behind the door.

The doors to all three bedrooms were open. When she opened the bathroom door she could see into the box room. The curtains on the window were closed. There was a chest of drawers, open top and bottom. She started down the stairs and caught a glimpse of a pair of bare, hairless legs curled on a bed in the front room.

Ryan was smoking in the sitting room door.

'What did I tell you?' she said.

'It's not a fag,' he said, 'and I'm not giving you any.' His tone had changed now that he had Other Ryans watching him.

'What's the matter with your father?' she asked the sitting room as he inhaled, and the biggest Other Ryan answered, 'Pancreatitis.'

'An awful dose,' she said. She stepped into the room and stood with her back to the window. On the mantelpiece was a row of frames containing dark-haired, dark-eyed kids, none yet into their teens. One wedding photo: Tony, holding a small fella and smiling at the Italian girl, who was holding a little girlín and beaming at the camera.

'He's had it for months,' said the biggest Other Ryan, as Actual Ryan exhaled and said, 'You can go, Maureen.'

'Did you say you were going to see him?' she said.

He took a step into the sitting room and held the joint out to the three. 'I don't have a car,' he said. The biggest Other Ryan leaned over and took the joint from him. 'So if you're after a spin you can forget it.'

She smiled at the biggest Other Ryan. 'Which one are you?' she said, as Actual Ryan went past and opened the front door.

'Cian,' he said.

'Cian. Roy Keane, is it?'

His eyebrows shot up. 'Is it what!'

Maureen pointed at the other two. 'And you? And you?'

Cian answered for them. 'Cathal and Ronan.'

'Bye, Maureen,' Ryan said, from the hall.

'He's kicking me out,' she explained. 'I don't like to annoy him. See you again, lads.'

'You won't,' Ryan said, following her on to the footpath. 'They're not involved in anything, all right?'

'Sure what's that got to do with it?'

'It has everything to do with it,' he said.

He stood at the gate and she stood facing him. He put his hands in his pockets and looked to the top of the terrace. She thought, *Well, that's it, then*. It has everything to do with it. She was the mother of the merchant prince and if Jimmy chose to hoard and to torment then by association she'd be loathed. And if she decided to denounce or deny him, she'd be nothing at all.

'What hospital is he in?' she asked Ryan.

'Why?'

'Fine,' she said. 'Don't tell me.' She went a few steps and turned back. 'Did you find out who's claiming you?' she asked. 'On the internet?'

'Not yet.'

'Aren't they awful fuckers?'

'Doesn't matter any more,' he said, but when she asked why he shook his head and clamped his lips.

*   *   *

222

Tony Cusack was in the hospital nearest her old residence, the burned brothel. It was easy enough find him. All she had to do was phone around as the bus brought her back into town. When she'd located him they told her which ward he was in and relayed the visiting hours.

She arrived on the ward and a student nurse directed her to a room with four beds, in each a miserable man staring at the ceiling. Tony Cusack was in the fourth bed, which was placed at a right angle to the others. He was hooked up to a drip, and there were tubes in his nose. There was a single chair to his left, in which sat a dark-haired girl, wearing headphones and staring at her phone screen.

'Hello!' Maureen bellowed, and the girl looked up and pulled her headphones off.

'Hi,' she said. It sounded less like a greeting than a correction.

'I heard your father was sick,' Maureen said.

'You heard right.' The girl was pretty, in a furious sort of way. She leaned forward. 'Who are you?' she said.

'Mo Looney,' Maureen said. 'An old friend of the family. Hello, Tony! Tony? Hello.'

'Mo Looney?' the girl said, as if the name had an unusual smell.

Maureen leaned over Tony and waved at him. 'Jesus Christ,' he said.

'Painkillers,' his daughter said. 'Not that you're usually much quicker, Dad.' She turned narrow eyes on Maureen. 'Are you a friend of my nana's or something?'

Maureen thought of Noreen Cusack, still whippet thin after four children and a dreadful bat even before she hit forty. But then, her husband was a drunk, and such traits drunken husbands bring out in women. And Tony'd learned it from him, and now Tony had a front room full of drugged-to-the-gills young fellas.

'We wouldn't be terribly close these days,' she said. 'What's your name?'

'Kelly.'

'Where do you come?'

'Second.'

Maureen nodded. 'And Ryan is the oldest.'

'Allegedly,' said Kelly.

She got up and waved Maureen into her seat.

Tony turned his head. 'What are you doing here?' he asked. 'Is this something to do with Ryan?'

'No,' Maureen said.

'After Jimmy came looking for him,' Tony said.

'No,' Maureen said again, and then nodded and said, 'Ah.' She rubbed her thighs. Kelly sat at the end of the bed and looked back at her phone. 'When was this?' Maureen asked Tony.

'Last night,' he said. 'I think. What day is it now?'

'Friday.'

'Why doesn't he leave him alone?' Tony said; she leaned closer. 'He's out of all that now. He has a small fella.'

Kelly put her phone face down on the bed.

'I heard you were a grandad,' Maureen said.

'I am,' he replied. 'He's a lovely little lad. And my fella's trying. Will your fella not leave him try?'

'Sorry now.' Kelly Cusack stood up. 'Who exactly are you, Mrs Looney or whatever?'

'Or whatever,' Maureen agreed, and leaned closer to Tony, as though she might hear his confession.

'What do you want with him?' Tony said. 'The pair of you.'

'Maybe he's still working for him,' Maureen said. 'You wouldn't know, Tony. They don't tell me. Either of them.'

'My dad', Kelly said, and stepped so close that Maureen stood up in shock, 'is on painkillers, in a hospital bed, so this can wait, can't it? And,' she said, 'and! If this has something to do with my brother, you'd want to all back off and let him alone. I swear to God this city's full of vultures. Doesn't matter what he does, he's fucking wrong! Go on, now, and leave my dad sleep, or I'll cart you out myself.'

'Who do you think you're talking to?' Maureen said.

'Who do you think you're talking to?' Kelly said. 'You saucy ould bitch.'

Maureen put her hands on her hips. 'My name,' she said, 'is Maureen Phelan. My son used knock around with your father, years ago. He used employ your bould little fecker of a brother, not that any of us should be happy about that. I am here to see your father, because your brother told me he was sick, and years back now your father did me a great turn, though it's left him frightened of me and more frightened of my son. And I would like to set something right for once in my life, why is that so hard to believe?'

Ryan Cusack walked in in the middle of this declaration, and sat where his sister had just been sitting, and put his head in his hands.

'Don't be so fecking dramatic, you,' Maureen said.

The eyes of the men in the neighbouring beds flickered over and back. A reporter on the telly employed long vowels to talk about happenings in the Special Criminal Court. A nurse called to a colleague out in the corridor.

'Take your head out of your hands,' Maureen said to Ryan, and he complied, red-eyed and unfocused. 'By God, I won't be told,' she went on, 'by you, or by Jimmy, or by myself either, that I should have let you jump.'

'What the fuck does that mean?' said Kelly.

'Ah,' Maureen said, furiously. 'It means pray for the dead, and fight like hell for the living.'

Track 8: A Vandal Speaks

The night before it happened, just before visiting hours were over, my dad says to me, 'You'd want to be a bit nicer to poor Linda.'

I'm trying to play thick then, like, *Wha'*? and he goes, 'Rocky, don't be acting the bollocks. She didn't have anything to do with it, did she? You're a parent yourself now, how would you like it if someone was a bollocks to Diarmaid over shit you did? I wouldn't like to think that someone could be a bollocks to you over something I did.'

Then there was a long pause because I didn't know what the fuck I was meant to say. After a while he says, 'I could hear bits of what you were saying to her back at the house before the ambulance came.'

'No you fucking couldn't.'

'Bits,' he says. 'Rocky, yer wan is gone and isn't that justice enough?'

I could've asked him to elaborate, I could've asked him exactly what he heard but the idea of him hearing any of that, when he just thought yer wan took advantage and didn't know she'd taken a lot more . . . But I didn't. I was embarrassed. I was angry with him for making me embarrassed. I was angry because he was right. It wasn't Mel's fault. It wasn't anyone's fault any more. So I just got up and said, 'I'll see you tomorrow.'

I spent so much time giving out about my dad you'd be forgiven for thinking the man was a full-time cunt.

He sat with me for hours after I told him you were pregnant. You were so done with me at that point and the shit that was going on, you were right to be done with me. I was in a bad way.

He told me it wasn't hopeless and when it was obvious I wasn't listening, he told me again. He still thought I could make something of myself. He told me that it'd all change once I had Diarmaid in my arms. He told me I was going to be a great dad, and he believed it. I know now where that faith comes from because I think Diarmaid's amazing but it's weird to think that my dad could love me the way I love Diarmaid. Coz you almost think that kind of love is unique to you, don't you? And in other ways he was so fucking—

I remember him playing football with me when I was very small. Jesus, he'd only have been a couple of years older than I am now. I remember when Kelly told him I had a girlfriend. We were together only two, two and a half months. He took the piss but then later he comes in to me in the kitchen and goes, 'What's she like?' I didn't know what to say so I said, 'I dunno.' He breaks his hole laughing, 'What d'you mean you don't know what she's like?'

He made me show him a photo of you and he goes, 'She's lovely, boy.'

And I'm like, I know, and he says, 'You'd want to look after her.'

He wasn't great for advice and sometimes when he tried it was just . . . like I laugh now, but at the time . . . He was mouldy one night and he started on at me about sex. Fucking stocious, like, the sentences weren't coming out right at all.

'Rocky, I swear to God, boy.

'I swear to God you'd want to fucking watch yourself.

'Coz I knows full well what you're after and she's only a fucking young wan . . .'

And you four months older than me, like—

'If you're giving her what I think you're giving her, you better not be.

'Coz I'll let her father skin you.'

Still, he didn't stop us going up to the bedroom and pushing Cian's bed in front of the door. He knew well, like, he was just glad I wasn't being arrested any more. He always liked you. He used to say, 'She's too good for you, boy.'

But then, the morning of Diarmaid's christening, I said something about Gary not liking me and being right not to like me, and my dad says, 'I don't see Karine speaking Italian or playing the piano.'

I says, 'Dad, what're you on about? She's a fucking nurse.'

And he says, 'I never said she wasn't great in her own way but you're great in your own way and d'you know what? If anything she did well for herself with you.'

I remember him coming to the Garda station after I'd been caught with that cocaine. I hadn't seen him in ages. I was living in Dan's stash house. I thought I was fierce grown-up, but . . . D'Arcy, I was so glad he was there with me. It was all I could do not to hang on to him and bawl.

He broke yer wan's window, didn't he? He did that for me.

The last time he hugged me was when I came home from Bofin and if I'd known then what was going to happen I wouldn't have let go so soon

and I'd remember it better now.

So

'A Vandal Speaks' is about my dad. It didn't exist – in melody, in lyric, in any concept – until afterwards. I didn't know how to get it out but I knew I had to because it felt like I was buckling under it. I tried writing down how I felt but I didn't have the words and I still don't. I mean, I'm so angry

and guilty

and ashamed and why should I be ashamed?

and sorry for myself. Because why does everyone else get a normal family? Why do you get a normal family? A mam and dad who aren't mental or alcoholics or who don't kill themselves with their stupidity and selfishness?

It was the kind of anger I couldn't act on, I couldn't get the muscles on my face to show it

Maybe it was grief, with it, that made it so fucking—

Oh God, I dunno. I don't know how I'm going to carry this.

I wake up even now thinking it's all been a dream and that he's still there and we can still fix everything that went wrong and no all I can do is put words in his mouth in a song but

is that just the most selfish thing you've ever heard, D'Arcy? That all I wanted was for him to acknowledge the shit he pulled because I was only a kid, however bad I was, I was only a kid, his kid, his son

and say sorry to me.

If I think of him as a vandal, someone careless and mischievous, I don't have to think of him as

I dunno

a self-centred cunt who drank himself to death despite us screaming in his ear that we needed him.

I need my dad, like.

I'm not that much of a grown-up that I don't need my dad.

I still can't believe that it's gone. The chance to fix it or

hear him say he's sorry

and that he loves me.

I won't sing this live. I won't play the piano line. I won't explain it. Just sometimes you

take what's hurting, freeze it in time so it can't grow any more

– I know how to do that –

and you just

There's no one to take it from you so you just go on carrying it.

D'Arcy, I said I'd see him tomorrow.

I miss him so much.

Karine was half-watching the end of a film with her parents and Yvette when he phoned. He was no longer likely to call at all hours, but it was still so familiar an imposition that she picked up without thinking of how late it was. She left the room as she answered. 'Hey,' she said, on her way to the kitchen.

'Story, girl?' he said. 'What are you up to?' and she stopped at the kitchen window and shook her head and wondered was he actually, *was he seriously* phoning to see if he could score her? After everything? And yet the possibility wasn't unwelcome.

'I'm at home. Going to bed in a minute.' Because he said nothing she went on, 'Why, where are you?'

'I'm in the hospital.'

Her first thought was that he'd been attacked. 'Are you OK?' she asked, hand to her chest.

'Yeah,' he said. 'I'm grand. My dad has . . . this pancreatitis thing was at him.'

'Oh,' she said. 'OK, well, hospital's the best place for him, then. What happened?'

'Two days ago . . . We'd to call an ambulance coz I'd no car, like.'

'Two days? You never said.'

'No, coz . . . I got a call then around seven this evening to come down coz he was . . . He wasn't doing well.'

'OK.' A jump in her chest. 'So what's happening now?'

He said, 'He died.'

She closed her hand around the edge of the draining board. 'Oh my God.'

She heard him breathe and she couldn't remember if she could usually hear people breathe on the phone. Was it a norm she hadn't noticed, or a sign he was breathing too quickly?

'Jesus,' she said. 'What happened?'

'They said septic shock and that maybe it was something that ruptured in him. I don't know, really.'

'I'll come down to you.'

'No, don't. It's OK. We're all here anyway. I have people to ring and stuff. I just wanted to let you know coz I guess you'll have to tell Diarmaid, not that he'd understand, but . . . I can call you again in the morning.'

'Ryan,' she said. 'I can go to you. It's not a problem.'

'I don't want you to.' She listened to him inhale, exhale, inhale, exhale. 'It wouldn't do me any good.'

She wasn't certain what he meant. She asked if he was sure, and he told her he was. She couldn't find a way around asking if he'd be OK. He laughed short and low and said, 'Who knows, girl?'

'Will you call me if you need anything?'

'Yeah.'

He didn't hang up, so she told him, 'I don't know what to say to you, baby boy.'

And he replied, 'Don't say that, anyway.'

No one who loved Ryan could have been fond of his father but it seemed such a horror for that to be all the life that was due to Tony Cusack; Karine thought that he had been a young father and a young husband, and so he must have had plans because these were the kind of occupations that inspired plan-making. She thought of times she could have been kinder to him. She wished she hadn't taken Diarmaid from his arms that day in town.

'God love them,' her mother said. 'What age is the youngest?' When Karine said that Ronan was fourteen her mother put her hand to her sternum and tapped as if miming a heartbeat, and said, 'God, Gar, isn't it awful?'

'It's shocking,' said Gary. 'Jesus Christ, wasn't he a young man?'

'He was an asshole,' Karine said, 'is what he was.'

'Christ, girl,' her father said, and Karine had to stick her chin in the air to keep her eyes from spilling over.

'He was,' she said. 'Y'know, you've been down on Ryan for years. He can't do anything right.'

'C'mon now, girl,' said her father. 'Me and the young fella had our differences, doesn't mean I wouldn't be sorry for his loss.'

' "The young fella",' Karine coughed out. 'His name is Ryan, Dad. Not "that other langer" or "Brian" or "Kim Jong-un" or "Luciano Pavarotti" or whatever other bloody hilarious thing that pops into your head.'

'Sure I'd only be messing with him,' Gary said. 'He knows that.'

'I'll tell you what he knows for sure because you never let him forget it. He knows you think he's not good enough, that he's rough and we're respectable even though we're all from the same place. And d'you know whose fault it is, Dad, that you think he's not good enough? Tony Cusack's. All the things Ryan did wrong he did because he didn't have anyone to tell him what to do right. You're worried now about Ronan? When Ryan was Ronan's age his dad was belting him. Ryan was selling drugs because his dad drank every penny they had. His dad sold his piano, like, the one thing he was great at and God, if you'd spotted the marks on him or asked him once in a while if he was OK, instead of, I dunno, going on some stupid dad-crusade about your daughter's honour or virginity or whatever, which, by the way, Ryan had well gone before you even knew I was meeting him.'

'Karine,' her mother said, 'for God's sake.'

Karine said, 'Ryan didn't have a father worth a shit and you didn't once think he could have done with you, Dad. You could have been nice to him.'

'All right,' her father said. 'All right, Karine'. And he made her a cup of tea and watched her while she cried into it.

Mid-morning Karine told Diarmaid that Nonno had died. She didn't mention heaven or God and she was careful to stress that

Diarmaid wasn't going to die, too, but he didn't react in the ways the articles online said he might. He just said, 'OK,' and continued moving his bricks from one side of the room to the other. She was afraid that he'd blurt something later on that would distress Ryan, but more afraid to belabour the point.

She phoned Ryan. He said he was fine. He hadn't really slept, no. He would. There was nothing else to do for the time being.

He called over in the late afternoon, when it was only her and Diarmaid in the house. He watched her sniff back tears. She enquired again about the fading bruise on his jaw, which last time she'd seen him he'd explained as 'Stupid shit'. He shook his head. He would let her think it was a bad flashback, some psychic injury. He told her to continue with whatever it was she was doing; he didn't really have anything to say. She made Diarmaid's dinner while Ryan sat with him on the sitting room floor, building cars and aeroplanes out of Duplo.

Tony's sisters took charge of the funeral arrangements. Two were older: Eilish and Emer, whom Karine had met only a handful of times. Then there was Joseph's mother, Fiona, Tony's twin. She'd spent her twenties working in hotels all over the world, had adopted a broadcaster's accent and was definitely a little bit tapped. She got involved in every family mishap because she wanted people to know she was indispensible. This Karine had heard from Joseph, who had been let down by his mother quite a bit in his twenty-five years, and who was vociferous about what a steady person his father was.

The removal was as horrible as she thought it'd be. She left Diarmaid with her parents and stood at the end of the funeral home, eyes on Ryan, who stood with Kelly on one side and Fiona on the other. Tony lay on white silk in the middle of the room. Ryan looked through the mourners at his father, and Karine felt an ache in her middle, drawn to Ryan but snagged on some outlandish, novel difficulty. Her Ryan, like. She had to cry in case she laughed.

Natalie stood not far from her. She didn't greet Karine. She didn't look over. Karine wondered how many of those attending wondered why Natalie was there instead of her and how many wondered what Karine thought she was doing, standing there, all sorrowful, when she wasn't Ryan's other half any more. She followed the instructions of the undertaker and stood outside at the end, when they were closing the coffin and needed privacy for the family. Natalie stepped out twenty seconds after her and she was never so glad to see the odious bitch.

More awfulness. Carrying the coffin. Ryan and Cian, Cathal and Ronan, Joseph and his father, Mark. Prayers at the church. Ryan didn't believe in God. Karine couldn't imagine Tony had, either, but who knew what corners he'd fled to these past few years? And then they were standing outside again, the light stretched thin across the sky. Natalie beside Ryan, holding his arm. Him listening to something his grandmother was saying. Natalie's thumb moving up and down on the fabric of his jacket.

Does your nana think she's a decent girl? Karine shouted at him in her head as she walked home. *Can she smell the fucking prestige off you?* If he was an ugly bastard, like Louise's ex Jamie with the wiry hair, no one from Rochestown or wherever would look twice at him, he wouldn't be worth the dodgy past or the pungent accent, though his voice was softening, something she'd put down to his having to knock its edges off if he was to be understood in places like Berlin or Seoul but now thought a directive Natalie had given before introducing him to her parents and accountant friends.

Natalie was not a decent girl. Natalie was the one who laundered the cash, and Ryan was not the first dealer she'd slept with. The line between rough and respectable didn't matter to Natalie, nor to anyone who had a say in how the city moved and breathed. It only mattered to people like Gary and Jackie D'Arcy, because telling lies to and about one another was the only way to feel like Cork City gave a shit about them.

When she got home Karine texted Ryan:

Are you OK?

He texted straight back:

Yeah. Don't worry.

Who's with you?

It took him longer to reply, and the suspicion that the delay provoked made her less sensitive to the crash when it came.

I'm at Natalie's.

She didn't recognise the number when it appeared on her screen. She had dressed Diarmaid in the dark trousers and white shirt she'd purchased in town the day before, and was alone in her bedroom, finishing her makeup.

'Hi, Karine? It's Natalie Grogan here.'

'Oh my God, what's wrong?' Karine said, and Natalie was irked.

'Nothing's *wrong*. Except, obviously, we have to go to a funeral. Look, do you think you could bring Diarmaid over? I think it might help.'

'Help what?'

'Help. You know. Help lift his father's spirits.'

'Why didn't Ryan call me?'

'Well,' Natalie said, 'he's being a bit difficult.'

Natalie lived in an apartment in a converted Georgian house in the south city centre. Gary agreed to the drive given the day that was in it. He was ready to go in dark chinos and his black bomber jacket. She thought he looked like a football hooligan trying to go straight as a McDonald's bouncer. More and more these days the love of him was giving her heartache.

He pulled in on a double yellow line. 'I don't like it down here at all,' he said. 'It's very dirty.'

'Bet it's not dirty inside.' Karine got out of the car and opened the rear passenger door to get Diarmaid.

'Mammy,' he told her. 'It's dirty.'

'Don't mind Grandad. He's just trying to make himself feel better.'

'I am not,' Gary said. 'I always said town was dirty. You couldn't pay me to live down here.'

'I'll only be a minute,' she told him.

The door had a number of steps up to it. She pressed the buzzer and waited. Diarmaid pulled back on her hand. 'Andiamo!' he shouted.

There was heat in the sun; it wasn't proper weather for a funeral. Karine was wearing a black, knee-length bodycon dress. It made her self-conscious about her belly, so she'd borrowed a blazer from her older sister, Claudia, who worked in an office and had a collection of blazers. Her stiletto sandals completed the rigout and she imagined begging off the whole thing to sit on the Grand Parade boardwalk with Louise, sunnies on. Smoke a joint or two. Suck her belly in, pretend she was an Instagram model.

Natalie came to the door in a similar outfit, and Karine could think of nothing she'd rather do less than sit with her on the Grand Parade boardwalk, smoking psychoactives. She didn't greet Diarmaid; she looked straight at Karine and said, 'So, he won't go.'

'What d'you mean, he won't go?'

'Will you talk to him, please?'

'Why do you want me to talk to him?'

'Don't be coy,' Natalie said.

She walked Karine and Diarmaid through the apartment. The walls were painted a vivid white. There were framed art prints in the hall, and in the kitchen Karine saw a photo collage on canvas and glimpsed Ryan in a couple of the pictures. His arms around Natalie in one. In the other, both of them wearing sunglasses. Maybe Naples. Karine had been there with him, once.

There was a terrace through the sliding door at the back. Natalie let them through and closed the door behind them. Ryan sat smoking a cigarette on top of a wooden picnic bench, feet resting on the seat. He was in jeans and a red checked shirt and white runners.

Karine picked up Diarmaid. 'Put that out,' she told Ryan.

He exhaled and stubbed the cigarette into an ashtray. He held his arms out, and she let Diarmaid go to him.

'You've to get dressed,' she said. 'You don't even have an hour.'

'I'm not going,' he said.

'You are going.'

'No, fuck it,' he said. 'Why should I? He's not going to know either way. He didn't have to die, he made that decision. They told him to stop drinking. Fuck him.'

Diarmaid tried to climb on to Ryan's shoulders.

'You can't not go,' Karine said.

'Watch me.'

She shook her head. Ryan caught Diarmaid and brought him into his lap. Diarmaid wouldn't stay still. He cocked his head to his father's kiss and squealed and tried to crawl off the edge of the table. Ryan didn't look at her. She challenged his silence with her own. And so in the end he said, 'I don't care what anyone else thinks. All I got from him was shit, my whole fucking life. I'm supposed to turn up now and look all miserable and be all, I'm sorry he's gone. I'm only sorry I didn't kill him myself.'

'You don't mean that.'

'I mightn't have meant it if this had happened before Diarmaid was born but I know now what you're supposed to be when you're someone's father. So fuck him.'

'You have to go,' she said, 'and I'm not saying that because you should feel sorry for your dad. I get it. But I know you, and if you don't go you'll never forgive yourself. And you'll never be able to take it back. This is it, Ryan, there won't be another funeral.'

'I'll get over it,' he said.

'You won't. And not a hope in hell I'm going to let that happen. Get dressed.'

Diarmaid climbed off the bench and ran to explore the boundaries of the terrace. Ryan watched him, elbow on knee, chin in hand.

'Ryan,' she said.

'What if I fuck it up?' he said.

'Staying here would be fucking it up.'

They went back in. Natalie came out of the bathroom, fixing the clasp on her necklace. Ryan walked past her and through a different door. Karine hovered in the hall, Diarmaid squirming in her arms. She was half inclined to let him down so he could leave fingerprints on glass or pull things out of cupboards. What was stopping her? Being respectable, probably.

'Is he going?' Natalie asked.

'Course he is,' Karine said.

Natalie went back into the bathroom. Karine followed Ryan.

This was a bedroom. White walls, grey bedclothes, rumpled; Ryan had laid his black suit and white shirt on top. There was a holdall on the floor beside a chest of drawers. The room was too empty to be the main bedroom. The window looked out on dancing foliage.

She put Diarmaid down and told Ryan she had to ring her father. She asked Gary if he could hold on. Ryan told her that he could come in and have a coffee, if he wanted. Contained on all sides by his own respectability, Gary didn't know what to say. 'I'll hang on here,' he told her, and hopefully, 'Sure you won't be long.' Karine hung up. Diarmaid climbed on to the bed. Ryan was still looking at the suit.

'Is this your home, like?' She cast a glance at the holdall.

'My home?' Ryan said.

'This apartment. Do you live here now?'

'I live in Gwanak.'

'You don't, boy.'

'Well,' he said, 'I don't live here either.'

He removed his shirt and let Diarmaid poke at the cloud-obscured moon for a bit. Karine considered his skin and what it meant that he would still do this in front of her. Maybe he didn't think of this as vulnerability, or intimacy. Didn't think twice about taking his jeans off, briefly cupping himself before getting into his suit trousers. Trust or just ancient history, she couldn't ask.

He put on his shirt and tie. She fixed his collar for him, put her palms on his chest, and said, 'Come on.'

She sat with her parents and sisters at the Mass, close enough so Diarmaid, in the front row with his father, could see her. Diarmaid didn't give her a thought. His aunts and uncles passed him back and forth as he demanded. He made the most of the attention of his Italian great-grandparents, who sat in the third row. They had smiled at Karine as they came into the church. When Karine had gone to Naples with Ryan, he reported that Nonna Cattaneo had given him a long lecture on respecting women, by which she meant he shouldn't sleep with any. He told her that he was twenty years of age and knew what he was doing. What Nonna had thought once he'd come to her with Natalie, saying, 'This is my new girlfriend and by the way the last one's pregnant,' Karine didn't know, but she dearly hoped Nonna had boxed his ears.

A priest said a dishonest homily about Tony being a devoted father. There were flower arrangements around the coffin. D A D spelled out in red and white. Sprays of lilies and carnations. A floral teddy bear with a ribbon that Karine thought said Grandad. She didn't know who might have ordered it for Nonno.

The service ended, and Gary and Jackie left the pew to join the line of mourners offering condolences.

'Oh Christ, do we have to do that?' Yvette said.

'I do anyway, I've to go back to work,' said Claudia.

'I'll tell them later,' Yvette lied, as Claudia followed their parents.

When Gary reached Ryan, to the right of Nana Cusack and second from the end, he took Ryan's hand in his, then closed his free hand over it. Jackie reached in, hugged Ryan, kissed his cheek. Claudia, ancient and wise, followed suit.

The boys carried the coffin to the hearse and mourners dispersed to their own cars. Gary drove to the graveyard, Jackie beside him, Yvette and Karine squished in the back beside Diarmaid's car seat. 'It's too hot for this craic,' Yvette said.

'It's 18 degrees,' Gary said.

'It's 22 degrees.' Yvette pointed at the dashboard.

'Era that's off.'

'It's roasting,' Yvette said, with feeling.

The coffin was lowered into the ground and the priest led a decade of the Rosary. Niamh took Diarmaid and busied herself with busying him, moving around the outside of the circle of mourners, speaking softly. Nana Cusack stood glaring into the grave. Fiona held on to Joseph and wept. Cathal and Kelly cried openly. Cian stood, red-eyed, an arm around Ronan. Ryan stared at a patch of earth far enough in front of him that he didn't have to bow his head. And the sky was a brilliant blue above them.

More handshaking, kisses and hugs at the end. There were a fair few neighbours. Friends of the Cusack siblings. Fellas in dark shirts who looked like they might join Tony any day now. Davy and Orson from the band waved faintly when Karine made eye contact. Mel Duane stood talking solemnly to Colm and Natalie. Louise joined Karine, wearing a black skater dress and fake eyelashes; Karine hadn't seen her at the church. The woman Karine had met on the Grand Parade was there in a great overcoat, and must have been boiling.

Joseph announced that there would be refreshments in Nana Cusack's house for anyone who wanted to come. 'I suppose we should make an appearance,' Gary said. He watched Ryan's grandfather pinch Diarmaid's cheeks. 'He must have been a fine man in his day,' he said. 'What age is he now, Karine?'

'I haven't a clue.'

'Seventy, I suppose,' Gary marvelled, inexplicably.

Mourners started making their way back to their cars. The breeze blew Karine's hair on to her face. The cemetery was in bright green countryside. Didn't seem right to plant him here, away from the noise. Moving him from what he'd known. Casting him out. She wanted to go to Ryan but Natalie was now fastened to his side. Be silly to cry now when they'd all stopped crying. Jackie put an arm around Karine's waist. Louise agreed with Yvette that it was terrible, wasn't it? Awful. Karine caught Ryan's eye. How selfish was this? She couldn't bear the arm around his.

Ryan brought Diarmaid over. 'You coming to my nana's house?' he asked.

She nodded.

'C'mere,' he said, and touched her upper arm with his finger-tips. She half-turned. He looked over her shoulder. 'See the fella there by the gate?' he asked.

She looked. 'Which fella?'

'The lad in the green coat.'

A trim, bald man in a khaki pea coat leaned against the wall, looking through the passing mourners to Ryan.

'Is he a guard or something?' Karine asked.

'That's J.P.,' Ryan said, head bent by her ear.

'What the fuck does he want?' She moved Diarmaid to her other hip.

'He was buddies one time with my dad,' Ryan said. 'He told me he was sorry for my trouble. He gave me the knock on my jaw. And I'm such a coward I can't tell him to fuck off.'

'That's fine, don't you be brave.'

The lady from Centra came up to J.P. and stood beside him, her hands in the pockets of her overcoat.

'Who's that?' Karine asked, and Ryan looked.

'His mother,' he said. 'I'm not brave enough for her, either.'

Men were brave and women were brazen. A woman's courage was more defiant than valiant, owing to how so much was stacked against her. The rest of the world always found some evil in a woman's courage. A woman's courage involved the word 'No' and that's why it was brazen.

There were times when it was best to be brazen and Karine had learned only some of them because so much of the knowledge came with age. She watched as J.P.'s mother turned up at Noreen Cusack's house and came into the kitchen for a glass of wine. She was not brazen enough to ask her what she was at. Instead she followed Diarmaid around, sick to her stomach. J.P.'s mother was just one invasion. There was Natalie too. She had a couple of years' advantage in terms of brazenness. She would not, *would not* leave Ryan's side. She pursed her lips and nodded when people talked about Tony. She stood steadily in her heels.

'She'd to call me this morning,' Karine told Louise, 'to get him moving. She'd to call *me*. Look at her there, then. Like she fucking owns him.'

'He shouldn't have her here at all. What are you, his mistress? You're the one who's supposed to be family, like.'

'Yeah, except he hates me now, I told you.'

'If she'd to call you to get him moving,' Louise said, incredulous, 'then obviously he doesn't hate you.'

Ryan turned a tumbler of whiskey in his hand. A few times his eyes went to J.P.'s mother. A few times they went to Karine. Other than that she was sure he didn't focus. She heard the ringing in his ears and had a second glass of white.

Niamh and Ronan and the Italian grandparents took Diarmaid into the garden, so she followed. Her mother and father were sitting out on the little deck at the back. Her mother had her jacket off and had moved her garden chair out of the shadow of the house.

'We'll bring Diarmaid home now in a bit,' Gary said. 'You can stay on.'

'I don't know if I'll bother,' Karine said. She was going to develop a headache. She was going to puke. She saw the way Nana Cusack looked at Natalie: *Who in God's name is this?* None of this was right. Graveyards in the open countryside and gangster mothers wafting in like foul smells. She needed to be with him. Selfish bitch! And his father just gone! This hurt worse than Seoul. She put her face to the sun.

'That's the girlfriend, so,' her mother said, gently.

'Yup,' Karine said.

'She looks like an accountant all right. Doesn't she, Gar?'

'I'd say she's a fucking dose,' he said, loyally.

'Like you're not delighted.' Karine closed her eyes.

There was no response. She imagined her parents exchanging glances. She looked at them, bright spots in her vision. They seemed placid. 'I should stay,' Karine said. 'I should talk to people.

Kelly. Joseph. Say a proper hello to his grandparents. Actually, that's all I can say. *Buongiorno. Come state?* Fuck's sake and I bet she's Duolingo'd herself into fluency.'

'Love—' Her mother.

'I'm fine,' Karine said. 'I'm fine, don't worry.'

She was not, even after the fourth glass. Her parents, Yvette and Louise had gone home. She was sitting on the deck with Kelly, lightheaded. Her black dress caught all the heat in the afternoon.

'We're supposed to know what to do now,' Kelly said. 'Like any of us have a clue. Taught nothing, like. D'you know how long I was the mammy in that fucking house?'

'I know, girl,' said Karine.

'I've been for two walks along the road with Cathal already,' Kelly said. 'To smoke a joint. Back then for more gatt. That's how Cusacks cope. What are we gonna do, like?'

Karine sighed in solidarity.

'That wan inside, then!' Kelly said. 'Natalie. All advice. You can tell she thinks this is brilliant, like. She's so comfortable with the common people.' She scoffed. 'He's only flahing her, is all.'

'For the last three years. It's hardly just flahing, is it, girl?'

'He's only flahing her,' Kelly announced, and looked at Karine and said, 'Of course you'd say that, isn't he still flahing you too?'

It was time to call it a day.

Noreen, her daughters and her pals were still in the kitchen, and J.P.'s mother among them, no longer the recipient of curious looks; they seemed cosy. Noreen kissed Karine on the cheek and thanked her for coming. Karine said her goodbyes, looking straight at J.P.'s mother. The woman returned her stare. Karine thought what she'd like to say, the order those words should leave her clenched jaw, the reaction that would be appropriate, and that it would be evil to say anything at all, egotistical to make herself the prosecutor, to be righteous and adamant and centre of the room . . . This was another of Ryan's stories that wasn't her own, and her anguish wasn't the fucking point.

Niamh and Ronan were sitting on the stairs, looking at a video on a phone. In the sitting room were the Italian grandparents, Cian and Cathal, Joseph and his father, and Ryan in a chair by the fireplace, still holding a tumbler. Natalie perched on the arm.

'I'm going to head,' Karine said, and Ryan came to her.

Natalie threw a glance at the floor near Karine's feet, and continued the conversation. 'But you see,' she said, 'the thing is . . .'

Karine opened the front door.

'You didn't need me in the end,' she told Ryan, and she was neither brave nor brazen, just four glasses drunk.

From the sitting room she could hear Natalie saying, 'Anger's natural. But you can't indulge it, because it never lasts.'

'I'm glad,' Karine told Ryan. 'Honestly. You could have been hanging off me all day, just trying to fortify this old thing . . .' She gestured back and forth, her heart to his. 'But you stood on your own two feet, and that's healthier, Ryan, isn't it?'

Natalie was saying, 'Of course you'd be angry with a parent for leaving you so soon, even when it's down to an illness, but it's ruinous to think like that.'

'D'Arcy,' Ryan said. 'I don't know what I'm—'

'You do know,' Karine said. 'You were a grown man today. And something made you like that, something's driving you forward.'

'Uh-huh,' Natalie went. 'Uh-hmm, exactly.'

'And if this shitty day means anything it's that we have to move forward,' Karine said.

'I said to him, Ryan, you'll come to terms with this, you'll realise that your father—'

'Sorry,' Karine said, pushing past him. 'For fuck's sake!'

She went back to the sitting room and shook her head at Natalie and said, 'Do you ever, *ever*, get sick of the sound of your own voice?'

Natalie laughed. 'Excuse me?'

'You are so full of shit, like. I'd be hacking my throat open if I sounded like you. I'd be inviting medical students to look up into the cavity and see if they could find my alleged brain. You know what?' The wine boiled across her forehead and neck. 'You clearly don't know a thing. Ryan is right to be angry, don't you dare tell him that he's not to be angry.'

'Oh my God, calm down,' Natalie said.

'You know nothing.' Karine sniffed violently. 'Just shut the fuck up and let him do this whatever way he needs to do this. And if you can't do that, then go back to where you came from and leave him alone. He does not need this righteous shit, you leave him alone!'

It was wrong to rush out, theatrical and attention-seeking and typical of a nutty ex-girlfriend, but her eyes were streaming, her nose running. When she got back to the road she took off her sandals – four glasses to cushion her feet – and quickened her pace. It was too bright still. The small of her back was damp. She got home and opened the front door too quickly and bumped it off the wall inside.

'Which of you is that?' her father called, from the sitting room.

'It's me,' Karine said. She ran upstairs to the bathroom and wet a cloth and pressed it to her face. She sat on the toilet and opened her bag for her phone. There were no texts, no missed calls. She thought of that room full of Cusacks, exchanging cringes. She dabbed under her arms with the cloth. She thought of Ryan, apologising to Natalie on her behalf. She thought of the Italian grandparents telling him this is why you respect women by not sleeping with them. Kelly, rolling her eyes, saying *It's coz he's still flahing her*. And Ryan, edges filed from his voice, full of private stories, holding Natalie's hand, thanking her for trying to make him a better person. Karine looked at the static screen of her phone and her hand shook.

She cried, then held the wet cloth to her face again.

She put her head around the sitting room door. Her dad was in the armchair, a pint of lager beside him on the floor. Her mother sat on one end of the couch, shoes off, glass of wine on the coffee table. Diarmaid was snoozing on the other end.

'It's too late for him to be napping,' Karine said.

'He's had a busy day, love.' The two of them like fucking owls, unblinking.

'How's Ryan?' her father said.

'I don't know,' Karine said. 'Ask his girlfriend.'

'Get a glass,' said her mother. 'Come in here and have a drink.'

The text came in as she got to the kitchen door.

Ryan.

The whole thing in the lock screen preview.

Hey I'm outside

She turned back. She opened the door.

He was still wearing his jacket and tie. He wrinkled his nose.

She stood back and he came into the hall. She closed out the door and he looked at the floor and the wall and then at her. There was an attentive silence from the sitting room.

He said, 'I keep thinking of him up there, in the ground.'

And she took his hand in hers.

'I did need you today.' His voice went to a whisper. 'I don't understand it.' He put his weight on one foot, then the other, then back again. 'I kept seeing you and I thought maybe you'd come to me and that's all I could do, think, I couldn't move. Karine. And once I made myself move I knew that running after you is as much as I can do. I don't want to go forward,' he said. 'I don't want to fuck it up. Can I stay here with you?'

She took his other hand and he looked past her and pulled his lips back in a desperate approximation of a smile as she told him of course he could, that it could never be any other way, that she was wrong and that she knew all along she was wrong, though the lie was kind, at least. It came from her loving him, and so what could she do but make a glorious hames of it? She put her hand on the back of his neck and held him close so he could cry. 'Baby boy,' she told him, 'I won't take another step without you.'

Georgie should have been able to find herself in her parents' house. It seemed like the kind of thing that would happen. She would explore her old home, and in her old room find a stash of half-remembered novels about teenaged toffs solving mysteries on moors, and remember the principled kid she used to be. She would imagine that kid suppressed by dark circumstance, or, very literally, by ugly sweaty randos, and do something dramatic like furiously strip the paper from her bedroom walls and find underneath the torn scraps something like *Georgie 1999* in looping handwriting on the plaster. And this would make her determined to rescue that principled kid in some Hollywood way. Self-care by way of a hallucination. She would visualise herself at fifteen, tearstained and bound in cloth, with the older, stronger, made-kind-by-trauma Georgie wiping her eyes, freeing her. 'You're safe,' the older Georgie would say to the younger, holding her close. They'd bawl, and Georgie would wake with a start, and a smile would come over her face, and she'd feel whole and wholesome, all that shite.

She went into her old bedroom and thought hard but was not overcome. She remembered being the child who'd once lived in this room and the recollection was pleasant, but there was no thread between past and present, no full circle travelled. She found a box of novels under the bed. *Heidi*, *Lorna Doone*, a few Agatha Christies, once-trendy paperbacks with lugubrious titles and contemplative girls on the covers. She sat on the bed and read a few pages from this one and that one. The sentences didn't revive the girl who'd lived in the room. She was Georgie and at the same time she was long gone. Georgie thought that her mother was wrong in lamenting the loss of her teenage and young adult years, because it didn't much make a difference whether you were present or not; a person would still change, shed old personas, keep secret much of the process, fail to update you. The world was populated with fluctuating spirits, secretive and inherently dishonest. The family was a construct clung to for the sake of sanity. We come into the world alone and we leave it alone. She returned a lugubrious novel to the box and shook her head.

Having told her parents about Harmony, she was encouraged to feel a need to see her. If she didn't, that'd be a sorry tale: a distant daughter with a distant daughter. Trauma bequeathed. She might as well ask to be committed.

She did want to see Harmony. Just not with the way things were, with her spending her days recounting filth for Medbh to pore over and watching Medbh grow ever more frustrated because her male filth-peddler wouldn't talk to her. Her head wasn't in a reunion, even if her heart was. It was proof of good mothering, not wanting to expose her daughter to this turbulence. She sat in the kitchen in Millstreet a couple of days a week and tried to put her own mother off the idea. Her mother had no sense for the stirrings of the city. When in Cork, Georgie felt like the concrete might crack under her, or the windows shatter as the streets shifted. Something ancient, waking underneath. The river changing course. The people marching. Some cataclysm. She'd given up her life in London and it was important that it was for good reason. Naturally things felt more fragile.

London, she told her parents, was very fragile. Brexit, disastrous Brexit. Neighbour spat on neighbour while the Westminster lunatics giggled and rocked and counted their bank balances. There was the Windrush scandal, then the tabloids turned on the Irish, and so the dogs were preparing for the worst. She was better off out of it. This was why she ignored Jessica's texts and phone calls. This was why, in the end, she blocked Jessica's number.

In the mobile home by the sea, she wrote her latest assignment. She didn't feel the same distance from this recollection that she felt from her childhood memories, which felt unfair.

It all changed in March of 2010. I had a scapular that belonged to my mother and I used to bring it to work because it was, I suppose, a sort of talisman. A scapular is a religious item, made up of two cloth tags on a string. This one had pictures of the Virgin Mary on the tags. It's supposed to show the wearer's devotion. I used to wind it around the handle of the bedside table in the room where I worked. Punters didn't notice it. I wasn't very engaged in the work so I tended to appeal to the rougher men, the ones who weren't kidding themselves. Every so often I'd get one that wanted to save me but otherwise the ones that came back were the ones who got off on fucking a girl who didn't want to be fucked. Weakness attracts predators, unfortunately.

The brothel was moving location as it did every so often. I had forgotten to remove the scapular from the handle of the bedside table and when the furniture arrived at the new house it was gone. I told Robbie about it and shortly after that Robbie went missing. For a long time I wondered if the scapular really was a talisman because once I lost it, I lost Robbie, and then because I didn't know what to do except wait for news, I was stressed, I drank and I abused cocaine and speed. The boss/manager/pimp at the brothel lost the rag with me because he was getting complaints and because he thought the scapular meant I had found religion, which wasn't true at the time, but that period of my life was only around the corner . . .

She put her head down on the plastic table top and stared sideways at the fridge.

That period of my life was only around the corner. For a while I pretended to convert and in return for that deception they took my daughter from me. Is it very bad that I don't think they were wrong? They went about it in an infuriating manner and for that I'd cheer if a gust blew them backwards off a cliff, but I was essentially homeless and even more essentially feckless, so : . . .

She got up and walked the few steps to the fridge, but not being hungry she just considered what she had within and went back to her seat. She would have to ask Medbh how to get to the next bit of her story. There wasn't much grit or grime to her life in the commune, except in a literal sense. Medbh had mentioned something about drawing parallels between punters and David, in the sense that David had also been happy to fuck a construct rather than a real human woman. Georgie didn't think that was fair – how would David know any better? He was soft as a boiled turnip – but Medbh was always able to draw patterns on a scattered life.

That was why Georgie couldn't forget what Medbh had said about Ryan. Of course she had always known that many of the details overlapped; the men calling the shots were the same, as was clear when it had been Ryan who had come for her, instructions rattling in his head, pistol in his sweaty little hands. Thoughts of his story encroached now on thoughts of Georgie's own, what he might have been submitting to Medbh at the same time Georgie was sending on her memoirs, had he given in to her coaxing:

They gave me twenty-five wraps and told me if I didn't have them sold by Sunday they'd break my arms. I was scared.

Jimmy Phelan was the boss of the whole city. The boss of me. He said jump and I said how high and out of any particular window?

Jimmy Phelan told me to kill a girl called Georgie Fitzsimons, who I sold coke to when I was in the mood (I had been known to refuse her coke because she was a whore, an occupation I didn't approve of because even vampires have standards). I didn't want to be a murderer. I mean, other people could overdose away on my stuff, I didn't give a hoot.

Or maybe I did give a hoot. Yeah, it used to keep me up nights. That's why I got out of the business.

Anyway I didn't want to be a murderer so I sent her into exile. I bet she has a little shrine to me and my kind heart. I bet she'd write me love letters if she knew my address. I bet she pulled herself together. I bet she created a whole life for herself, one that involved jobs and friends and hen parties and trousers bought in Zara.

Georgie went into the tiny toilet with a bottle of strong cleaner and a cloth. She rubbed at the hair-dye stain and hoped mechanics might show her the way forward, in terms of endorphins released on the workings of her muscles. She worked on the hair-dye stain every day and it was fading, but not lifting. She wondered if she could make it a metaphor and run it through the memoir. Such was the nature of shame. *He's ashamed of himself*, Medbh said. So they shared this, too. For the first time she wondered whether he was ashamed before she'd ever started writing comments. Maybe shame wasn't new to him.

She rubbed harder.

Of course it was new to him; the ashamed don't run off to Berlin and Seoul and record music for sale or supply.

The night she'd been exiled, he freaked out all the way to the airport. He was white as a sheet and swallowing hard.

She kicked the bottom of the sink. 'For fuck's sake!' she roared, and caught her breath and muttered, 'I'm going crazy here, I'm fucking losing my fucking mind.'

She got her jacket and bag and locked the door to the mobile home.

Prescribed recollection did this to her. Being asked for further detail made her homicidal. Medbh's pruning and padding. Having to come up with aliases. Dwelling on the clients' fetishes. What did that look like? What did this feel like? If this was a story that needed to be told, then Ireland's priorities must have changed drastically in the time she was away. What would her story change? Nothing. Who would read it? Those who yearned to be horrified and those who got off on their own great empathy. What good would that do her? No good at all.

'I'm not surprised you're doubting yourself. I'm surprised it's taken so long.' Medbh shook her head as Georgie sat on her couch. 'Something like this isn't supposed to be easy.'

'How would you know?' Georgie said, and Medbh smiled.

'Obviously in terms of your exact situation, I don't know. But in terms of everything important needing time and effort and attention, that's something everyone knows. You can do this, Gia.'

'I know I can,' Georgie said. 'But I don't know why I'm bothering. It's not like people in Ireland don't know that prostitution happens.'

'Well, they shouldn't be allowed to pretend it doesn't.'

'They don't pretend it doesn't.'

'Look,' Medbh said. 'Tell me where you're stuck and we'll find a way forward.'

Georgie talked about the transition between the scapular and the religious commune. Medbh offered ideas. Georgie half-listened. She looked around Medbh's living room, at Medbh's bright plastics and patterned fabrics.

'You know I know fuck-all about you?' she interrupted.

Medbh sat back. 'OK,' she said.

'I thought you might try to argue,' Georgie said, unhappily.

'I don't talk a lot about myself, I suppose. Is that what's wrong?'

'I don't need to know anything about you but you need to know everything about me in order to finish this book or whatever it's going to be.' Georgie paused and thought about it. 'Maybe I'm the problem. I'm not nosy so I don't understand why anyone would be nosy about me.'

'You're making it sound unsavoury. It's not about assuaging nosiness.'

'But it is, girl. Not for you, like. For you it's about making money.'

Medbh laughed. 'Excuse me?'

'This is your job, isn't it?'

Medbh considered and conceded.

'At the beginning,' Georgie said, 'I just wanted to talk about him. You said I was far more interesting and so for a while we talked about me instead. And now you want to bring him back into it, because my story isn't complete without his.'

'Yes, well, this part of your story isn't about him.'

'Did he contact you?'

'No. But the profile piece is finished. We're trying to get a photo to go with it. Usually we'd send a photographer but finding a time that suits is proving unusually difficult. Wonder who's being awkward there. I think Natalie Grogan's heart is broken with him. I wouldn't mind,' she said, rising, 'but it's a flattering piece.'

'How did you mention the allegations?'

'I didn't,' Medbh said, and left the room, an action that insisted Georgie either sit and simmer or follow and force a confrontation, and as the second would go badly it could hardly be an option at all. Medbh was leaving to make Georgie prove she was going to be good.

After a few minutes she came back with a glass of water and sat down.

Georgie looked towards the window. 'So you're still trying to keep him sweet in case he decides to give you his gangland recollections.'

'That's the long and short of it.'

'Anything you want to know about him, I could tell you,' Georgie said. 'Boys like him were two a penny.'

'I thought you said he was remarkable? Accomplished for his age? Rolling in it? Canny? Scary?'

Georgie tucked her fists into her armpits.

'I need to keep working on Ryan Cusack because he could be the key to something huge,' Medbh said, sitting forward. 'He doesn't have family members in the business, he's like a wild card, and therefore in a very privileged position.'

Georgie said, 'You have to know none of this disclosure crap is compatible with his music. And you think he's going to come clean voluntarily and fuck his chances of going on the *Late, Late*? You're mental.'

'It will fuck his chances of going on the *Late, Late*,' Medbh said, 'but I'm hardly going to tell him that.'

'You don't need to tell him, he's smart enough to know.'

'Sure,' Medbh deadpanned. 'He's got a wild intellect.'

'I guess he's smarter than me,' Georgie said, and got up. 'Finish my story however you like, Medbh. You have the long and short of it and the actual truth doesn't matter a fuck.'

'It does,' Medbh said. 'Which is why I'm doing this.'

'You're doing this coz you think you'll make a mint out of it. And the truth is whatever looks good on the page.'

She moved towards the door and Medbh said, 'Gia, are you storming out again?'

'I'm not storming out, I'm finished. Fuck you and whatever nonsense portrait of Cork you're trying to sell.'

She turned at the door. Medbh was shaking her head and laughing through her nose.

'He's never going to talk to you,' Georgie said.

'We'll see about that.'

Georgie thought five minutes later that Medbh could have used the same infuriating certainty to predict what she'd do next, because she wanted to turn back, apologise and pledge to get stuck in anew, and not because she was fond of Medbh, or that she thought she had been unfair in her assessment. She stopped a street away from Medbh's flat. She turned around. She put her hand to the wall to her right.

Because she had nothing better to do. Nothing else expected of her, nothing anyone was waiting for.

Titillate with all you did wrong before segueing into a detailed account of all he did wrong.

Well, as a long-time observer, as a one-time associate . . .

As someone who took what he had to offer . . .

As someone who watched his fingers pinch the baggie shut, his brow furrow in concentration, his shoulders tighten in shows of capitalist male aggression . . .

Let's talk about what men do wrong.

Let's talk about what men do.

This one liked me to piss on him and that one liked school uniforms and this one disclosed that his father had dementia and then fucked me with his hands around my neck.

It was a day with a low and heavy sky and an irritant breeze, an unhealthy day. Georgie felt incubatory. She suffered an idea as she walked along the river towards the bus station. She would phone a radio show and, if they could guarantee her anonymity, she would tell Cork about Ryan Cusack's sins in real time.

She leaned on the railing, her back to the water, and her call was taken by a perky producer who asked what was on her mind.

Georgie said, 'There's a local band called Lord Urchin.'

'There is indeed,' said the producer.

'I can confirm,' Georgie said, 'that their lead singer used to be a drug dealer.'

'You can what?'

'Confirm,' Georgie said.

'See now, that'd be a thing you'd tell the guards,' said the producer, and wouldn't be pushed past, but spoke instead of legal vulnerabilities and listeners' interests.

'I'm a woman trying to tell a story,' Georgie despaired.

'Of course you are,' said the producer. 'But tell it first to the guards. And then sure if you have a story about how you got on with the guards, get on to us again. That'd be more in our line, you see?'

So there was no way around it: a criminal man was in no way as sexy as a transgressive woman. This must have been what Medbh had meant those few weeks ago when she told Georgie about the appetite for women's stories. And as Georgie was a bit long in the tooth for sitting on the footpath crying, she wandered despondently, as might wander a muse aged past the point of allure, or a cow through a tumbledown fence. She thought about what people did when they weren't troubled by their pasts. They went to work and came home again. They met people on Tinder and had brunch on Sundays. They adopted sanctuary donkeys. They developed interests in gardening and running. These were things she needed to cop on and do. Above all, the untroubled could read moods. They knew when to talk and what about. They did not frustrate themselves screaming into the wind.

She paused by the window of a recruitment agency and read notices for office jobs. She moved on and looked around her. There were women she might look like. Shops she might buy from. The problem would be in sharing the city with men like

Ryan Cusack, and watching them enjoy their spoils even if she was enjoying her own. But then the women she might look like, they were already doing that, none the wiser. And so she needed to tut the way the rest of them tutted and whisper darkly and say, *God, isn't it shocking?* when appropriate and just fucking wear straight-legged trousers and attend hen parties and get the fuck on with it. It was not her responsibility to elucidate when everyone already knew where the light fell and didn't fall.

She decided to return to the bus station. She took a side street off Oliver Plunkett, keeping near to the wall. A door opened from the pub on the left, a few feet in front of her.

Ryan Cusack came out on to the path.

Her throat closed. He took a box of cigarettes and a lighter from his pocket. She could not stop. If she stopped, he'd look over. She bore right and looked right. She saw his reflection in the windows on her side of the street. He curled a hand around the tip of his cigarette and the lighter. She hurried her step. She had to look back to see if he was moving, and he was walking in the same direction, smoking. She looked at him and he looked at her. She looked forward again and trotted to the end of the street. She turned right. He wouldn't know her. Four years and twelve or thirteen kilos. Wardrobe and aura.

Just a couple of metres behind her, he said, 'What the fuck are you doing here?'

She was already running when she thought, *He can't possibly run after me because how bad would that look?* She could run and be unexceptional so long as she didn't cry for help. She got to Parnell Place and its multiple lanes of traffic. She danced, panting, at the kerb, looking for a chance to dart across, and without one decided to duck into a Spar. She hid down the back with the toiletries. She gasped. She dragged the back of her hand across her forehead. The small of her back was already damp with sweat. She took out her phone and called Mr Love. It rang out and went to voicemail. She jumped and dropped the handset before Mr Love's message finished playing; when she went to pick it up she kicked it and it slid across the tiles and hit Ryan Cusack's left foot.

He picked up the phone, held it to his ear briefly, then hung up for her.

'Gimme my phone please,' she said.

He held it face-up in the palm of his hand. He said again, 'What the fuck are you doing here?'

She had thought about what she might say if she was recognised by a lesser demon. Visiting my daughter. Minding an ailing parent. Renewing some legal document. To this more significant evil she could manage one word: 'Funeral.'

'Mine,' he said, 'is it?'

'I don't want to be here so if you just give me my phone back I'll go.'

'I don't want you to be here either because you're meant to be dead.'

If they taught them how to sound threatening, the big lads to the baby dealers, then he had either forgotten or failed the class. Was that another ridiculous thought, that such instruction took place? Did that business not simply attract the power-hungry, the way hers attracted the desperate?

'I know,' she said. 'You told me before. I'm sorry. Just give me my phone, thank you, I will go.'

'Go where, though? Coz this is making me pretty fucking anxious, Georgie.'

'Away from the city.'

'Away from the city where? is what I'm asking you.'

'Anywhere,' she wittered. 'Just away. Promise.'

He grimaced, and she thought that if she didn't start making sense now she was not going to get away with this, though he, standing there between the deli counter and the deodorant tins, seemed willing to let her if she could only say something soothing. She did not even have time to rack her brain. 'My parents' house,' she began, as her phone rang in his hand.

They both glanced at the phone and at the name 'Medbh Lucey' across its screen.

Ryan said, 'Oh, you daft fucking cunt,' tapped the screen and held the phone to his ear.

'Hey,' he said, and then, 'Gia,' slowly, tasting the name, finding it bitter. 'No, Medbh, you don't have the wrong number at all, girl. Naw, naw. You tell me.' He looked at Georgie as he spoke. Georgie saw herself bolting and running in spurts through the city, flapping her hands and quickly sick with exertion. 'Why would you want to call the guards?' he said. 'Sure we're right here in Spar. Do you want to say hello?' and he passed the phone to Georgie.

'What the hell is going on?' Medbh said.

'Hi Medbh. I just ran into Ryan.' Georgie looked up at him and then away. At the other end of the phone, Medbh barked, 'What is this? Have you been wasting my time?'

'No. I haven't.'

'What do you want me to do? Should I call the guards?'

'I don't know,' Georgie said.

'You don't know? How do you not know?'

'I don't know what to do now.'

'You can hang up,' Ryan said, 'and tell me if you're really that fucking stupid?'

'No, I don't want to hang up,' Georgie said.

'Hang the fuck up.'

'No, I don't want to.'

'Why don't you both come to my place,' Medbh said, 'and we can be clear about what's going on?'

'What did she say, come to her place?' Ryan asked Georgie.

Georgie nodded, eyes to the front of the shop, the street outside, and the plenty strolling it.

'I hope you can hear me, Medbh,' he said, though he didn't raise his voice. 'Go fuck yourself, you liary fucking jackal.'

There was a pause on the other end. 'I did hear that,' Medbh said.

Ryan waited till Georgie looked at him. 'Tell me, Georgie, have you lost your fucking mind?'

Georgie said nothing.

'What did I ever do on you?' Ryan asked.

Georgie imagined Medbh straining to hear, opening a new document on her laptop, stretching out her fingers.

'I saved your fucking life,' Ryan said.

'You threatened to kill me—'

'I didn't kill you, though, coz you're standing right here!'

Georgie could think of no reply but to repeat, shakily, 'You threatened to kill me.'

'I couldn't think of another way to get it through your thick, coke-broken skull that saving your life could have fucked us both. I'm sorry you think I should have been more gentle, Georgie, but y'know, I think this proves that I was far too gentle as it was.' He looked at the ceiling and jutted his chin. 'No good deed. What are you trying to do to me?' And in case she thought the question was rhetorical he looked at her and said, 'Seriously, tell me.'

'People should know,' she said.

'Why? Why should they know?'

'They should know what kind of place this is.'

'What, Cork?'

She tried to shrug.

He pressed her. 'People need to know that there are drug dealers in Cork?'

'Yes.'

'Georgie, that there are dealers in Cork comes as a surprise to fucking no one.'

Rehearsed, she said, 'It's not fair how some people come through the muck they were involved in and some people don't. If you had a hand in what went on then you should be honest about it. My boyfriend died.'

'I didn't know your fucking boyfriend, I was a fucking child.'

'People can decide for themselves whether or not to hold it against you.'

'Jesus, you're so Irish,' he said. 'What're you going to do if J.P. sees you here?'

'I don't think he'd recognise me,' she said, and he thought about this. She watched his chest move up, down.

'You might be right,' he said. 'How many of his fellas did you fuck, back in the day? Would they know you?'

Georgie took her phone from her ear and ended the call. 'Don't talk to me like that,' she said.

'No, I will,' he said. 'You're being fucking rich. One mention of your past and you hang up on Lois fucking Lane like a shot. Shouldn't people know that about you, can't they make up their own minds?'

'I never hurt anyone.'

'Naw, unless they paid well for it.' He looked over her shoulder, towards the deli counter. His eyes unfocused. At the top of the shop, a young fella with a moustache leaned on his elbows on the counter, looking down as if reading. 'What the fuck am I going to do now?' Ryan said.

'No one cares what you do,' Georgie said. 'Or cares what you did. Medbh doesn't even care. So you can just carry on as before, you're going to get away with everything.'

'No,' he said. 'You know who does care? J.P. cares. He thinks it's a big fucking deal. See, the connection is indelible now: Ryan Cusack and Ireland's underbelly. There won't be a Lord Urchin, d'you understand? I'm not allowed it, in case more Medbhs show up, or more interfering, judgemental fuckwits from Millstreet. In case there's ever a trail back to him. I don't know if you can see this—' he pointed to light discoloration on his cheekbone – 'but I got it from him, for his own entertainment, not as a warning, the warning was much worse. If I continue to be so reckless with my hobbies, the next time I see my son it'll be for sale on the dark web. Wouldn't you rather he'd kill you than have to hear that?' He sucked air through his teeth and shook his head. He put his hands in his pockets. 'There are four other people in Lord Urchin,' he said. 'More in Catalyst Music. It's not just me you fucked over. Does it make you happy, Georgie?'

He smiled, flat and hard, and blinked hard also, and shook his head, kept shaking.

Bravely, she said, 'If you expect me to say I'm sorry—'

'I won't hold it against your kid,' he said, 'because I hope someone got a decent parent out of this. Fuck you, Georgie. Go live your fucking life.' And he swiftly turned and left the shop, turned right, and was gone.

Medbh rang Georgie's phone again.

Georgie answered, confirmed that she was fine, and that there was nothing to tell the Gardaí. She said her goodbyes. Thank yous. Sad sorries and then more defiant sorries. She asked Medbh not to call her again, and told her she meant what she said about the book. No, no. Medbh could augment it and finish it, and sell it and make money off it, and the people of Cork could read it with one hand down the front of their trousers, going, *Isn't it desperate, isn't it awful, isn't it a page-turner, isn't it stranger than fiction?*

At Tony Cusack's funeral, Mel saw the man with the shaved head who'd come a few nights previous and hauled Ryan away. He was familiar, which was why she thought first he was an old neighbour or an acquaintance of her mother's, the kind of man who'd come to Mel's bedroom door in the middle of the night, eyes glinting, to *plámás* her. Instead of making her angry or disgusted this made her sad. That her mother knew such pathetic people. That they were all that was available to her when she tried to build her tribe. Tara's friends had tended to come in hard, as though completing a set; this lasted until something precious was broken, and then Tara drifted about searching for a new consort. To Mel's mind came laneways in the dark, queues in which bodies swayed and voices cracked, post-club gatherings, cigarette papers, pleading through the wooden panels of locked bathroom doors.

Once they'd buried Tony and mourners were commiserating, she hung back to observe the man with the shaved head, and he caught her at it. He approached her. 'Who are you, anyway?' he asked. 'You're not one of them.'

'Who am I? Who are you, more like?'

He considered her wryly and said, 'Ryan didn't tell you, which means Ryan doesn't want you to know. Maybe he's right and I'm not worth knowing.'

She shrugged.

'G'wan,' he said. 'Tell me. Are you a girlfriend? Home help? Am I to be sorry for your trouble?'

Mel said, 'I'm only a buddy.'

'You wouldn't be one of the little bandmates, would you? Dirty looks you're giving me, like.'

'Why would I be giving you dirty looks?'

'Not sure,' he said, 'if you don't know who I am,' and Mel had the gist of things. Something to do with the band, and Ryan's insalubrious mistakes, because it warranted a late-night crack on the jaw. Had to be a gangster type, and Ryan had warned them one would come along. Expected dirty looks, because he'd decreed something terrible. She didn't want to be a bandmate in that moment, so she said, 'I grew up next door to the Cusacks.'

'You weren't Tara's young wan?' he said.

'I am.'

'Isn't that gas? You don't look much like her. Was that intentional?'

'I don't think a person has a say in that.'

'I meant the hair and the clothes.' He looked over her shoulder, eyes darting. It reminded her of the way teachers ended interrogations in the corridors. 'And you get along with the small Cusacks, do you? There was no love lost between their dad and your mam.' He stepped back and said, 'Don't be giving me any more dirty looks.'

'How do you know my mam?' she asked.

'Your mam was a woman who made herself known.'

Kelly took to saying things like 'Life goes on', in the manner of a sad sack of yore whose children kept falling to airborne maladies.

'It's OK to grieve, like,' Mel told her, and Kelly replied, 'Oh my God, Linda, fuck off.'

Kelly was right in that there was a lot to do, complicated decisions to be made. Ronan and Niamh were still minors and needed a guardian. The tenancy of the house had to be sorted and it looked like it would have to go to Cian, being the oldest child resident there; Cian didn't like this one bit. Entities had to be informed, accounts closed or agreements transferred. There was intermittent but vicious quarrelling, which Mel supposed was to be expected considering how their father had died.

Septic shock. A cyst had ruptured and poisoned him. Complications from chronic pancreatitis, brought on by alcoholism. He couldn't stop drinking even when it hurt him.

And whose fault was it? His own? Sometimes. His children's? More times. Cian's, because he lived there and was too easygoing; Kelly's, because she'd moved out; Ryan's, because he'd put himself first and left the country; the youngest three, because they were wild. Mel wanted to make them understand one another, but thought they might turn on her for trying. Tempers were running high. She had her own concerns.

There was no love lost.

She felt that it wasn't wrong to expect the city to open to her. Being a native had to mean something. She took to walking from the terrace into town and back again, giving her host family their space and reconnoitring her own. She didn't expect that people would put a name to the face and rush out and confess to her – a rundown of her mother's carry-on, an in-depth explanation of why Mel was poisonous, too – but she expected to be asserted as Corkonian, and perhaps to feel her mother's presence as well.

Cork didn't want to hear about her mother. It offered river and food and flow. It told her she was in a good place. *Don't mind grubby*, it told her, *how about grub?* How about pulled pork, or pear and blue-cheese pizza? The Farmgate for something hearty; look down at the shoppers in the Market, the teenagers sitting at the fountain, all the yellows and browns, that art deco floor. Iyer's. Orso. Izz. All the good stuff and around the good crowd. Down to Denis in Cafe Paradiso for something swanky with samphire. Up to Mr Miyazaki to have her mind blown. Absinthe in Arthur Mayne's. Out the back door to the Crane Lane with whoever she picked up. Jump up and down in front of whoever was playing that night. This was the tone of the place. She could rip the streets up but all of a sudden she wasn't sure she'd find the foundations she remembered. *It's just you who were warped, Mel*, Cork said. *It's family that got you, as it is that got Ryan and Kelly and the rest of the Cusacks. Don't you blame me; I'm the Rebel City; I'm the Real Capital; you're what's incongruous, and still I'm going to wait for you.* And this was made clear in the news of urban renewal, the painted electrical boxes, the new diversity, the Instagrammed tasting plates and coffees on the Grand Parade.

She traipsed old haunts, trails they'd made as children either side of the North Ring Road. Once she happened across a boy and girl of nine or ten years old, off the path and behind the bushes. They were standing two feet from one another, trousers around their knees. Her pastel pink underwear, a flash of his most tender skin before they squealed and crouched and held their hands in front of themselves. She laughed and retreated. She could have made them feel better by telling them the game was old as time, but memory embarrassed her.

Once she went to see her grandfather and he made her a cup of tea as though she were a smirking creditor. She sat in his teak and Formica kitchen and told him a sanitised version of the Cusacks' turmoil; she thought he might connect with funerals and decisions, that kind of administrative rigmarole.

'I didn't know the man at all,' he said.

'He lived next door.'

'But sure not to me.'

Mel's grandfather had not visited often but she still thought this was rude, aggressively distancing. She said, 'I'm only telling you.'

'But sure what are you doing there at all, girl? Did you not get a job?'

'I told you, I'm playing for a band.'

'That's not a job.'

'I get paid.'

'Not enough for rent, by the sounds of it.'

'They were nice enough to let me stay when I had nowhere else to go.'

'Don't be like that with me, now. They that brought you to Cork. I told you I had no room.'

'That's fine,' she said. 'I didn't want to stay with you anyway.'

'That's very childish.'

'*Childish* like I'd only be up all night roaring? I don't expect you to know better. You never came to see me when I was living here. Did you just not like my mam?'

The offended puss on him. But she thought it wasn't a stretch to wonder if Irishmen of a certain era had simply not been expected to love their children or their grandchildren.

'I was told there was no love lost between my mam and Tony Cusack,' she said. 'Did you know that? Did the guards ask things like that when she went missing, whether there was anyone who might wish her harm?'

'Of course they did. But your mother would have fought with her own reflection, so of course she fought with the neighbour, she'd either be fighting him or in bed with him.' He had gone flaming red. 'Go on,' he said. 'Go on now, Linda. Don't be vexing me, girl.'

Mel kept walking. Down to St Luke's or out to Dublin Hill. All the way out to the Commons Road. Once to the hospital in Wilton and back again. While the air favoured it. While the days were in it. She stamped through the city that wouldn't suffer her mother.

Do you make a home or are you just stupid enough to assume it? Had Tara ever wondered? Had she fuck. She'd just assumed, and tried too hard to bend the city to her will, and was expunged because of it. No love lost; wasn't that suggesting that her mother was otherwise loveable? Owed love? That it was the way of things to belong and to be wanted and that she and Tony Cusack had curdled what should have been pure?

And them fighting over roles, the Cusack siblings. In front of her, with no home, a disappeared parent, no real notion over who she was – or *he was* or *they were* – fighting over how full their heads were with each other when Mel was only another placeholder name for a placeholder guitarist.

Two mornings after her visit to her grandfather, she woke to a message in the group chat from Ryan. He said he'd been at the studio, and would they come down?

He'd been forming a habit. During the day, before he'd come

home to his siblings to argue and blame, he would go to the studio and refine the songs. It kept him occupied, he said. She, Joseph, Orson and Davy stood in the control room and gaped at Ryan, who sat at the desk and went through all he'd done. He said to everyone's knees, 'I've got a few sounds I need to track down. But we're close to putting it to bed.'

'What about the lyrics?' Orson asked.

'They're written. They have been for a while. Just had to get my head around what I was saying.'

'But not recorded,' Orson said.

'Naw.' He rubbed his forehead and closed his eyes. 'I think we need to do a gig, actually.'

'At some point that'd be deadly,' Joseph said. 'But not any time soon, for fuck's sake.'

'If not a few gigs,' Ryan went on. 'I want to finish the album and I'll only know how once we see how the songs work live.' He seemed as uncomfortable as a doctor bound to give a ghastly diagnosis; he lifted his head high enough to speak to their torsos. 'But I shouldn't be up front, I was daft to think they'd ever let me up front.'

They referred to neighbours, old school friends, people he used to deal to, girls he'd slept with, the rest of Ireland. 'It didn't feel like a decision at the time,' he said, 'but that's what it was and I have no business complaining about it now.'

His risking the attention of further Medbh Luceys would put more than himself in jeopardy, and whether the rest of his bandmates felt any sympathy towards those people was beside the point. Big gangsters, yes, atrocious cunts who wouldn't appreciate a spotlight thrown on their deeds. Smaller gangsters too, young fellas who might have come off the rollercoaster and didn't deserve re-association because an old accomplice wanted to sing songs for a living. Various mammies and daddies and grandparents and siblings and romantic partners and exes and sons. And what did it say about Cork, anyway, that a langer like him could be forgiven? Sure then any cunt could be forgiven. Where was the moral? Where were the ethics?

'What are you suggesting?' Joseph said.

That he didn't mind the studio so much. His favourite thing about listening to music was admiring the background stuff, the points at which a producer had decided a song needed augmentation or stripping down. He could still write songs, plenty of lads sold songs. He'd sold music. He'd scored that video game. God knows how many YouTube videos featured his compositions. He could still play piano because no one ever looked at who was on keys. The singing was all he had to knock on the head. He wasn't a natural frontman anyway, he was too self-conscious.

'That's bullshit,' Joseph said.

'Naw, it's not, I'm a nervous cunt.'

'So who's gonna get up and sing your songs for you?'

'You can,' Ryan said. 'Mel can.'

'Me?' Mel said. 'Who says I can sing?'

'I say you can sing coz I've heard you singing. You've a grand voice.'

'It's too high,' Mel said.

'It is not.'

'It is. I hate it.'

Joseph said, 'What about *The International Recordings*?'

Ryan sucked his teeth. 'Things have already changed. You'd no problem getting rid of Izzy.'

'Actually, I'd a big problem with that,' Joseph said.

'Bring her back, then,' Ryan said. 'Let her sing.'

Orson laughed. Davy met his eyes and laughed brusquely with him. Joseph said nothing for long enough to let them know he was ignoring this smartarsery, then he said, 'Cuse. You're not thinking straight. We can't sing your songs for you, it wouldn't be right.'

'Bollocks. Never bothered Billie Holiday. Or Nina Simone. Or Marvin or Sinatra. Plenty of bands out there where the lyricist isn't the frontman. Anyway, it just turned out I had something to say, it was timing, is all. Next time you might write the lyrics.'

'You're not thinking straight,' Joseph said again. 'You're only coming through a tough spell and you need to take it easy on yourself.'

'My dad has nothing to do with this,' Ryan said.

Natalie and Colm were let loose on the city. They listened carefully to Joseph's declaration that Ryan was rushing things, then booked the live room of a bar in the city centre for the first gig and pencilled in a second in Dublin, a third in Galway. They timed an announcement on social media. They invited bloggers and arts journalists, Medbh Lucey and all, for the craic.

At the Cusack house the turmoil continued. Ryan came by each evening, Karine at his side, and had to be stopped from tearing his hair out. He didn't mention the gig, or seem capable of caring about art. The language he used here was nothing like what he said at the studio; isn't it funny, Mel thought, how the terrace forced out the worst in them?

The day before the gig he was home earlier than had become usual. He did not have Karine in tow. He came upstairs and found Mel repeating Izzy's riffs on Kelly's bed.

'Will you do me a favour?' he said.

Mel thought *Well, isn't that funny?* but she did not really find anything about Ryan curious, having observed him so closely for so long. So she didn't leap off the bed, join her hands and say, *A favour? Thank God we've moved past all of that unpleasantness.* Why wouldn't he have been able to focus on one thing and ignore another when it suited him? Everyone was capable of mental blocking and draining; Ryan Cusack was not special and had never been special, he was merely proximate. So without moving her hands from the strings she said, 'Yeah, what?'

He wanted her to come with him to the venue so they could go through the songs. The rest of the bandmates couldn't get it through their heads that he was serious about not being up front, but Mel, having come in last, didn't have any pesky set ideas. The more he thought about it, the better a roving mic sounded. Maybe he'd take a song, then her, then Joseph. Play it by ear. Ha ha.

They got the bus and stood near the front, holding opposite sides of a metal pole. She assessed his nails, bitten to the quick. He was animated. He listed the songs he thought she could definitely sing. Did she have any objections? What didn't she think would work? Why?

When they got off the bus she said, 'You never even asked if I wanted to sing.'

He squinted at her. 'Don't you?'

'Not everyone can stand the thought, Ryan. You grew up with a musical parent, so singing to a crowd doesn't freak you out. But to most people, you'd be a bit tapped, like.'

Ryan watched as the bus pulled back on to the street behind Mel. When the city hum had come back to the right level, he said, 'Why would you only bring it up now if you didn't want to?' He started walking. 'You're not most people,' he said out in front of him, as though whether or not she heard him was irrelevant.

She only brought it up again half an hour later, as she slung her guitar over her shoulder on the stage. Ryan stood at the front of the floor, hands in his pockets and shoulders up. The venue manager, a bearded fella with a pot belly who irked her for looking so much like a venue manager, pissed about behind him. They ignored one another, as men had the luxury of doing.

'What's that mean?' she said. 'I'm not most people?'

'Ha?'

'You said I'm not most people.'

'Oh. I dunno,' Ryan said. 'You're a musician. To most people I'd be a bit tapped but you're of the same inclination, therefore you're not most people. Don't read too much into it.'

'Why not? In case I'd think it was a compliment?'

It smelled good here, deeply alcoholic, like it'd gone into the walls. It smelled dark even with the lights on, like the kind of place you could grow myths, find a tribe, lose a crisis. Like the studio, it was as it should be. And so if all of these things were as they should be then it was Mel that was wrong. Clashing with the confines, likely to hurt something.

'You can think it's a compliment,' Ryan said, slowly.

'Yeah, but keep it professional, right? Maybe you go through life like that—' and she pointed – 'careful with compliments in case someone gets the wrong idea. Is it my mam has you that way?'

'Is there something I can say that'll put that out of your head?' he said, at last.

She said, 'I never liked you.'

'OK.'

'You're rude to me because of something you did with my mam. It's not fair, but it is expected. Maybe outside of that you're a dote, I don't know. I never knew you as a nice person.'

'OK.'

'What's really important to me right now is that you don't think I like you.'

'You don't have to like me.'

'You want to put me in your place at the front of the stage. Are you sorry for me? Are you sorry for what you did with my mam, you think this'll help?' When he didn't answer she pointed to her chest and said, 'I've never been in a band before, like.'

'I'm not trying to compensate you. If I never saw you again that'd suit me down to the ground. It wouldn't make me brave but it'd suit me down to the ground.'

'See what I mean? You're not a nice person.'

'No.'

'So that's why you want me to substitute for you, because you're trying to be brave? Is it that much of an effort to be decent to me? None of it was my fault, Ryan. You fucked my mam. You did that.'

He did not even look to see if the venue manager had witnessed this, so it must have been a shock. She was chastened by his shuddering in his spot on the floor but she would not tell him that she was sorry.

Then he said, 'Yeah, I was trying to be brave.'

She rolled her eyes and jumped off the stage.

He turned with her and said, 'I thought it might draw a line under it. If we moved forward, fuck whatever went before. After my dad it seemed important.'

She put her elbows on the bar counter and took her weight off her feet. 'There was no love lost between your dad and my mam,' she said. She made note of the different bottles in the fridge behind the counter. She wondered which of them she might drink on stage. Swig something that told of the person she was attempting to be, an actual person, at an actual point on a spectrum.

'That was coz of me,' Ryan said, behind her.

'Naw,' she told the fridge. 'No one fucking loved her.' She was being theatrical, so she straightened and looked to the left, forearms still on the counter. 'When we were small, I was jealous of you. So I should be delighted you want to give me your place. Did you know that?' She turned to face him. 'That I was jealous of you?'

He shook his head. 'Because of the music thing?'

'I just wanted to be you.'

'Why?'

The thought that she might tell him flared and fast went out. 'We were small,' she said. 'Kids are stupid.'

'If it was you, though . . .' He could not stay looking at her. 'If it was you it would feel positive, just coz there was no love lost. And you're like me. From the terrace, I mean. The stuff that makes sense to me makes sense to you.' He folded his arms and tucked his chin.

She didn't know if she was reading him right or just imagining herself literate; he was anxious, he was embarrassed, he was on to something in thinking that they were alike, in that case. Fuck's sake, did anyone's skin fit right? Couldn't he have stayed self-possessed and useful? Had he ever been self-possessed or was that more of her projection? Had his assuredness dissipated once it had gotten him where he needed to go, between her mother's legs? Ha ha, another place they'd both been and come away from.

'The days I wanted to be you are gone,' she said. 'If I went up front in a band it wouldn't be to sing your songs, considering your history with my mother.'

'Stop, Mel.'

'For your benefit? Ah, no. I'll say what I like about her because that's all I was left with, speculation. Mothers mean something, even when they're the world's worst. And no one will give me clues except, *Ah, there was no love lost between your mam and Ryan's dad.* Your dad could have driven her off, your dad could have killed her, I'm not allowed to know. Still, Mel, come back to the Northside and pretend nothing's happened, do Ryan Cusack favours he hasn't earned.' She clenched her jaw. 'I don't want to sing your fucking songs, Ryan. Couldn't one or two be about my mam?'

He shook his head, mouth tightly shut, for her last few sentences, and when she stopped he said, 'This is sick.'

'Fire me, so, the way you fired Izzy for telling inconvenient truths. You fucked my mother. Didn't you fuck my mother? Didn't Izzy say own it? Listen, one crazy bitch about another, Izzy knows her stuff there, like.'

'I didn't fuck your mother,' he said. 'I wasn't conscious.'

'What's that mean? You weren't aware? You weren't woke?'

'I wasn't awake.'

'You're gonna have to expand on that a bit, boy, because I haven't a clue what you're saying to me.'

'Your mam gave me a hape of drink and once I drank it she hopped on top of me. And all I can remember is realising what she was doing and throwing her off and running home and saying nawthin' about it for fucking years, till I had a belly full of yokes and Izzy was there, asking me why I was such a cheating scumbag.'

He turned around. He looked away. He made weak motions close to his body as if furtively blessing her with the hope he might be lying and so after a while she said, 'Right. Right so. Thanks.'

'D'you think it felt good to tell you that?' he asked, as he started to fracture. 'D'you think I'm here to shed light on your twisted fucking cunt mam for you? You can have her, girl, she lives in my fucking head, she's here with me right now, she won't fucking leave.'

After that Mel flung herself through the city centre, furious with an intensity that could not stand examination. She rattled off subjects she'd rather took up space in her head. *Drawing. The flow versus scratch of a pencil. Photorealism in ballpoint pen. Fonts. The graffiti-style logo for Lord Urchin. Street art. Political awakenings. Being a political artist. Smashing the gender binary. Smashing the patriarchy. Getting smashed. The liver having considerable powers of regeneration. The fear of aging skin. Whether or not one should wear SPF all year round. Vitamin D deficiencies. Staying healthy given this new profession. Late nights. Foggy brains. Fans. Stans. Anti-fans. Groupies. The essential sex appeal of lead singers. The essential anguish of lead singers. Lead singers and her mother.*

She steamed as far as the Lee Fields to look across at St Anne's, no lunatic asylum any more, but apartments, though from this distance it looked the same as it had when she was a young wan, all dolled-up for drinking tins in the bushes. She went back to town via the university and the Lough, and all down Barrack Street was the same: places for lunatics, repurposed. *Is this how you're opening up to me?* she asked the city. *Seems a weird sell for your prodigals.* Cork did not concede that it was. It threw more beautified shopfronts at her. It was happy with this redefinition, not a care at all to what or who it was fucking.

Off Pana, two hours later, Mel thought of her belly.

She bought a doughnut and a shot of espresso in a place with exposed brick walls and distressed metal fixtures. People said about such places: too gimmicky, too slick, was it fuck authentic! Now, had the brickwork been there before, and carved with the names of the fallen, then that would be more in their line. When Mel had been Linda she'd have given her liver for a place like this; with a place like this she wouldn't have needed her liver for bushing, or the courage for those games as old as time. *What are you at complaining, so?* Cork asked. *You can only nitpick what's been fixed if you didn't mind it broken.*

On the windowsill outside the shop sat a dishevelled guy, back to the glass. He was jiggling as if he was listening to music. As Mel was heading back out she made use of a trick of the light, and imagined passing through the glass, knees bent, arms low, settling into this man's body, opening her new eyes and thinking new thoughts for the new old city.

Sunlight bounced aggressively off windscreens and shopfronts. Mel stood on the footpath, looked left and right and then down at the man, who was looking right back at her.

'Howyeh stranger,' he said.

'Jesus, Traolach, boy! What are you doing in Cork?'

'Had a few days free. Wanted to pay my respects to himself. Terrible thing, what happened him. Have you a father yourself?'

'Yeah, boy, I'd have a father all right.'

'Well biologically you would, I suppose. I'm asking in a more everyday sense. I have one. Sixty-one years of age. Riddled with gout. Gone mad with his own expansion, 'tisn't healthy.'

'Mine lives in Glasgow,' Mel said. 'He's healthy as a trout.'

'Lovely stuff,' said Traolach. 'Will we go for a wander?'

'Sure why not?' she said.

Traolach got up and stretched. He had a canvas backpack, and pulled it on to one shoulder. They began to walk towards the Grand Parade. 'It's a shame about the *rírá* on Bofin,' he said. 'That Izzy is an awful *pleidhce*.'

'She put a video on YouTube saying she'd been kicked out because she didn't fit the aesthetic.'

'I'd say you prefer the lie, do you?'

They hit Paul Street and had to dodge striders and preachers, women with shopping bags, children with precarious ice creams, the vigorous youth. Mel and Traolach parted and came back together. Outside the coffee shops, brown-eyed boys chatted and sprawled. A tide of Italians and hijabis and loud students at TK Maxx. Drunks in sagging trousers, grousing. Multitudes, and inharmonious, and evasive in terms of their loyalties.

When she and Traolach fell back in step, Mel said, 'Ryan told you what Izzy said, so.'

'Sure I met him afterwards at the pub. He was in an awful way. Took the first fag he'd had in two months off me. The little missus came and brought him off to talk him down, but he was back to me an hour later. She'd ballsed it up. Tried tough love, wanted him to confront the big bad memory. I prescribed whiskey. Why confront the memory? If you've got it contained, you should keep it contained. Of course, it helps if no one goes ripping the skin off it in front of a crowd.'

'You know it was my mam?'

'I do.'

'And you think it's all right to say to me "big bad memory", do you?'

'Don't get offended on behalf of the guilty,' Traolach said. 'Do you remember being fifteen?'

'I was an old fifteen.'

'Himself thought he was too.'

She asked him to clarify the 'himself' pet name. It seemed an unearned fondness. It was a word for the lips of a doting old wife, or the star-struck housekeeper of a convivial bishop. He didn't explain it. He asked her where they should go.

'I dunno. The peace park?'

They found a place on the grass and sat down. Mel tried to pretend she wasn't expecting therapy; she leaned back with her hands on the ground, but could prepare no responses because she was sorry more than she was offended.

Traolach dug into his backpack and with great care, produced a colourful square on the tip of his finger. 'The cause of all this ruckus,' he said.

'Is that acid? Will you go on away! You know I'm staying with Ryan's family? I can't be heading back up there tripping, I'd be shot.'

He shrugged, put the square on his own tongue. 'The body of Christ,' he said.

'Don't you have to go and see Ryan yourself?' Mel asked. 'What are you at, like?'

'Seen him already.' He pulled his bag on to his lap, and, Poppins-like, produced a net of oranges, four kiwi fruits and two 2-litre bottles of water. 'Did you ever eat a kiwi while tripping?' he asked. 'It's a fine thing. A mad thing. Do you believe in madness?'

'Don't you?'

He waved a hand. 'It's all in our heads as is. Doors open when we take acid, or DMT, or mushrooms. Fuck me, this is the mushroom park! Wrong fucking drug!' He laughed and chanted at her. 'My! Brother! Knows Karl Marx!'

'If you've seen Ryan already—' she began.

'Ever do DMT? You meet angels, Mel. All in here,' and tapped his head. 'Madness is difference, or a brain at full potential. I woke up on the operating table. Couldn't feel a thing but I could hear and see everything. I wasn't scared.'

'We were arguing,' she said, 'so if you've seen him already and you're on your own again now, I guess he's in bad form. I don't even know why I was angry with him. I know it couldn't have been his fault. I know I was being a prick.'

'Oh yeah, you definitely made him miserable. D'you know what I told him to do?'

'Was it acid?'

'He wasn't having any of it. Afraid of his own head, that lad. But who am I to tell him he's wrong, knowing what goes on in there? Take it yourself, if you like,' Traolach said. 'It won't be seen as an insult to the hosts. I told him I'd talk to you. He knows I've come bearing gifts, that I'm a chemist and a peacemaker. Texting him now, so he'll know where to mop us up.'

Mel pushed this around in her head for a bit, then craned her neck to say, 'Do you know how weird that sounds? Like you're some sort of gruesome twosome, and you barely know him.'

'Did drugs with him outside of Café del Mar. I couldn't know him any better.'

'Try growing up either side of a wall as thin as your fucking fingernail.'

Traolach went, *Mmm*, tapping at his phone.

'You don't know this place either,' Mel said. 'Or how it feels to be told by this place, which is only a malignant growth of buildings and strangers, that you were wrong to want to know what happened to your missing mam, and given something worse instead.' There was no love lost between her mother and Ryan's father and it was no wonder and it had been corrected and here she was now, in Bishop Lucey park in the centre of Cork City, with no reason at all to be here instead of Glasgow, would she like some warbat or some dosas or nigiri or glazed pork belly?

'I don't know if I've the right frame of mind for acid,' she said.

'Doubt is the sound of your mind changing.'

'You might be right.'

He put a square on her tongue and lay back on the grass, his knees bent, his arm over his eyes. 'Only thing,' he said, 'is there was a fair dose in what I just gave you. It was for himself.'

'The argument today started coz he wants me to substitute for him,' she said. 'Anyway, not my first time on the spaceship.'

Traolach removed the arm from his eyes, smiled at her, replaced the arm.

She waited. She thought about songs and spaceships. Space Oddity and Ashes to Ashes. Wide Open Space. Supermassive Black Hole. Calling Occupants of Interplanetary Craft. Every Planet We Reach is Dead. Rocket Man. The Final fucking Countdown.

'I like Ryan's songs,' she told Traolach.

'Yeah, they're nifty enough.'

'I mean I like them enough to want to perform them. He said if he never saw me again, that'd suit him. And still he's trying to find a place for me. Cork never shut a door but it opened a window.'

Traolach said 'Ha ha' rather than laughing.

'It's like Cork's changed,' Mel said. 'It just put on a snazzy outfit and said I can hang out as long as I don't mention or question what it was before.'

'Like yourself,' Traolach said.

'I'm just me.'

'We both know that's not true.'

Alex Grey shit starting to pop. Texture in the grass that hadn't been there moments before. Where one reality ended another began. What was artifice, what was all in the mind, what was bias and what was wishful thinking? She thought about all the colours bees could see. Tried to imagine the difference between one ultraviolet and another. Imagine seeing all of those colours and not having the time to make sense of them. *Busy as a bee. Drone. Hive mind. Fume*, meaning to smoke. Smoke to dull the bees' defence responses. *Fume*, as in *vapour*, as in *attack of the vapours*, as in emanations from the womb causing hysteria, causing depression. Generations misunderstood, condemned, corseted to the point of fainting and then dismissed as hopeless. *Bees in their bonnets. A gathering in the head.* Nellie Bly spending ten days in the asylum. Busy bees subdued by smoke, narcotics, censure. *Anger, jealousy, over-action of the mind, political excitement, uterine derangement, female disease.* She remembered a list of reasons women had been committed to a lunatic asylum in the 1800s. It was hilarious and horrifying. Imagine such a list particular to Ireland. *Religious disregard, starvation,* ag labhairt as Gaeilge, *won't take the soup, rude to the British.*

'I feel like I crawled out of a hole in the ground,' she told Traolach. 'I could laugh at how sorry for myself I feel.'

'Laugh, then.'

Imagine such a list particular to people only shaped like women ... though that was all of them. Only shaped like. Designated. Whether they were invested in it or disgusted by it was irrelevant, into the asylum they went! Madness was a contagion spread by foul mouths. *Unbecoming language, wearing of trousers, sprinting, cutting of the hair, playing of externally amplified stringed instruments, sporting of surface piercings, discomfort with pronouns, fear that discomfort is not enough at all.*

She picked up the orange and wondered if she was meant to peel it.

How dosed was a fair dose?

This was for himself, the dose or the dosing?

Now she could see the auras of those around her: mostly strawberry-red, the odd doused in a royal purple. Could she read them? Would they confound her too? One hue flashing to another. She opened a bottle of water and gulped. Traolach. Disciple with the chest scar. 'For himself.' Groupies again! Guerrilla warfare. *Chemical* warfare.

Ryan's was the bloom of oil spilled in water. Blues, greens, purples. He came across the park with his hands in his pockets.

'He'll ask if we're OK,' Traolach said, when she nudged him.

'What should I say?'

'You could be dishonest, but I don't know how you'd do with it. He might have hid your mam's secret for her for years but otherwise he's a truth teller.'

'What if I tell him I forgive him?'

'What if he tells you to go fuck yourself?'

The blue above flashed with Aztec patterns, or Mayan patterns, something ancient and overwhelming. Mel had an orange in one hand and a kiwi in the other and when Ryan furrowed his brow at them, she offered no explanation but a batshit smile.

Two hundred and thirty-two people showed up for the gig, more than even Natalie had been expecting. Ryan was last up on stage. Several clusters of people had stopped him to tell him to break a leg. The venue manager had left bottles of water on the floor beside their instruments. Mel took a professional-looking draught. She was already sweating: her neck, her temples. She was waiting for Ryan to panic, which was worse than expecting it from herself.

Natalie and Colm stood in the right corner with Triona and Senan. To the left, at the front, stood Karine D'Arcy with a couple of the wans she'd been in school with. Kelly, Cian and Cathal stood behind them. There were others Mel recognised; they slipped in and out of the crowd. Traolach, too, at a different spot each time.

Joseph spoke into his mic. He said that this wasn't a regular gig – there'd been no cover charge, no warm-up act – that Lord Urchin were previewing the album and that the audience were as welcome to react negatively as positively. There was a warm cheer and a smattering of whistles.

They started with 'No Soul to Sell' from *The International Recordings*, with Ryan taking the mic. He sang it as it was meant to be sung, stirring and confrontational. He showed no signs of panicking. He deserved his cheers. If Mel was a conspiracy theorist she would suspect his declaration in the studio to have been a sort of baiting of her ego, or his cousin's ego, that he meant to continue as their frontman and was going to sneer at them for thinking they could do what he could do. She was too happy with her own performance to take the thought further. No one had thrown anything at her for not being Izzy King, so Ryan could do what he pleased with his mouth.

She shot him a look and he returned it as he thanked the crowd.

'So we're Lord Urchin,' he said, and casually flipped a thumb at each of his bandmates. 'Davy, Orson, Mel, Joseph. I'm Ryan.'

More cheering, and he looked down and grinned, then lifted an arm and crossed it behind his head, looked off into space. 'I got myself into a bit of trouble on the internet,' he said, which reignited the crowd; someone shouted, '*Maith an fear!*'

'Which didn't necessarily come at the wrong time,' Ryan continued, 'because it helped us work things out, line-up wise.'

A cheeky 'Whey!' went around the room. Izzy would have expected better.

Ryan said, 'The album's nearly done. Remains to be seen whether I'm nearly done. So let me clear this up.'

Mel thought that the bar must be selling well, so generous were the crowd's reactions. A petty part of her wanted to take the mic and tell them that Ryan was actually anxious to the point of cowardly, an unworthy son of the Rebel County. She was more subject to hero worship than most; she had been cursed and calmed by it; she understood that it sprung not from him as he really was but rather what he represented. Happening by at the right time, in a pleasing shape, and absorbing the furious desire of an onlooker badly in want of a complete self. So she considered people like her, who knew that they were lacking, and people like Ryan, just as lost who nevertheless could seem whole, if you put them in the right light. Ryan did not have to know that this was happening. He was not instigating it.

He was alternating between telling the stage and telling the back wall of the room that fuck-ups of this magnitude couldn't expect exoneration so he wasn't asking them to be nice about it.

'I'd put it at the top of the list of stupidest things I've ever done,' he said. 'But y'know, young fellas are fucking idiots.'

The young fellas roared affirmation.

'And desperation is a fucking dose.'

This, too, pleased them.

'And if someone knows what the fuck I'm meant to do next, I'm all ears.' He didn't wait for the crowd to calm, he said, 'I'll do a new one for you,' then covered the mic and said to the bandmates, 'How It Feels to Be Tamed'.

As if he'd know how it felt to be tamed. He was spot-on, his delivery deepened, tougher, and again Mel considered that he might be fucking with them all. But he said to her, 'Will you do "Believe in No One" with me, so?' and as soon as she nodded Orson began the intro.

Then it was half past one and they were in the venue's outdoor smoking area, a covered lane threaded with ivy, hanging baskets, iron lanterns. They were sober but keen to be less so.

Three things were interesting. One: how easy Mel had found it, despite not having played to an audience before, how easy it was to sing harmony to Ryan's melody when she imagined her voice as belonging to someone else, someone more certain who didn't mind its pitch or care that it was shot through with pink. Two: that Natalie was sitting here unashamed when it was clear that Ryan clung to Karine the same way in elation as he did in grief. Three: how easily swayed that crowd was.

They sat behind pints of IPA and cider and balloons of amber liquids, suggesting, countering, planning. Something powerful had happened. The crowd was emphatically on Ryan's side. The city had just told them it wanted him throaty and impudent. Now his friends took turns telling him. He gave them odd smiles in return; first one side of his mouth would lift, then the other. His nose would wrinkle. The black eyes would narrow and focus on things either side of their heads. He wouldn't be drawn. Mel had sung harmonies and Joseph had taken on a couple of songs himself. Anything Ryan could do, the other urchins could do just as well.

'That's not true,' Joseph said.

Ryan shrugged. 'It is true.'

He said he could finish the album now. There were some session musicians Triona would help him track down. He wanted to drop some sounds and strengthen others. There was a sample he couldn't get out of his head; he'd made up his mind now to clear it. But it was good, what had happened. It was hard to be nervous about performing when he was snatching what moments he could; he knew how little time he had left so he could pour himself into every second.

'But Ryan.' Natalie leaned forward, breasts swelling over the neckline of her dress in a way Mel found intimidating and certainly designed. 'They like *you*. Yes, Lord Urchin, but with you up front.'

'They like me tonight, they might hate me tomorrow,' he said. 'They have short memories.'

Much later. After four. Back at the terrace, in the Cusack house. Cian guffawing in the sitting room with Traolach. Mel with a can of lager snapped open on the kitchen table in front of her. Ryan on the other side of the table, with a mug of fucking tea. Clear as a bell. His voice. All night. He was too pleased with it to threaten it with gatt. Mel was slow to get words out, heavy-tongued. Would feel it tomorrow. Italian hip hop from the speakers. No, he said, Neapolitan. Karine, by the worktop, with a pint of tap water. Ever watchful. The little missus. Ah. Unfair. Was her own self, too. Just so much whispered between the two of them; every time she touched his wrist, caught his eye, transmitted a warning, Mel felt simultaneously better and worse for being alive, where she was and when she was.

They were talking about Medbh Lucey and her interest in working-class voices. Nice and guttural. Her bit done for structural inequality. Karine was laughing. Said she was more working-class than Ryan. *She* didn't speak a handful of languages. Had never been to *Seoul*. Grandad wasn't a *pharmacist*. *Never* had music lessons. Or notions. 'Notions?' he cried. Big home-improvement credit-union heads on Jackie and Gary! She doubled over. He put his head on the table. Both of them in hysterics. Mel thought of learning Russian and making homemade cosmetics and Kayla Lam. Of being Melinda.

'At least you kept your names,' she said.

'Our names make sense,' Ryan said. She thought of his blood and muscle, skull and ribcage, Adam's apple, the pattern in which hair grew on his face, his pianist's fingers. That he'd fathered a son. She thought of him inside Karine, her underneath him, accepting. How the male and female fit together. Where she'd gone wrong. She thought of her mother climbing on top of him and shut her eyes tight. He was fifteen when she fell out of love with his gatch, deeper voice, broader shoulders. Let her down. Wrong to hold it against him and here she was.

'Mel sounds Scottish,' she said, as if nationality was the point.

She opened her eyes again. Karine had left the kitchen with her glass of water. Ryan still had his head on the table. Droplets on the surface from the heat of his breath. Imagining it, maybe. Black hair, styled well in that it was masculine, handsome but not in a way that drew attention to itself. If she did that it would draw attention to itself. Look at the wan. Butch. Lesbian. Head on her.

'Remember when Izzy thought D'Arcy asked why was it male, instead of why were you Mel?'

Just about.

A long silence.

'Is that what you meant when you said you wanted to be me?'

She didn't reply.

Didn't seem imperative.

'I wouldn't wish me on anyone,' he said.

'I'd have made a better go of you,' she said.

'Maybe. I'm trying.' He sat up and pulled up the right sleeve of his T-shirt. 'I won't tell you how much that ink cost but it was worth every cent. It's not the body my dad kicked or the one your mam took for herself.' He shook his head. 'Fuck it,' he said. 'Fuck it all, Mel, the water's rising and we are completely fucking fucked. You might as well be who you want to be. Make a song and dance about it. Maybe that's what you're here for.'

'But not you, if you're fading into the background, no song and dance for Ryan.'

'I'm here for Diarmaid. Everything else is extra. If I can't have it, I can't have it.'

She locked eyes with him and said, 'It's not fair.'

'Most things aren't fair.' He jerked forward. 'Be who and whatever the fuck you like, Mel. Don't be a gutless cunt about it when there's no one standing in your way.'

'I'll be a gutless cunt if I want.'

'That's the spirit, boy.'

Track 9: You'll Answer to Me

Natalie made her own recording of the interview I did with Medbh Lucey. We listened back immediately afterwards and Natalie says, all long-suffering, 'Could you have been more abrasive?'

'Yeah,' I says. 'I could, actually.'

The night of the interview, all that I'd said was underlined for me by a lairy cunt going slowly mad because his power kept shrinking the world. He drove me to his *síbín*, a place I'd been a handful of times, none of them positive. He got in my face and promised me damage. He held it against me that he had to make these promises. I wasn't saucy with him. I told him I'd kneel for him, I told him I was sorry. Sorry! For making him think about a shrinking world at all! Still he gave me a dawk and held his hand high against his chest afterwards. 'How much singing do you think you'll be able to do,' he asked, 'if they have to set your broken jaw for you?'

But that's the thing about lyrics. They shroud the reality of things, don't they? They're ugly when direct. J.P. would have said I'd sung for Medbh Lucey already, except, of course, I told her nothing she wanted to hear, which was evident in her telling me she'd put the words in my mouth if she had to. I stood in J.P.'s *síbín*, rubbing my cheekbone and thought, This is the story of the rest of my life.

'You'll Answer to Me' was the second last song to come together. I thought it was finished before it actually was. It had a different name, then, and though it was going in the right direction the path it was carving was wider. It wasn't defiant. It was self-pitying. It was about fear, because I was afraid, but in the nature of songs it was skirting around the reasons I had for being afraid. That's all right, boy, we'll say it's about anxiety! Everyone has anxiety, everyone has the gnawing fear that they've done something wrong and everyone hates them. Except, of course, I had done something wrong. All of those people walking around only just holding themselves together, worried about their mental health, and whether they're overeducated, and how to read their friends on social media, and me, here, hello, what's the story, a genuine fucking disaster.

Then my dad died and wiped my head clean.

I remembered the interview only after I met Georgie in town and realised that the violent truth was being wielded against me by another fucking idiot disaster. And then when I thought about the interview it was through a red haze, it was at inadvisable temperatures. Medbh Lucey was prodding me to implicate myself and I was lying through my teeth so Jimmy Phelan wouldn't feel the slightest twinge. I was fucked because to Medbh, to the good people, I was corrupt. I was unrepentant and no one gave a fuck that it was by necessity. I was, therefore, unsympathetic. A scumbag. The wrong kind of rebel. And what was I doing? Proving her right by protecting a man who said he'd slit my throat.

And then I wasn't despairing, D'Arcy, I was murderous, and the lyrics rewrote themselves.

'You'll Answer to Me' doesn't implicate me because I no longer give my temper free rein. I give it a loose rein, though. I kept the words spitting and scathing. You know what I'm doing in 'You'll Answer to Me'? Talking to J.P. Telling him he underestimated me. Like anxiety, the desire for revenge is universal. People get off on the idea. I was getting off on the idea and my mood was an unsafe one.

So once I finished the lyrics I took Natalie's interview file and uploaded it, shared the link, held my phone in front of my face and said, 'I see your offered second chance, Ireland, and I don't fucking want it.'

Proximity to danger is not something I feel with any consistency. I've sat into cars with fellas who swore to kill me. I've stood over fat lines of coke and felt like my heart was going to burst and still crouched to snort another. Reality is a pier alongside which you bob in your skiff. Sometimes you can gauge the distance. Sometimes you miss the jump.

I use 'you', as in, 'one', as in, I'm speaking for a hypothetical, but that's just a method of distancing. I mean 'me', 'I'. Reality is a pier alongside which Ryan Cusack bobs in his skiff. I can talk to you like I'm wise and like this is a universal but I can only speak for me, because I'm not that empathetic and I'm not that fucking smart. But I know what I've done and what's been done to me isn't usual. I know that anger, in me, can be righteous and blinding and pure. Can lift, for a few lightheaded moments, the burden of damage I've done and the damage done to me.

Had there been great and evil nuns running rampant on Jimmy's childhood he wouldn't have so many big ideas about himself now, but it wasn't fair to say that more religion would have done him the world of good when less of it would have done Maureen the world of good. Her own son and she wishing Catholic Ireland on him.

He could stand across the road glowering at her all he liked; it wasn't her job to deliver him from wasting his time.

She had four wans and one fella in anoraks in front of her. The first two happened along as she stood in wait, and when they stopped to read Mother Jones' plaque she began to regale them. The other three had stopped on their dawdle up the road, made curious by the oration she'd practised in the middle of her kitchen.

'She claimed to be older than she was—' she winked – 'because youth cannot demand respect and youth gets feck all done. A young woman is to be conquered but an old one is to be feared.'

She made a snapping motion with her jaw and the anoraks jumped and laughed.

On the other side of John Redmond Street, Jimmy fell back against the wall, hands in his pockets. He put her in mind of a midweek arse-scratcher.

'Do you know,' she went on, watching him, 'she didn't get on with the suffragettes at all?'

Jimmy shook his head.

'What a shame,' said the lime-green anorak.

'The way Mrs Harris Jones saw it,' Maureen said, 'the freedom of the workers, regardless of their sex, was more pressing. I suppose in the same way that today they're all me-tooing, and nothing at all about the craiturs abroad in Saudi Arabia.'

She continued with the March of the Mill Children, President Roosevelt refusing to meet Mother Jones, her arrest in West Virginia, and how she was called a fake at the Battle of Blair Mountain. This last detail had made Maureen soft on Mother Jones, for it was an awful thing to have your bluff called, and good to see that even formidable biddies could be hopeless on their off days.

She asked the anoraks where they were off to next and took three of the five with her towards the river. Jimmy sauntered after them.

She crossed with them at North Gate Bridge. She did not point out her old home, or tell them about lads wanting to jump into the Lee from the handsome footbridge further down. She assumed Jimmy was still following but she wouldn't please him to check. She brought her tour down to the Coal Quay, across to Paul Street, down Carey's Lane. They crossed Pana and went into the English Market. She told them it was more than two hundred and thirty years old, that Mrs Windsor had come over for a gawk a few years back, that it kept going on fire in the 1980s but she was over visiting Mrs Windsor herself at the time so she couldn't say how bad it had been.

The tourists asked her a few questions and were charmed when she announced, abruptly, that her time with them had come to an end. 'Not at all!' she said, when they offered her money, taking a chance that they'd know she was only being polite. They did not insist. Lime-green anorak asked for a photo, which Maureen coldly declined.

She left them and went out on to the Grand Parade, where Jimmy stepped up to put an arm around her shoulders. She gave him a cross little shrug.

'Maureen,' he said, 'what in fuck's name are you doing now?'

'What am I doing, what are you doing?' she said. 'Following me around town like a lost dog.'

'I was driving past,' he said. 'Your beady little eyes is what made me wonder what fuck-acting you were at now.'

'Fuck-acting! A fine way to talk to your mother.'

He laughed very jovially and said through his teeth, 'What are you at, Maureen?'

'Socialising.'

'You are yeah. Hanging around John Redmond Street like you had an appointment. Waiting on the fuckers, whether or not they knew it. You're not starting a cult, are you?'

She stopped. 'Have you nothing else to be doing? Have you no scuts to torment?'

'You hardly think I'm tormenting you,' he said. 'I have plenty reason to worry about you.'

People walked past, some fast and close enough that they had to dodge. Plenty of scuts, with it being summer. Not that they'd be pursuing their educations otherwise, only that the meagre sun tended to draw them out. There they were in short sleeves, showing off their tattoos. Territorial as crows, noising and scratching and lepping around. Her grandson Conor wouldn't have been able for them; he was good for nothing but backchat. She doubted Jimmy would afford bluster to someone else's scut. Her merchant prince needed subjects and subjects needed minding, or keeping, or directing or tormenting and really he should have had other things to do, in a true and free and just Ireland: minding his children, keeping his friends, directing his talents, tormenting bishops and landlords and kings.

'What are fellas supposed to look like,' she said, 'when they're forty-nine?'

'Ah, for fuck's sake.' As she peered, he laughed. This time she caught a note of self-pity, melancholy's most honest form.

'Jimmy,' she said, 'you're a miserable boy.'

'I'd be considerably less so if I didn't have you to bother about.'

'I don't think that's true at all.'

'What are you at with the tourists, Maureen?'

'I'll tell you,' she said, 'if you buy me a sticky bun. I've come up a bit short.'

In the olden days the merchant princes would have cut opulent figures and been followed around their cities by sycophants, beggars, boys looking for work. Not the case with her fella in his T-shirt and jeans, though the anonymity was its own ugly prospect. She had her favoured places for a sticky bun and they were patronised by all shapes and sizes of mammies, among whom she felt her own anonymity; she wouldn't dilute it with his. She took off across the road and away from the centre and found a modern coffee shop occupied by young lads with beards. They didn't have any sticky buns, but what could she do except sigh and let her son buy her an almond biscuit?

She began, 'Did you ever hear of Mother Jones?'

'Course I did.'

Their coffees had foam fronds on top. She was put out that he knew what coffee to ask for. The merchant princes would have been worldly, and a captain of industry should know how to use all that Cork made available. Still she was not keen on the overlap: the bright city, the black city.

Mother Jones had no time for captains of industry.

Maureen said, 'Jimmy, it's a terrible thing.'

'What is?' He folded his arms on the table.

'The way the country's gone.'

'Have you joined that People Before Profit crowd? Aren't you always banging on about how great the country is, compared to what it was?'

Maureen welled up and widened her eyes, horrified at herself. She looked at the wooden tabletop, the young fella behind the counter, the colossal coffee machine, the bags of beans they'd lined up by the till.

Jimmy said, 'Maureen, what's wrong with you?'

'I'm nearly seventy,' she said.

'What about it?'

'What have I to show for it?'

'You've me,' he said.

'Jesus Christ.'

'G'wan, I'm only codding you,' he said. 'What do you want to show for it? Leading tourists on fucking goose chases, what?'

292

'I thought I had the measure of this place,' she said. 'Cork. Being a very male sort of city and that's why it was so bad to me.'

'Oh, Jesus,' Jimmy said, and looked at the ceiling.

'But then there was this fecking Jones woman, and everyone and the cat knows about her, but I didn't at all.'

'So?'

'I'm only trying to understand this fecking place!' She put her head in her hands.

When she looked up again Jimmy was staring at her askance; he said, 'You're not going doolally on me, are you?'

She pointed at him. 'You're an awful bollocks.'

'Stop, you're too kind.'

'You are. It's not right, all that you do.'

'What do I do? I do nothing.'

'Then you have a wan like Mother Jones, starved out of it, off to America, lost all her children to fever and emancipated the working man! People should know.' She blinked, cleared her eyes. 'I want to make this place make sense to someone.'

'This is a really odd way for guilt to manifest,' he said.

'I'll talk to tourists if I want to,' she said.

'I'm only asking what you're telling them.'

'I'm telling them,' she said, 'about the Lee, and the harbour, and Atty Hayes, and Jack Lynch. I'm telling them about Mutton Lane and Rory Gallagher and how Mrs Windsor bought fish from O'Connell's in the English Market and about the Idle Tower and butter vouchers and Mother fecking Jones! I am trying,' she said, 'to put manners on the place!'

He let her recover, then he said, 'Only I wouldn't like to think you were making any points off the backs of those here present today.'

'Why would I want people thinking less of me?'

'You might be worried that otherwise they wouldn't think of you at all.' He leaned forward, locked eyes with her, let his voice go soft. 'You want to tell the story of the place and that's fine,' he said. 'You want to have them hang off your every word, that's fine. You want to feel like you belong to Cork, or that it belongs to you, fine. But Maureen, guilt is treacherous. It always asks for more than you have to give, do you understand? And it has no right to you, girl. You've done nothing wrong.'

'I'm nearly seventy,' she said, 'and all I have to show for it is you.'

'And I'm a bollocks. But I am not your fault. And putting manners on me is not your right.'

'Why wouldn't it be?' she said, but she was shaking her head as soon as she opened her mouth.

'Don't try to be my mother,' he said. 'It's too late, Maureen.'

This interfered with her research and her practising her speeches in the middle of the floor. That she'd had a child when she did and in the circumstances she did had overtaken everything else about her, and she couldn't remember who she'd been before Dominic Looney had his way with her. It was one thing to be a bad mother but to not even be allowed that was unimaginably dreadful. Ireland would have erased her, and now that Ireland was throwing parties in the Mansion House for the likes of her, her son wanted to erase her. What was she at all, then? A spinster. An old maid with a bone to pick. She was gone past fury; she missed fury, was lonesome for it.

She did not know what to do with herself in its absence. There were no tourists she liked the look of, and the scuts basking in the sunshine looked to her past the point of rescue. She kept away from John Redmond Street. The city didn't notice.

She didn't think often, those few days, of Ryan Cusack. He seemed ensconced in normality and didn't need her thoughts. The Cusacks would pull together. The loss of a parent was nothing so terrible if at least you'd had the parent in the first place.

She had gone to the funeral to pay her respects, said a few kind words to Noreen, and had been invited back to the house. She'd shaken Ryan's hand but had otherwise avoided him. She had enjoyed the chat with Noreen and her daughters and their old friends and neighbours, the good women of the Northside, from whose ranks she'd been hounded so long ago. She would never say so out loud but it felt like falling through a dimensional crack into a parallel life. What would have happened, what might have been. It was no great shakes but nor did it set her teeth on edge, which she would always have haughtily predicted. She did not arrange to meet Noreen again because she assumed she would meet Noreen again. They had enough in common. Their sons had gone to London together—

She did not have a son; did he not make that clear?

On that basis it would hurt to think of Ryan – him being once a sort of son to her himself – so she couldn't chance it. But one lightly clouded morning, she came out of the apartment complex and on to the footpath and there was Ryan's blonde girlín, holding their son in her arms.

She was still and tense, unmistakably waiting, but as soon as Maureen met her eyes she turned and walked away.

Maureen closed out the gate of the complex and stood with her hand on the metal bar. 'Hello?' she called after the blonde girl, and when she didn't hesitate or turn her head Maureen set off up the path after her. 'Hello! Hello, Ryan's young wan!' and at his name the girl stopped. When Maureen drew alongside her she shifted the little fella from one hip to the other. 'Are you looking for someone?' Maureen asked.

'You,' said the blonde girl, 'but it was a bad idea.'

'Why would you be looking for me?'

'You're Mrs Phelan, aren't you?'

Maureen said, 'I'm not Mrs anything,' but softly, the blonde girl looking like the wind could carry her off, even with the child in her arms.

'But you're Jimmy Phelan's mother.'

'Just about.'

The little fella stared at Maureen, mouth downturned.

The blonde girl said, 'I met you before, I don't know if you remember. On the shop on the Grand Parade, I had Diarmaid with me.'

Maureen nodded.

'I saw you at Ryan's dad's funeral,' said the girl.

'You did.'

The girl closed her mouth, raised her eyes to heaven, opened her mouth again. 'I know Ryan hasn't been Ireland's greatest citizen or anything. But he's trying.'

Maureen waited and when the girl did nothing but let her chin wobble she said, 'Well, it'd be time for him.'

'Yeah,' said the girl, bitterly. The small fella put his head on her shoulder. Maureen thought that she could pinch his cheek, put her hand out for his. She had the feeling that if she tried to pet the child the blonde girl would flatten her. Perhaps that came from nowhere but her own morbid sadness. Still, the blonde girl's presence was a weight to her drifting and better yet, nothing she'd seen coming. So she straightened.

'Yes, I am Jimmy's mother. What is it you're after?'

'I wish he'd leave Ryan alone,' the blonde girl said.

'I can understand that.'

'I don't know if you can do anything about it, or if you'd even want to do anything about it, but he's worth a try, even if he doesn't think it himself. You know he plays music.'

'I do,' Maureen said.

'I know some people are worried that if he does make music, the likes of fans or journalists or whatever will ask him to talk about what he used to get up to. But Ryan isn't like that. He doesn't want to talk about it, he's not proud of it.'

'My son doesn't tell me anything,' Maureen said, 'and doesn't pay a blind bit of notice to anything I tell him, either.'

'If Ryan can make something of himself it's good for him and me and Diarmaid. He'd never jeopardise that by telling tales on anyone. And you're a mother, so you might . . .' She looked at the heavens again. 'I am asking you if there's anything you can do, given that you know Ryan and his family, given that it's your son who has the problem with him. I know me coming down to talk to you looks crazy. Ryan would have a conniption if he knew I was here.' She exhaled through pursed lips. 'Two nights back, Ryan's band played a gig. Live testing some songs, rather than a proper performance. I don't ever get to see him like that, and it suits him, and it strikes me as insane that he can't make a go of it because of some stupid shit he did when he was a teenager. If you can't say or do anything to help, then at least I want you to know that it's wrong. It's just wrong.'

She turned to leave and Maureen said, 'I bought his songs.'

The blonde girl turned back and the little fella, irritated, bounced in her arms and said, clearly and louder than Maureen had expected, 'Mam!' She shushed him.

'Ryan has talent,' Maureen said.

'I know that.'

'I don't want you to think that I don't care.'

'Thank you,' said the blonde girl, with effort.

She walked on, and Maureen followed. The little fella watched her over his mother's shoulder. 'He must be heavy,' Maureen said. The blonde girl's head jerked around.

'A little bit,' she said.

'You'll spoil him.'

What she could see of the blonde girl's expression was not pleasant.

'An awful stupid thing to say,' Maureen admitted, 'given the state of my own lad.'

The blonde girl did not reply.

'What's your own name again?' Maureen asked. There was not enough room on the path to walk beside one another.

'Does it matter what my name is? We're talking about Ryan.'

'He's not so important you'd lose your name, is he? All we do is talk about and worry about and wait on fellas in this city.'

The blonde girl stopped. She put her son down, clutched his hand, pushed her hair back from her face. 'This is about a fella,' she said. 'How do you want me to ask for help on behalf of my ridiculous langer of a fella without talking about him?'

They had come to the end of Maureen's street and stood on a thoroughfare. It being only mid-morning, and grey, and not particularly warm, scuts were thin on the ground. Temper had reddened the blonde girl's cheeks.

'Where's Ryan now?' Maureen asked.

'Why?'

'There aren't so many young fellas in town at this hour. They sleep in. Maybe they get their young wans up to fight their battles.'

'You're damn right I'll fight his battles,' said the blonde girl.

Maureen let her go. She wanted to sit down somewhere to quarrel silently with the word 'mother' and all of its unfair connotations. She considered going where mammies gathered, so that she could upset someone undeserving of her. She considered going back to the coffee shop she'd been with Jimmy, so as to bother a captive audience of young fellas about whom there was nothing gammy. She wandered. She forgot what she'd left the flat for.

She did a loop of the city centre and ended up back on the Grand Parade as the young fellas began to show their faces. There were six of them at the fountain as she came back around, looking at their phones, tilting the screens towards one another. Maureen stopped a few feet away and waited for them to notice her. 'Would you do me a favour?' she said, to the first one who looked up.

He was nonplussed. Slouching, no oil painting. He googled Lord Urchin for her.

'That's yer man's band,' one of his pals said. 'Yer man with the fuck your second chances interview, he's unreal.' When Maureen asked him to elaborate he smirked and said, 'You wouldn't know him anyway, girl.'

She did know him, she said. He was a grand lad, talented, and it was a shame that so many people thought art belonged only to the innocent or the sanctimonious, though she wasn't sure if she could stretch that far; it wasn't necessarily someone's own fault if they were squeaky-clean, but it was dull to exalt the squeaky-clean, wasn't it?

The scuts nodded hotly.

'Is there a video or something?' Maureen asked, and the first scut disconnected his headphones and held the screen so Maureen could see. The other scuts gathered around, blocking the sun's glare.

*   *   *

What had Maureen done since she'd come home from England? Wander. There was a case to be made for her having been wandering since they'd taken Jimmy from her. At times what she was sure had been direction turned out just to have been anger, setting her this way or the other till it waned, leaving her in the middle of rooms, pages, conversations, wondering what she was doing. In Cork she lived among ghosts and struggled with déjà vu. Once she had burned down a country church and no one had come along to blame her. Once she had killed an intruder; her son made the problem go away. Once she had saved a little musician from the Lee and he might have thanked her, if her help didn't come with complications. Her crooked son, corrupting everything he touched. She couldn't blame herself when she hadn't been allowed to raise him. She couldn't blame Ireland when Ireland had such a capacity for making wrongs right.

Something the little musician said in the video she watched with her scuts:

'D'you know how fucked we all are?'

To which came roars of laughter.

'D'you ever think you should be marching?'

By the sounds of it, they did.

'Housing crisis, climate crisis, political crisis, if Brexit doesn't kill me Salvini will. I've a son, like. Fucking hell . . .' And then, timed perfectly, 'Don't sell drugs though.'

The audience hooted and whistled.

'If the odds are stacked against you, don't get so brave as to think you might bend the rules.' As if he was talking to someone in particular, he said, 'D'you know what I mean?' Waited for a muffled answer, smiled. She could hardly reconcile this Ryan with her Ryan. He was relaxed, serene, even, yet every word was a shard; there was great hate in him, and it thrilled her to hear it. 'Legalise the fucking lot,' he said, then the next song began.

Something the little musician said in the interview the scuts told her about.

'I see your offered second chance, Ireland, and I don't fucking want it.'

Maureen wandered further and found sons all over the city, underdone, still malleable. Long-limbed boys in cotton tracksuit bottoms with photos of their babies on the lock screens of their phones, dirt under their nails. It was said that they had no respect for women but Maureen found them amenable when perplexed. Maybe it was her grandmotherly semblance. Some were already devoted to Lord Urchin, some had heard bits and pieces and were pleased, others were unimpressed, others ignorant. She didn't do any advertising, rather, market research. *Was it all worth it?* was the one question. What Ryan Cusack was good at, was it worth the hassle for him, and was it too pure a thing to bear Jimmy's suspicions? She got the scuts to show her videos on their phones and asked them what they thought. She read a review of the gig in the *Echo* and recounted it. The writer had said the show was politically charged. How much would it take to get the scuts politically charged, she asked? *Fuck the politicians*, they said. *Eat the rich*, and they laughed.

She met these boys all over town: on the Grand Parade and Pana, out at the university, in Fitzgerald Park, in coffee shops where she broke through frond after frond. The girls they had with them were less easily agitated but Maureen learned to tailor her methods. She found that they didn't care much about Catholic Ireland. History didn't move them. They faced forward.

She resumed practising her oration in her kitchen. She read about Mother Jones, Mary and Muriel MacSwiney, Hanna Sheehy-Skeffington, Leonora Barry, Mary Elmes, and even Nano Nagle, borrowed crosier forgiven for the sake of the theme.

Familiar now with the qualities of the boys in town, she chanced following Jimmy as he went about his days. Depending on the traffic she could do this on foot or sailing along on one of the public city bikes. He spent most of his time en route from one drab location to another; in the movies men of his vocation had fast cars, buxom girlfriends, polished shoes.

She sat two feet from the window of another fancy coffee shop on Barrack Street – vociferously surprised that there were fancy anythings on Barrack Street – and watched Jimmy and his buddy Tim Dougan, who she thought must be pushing sixty, carry tables, stools and boxes out of a pub cellar to pack into the back of a van. Later she caught up with him in a hotel lobby, where he sat for ten minutes with a man only slightly more hirsute and just as glum. The other sites she managed to follow him to were a hardware shop, a supermarket, a tyre yard and a selection of pubs. Only once did he catch her. He looked around as she walked in the side door of a bar off Oliver Plunkett Street and his face contorted with presumption. She played stupid.

'Should I say hello to you or not?'

'No,' he said.

She tutted at the ceiling and ordered a gin and tonic.

It was enough to make her sorry for him; his days hardly seemed exciting enough to warrant his fatigue, or the relentless surveillance of his surroundings. Perhaps he spent his late nights doing terrible deeds. She hoped so, in a way.

She visited the flea market to make faces at the man with the denim jackets and to find a gift to bring Jimmy. She did not know what it might look like, but it had to be symbolic of the link between them. Not only mother to child but mother to son, specifically.

She had once been a great woman for knick-knacks. Her eye went naturally to the kitsch and the ugly. She spent almost an hour in the flea market, picking through pieces that almost suited, until she thought to make a sort of diorama of gifts, a Mass's offertory. She wheeled a plastic folding crate from a woman selling records and into it put a *Lola Versus Powerman* LP, three antique green glass jugs, a decorative copper wall plate, a biography of Michael Collins and a bronze sculpture of a crow on a tree branch almost the length of her forearm. This set her back a few quid but she thought it magnificent. Sticky buns, the occasional treat for Conor and Ellie, fivers for her favourite vagrants: this was what she spent Jimmy's standing order on. But now she wanted to be abundant as the womb.

Just before eleven on a Friday morning on which the temperature had risen and the Irish had sagged under it, Maureen arrived at Jimmy's city centre apartment with her plastic crate of yokey-majigs and wossnames. He had what she had dubbed his brandy head on him, though now she wondered if it was ennui that had him wincing, if he was not, in fact, succumbing to thoughts of what must amount to vain enterprise; how much of the effort of scuts and pups and bollockses was doomed to futility? Jimmy took the crate off her. She followed him in, opening and closing her sore hands. She bet that no one had time to be world-weary in Mother Jones's day.

'What have you got here?' Jimmy asked, rummaging.

'I was at the flea market. Some baubles I thought you could do with.'

'Could do with?' He flipped on the kettle without taking his eyes from the crate.

She demonstrated. 'The little green glass jugs and the wall plate because it'd suit you to have things of this vintage here, they reminded me of merchant Cork. The Kinks record because I'm nearly sure it came out the year you were born. And what Corkman doesn't need a book about the Big Fella? I don't know about the crow, only I liked it. I'd nearly keep it for myself.'

'What brought this on?'

'Just to show I think of you and I have hopes for you. I am your mother, Jimmy.'

'You know what I meant, Maureen.'

'I do. I'm to stay out of it, and not be trying to put manners on you. Only I've a favour to ask.'

'If you're hoping to open a tourist office I'm going to have to pass on investing.'

She didn't smile. She said, 'Will you ever leave Ryan Cusack alone?'

'Oh, for fuck's sake.'

'I know you went for him over this music thing. I don't see what good it does you.'

'Maureen, keep your nose out of it.'

'I would if the whole shebang looked complicated, Jimmy. But it's simple. He doesn't work for you any more. He has no interest in second chances. He wouldn't open his gob about you.'

'Did he petition you, or something? Isn't that opening his gob?'

'He did not,' she said, and put it to him that she'd been moved only by Ryan's singing voice and the mood he'd drawn out of the audience at the gig she'd seen on the scuts' phones.

'What fucking gig?'

'Testing songs,' she said. 'It wasn't a real concert by any means. Listen.' She took out her own phone, stored on which was the second chances interview file.

'I've no interest,' Jimmy said, 'in that little prick's band.'

'I'm not playing you music. Listen, I said.'

She played the interview for Jimmy.

When it was over, he said, 'You know when I say I'll have him shot, I'm not exaggerating.'

'He said nothing about you.'

'It's another step down a fucking path I told him not to walk!' Jimmy said, and made a move for his phone on the kitchen island.

Maureen applied a halt to his gallop. She grabbed the Michael Collins biography and fucked it at his head.

It hit him over the ear. He put a hand up, inhaling through his teeth. He said, 'You fucking—'

She flung each of the glass jugs at him. He ducked and put his arms over his head.

'You're a pup!' she roared. 'What are you?'

She frisbeed the LP through the air. It hit him on the arm. She held the decorative copper plate over her head and bounced it off his chest. She seized the bronze crow and held her arm back and he looked up at her over his wrists.

'Don't think I won't take your fecking head off with this fella,' she said. 'You know how dangerous I am with heavy ornaments.'

'Have you lost your fucking marbles?'

'It wasn't that I lost them when I killed that poor eejit on Bachelor's Quay or when I burned down that church. It wasn't that I lost them when they took you off me, God no. Only now that I see all I could and should've been doing, cursing the dead and putting the shits up the living!'

He rose in increments. 'Maureen,' he said, 'for fuck's sake.'

'For fuck's sake, you,' she said. 'This is how you were reared, as an oppressor and a bollocks. I'm ashamed of you!'

'That's fine, no one asked you to be any other fucking way!'

'I am asking you to do one simple thing, Jimmy.'

'And you can ask all you like, girl, but I don't share your simple way of looking at the world. If you were standing where I'm standing you'd know what's at stake.'

'From where I'm standing your head's at stake,' she said. 'Because if you don't do as you're told for once in your life, I will make what's left of that life miserable. I'll spend the rest of my days procuring blunt objects to attack you with. You can tell them I've lost my marbles and lock me up and I'll tell them so much about you that your ears will bleed from the other end of the county. The city's at stake, Jimmy. The country. We don't know what good that lad can do but I'd say it's more than the pair of us could manage. You'll interfere with him no longer, unless it's over my dead body.'

He lowered his arms. She flexed hers.

'You utter crackawly,' he said.

'I'm thinking—' and here she lowered the bronze crow, and raised the first finger of the opposite hand – 'about what kind of a town this should be for Conor and Ellie. Ryan's enterprise is good and true. Can't you hear it coming out of his mouth?'

He tried threatening, then he tried reason. He told her that leaving Cusack to run unchecked around Cork constituted Jimmy's having a bit of a wobble, and as he'd told her till he was blue in the fucking face, if you had any bit of a wobble all around you langers were getting big fucking ideas. He watched her until she put the bronze crow on the counter top; he made to grab it; she picked it up again. He asked if she thought there weren't a dozen better weapons in this kitchen he could use in retaliation. She said she knew that but she also knew he didn't have the will to do any such thing, because he wasn't an utter crackawly.

'How do I know that if I did you this turn, you wouldn't keep asking for turns?' he asked.

'You don't,' she said. 'You know what's right in front of you now, focus on that.'

She offered up her flat as a place both parties could find their way to. He made the phone call. She left triumphant, the bronze crow still in her hand, but as soon as she turned the corner on the street outside she had to slow down and walk with a palm on the wall to her left. All her adult life she'd relished confrontation but this left her weakened. She was not afraid of him. It was the victory, gone to her head.

She began to shake as the time came for them to arrive. She drank some lavender tea and looked up breathing exercises on the internet, but had only made it through one sequence before the first knock. It was Jimmy, ten minutes early. He had Tim Dougan with him, who asked how she was. Grand, she told him. Mighty, in fact. He refused to sit, though she told him twice. Sciatica, he said.

The second knock was five minutes late, which she would have put down to nerves, only for the strut of yer wan who came in the door.

Her name was Natalie Grogan and she had been to Maureen's flat once before, years ago. She was a striking girl with childbearing hips and the look of a tax collector off her. Ryan came in after her, looking how Maureen felt. Natalie beamed around the room. She shook Jimmy's hand, nodded at Dougan, and to Maureen said, 'Mrs Phelan.'

'I'm not Mrs anything.'

'I'm sorry,' Natalie said. 'Ms Phelan.'

None of the four wanted tea. Maureen made a second cup and stood back. Ryan sat in one chair, Natalie in its partner. Jimmy on the couch opposite, arms stretched over the back, legs spread. Hateful grin. Burr of a voice. Maureen sidled to the shelf where she'd left the bronze crow and ran her fingertips over its near wing. Jimmy's eyes went to hers and rolled back, quickly, in his head. Like a bold teenager, and she thought she would hold tight to this. Who knew what a son was, anyway? This was what she had to work with. This was hers.

And her other one, kind of, sitting in the chair with his elbows on his knees, half the world from the fella on stage in the video who spoke of waters rising and marching and protest and everything being fucked, fucked.

'I'm curious,' said Jimmy, 'as to how you could afford any of this craic. Jaunts to Berlin and Seoul aren't cheap.'

'Mr Phelan,' said Natalie, 'can we speak plainly? I'm busy. You're probably busy. Let's take it as established that we're both very articulate and clever.'

This rattled Jimmy's grin.

Natalie turned and looked at Maureen. 'Can we speak plainly?'

'Don't be cute on my behalf,' Maureen said.

'The place isn't bugged,' Jimmy said, 'and it'd be good for my dear mother to hear exactly what a venal little prick Ryan Cusack is. Speak plainly. I am fucking busy.'

Natalie smiled. 'What Ryan did for you a few years back was lucrative for all of us. You must have expected him to charge a broker's fee.'

'Never something I put past him.'

'Well, we invested wisely. It was washed clean and our fee pumped into Catalyst and a few other businesses. It all adds up.'

Jimmy said, 'You can see why I would think I had a say in your businesses now.'

'Exactly,' Natalie said, and the men cocked their heads, even the young man who Maureen thought should already know where this was going. 'Mr Phelan, I'm not here to get one over on you. I expect you to ask for your dividends and I have them for you. And a portion promised to an investor.'

'Investing in what?' asked Jimmy.

'Catalyst Music. The company, which consists of a label, production services, promotion services, management services, all kind of in-house, Korean-style. Purely as an investor, and then only through a holding company.'

'So we all get into bed together.'

'We're already in bed together,' Natalie said. 'We have been since day one.'

'Pay me off,' Jimmy said, 'so that Ryan can go on doing what he loves to do, despite the fact that the public eye is the last fucking thing I need on me—'

'The last thing you need on you is An Garda Síochána. The National Crime Agency. La Guardia di Finanza. Interpol.'

Ryan was the first to break the silence. 'Natalie, what the fuck?'

She held up a hand. 'I'm speaking plainly. I don't want that to happen. God forbid, right? The shit I'm up to my ears in?' She laughed.

Maureen tried to catch Jimmy's eye, but he was transfixed.

Natalie sat back. 'Mr Phelan, if anything were to happen to me, my lawyer has his brief, and a great big file in a safe. It would all come crashing down. You'd be fucked.'

Jimmy said, 'You think I haven't heard this kind of shit before?'

'Oh, no doubt, but from someone who you knew meant it? And just so we're clear, if anything happened, Ryan would be equally fucked. He is such a good frontman. Always has been. If he wasn't so insistent on fucking his ex-girlfriend all the way through our supposed relationship, I might have been more inclined to obscure his involvement in your operation to the extent I obscured yours in ours but, fuck it. Live by the sword, right?'

Ryan went so still Maureen thought he was not even breathing.

'Plain-speaking woman,' Jimmy said, 'what exactly is it you're threatening me with?'

'Nothing,' Natalie said. 'If it wasn't for you I'd be working for KPMG and people would be on at me to get a diagnosis. No, no, I am very fond of you, Mr Phelan. I am telling you that I have safeguards in place. This could make you wary of me, or it could make you think that I'm the kind of person you should stay in bed with. I'm going to continue making legitimate money, but I can make more if Ryan is on a longer leash. He's not going to tell tales about you, because it would lead to Armageddon. I'm not going to tell tales because I like show business. You're gonna like it too. Your kids will like it. Your mother will be proud of you. And it's all clean, Mr Phelan. Not a cent can be traced back to the nonsense that brought us all together.'

Jimmy looked at Maureen. 'I'd have to sit down with your money man.'

'I'm my money man,' Natalie said. 'And we can sit down now, if you like. Only I don't want Ryan here for it. It doesn't concern him.'

'It doesn't concern him?'

'He gets a salary,' Natalie said, dismissively.

She opened her laptop. Dougan folded his arms. Jimmy leaned forward.

Ryan and Maureen were sent to get coffee.

'He's going to kill me,' Ryan said, as they went through the metal gate on to the street. 'She's just told him he can't kill her so he's going to kill me, isn't he?'

'He won't touch you,' Maureen said.

He went down on his haunches in the middle of the path. He covered his nose with his hands. She placed a palm on top of his head, ruffled his hair. 'How did I get myself into this mess?' he said.

'Is there a way out of it?'

He shook his head. Strands of his hair moved between her fingers.

'Well, then. What did I always tell you?'

'You go through it.'

'That's it, boy, and stop for no one.'

He did not get up, so she cleared her throat.

'Jimmy and Natalie are merchant princes. They're going to spend their lives shafting you, but I'll do for you what I can.'

'Who do you think you are?' he despaired, but it was as though she'd put the question in his mouth. She looked straight ahead, towards the city centre, and said, 'I'm Mother Phelan.'

*   *   *

308

It did not end on Natalie's leaving, nor on Ryan's promise that he would never utter Jimmy's name, never even curse him. It ended only as Jimmy readied to leave, and on Maureen's intercepting a look between himself and Dougan; she called Jimmy to her side and took his hand.

'I am your mother,' she said.

'Definitions, definitions.'

She squeezed him, hard. 'Whether or not you believe that Natalie divil,' she said, 'with her legitimate money and her nerve, believe me. When you go home tonight and find green glass between your tiles, and see the dent on your wall plate and the spine fecked on your Big Fella book and the cover bent on your LP, remember what I said. Not a hair on his head, Jimmy.'

'Do you not think she was persuasive, Maureen?'

'She was,' she agreed. 'She was. But that's merchant-prince bluster, and I'm not fluent in that at all. This is what I know. I am your mother.'

He smiled, thinly, as she leaned in, locked eyes, and put him straight.

'I brought you into this world,' she said, 'and by God I can take you out of it.'

Track 10: Tall Tales

How it Feels to Be Tamed, the debut album from Lord Urchin, could stream in the zillions and sell out on commemorative vinyl. It could flop and be forgotten in the span of a week. It might lead to nothing but a brief spike in the blood pressures of fine people who've never made mistakes. The video for 'Up and Lose' might go viral because I move really well when you're directing my steps.

It does and it doesn't matter.

It matters because this isn't just about me. It's about Joseph, Davy, Orson, Mel. Everyone behind the scenes. Cork, maybe. People who put their faith in me have it vindicated.

It doesn't matter because I found a way to say the things I had to say and you heard them. I found my way back and you wanted me. And I can't tell lies any more.

I mean to myself. It's all I used to do, I didn't even have to open my mouth. It happened just in the course of me moving through this city, leaving the house with my chin held so-high, my hands ready for fists. Or cycling through languages to think in, so I could remove myself from the rot I was generating. Layers of Ryan between heart and action. All that energy I wasted, D'Arcy. The closer I get to you, the more calm I am. It's like at the beginning, when my dad phoned looking for me only to find I was already close, just up the stairs, doing things with you in my head. Is that healthy? I'm sure it has to be. I've told lies long enough that I have to know how truth feels.

'Lies' being a strong word when I'm trying these days to be kind to myself, let's say 'tall tales' instead. Let's put a quirky beat to it because it should feel the way questioning health and truth and sanity feels when you're happy. Let's make it driving and infectious. Let me open my mouth wide and admit to beautiful greed. I want to occupy you. I want the fucking air you're breathing.

You asked me before if it mattered that you knew about what had happened to me in the house next door when I was fifteen. I told you it did, and it does. My answer was right but the rough work was wrong. I thought I needed a good self to sell to the girl I loved because she had to believe that I was a solid fella. A grown man couldn't be broken.

I didn't understand. I wasn't broken, but I was in bits. And once you understood them all, that was it. I was complete.

A musician, a miscreant, a bad son and a good dad. And yours.

Because haven't you made those tall tales irrelevant?

Because haven't you already saved my life?

The frame around which one builds one's life is a brittle thing, and in a city of souls connected one snapped beam can collapse all that is rotten and inspire solutions to problems old as the hills. Cork City had redrawn its boundaries and doubled its population. It did not notice Ryan Cusack's first brave steps but it was open to racket and roar and now that his foot fell heavier, now that he'd filled out a bit, Cork was all ears.

It didn't feel dramatic because cities would rarely please you to make an obvious fuss. It was dicey, for a while. The Irish were pass-remarkable. Tough. Believers in just deserts. Receptive to charm. Fond of cute hoors. A contrary lot. It could have gone one way or the other. It was said that Ryan Cusack was the worst young fella in the city. No one cared whether he was sorry because the damage was done. But then he opened his mouth and said, *Well, I dunno, look at the fucking state of the place, like, don't look at me*, and the people who mattered, those who would download music and come to gigs, said, *Jesus, he has a point, like*. They got political about that point. It helped that there was nothing gammy about him. He had a smart mouth, an ink wash tattoo, four languages, two rare lungs, a beautiful son, and a girlfriend who knew his history, his politics, his humour, how he moved, what he wanted. He was the love of her life and he made the breath catch in her throat. He was lying on her bed in her parents' house at half-eleven at night, bare, in a bit of a state, even if he was trying to hide it.

'I won't hate it,' he said, 'coz it's you and I can't hate anything you do.'

'That's not how it works, boy.'

Karine was astride him, leaning forward so that her palms were on the bed either side of his chest. She was naked too, and sensitive to his being in a state, more so than he was, his being so intent on kicking consequence up the road. But this had been the way now for nine years of their lives.

He brought both his hands to her breasts and in the course of caressing her coaxed her into sitting upright. She ached to but didn't dare move down. He pulled his hands down over her belly, rested his palms on her thighs, pushed his thumbs between her legs.

Gruffly, 'I wouldn't be doing this if I didn't want it.'

Even that statement she'd have thought too redolent, but she wanted him and would be easily persuaded, so she leaned forward again and put her hands on the bed, shuffled backwards and took him in her mouth and went slow, used her tongue. He made noises as if his teeth were locked over his bottom lip. She could have kept going – he would have let her – only for the recklessness of being wet; when he told her he had to come inside her she moved back up and sat upright and reached down for him as he reached up for her and swung her beneath him.

Afterwards he said, 'I felt too good, I didn't want to risk it.'

'You were right,' she said.

'I'm a coward.'

'You didn't feel very cowardly to me.'

He was silent. She put her head on his chest and a hand on his belly and slid down, proprietarily.

'There's a gap in my memory,' he said, 'and I keep imagining monstrous occupants for it. If I can overwrite that with something good . . . I don't know.'

'We have all the time in the world.'

'I'm glad you said that.'

She climbed on to him. He put his arms around her and she kissed his mouth.

'I'm all yours,' she whispered, and then, because she got such a kick from it, she said it again.

*   *   *

All was as grand as Georgie could hope for, given the circumstances. She had failed, in that she had wanted him ruined and he had rallied, but her conviction had suffered as her plan had progressed, so on some level she thought she might be relieved. Medbh was a lesson: no one gave a shit about sin if the sinner was interesting enough. Settling scores, therefore, took up too much energy. You were not guaranteed success. Sensible people knew when to let go. Besides, meeting him on the street, being confronted like that, would have made her iffy even if she'd been adamant. He'd made points and when she muttered them back to herself they left a sharp taste in her mouth. And he'd just walked away. It was an affront that he might have a high road open to him.

That he had dared to mention her daughter.

She alternated between fury and misery for the first few days, keeping an eye on the land around the mobile home, in case Cusack sent a squadron after her. She found her way to acknowledgment and through there to acquiescence. This she thought to be manipulation on his part, and she became angry again. Felt rough. Slipped back into acquiescence. Maybe he'd been on to something, in his own stupid way. God, how she hated him. Then hated herself. Then felt bad for both of them.

Things had moved on for him online. The commenters who were on Georgie's side were outnumbered now by keyboard scholars who talked about nuance, neo-capitalism, inequality and the right to game the system. And they were outnumbered in turn by shamelessly shallow people who loved Lord Urchin's songs or their frontman's big eyes or intricate tattoo or trim little arse. Georgie saw footage of a gig played in Cork city centre, read a profile not written by Medbh, and followed the band's social media channels; he got a lot of Likes, Ryan. Georgie thought that in her next life she'd come back as a handsome boy and if it all went to fuck, then she could just sell drugs and be forgiven for it and suffer no pangs of conscience and not worry about which old customer might see her any old where.

The point was that the abiding memory shouldn't be one of his disappointed face. He had some neck to be disappointed.

It was a complicated journey without a car. She had to get a bus to town and then a bus east and then, dropped outside the post office on the main street, she had to open the map app to find her way to the building where David lived with their daughter.

He had complained the night before that she had not given him enough notice. This was a man with custody of a small child, capable of making the noises of a small child himself. Georgie told him she was headed back to London so this was all the notice she could give. He emitted some minor blasphemies.

She located his building on the opposite side of the road. She stood, going over conversations she'd practised, then shrank into the doorway of a derelict shop as the heavens opened. Low, glowing clouds, fat raindrops, the light almost green. *Hello, Harmony. Do you know who I am?* Surely he'd have told her. *I'm very pleased to see you again!* He could have been imprecise; he had always been watery. He could also have been condemnatory, now that he was Born Again. Strange to think that she might have given birth to a devout girl. *Do you rebel? Don't. I tried it, it doesn't work.* Would it be right to say she was pretty, or did he discourage that kind of thing? *I named you. I wanted you to have a name that people would smile at, I wanted you to feel ordained. I did want things for you, Harmony Faye.*

The sun shower ended but Georgie stayed pressed to the flaking door. She wanted to cover dialogue eventualities. She wanted to at least be smooth. *She wanted.* She had ideas about herself, ideas about their implementation. She worked the nine-to-five in the London rat race. This was what David Coughlan knew of today's Georgie and it was this Georgie she'd swoop in as. *Hello, David. It's good to see you again. How have you been? Well, of course, it's so difficult to get away. All the hours God gave me, David. It helps when it's a role you're passionate about.*

The door of the apartment building opened and David came out holding Harmony's hand. Father and daughter looked up and down the street together. She was chattering, though Georgie could not make out the words. David was smiling and Harmony was focused more on him than on watching for Georgie, which was all the excuse that Georgie needed. She hurried back the way she'd come. She thought that the logical thing for David to do, if he was looking for her, would be to come towards the bus stop, so she hid in the post office. And when the bus came she scurried outside and boarded.

On the way back to the city she started an inner chant for a sign. *If I am doing the right thing, give me confirmation. Make it blatant.* She was never who she said she was, and sure about nothing these days.

She got on the second bus at the city centre station. At the stop in Douglas embarked two unwelcome faces: the hair-pullers she'd taken on weeks back. Georgie shrank into herself. The girls didn't see her. They swayed past and settled further back. The one she'd hit with the walling stone looked fine. The bus had just pulled away from the kerb when Georgie heard shrieking from behind her, which she assumed came from the undeterred wagons. What kind of sign was this? She was doing the right thing, because the girls were not worse for wear and neither was Ryan Cusack, and she'd put her back into breaking him? She was doing the wrong thing for precisely the same reason? She was ineffective, the weakest of poisons, and that was either admirable or it was repugnant; she didn't have the cop-on to tell.

The girls got off the bus in Crosshaven and moseyed on up the road, arm in arm.

Residents preparing for long-term stays had begun to arrive at the mobile home park in stuffed cars. They set about putting cushions out to air and scrubbing their patio furniture. Georgie saw the extra car by her mobile home and assumed it had nothing to do with her but then she put her key in the door and the door was unlocked and she had pushed it in, mind dulled by incantation, before she realised what was wrong.

There was a man inside, on the couch.

'Get in here,' he said.

Georgie said, 'No, actually, I don't fancy that at all,' and took to her heels.

You think you'd scream in such a situation. You think you'd fly along the ground but Georgie shambled like someone in a rush for the toilet. The man loped after her and only when he was close enough to grab for her and miss did she yelp. A woman in a white shirt and slacks opened her sliding door and ran out. 'Leave that girl alone!' she cried, which alerted a couple more residents, middle-aged men who came out of their mobile homes with purpose.

Georgie's pursuer came to a halt. Georgie stopped a head start away.

The man was tall. Had a squeezed-looking head with a mop of mousy hair. He did not look menacing but in Georgie's experience, they didn't have to. She shot frantic looks at the middle-aged men and the woman in the white shirt. One of the men said, 'What are you at?' and, then focused on Georgie, 'Are you all right, love?'

'Is *she* all right?' said Georgie's pursuer, affronted. 'Do you know who this is?'

The middle-aged man shrugged because no, how would he? No one had written an exposé on Georgie. Medbh had not disclosed her source and outed her as a retired sex worker. It was as she had the right to expect: no lay person could possibly give a shit who she was.

'Leave me alone,' she cried. 'I've done nothing wrong!'

Her pursuer's eyes bulged. 'Carmel. Carmel that installed you!' He swivelled his jaw. 'She has the right to her opinion, but I paid well for that fucking bay.'

The other middle-aged man said, 'Jesus, was yer wan in your place, Paschal?'

Georgie cupped her hands over her mouth and breathed through entwined fingers and said, 'You're Jessica's uncle.'

'I am,' he said. 'What about Jessica?'

'Jesus, you gave me an awful fright.'

'I gave you a fright? Who the fuck are you?'

She told him that her name was Georgie, and that there seemed to have been a misunderstanding. They spluttered and pointed and calmed, and the neighbours returned, tutting, to their own places, leaving Georgie and Paschal to thrash it out over a bad cup of tea in the mobile home. Georgie dubbed Jessica a flake and a witch and an awful eejit. Paschal asked what she was going to do now. She burst into tears. He frowned impatiently. She wiped her nose with the back of her hand and told him she'd go home to Millstreet, she wasn't destitute, just looking for peace and quiet. Cheek of him. He said cheek of her. She said she'd been a good tenant. He asked if she'd forgotten that she hadn't paid him a cent. She said she'd kept the place warm and clean. He said she'd splattered paint all over the bathroom. She said it was hair dye. He asked if she had fine motor skills at all. She said, 'Well, what did you do, anyway?'

'What d'you mean what did I do?'

'What did you do that made Carmel so cross? What did you do that made Jessica say you weren't going to be here this year?'

'What's it to you?'

'You don't have to tell me.'

'I won't.'

But he did, later. He'd had his head turned by a girl whose family had a mobile home near the entrance to the park. She was twenty-one; he stressed that he was a dope but not a pervert, and that he'd met her in the local pub, she didn't babysit for him or anything. It was only adultery.

Georgie said she could see why it had made him unpopular. Paschal said that there had been no fixing things with the wife long before this girl came on the scene. Georgie said wives had nothing to do with it, in her experience. He asked if that meant that she'd once been the other woman.

Well yeah. He could say that.

'Well then, you're as bad,' he said.

He'd stopped feeling guilty, and to hell with the rubberneckers. At least his wife, from whom he had separated, could blame him with a scandalous story. And it was good for his children to know that imperfection existed, that people who loved them could be dopes, that life was full and wonky.

Georgie said, carefully, that she'd been planning on spaghetti bolognese for dinner, and that she could still make it, if he wanted.

He thought about it and said, 'Why not?'

'I just need to make a phone call first,' she said.

David was annoyed at the start of the call, then incredulous, livid. A mobile home? Why would she tell him she still had the job in London, what was she trying to prove?

'David,' she said, 'I'm an idiot, which is not a crime. I was scared and it made me foolish. And now that I look at it, I see that this situation is messy enough, so I will be reliable, and on time, and honest. And maybe we can do something with that.'

He asked what that meant. She said she didn't know what any of it meant. She said the Born Agains never had to worry about what the bigger picture meant but that she wasn't being hateful, just curious as to how they coped, that in a sense having faith was a waste of the ingenuity that came from the fear of not knowing what was going to happen next. She said this was why he'd rebelled in the years before he'd met her. 'Don't hang up,' she said; she was just trying to explain what she had to offer their daughter. Chaos to his order. Imperfection to his virtue. Muddle and battle scars, or however he would like to explain it, whatever cold, dampening word men like him used to explain motherhood. And when he asked, in disbelief, whether she was OK, she told him yes, and thank you, she felt a lot better now.

Their friends said that it was sweet that in the midst of his tragedy they'd found each other again. It was not the right time to put anyone straight, even if the assumption made too neat a reunion story. Karine and Ryan loved one another but it was not a given that love would be enough. She had loved him since she was fifteen but it didn't stop him going to prison, it didn't prevent crisis pregnancy, it didn't stop them cheating on one another. It didn't make her parents like him. It didn't save him from Tara Duane.

Happiness was not all-encompassing. He could hold her and rage against his family, Cork City Council, the lads on Reddit, the CEO of Catalyst Music; he could hold her and cry for his dad.

Unless he couldn't. In some moments he could not access happiness even as a fraction of a larger mood. He could sulk, or go still in self-hatred, or snap, say things like 'You're not my fucking mother,' and, 'You have no idea what you're talking about, Karine.' She asked him who the fuck he thought he was talking to. There was always the worry that he wouldn't come back this time. She didn't like to think he'd do *something stupid* but she couldn't not think it. Young fellas did *something stupid* all the time.

She went dancing the week after Tony's funeral, hit it hard and clean, was inscrutable, did not ask for help with her squats. Louise was unjustifiably smug, as if she had not been predicting the opposite outcome. Friends could be awful frauds. They did some bad bitch facial expressions together, and then it didn't seem to matter.

She came home to find Ryan and Diarmaid and her father standing solemnly in the front room. Ryan was in front of the television, remote control in hand, cycling through a text menu on the screen.

'What are you at?' she asked them.

'I got one of them set-top boxes,' her father said, without looking over.

'It's a dodgy box,' Ryan said.

'It is not. I got it from one of the lads, it's preloaded, that's all, it's not dodgy.'

'That's the definition of dodgy,' Ryan said.

'Don't mind him, Karine, he's only stirring.'

'I dunno, Dad, that does sound dodgy.'

'It's not fucking dodgy!'

'Grandad, bold word,' said Diarmaid.

'You're right,' Gary said, and picked Diarmaid up. 'You're right of course, Derry. Aren't you the smartest boy we ever had in this house?'

'You'd want to change the Wi-Fi password,' Ryan said to Gary. 'How's anyone going to remember that string of nonsense?'

'Who'd be asking for it?'

'Anyone would be asking for it, they come in, they'd look for the Wi-Fi.'

'Wouldn't they be saucy!'

'Look,' said Ryan, and demonstrated on his phone. 'Yer manno next door called his ConorMcGregorIsSomeGowl.'

'He did not,' Gary said, admiringly.

'He's not wrong,' Ryan said.

Gary contemplated. 'Can you do that?'

'I can, boy.'

'And I can tell people then the password when they come in?'

'Yeah.'

'Call it KnockKneesJackie.'

'Jesus Christ, I will not.'

Karine said to Ryan, 'Isn't your son supposed to be in bed?'

'Yeah,' he said, to the television.

'Ryan.'

'Yeah, in a minute now.'

She left them to it. There wasn't much sense to be found in the rules this weather. That first night Ryan stayed over, the night of Tony's funeral, Gary had been careful and magnanimous. The second night he was puffed up on his own high-mindedness, and said he was proud of Karine for minding the young fella the way she was. On the third night, she told her parents she was afraid of leaving Ryan to his own devices, given the way young fellas tended to try *something stupid* when at the ends of their tethers. Any short time he spent with his siblings in the days after the funeral was marred by arguments; they took it out on each other that none of them knew what to do next. Natalie had ripped him a new one: he'd gone to her apartment the day after the funeral for his stuff and come out traumatised. Karine had been waiting for him in a nearby cafe. He said, 'I'm a piece of shit, amn't I?'

'Sometimes,' she said. 'Why, what did she say to you?'

'That I'm a coward,' he said. 'She says I made her the bad guy in my own head years ago and as long as I had a bad guy, I could tell myself I was a good guy.'

'You buried your father yesterday and she tells you this?'

'Yeah, I did. I did.' And he tried to continue but couldn't get the words out. She put a hand over his and felt the effort in his not jerking it away.

When she told Gary and Jackie that she was worried about Ryan doing something stupid they became determined to sort him out. Mental health was big on the radio and on Facebook; they would not object to his staying a few nights if it helped. Jackie made him scrambled eggs and Gary offered lifts and cups of tea and words of wisdom.

A few nights turned into a week, which turned into its own bubble, and possibly Gary didn't know what had come over him to be so amenable to Ryan's company. Karine was not surprised when they started talking politics and television and arguing about football and U2, only surprised that it had taken Gary this long. Maybe she had to be in her mid-twenties for him to accept that she would do what she did with Ryan. Maybe it was paternal solidarity. In a sense that was bad news for her: Ryan had always been soft on Jackie because his mother was dead, so maybe he'd be soft on Gary too, hereafter, and Karine would never again be in the right when she clashed with them.

Ryan came to Maureen's door unexpectedly in the early afternoon.

'I don't know how much you had to do with what happened with Jimmy,' he said. 'But whatever effort you made was welcome.'

She invited him in and made him a mug of tea. When she came out from behind her kitchen counter he was in the corner with the piano. He had raised the fallboard and had his fingertips on the keys.

'Sure play something,' she said.

'When was the last time you had it tuned?'

'Jesus, Ryan, I never had it tuned.'

'I won't play it, so. Wouldn't sound right. I'd be cranky.'

'Wouldn't be like you.'

He smiled and contradicted her sarcasm. She put the mug on her coffee table and gestured. He came over but didn't sit down; he picked up the mug and went back to stand with the piano. Then he said, 'Years back you were going to badger your daughter-in-law to sell it.'

'It's yours, isn't it?'

'I mean so I could take it with me at some point.'

'You can take it with you,' she said.

'What would your daughter-in-law say?'

'Era, I'd be shocked if she even remembered it's here. I'll worry about Deirdre. You worry about getting it out the door.'

He was moved and she feigned pragmatism. She looked at him from over the rim of her mug. He stood, side-on, looking at the piano. He was wearing a T-shirt in two shades of grey with a round neck, three buttons, the top open. It put her in mind of thermal underwear. The sleeves came just below his elbows, so she could see the lines tattooed on his skin. Pair of black jeans on him then that made her want to suggest he eat bigger dinners. But nothing gammy, nothing at all.

She said, 'D'you know what I'm after getting fond of?'

He looked over, eyebrows raised.

'Flat whites,' she said. 'Coffee, but with foamy milk. They can do designs on the top.'

'Really.' He was amused.

'Well they're new to me,' Maureen said. 'I only used to get Americanos.'

'All shite,' he said. 'Drink espresso, die as a man.'

'I wish I'd been a man,' Maureen said. 'To have such licence to be so full of yourself. Oh, I bet it's a trip.'

'How would you know what a trip is?'

'See, you're at it again. Come on up the road. I'll buy you an expresso.'

'Espresso.'

'What?'

He dragged it out and rolled the r. 'Espresso.'

'I'd clatter you,' she said, 'if I had you.'

It could have been warmer and brighter. The scuts didn't mind. The one walking beside her didn't have a jacket. He had his hands in his jeans pockets but didn't seem to feel any chill. She wanted to go to the trendy place she'd been with Jimmy, so they took the short stroll to the Grand Parade.

'Does everyone know who you are yet?'

He laughed. 'God, no.'

'Didn't I see you in the paper? I showed it to Jimmy, I made sure he saw you.'

Ryan said, 'Don't fucking rile him.'

'He wasn't riled.' Ryan did not look reassured. She continued, 'He has a few legitimate businesses, this isn't new to him.'

'That doesn't mean he wouldn't like to see me tied in a sack and fucked in the river.'

She acknowledged that this was true. 'I think he was taken by your Natalie, though.'

'Natalie'd give you pause for thought all right.'

'Where were you going with that wan?'

He said 'Ah,' helplessly.

'Away with the fairies!' Maureen said. 'And didn't say the nicest things about you, either.'

'She *would* like to see me tied in a sack and fucked in the river.'

'From what I gathered, you made her fortune for her. Was she expecting you to drop your drawers on her say-so, as well?'

'Maureen.'

'In Catholic Ireland,' Maureen said, 'they'd have said self-respect was a great motivator, but they'd have relied on fear to do the job.'

They were coming up on their turnoff, but beyond the fountain, outside the library where the teenagers congregated, there was a small crowd. Maureen took hold of Ryan's arm. 'Come on,' she said, 'and we'll see what's what.'

In the middle of a loose circle of young people was a great big girl with dark skin and a magnificent head of hair. She clasped her hands in front of her and recited a poem that was all vigour and decibel. Maureen kept a hand on Ryan's forearm. He remained relaxed, and she wondered afterwards why she had expected the poem to make him tremble.

The girl cried:

'You say this is what it is to be cared for.

'It is due consideration, it is a favour, it does not have to be love.

'There is no use for love.

'You say eat up, it's good for you.'

Maureen craned her neck and asked Ryan, 'What was that about?' when the girl had finished, and the clapping and whistling had died down.

Head bowed so she could reach his ear, he said, 'I dunno. Maybe direct provision or welfare or maybe just Ireland.'

'Not about a fella?'

'That's not really the way it goes these days.'

'Girls don't write angry poems about fellas any more?'

'Bigger things to worry about.'

'Funny,' Maureen said. 'I remember fellas running the world, dictating all the bigger things.'

He looked down at her and grinned. She flexed her hand over his arm. Another poet stepped forward, a boy with a thin black beard and worried eyes. He stood in the middle of the gathering, hands joined and head bowed, until people quietened. He looked around as if unpleasantly surprised to see them, and began to deliver. Ryan took his phone from his pocket and angled it so as to record the poet and Maureen wondered how, despite his youth and his arrogance, he had not considered it was his songs and his recorded anger that had roused the poets. Here he was now, capturing what the poet was saying in order to remember it, and she thought of the flow of knowledge or inspiration in the city, and thought maybe it was more primal than could be defined. Ideas, exchanged chemically. *D'you know how fucked we all are? Well, what are we going to do about it?*

She looked at the girl poet, who was nodding emphatically as her colleague performed. She asked herself was it a shame to be focused on Ryan more than the girl poet when the city preferred a man's voice and a girl could do with the encouragement? But she was, after all, a mother. Prone to maternal failure, but here a failure more benign than that which had preceded Jimmy's evil: the love of a wayward child and the desire for his success, even if it meant his taking someone else's spot.

She could not see his taking someone else's spot in this roiling Cork, so heavy with notions. Notions feeding notions, young wans and fellas singing songs and shooting films and doing pop-up poetry gigs on the Grand Parade. It was simultaneously the end of the world and the best time to be Irish; was it not all they could do to tell the story of it?

She looked at Ryan with her warmest smile. He did not notice. It did not matter. She wanted others to notice. She wanted the story built around her, so that people would know that Maureen Phelan was a great nationalist and a great mother, the kind who roused and riled and directed to the softest place, the best point to start tearing it all down.

It came to the day of the Dublin gig. Ryan needed to be at his father's house in the morning so that he could be ready for the road at lunchtime. Yvette could look after Diarmaid only for a couple of hours, so Karine would not be able to join Ryan for the trip. It shouldn't have bothered her. She watched him dress and imagined someone else watching him undress. She had only known him to cheat when unhappy and she could not say that he was happy. His father's death kept coming up on him in waves. He would be staggered, then furious that he wasn't surefooted. She tried to stop him reading anything online that might turn out to be an analysis of his wickedness, because he took it to heart. He talked about high-profile overdose cases, Colombian farmers, his old boss, the racial breakdown of prisoner numbers in the United States, sometimes in the belief that he, a blight of a human being, had contributed to it all, and sometimes in the belief that he was a victim of it as much as anyone else but that the truly culpable would never be dragged into the light.

He went off the fags again. He stopped drinking. He said he couldn't be sure it was permanent, but drinking didn't feel right to him, given how both of his parents had gone. Up at the Cusack house with his siblings he still smoked cannabis but no longer enough to make him incomprehensible. He would take a pill if it was offered, he said. Depending. But no more coke, he'd decided he was too old for coke.

Spending so much time with Diarmaid made him happy. Spending so much time with her made him happy. Suspicious as she was making herself, she knew it was true. It was in what he said and how he said it and while in the first few days she thought he could simply have been desperate to be held and kept safe, the days had gone on and he had not grown distant. In the best moments he was how he had been on Bofin: funny, thoughtful, hungry for her. In the worst moments – the swell and spill – he talked her through it as though it was compulsory that she be fluent in his distress.

They walked from her parents' house to his father's, and Karine stood by the kitchen worktop as the six Cusack children, Nana Cusack, and her daughters Emer and Eilish concluded on the course of action. Cian would take on the tenancy of the house and it seemed that the court might agree to his taking custody of his youngest siblings, so that they wouldn't have to live elsewhere.

'And sure Ryan, you might get yourself settled yet, boy,' Nana Cusack went on, turning to face him, and Ryan quietly agreed.

The business of the morning established and the conversation growing jokey, he went upstairs to the bathroom and didn't immediately come back down. Karine found him standing by the window in the back room, which still felt like his room though nothing belonging to him remained here. She remembered the first time she'd been in here, the way he'd done a nervous sweep of the room, moving his younger siblings' things out of his space. Dinky cars. Lego. Pyjama bottoms. The way he'd finally come to sit beside her on his bed, and how she'd sensed anxiety from him. Lust too, of course, but more importantly anxiety, and in that, sweet solidarity.

Now he said, 'I should be the one to mind them. I'm the oldest.'

She pressed against his back and put her arms around his belly. She didn't agree with or contradict him. The matter had been explored thoroughly. The house was the anchor and Cian would get the house.

He tilted his head towards his old bed. 'We'd hardly fit.'

'We didn't even fit when we were fifteen!'

He laughed.

She put her cheek to his back and said, 'Jesus though, we were so bold.'

She was expecting him to protest, but he said, 'I've been thinking about that. Us being that intense, we probably made it obvious. And having the video on my phone then, you'd have to ask if I left myself open to what happened with yer wan.'

'Ryan. Are you serious?'

'But you know what I'm getting at.' He unhooked her arms and turned to face her. 'I did a lot of stupid things because of yer wan and it just feels like sabotage on sabotage, like.'

She lowered her voice to match his. 'What stupid things?'

'Drink and drugs, like. And all that fucking around.' When they'd argued about the fucking around in the past he had deployed denial, deflection, then excuses, excuses, excuses. But not this excuse.

'I don't understand,' she said.

'I don't either, really. Only it felt like having control over . . . If I was gonna feel—' he cringed – 'dirty over it then at least I could earn it.'

'Would it make you feel better now?' she said. 'If I said you brought it on yourself?'

'I dunno,' he said. 'No. But if it was my fault at least it wouldn't be random.'

'If you say you're at fault because you were obviously sexually active then it stands to reason I'm at fault too.'

He was dismayed. 'No, it doesn't.'

She pushed her hands over her forehead. 'We shouldn't be talking about this now. You've to leave for Dublin in an hour and you can't go dwelling on this. If you were fucking around years ago because of her then imagine what it'll be like with forty girls, all down the front by the stage, eyes only for you.'

'I carried on like that when I was a kid and I couldn't cope with anything. I know who I am now.'

'Do you know who I am? You're telling me you're blaming yourself for the awful thing that was done to you when you were a kid, and all I can do is say, *Don't ruin our history, Ryan, don't fuck girls in Dublin.*' She stood back and narrowed her eyes. 'Don't you think I'm selfish?'

He faintly narrowed his own eyes. 'No.'

'You should. It wouldn't do you any harm. Maybe then you wouldn't be blaming yourself, you wouldn't be so sure you were so offensively happy at fifteen that the universe had to let in that cunt next door. Do you understand?' Though she could see that he didn't. 'I'm not perfect and sleeping with me is not the best thing you've ever done.'

'That's not what I'm getting at.'

'You're not saying that at fifteen you were soliciting. You weren't trying to score her. The only message you think you were sending is that you were too obviously in love and, fuck's sake, Ryan, why would you have been? I was not a great girlfriend at fifteen. I was terrified of your body, I was terrified of my own body, I was terrified of what my friends thought, I gave you shit just for being horny.'

He smiled.

'I'm serious, Ryan.'

'All right.'

'I am fucking serious! I've never been a good girlfriend. I cheated on you at my Debs, I was fifteen weeks pregnant with Diarmaid before I told you, I told my college friends you were in Italy because I was so mortified you were in gaol. And while you were in gaol I was with two other boys. I could have told you that, couldn't I? When you were fucking around trying to feel dirty with purpose I could have told you that, actually, you were the good one, you were the kind one, you were the honest one. And I'm only telling you now, an hour before you head off to an important gig during which you have to be confident, and brilliant, and the kind of fella that'll change people's lives.'

He said nothing for long enough for her to start crying, as she tended to do during arguments and after conniptions, either because she was weak or because even unconsciously she was manipulative and keen on the idea of girls being defenceless, delicate, pathetic.

'Two other boys?' he said.

'I was an eighteen-year-old idiot who was trying to pretend you didn't exist. How's that for a bad girlfriend?'

'It's pretty bad.'

'Why should you think I'm perfect?'

He thought about it. 'I don't think that's what it means to think someone's perfect. It's not that the person doesn't have faults. Just that their faults are irrelevant.'

'For fuck's sake, Ryan, how is that healthy?'

He vented a strangled cough. 'Yeah, well you do enough that drives me up the wall, Karine.'

'Oh, I do?'

'Course you fucking do. You're spoiled rotten. You talk about people behind their backs. You're very snotty sometimes when you talk to your mam. You think you know everything. You cheat on your fellas, don't you? Poor Dylan, like. Poor ould dote.' He turned a rictus grin at the ceiling. 'None of it means you're not perfect. I was made to fit around you, you're perfect for me.'

They stared at each other, then she sniffed and looked away.

'All sorts of stuff changed in the last nine years,' he said. 'Me wanting to be with you never changed. I'm not mad to think that this is it for me and you, that this is it entirely.'

'But I don't know what happens next,' she said.

He took her face in his hands. 'No one knows what happens next. The most boring fucking people in the world don't know what happens next.'

She put her hands over his.

'If I tell you', he said, 'that I believe you're perfect, let me believe it. But if you tell me I shouldn't think I let yer wan next door in, then I take your point. I'll work on it. I can think you're perfect and know my thinking is fucked at the same time. Fellas can be very fucking complex.'

'*Finished* finished?' Mel said.

'No, but finished from our end. Still has to be mastered,' Ryan said. 'It's good work, actually. Production engineer. I could still do that, if enough people decide they hate me.'

'*Enough* meaning more than those who think you're God's gift?'

He didn't respond. He was in front of Mel on the hired mini-bus, his legs stretched across both seats, his back to the window. Mel was leaning on a guitar case, eyes drooping. This after only three pints. Such were the problems of being a tiny man. Or girl. Boy. They/them. Gender rejection was supposed to be easier than this, in that it was supposed to be an act of revolution and there-fore lead to clarity of thought and conscience, verbal dexterity, a blinding sense of self. Mel felt as though in the drum of a great machine in which were tossed pronouns and politics and trousers of particular cuts.

Give it up for Lord Urchin. On guitar, Mel. Lead or rhythm, bit of both, not great but certainly getting there. Maybe a bit faster, if he/she/they figures out who Mel actually is. Melinda to Melvin, Melvyn (notions!), Mal (very Scottish but connotations of 'bad'), Meli (meaning honey), Melhem (cultural appropria-tion), Melody (musical but feminine; even abbreviated it would rankle; you'd need a beard to carry that off). Lead guitar or rhythm guitar, one to the other, depending on what the song asked of you. It was an achievement playing guitar when not reconciled with one's own body. Someone should clamber on to the stage, eyes shining, golden award thrust forward. *What leger-demain! What balls, if you don't mind! What name to inscribe on the plinth?* Mel would have to say, 'I don't know, actually. Leave it with me.'

Years ago, the hero-worship had given cause to look up the meaning of the name Ryan. It was of the surname, anglicised from Ó Riain (descendent of Rian). It was not certain what it meant. Maybe from *rí* (king), specifically, little king. At the time this felt significant because Mel would have liked to have been a king. There was another Ryan on the other side of the terrace and three more at school. Degrading, on bad days, to know there were so many little kings around when you were assigned 'princess' and given sparkly nails and fluffy cushions.

The Dublin gig had gone well. The audience was receptive, not as zealous as those at the gig in Cork, but open to radicalisation. If he'd been following his own plan, Ryan should by rights have allocated more songs to Mel and to Joseph; instead, he'd taken a couple back. Mel had sung low harmonies on 'Tall Tales' and 'How it Feels to Be Tamed'; this was good, felt as though pulled from a wilder place. Between songs Ryan spread the wryly pessimistic word.

'I'll tell you something I found out,' he said, slick of sweat on his forehead and one hand hooked into the back of his jeans. 'The ones who spent the most money were the ones who really resented me. The ones who were afraid of me, but were angry that they were afraid of me, coz I was only a scobe. Anyone else ever been the bad apple?'

Mel had suspected that most of the audience were not bad apples, but appreciated the suggestion that they could have been so influential as to spoil a barrel. In front of the bona fide their legs went to jelly. They got closer to the earth. They started to feel tremors, because loud music is its own psychoactive. So *Yes!* they roared. *Bad apples, demanding amnesty, with the cost of houses rising with the water!*

'We'll sing a song for bad apples, so,' Ryan had smirked.

Now, somewhere outside Cashel, Mel asked, 'Where did you get all that shit?'

Phone screen glow on his face. 'Hmm?' he said, without looking over.

'Bad apples. That spiel.'

'It's not a spiel. Just what was going through my head when I was writing the lyrics. You go away, no one knows what you're like, you get treated better, even though you're the same fella.

Personal history is a cunt,' he said, 'I'm not sure what good it does anyone.'

'It is a spiel,' Mel said. 'Who knew you were such a showman?'

'You try moving coke and yokes for a few years, see how you get by without plámásing and lying through your teeth.'

Half a kilometre on and Mel said, 'Have you any tips?'

'On what?'

'Making people think you're whatever kind of person you want them to think?'

He looked over the back of the seat. 'I told you,' he said. 'It's not a spiel. You've to believe it yourself first.'

This was going to be a task. First, to sleep on it. Back to the Cusacks' terraced three-bed and into Kelly's spot, woken mid-morning by a child in the throes of a tantrum somewhere outside. Niamh slept on, face swallowed by pillow. The flimsy curtains gave the light the colour of dirty linen.

The album was finished, an incentive to cement a sense of self before it was time to pose for promotional photographs. There would have been no Lord Urchin without Mel but Mel wasn't made on this terrace, Linda was, and increasingly it felt like what was built of Mel on stage was eroded again on the Northside. Mel had tea and toast and watched recommended videos on YouTube. Eventually another walk suggested itself. A walk to clear the head of cobwebs, various potential versions of Mel, bad apples.

The walk led all the way into town and Mel was here more comfortable, or at least with some degree of anonymity able to begin composing a spiel.

I play rhythm and I play lead so I am adaptable.

I can go from one to the other though to be honest I don't know which I prefer.

No, I don't know my own name, so what, like?

Mel went to Union Studios. With everything having been wrapped up without the full band present, it might be pleasant, and indicative of sureness of self, to thank Senan and Triona and say that, with a bit of luck, they'd all be working together on the sophomore release in a couple of years' time. Mel felt a pang thinking of Triona, and how she'd sought Mel's presence during the sessions because she thought they were both women and that Mel might have appreciated her. It was presumptuous, probably a bit sexist, but it was kind.

Natalie was at the reception desk, digging in a drawer for a set of keys.

'Oh, hello,' she said. 'Now's actually not a good time. I'm here with an investor.'

'I was looking for Triona and Senan.'

'No idea where Senan is. Triona went around the corner for coffee. Catch her there?'

'We're getting investors?' Mel said, and craned to see down the corridor.

'Catalyst Music is,' Natalie corrected. 'Not *we* in the way you might mean it.'

'I'm having a lot of problems with pronouns these days.'

Natalie smiled thinly.

Mel said, 'Actually, I wanted to ask you about payment and stuff. I don't know how it works if I become a permanent member of the band. Even if that's an option.'

'Sure, but Ryan is the man to talk to as regards line-ups. Payment, yeah. We'll talk about it. Just not this minute, because I'm meeting with my investor in the hope that he'll come in with me on a bid on this place.'

'The studio? Really?'

'Yes. We're thinking ahead. I'll call you.'

She took off down the corridor, and when she pulled open the door at the end Mel saw a familiar shaved head.

Which meant, perhaps, that there was no getting away from bad apples, only adaption in thinking, ingenuity in reshaping what it all meant. Mel expected to feel dismay but the brain-in-flux didn't come to dismay. Instead it fizzed with light let in. Mel left the building frowning. Was this part of it? Concoction and revision of personal politics, ceremoniously pushing people out and turning a blind eye when they crept back in again?

Mel messaged Ryan:

Where are you?

He responded twelve minutes later:

In D'Arcy's gaff, why?

Fancy a pint?

I'm off the drink.

Pint of Lucozade? Natalie said to talk to
you about whether I'm staying with Urchin.
Also my head is wrecked because of things
we were talking about last night. Town or
up home suits me.

Yeah ok. Not coming into town.

Up home so.

He was outside the Relic when Mel arrived back. He mirrored a wince.

Mel said, 'We don't have to go to the Relic.'

'I want to,' he said. 'But you've to buy coz I wouldn't please those cunts to put my hand in my pocket.'

Inside he took a table fifteen feet from the bar and stared at the barman as Mel ordered Lucozade in a pint glass filled with ice, and a gentle, soapy lager. The barman said he'd drop the drinks down. 'Ryan, I wanted to say,' he said, putting the pint in front of Ryan and the Lucozade in front of Mel; Ryan swapped them, still staring. 'We're all very sorry about what happened to your dad. We were very fond of the man, like.'

Ryan sat back and folded his arms and the barman didn't wait long enough to make himself look awkward; he scuttled off back behind the counter.

'What good is this doing you?' Mel asked Ryan.

'Just reminding the fuckers I'm here.'

'Ah, I don't think there's any chance of them forgetting.'

'You have to show your face even if you've been wronged. Don't give anyone a moment to bury what they did to you.' He sipped his drink and bared his teeth. 'Story, anyway?'

Mel said, 'Natalie said to ask you about whether I'm long-term.'

'You are if you want to be.'

'But you hate the sight of me.'

'And you say I'm not a nice person. Swings and roundabouts.'

'Why would you think it's going to work, then?'

'I don't,' he said. 'I don't know what the fuck is going to happen.'

'Water's rising.'

'That's not what I mean.' He sat forward, elbows on the table. He rubbed his mouth. He didn't look at Mel. 'I'm trying to be better,' he said.

'What am I, penance?'

Now he looked. 'Penance for what?'

'All right, then, not penance. Doing me a favour, so.'

'Why shouldn't I do you a favour? Didn't you grow up next door to me? Aren't you my sister's buddy? Who else would I be doing favours for?'

'Bit charitable, isn't it?'

'That's your insecurity, not mine.'

Mel said, 'The fella who took you away the night your dad got sick, is he part of Catalyst Music now?'

Ryan was rattled. 'How'd you know that?'

'I was at the studio earlier. Natalie said she was talking to an investor and then I spotted yer man.'

'That lad is a well-versed cunt,' Ryan said, 'and a long time running rampant. It wasn't my first time getting a box off him. But even well-versed cunts have mammies and kids. They start thinking about retiring into legitimacy. That's how the economy works, dirty money's still money. Natalie's sure she can handle him. Maybe she's right.'

'Yeah, but if you're gonna stand on stage and talk about bad apples—'

'You'll get bad apples, though. And wasps making use of them when they start to rot. Means the orchard isn't well-managed, d'you know what I mean?'

'Yeah, you mean it's someone else's fault.'

'Maybe. Or maybe it's all of our faults. Are you staying in the band or what?'

Mel drank, drummed fingers on the tabletop, said, 'Feels like I don't have a choice. I've nothing else going for me.'

'Spoken like a true bad apple.'

'Why would Cork even want me, so?'

'Fuck what Cork wants,' he said. 'Make it want you, boy. Keep on showing your face.'

Mel thought, *If my mother came back now, she wouldn't recognise me*, but did not say this because Ryan would not want to hear it, and because it was not at all clear that it would be a bad thing, anyway. Tara Duane had put no stock in her own fixed identity, and maybe this was what sparked rebellion in Mel. Tara clicked internet ads for a living but presented herself as a sex therapist and told sweeping lies to friends who lived too far away to ever see through them. Tara swore tearfully that she had no interest at all in fifteen-year-old boys, even as Tony Cusack smashed through the window. Tara had known all manner of bad apples but spoke of sugarcraft and loved inspirational quotes. What was a person, but a wavering mess?

Mel looked at Ryan, advocate for wavering messes, singing songs about being tamed but rejecting the process as a body rejects the wrong heart. Ryan looked back at Mel. It was not clear what he saw, but he was not looking to the door, nor to his phone. Mel thought that in the absence of sure self, there was something to be said for following a man that bit further along. And if Mel did not know who Mel was capable of being, then until it became clear Mel would accept the favours, be more than Tara as Ryan was more than Tony, and smile as Cork welcomed them both home.

* * *

337

They were in the sitting room when Cian came home from work and said, 'It's all kicking off in town.'

'What's kicking off?' Karine asked. Mel sat forward. Joseph came from the kitchen, bottle of beer in hand. Traolach cackled like this was a plan come to fruition; he had spent the last few weeks appearing and disappearing, racking up train tickets, holding court and presenting theories about Cork being a very volatile place. Ryan, standing in front of the fireplace with Diarmaid in his arms, looked at Cian only briefly, as though whatever this portended was irrelevant. Sons had to be looked after. Sanctuaries kept sacred.

Cian flopped on to the couch. 'Some protest or something outside City Hall. Started off grand but then the messers got in on it. There's things being thrown, I heard.'

'Not those fucking eejit ould fellas with their reflective vests?' Joseph said. 'Clowns can't decide whether they're annoyed about asylum seekers or broadband.'

'Nah,' Cian said. 'Young fellas.'

'What're they giving out about?' Ryan said.

Cian shrugged, eyes wide.

'I told ye all, this place is a powder keg,' Traolach said.

Ryan sat at his mother's piano, Diarmaid on his lap. His back to the room, he played one-handed while Diarmaid thumbed the low keys.

'Wouldn't be the right time for student protests, anyway,' Karine said. She was perpendicular to Ryan. He was looking at Diarmaid. Both serene, and making a racket.

Joseph googled. 'Reports of a small gathering in town on the RTÉ website,' he said. 'There's a photo here on Twitter. It's mostly young fellas but I see one nana so this one lad calling it a riot is probably being a bit hysterical. Mind you, his bio says he's a jackeen.'

'They're as bad as you,' Cian said to Traolach. 'Always making out that Cork people are loons.'

'I hope you're happy,' Joseph said, and though he did not use his cousin's name Karine could see that Ryan was listening.

'They're rioting in town over you. Go marching, boys. Bad apples of the Northside, unite!'

Ryan smiled. 'We go for a nose?' he asked.

'You will not,' Karine said.

It was fine, he assured her. He was just curious. He wasn't going to join in. It would probably have blown over by the time they got into town. But it might prove inspirational, or at least fodder for the music video, for the next gig, or for the expanded manifesto. He wouldn't go if she was dead against it but he was 100 per cent it'd be fine. They walked out of the estate together, holding one of Diarmaid's hands each, swinging him into the air every few steps till he was hiccupping with laughter. Ahead of them walked the others, Cian still in his work waistcoat and trousers, Traolach still banging on about the fieriness of the Corkonian soul. 'He'll get you into terrible trouble yet,' Karine said, nodding after him.

'It's me that's keeping him out of trouble,' Ryan said. They stopped at the corner and Karine picked up Diarmaid. Ryan stroked his son's cheek. 'I'll be back in a bit,' he told him.

'Don't be late,' Karine said. 'We have that viewing first thing.'

'I won't be late,' he said. He kissed her, then kissed Diarmaid's forehead, started after the others and then turned, walking backwards for a few steps. 'I loves yeh,' he said.

'Loves yeh back.'

It was a beautiful evening with an imminent red sky. There was no balm left in the air, but a delicate turn; it was the kind of atmosphere you could run and run in. Ryan caught up with the others and walked with his hands in his pockets, his head tilted slightly back. Karine could still see hints of the whorls tattooed on his arm. She thought of a lean, dark dragon parting cirrus waves, breaking into the lower atmosphere and laying waste to everything beneath him. She thought of Cork in flames.

She corrected herself.

She thought of his lovely low voice and she thought of people listening, rapt. She thought of his musician's sincerity, and how it would not be twisted to mean things it didn't mean. She thought of tomorrow's viewing of the three-bed semi in Glanmire and she thought of them curled up on a new sofa watching some Italian movie, bickering over music videos, being picky with house party invitations, making love like they had nothing better to do, putting together a cot for whoever was going to come along next.

But today she felt her dancer's body underneath the one motherhood had given her. She texted Yvette: *Any chance you could mind Diarmaid for a couple of hours if I go into town?* She stood, potential energy and stout belief, and alternated between watching the street the way Ryan had gone and watching her phone for the answer. The bubble appeared, indicating that Yvette was responding. And Karine could have picked out the notes, just then. She could have written it, the piece that was about to play.

And sure Cork? Cork was all ears.

Acknowledgements

Deepest thanks to Mark Richards, whose guidance has meant the world to me since the beginning.

To Jocasta, who jumped in with warmth and enthusiasm, to Rosie and Yassine, who are so bright and inventive, to Becky, Emma, Abi, Jess, Charlotte, Sara, Joanna, Grace, Nick, to everyone at John Murray and Hachette Ireland. An incredible bunch of people, committed and creative and kind.

To Luke Brown, who put manners on this book.

To the indefatigable Ivan Mulcahy. And to Marc, Sallyanne, Adrienn, and everyone at MMB Creative.

To Julian, Kat and Patrick, without whom I'd have gone stone mad on finishing this novel.

To the Irish writers. You keep my brain fizzing. Special love and gratitude to all of the stinging flies. And to those who keep the Irish writers ticking: the booksellers, the publishers, the arts administrators, the reviewers, the journalists, the translators, the academics, the editors, the multitudes. What times we've been through. Sure we'll keep going.

To Kevin Barry, for writing 'The Raingod's Green, Dark as Passion' and giving Maureen Phelan something to rail against. And for everything else too.

To those who shaped me: my family, my friends. I am lucky to have you.

To all whose interest or excitement or love for these characters means everything. To Shelley Atkinson. To Kate Gibb. To Tadhg Coakley, because I never got 'death or Carnegie Hall' out of my head (I hope you approve of how it actually turned out). To the whole of Cork.

And finally, to Aodh, a person so extraordinary you couldn't make him up, and to John, who's put up with so much of these characters' problems and never lost interest or patience, who loves them all, I think, almost as much as I love him.